PERFECTLY IMPERFECT

"EVERYTHING WILL BE OKAY IN THE END. IF IT'S NOT OKAY, THEN IT'S NOT THE END."

    —ED SHEERAN

Nancy—
Break The molds!

HARPER SLOAN

Cover Design by Sommer Stein with Perfect Pear Creative Covers
Editing by Jenny Sims with www.editing4indies.com
Formatting by Champagne Formats

To Contact Harper:

Email: Authorharpersloan@gmail.com
Website: www.authorharpersloan.com
Facebook: www.facebook.com/harpersloanbooks

Other Books by Harper Sloan:

Corps Security Series:
Axel
Cage
Beck
Uncaged
Cooper
Locke

Hope Town Series:
Unexpected Fate
Bleeding Love

Disclaimer:

This book is not suitable for younger readers. There is strong
language and adult situations.

PLAYLIST

I'm A Mess by Ed Sheeran
Tenerife Sea by Ed Sheeran
Distance by Christina Perri
Kiss You In The Morning by Michael Ray
Wasn't Expecting That by Jamie Lawson
Heaven by Matt Bomer
Rewind by Paolo Nutini
F**ckin' Perfect by P!nk
Glitter In The Air by P!nk
Love Myself by Hailee Steinfeld
A Little Bit Stronger by Sara Evans
Don't Let Me Let You Go by Jamie Lawson
Gravity by Sara Bareilles
Nothing Left to Lose by Kari Kimmel
Fight Song by Rachel Platten

To enjoy the *Perfectly Imperfect* playlist: https://open.spotify.com/
user/1293550968/playlist/6UECoRhmimeoS9vyeh77dV

Dear Reader:

I debated on whether or not to have a forward note in *Perfectly Imperfect*. In the end, I felt that **you** deserve to know why this book took precedence over each and every other WIP (work in progress) I had going at the time. The reasons behind why I felt this story needed to be told. And most importantly, why Willow Tate will forever hold the biggest part of *me* that I could ever put into one of my characters.

For the better part of my life, I've struggled with body image issues. Not something small, but big, ugly, crippling issues that have shaped me into someone I wasn't always proud to be. I went through high school hiding an eating disorder that most will be finding out—or maybe just confirm what they thought—through this message. You see, I was more concerned about the 'perfect' expectations that society mentally demands of us. More worried about maintaining my appearance as one of the 'popular,' 'pretty girls' than I was about my own health. I played right into the hands of the predator that hunts our self-esteem daily.

Then I got older.

And not so wiser.

I'll save the gritty details, but those image issues I struggled with got worse before they got better. People close to me making comments about how I was 'fat' or how I 'used to be so pretty.' They just compounded those issues until they were a snowball spiraling so fast I knew I would likely never catch it.

I still carry some of those issues around visibly, and I don't think I'll ever feel perfect. I struggle. Day in and day out. I *struggle*. The difference now is that I know I'm not perfect, nor will I ever be, but I have more confidence at this stage in my life (and body shape) than I ever did when I was at my mind's version of perfect. I still have moments, just like Willow, when I feel like everyone is looking at me and judging my body. Judging the choices that they *think* I've made. Judging me because of how I look.

But … I've learned through YEARS of struggling that I'm perfectly imperfect. I'm happy. It's taken me a long time to feel that way about myself and even though I have days when I feel just imperfect … I love myself.

The Internet is a mass of viral videos telling us who and what we need to be. Portraying anyone above a size ten as 'overweight' or 'plus size.' Public image personalities lashing out at people who aren't up to *their* standards of perfection. Telling <u>us</u> which point we need to be at to consider ourselves worthy of that perfection. Making us question, and most often hate, ourselves and the skin we live in. Willow—like me—felt that, feels that, and lives that. But she learned that perfect isn't what others expect you to be, but what you expect for yourself.

In the words of Kane Masters himself, *I want to give hope to those who need to know life isn't what others want for you, but what you want for yourself. Strength in the face of weakness.* That you *can* be the change that you want for yourself.

Willow holds so much of me. What I've felt. Things I've done. Thoughts that I've had. Experiences that I've lived. The fears, the highs, the lows, and the hate that she feels is real and raw for so many people out there. I know that not everyone has felt the things that Willow does. She might appear weak at times, but for those who have walked in her shoes … you know how strong Willow is. For those who continue to slip on those shoes day in and day out, I hope that Willow can show you how perfect is just an image. You, like Willow, are loved and if anything … I hope that through her story you can heal.

Like Willow – I found I learned that it doesn't matter what others think about *me* and the skin I wear. All that matters is that *I LOVE ME*.

And while I will never be perfect … I will be imperfect and rock it perfectly.

I hope you enjoy Willow and Kane's journey.

Love,

Harper

DEDICATION

To the little piece of WILLOW that may be inside of you.
I hope that through her story you see how stunningly perfect you
are regardless of the imperfections you may see.
Happiness is there – just waiting for you to take the leap.
And if you need a little helping hand…this is for the KANE
waiting for you.

PROLOGUE

MY BODY, STILL BRUISED AND broken, screams in protest as I pull myself toward the open door of the limo. My mind is working in tandem with my aching body and is objecting to my moving another inch. I don't want to be here. I want to be anywhere but *here*.

I take a deep breath and watch my father exit the vehicle before reaching out and offering his hand to help Ivy, my sister, as she climbs to her feet. At that moment, I wish with all my might for this to be just a dream. A terrible nightmare that I'll wake from at any second.

"Willow, get out of there, now," my father snaps his demand at a hushed whisper. His head faces forward, but his voice carries softly enough to get my attention.

Balling my fists and squeezing my eyes closed, I pray. To be a little stronger. To be able to get through this without breaking into a million pieces. To be the person whom my father wants me to be. Someone more like my sister.

When I reach the opening, I awkwardly swing my legs out, making sure not to bump the door with the hard cast around my left foot. My mind immediately realizes the error in my stalled timing when my eyes meet my father's sharp gaze, burning with hatred and annoyance.

Toward me.

Because *I'm* the reason we're here.

His arm is wrapped around my sister while her body is tucked tight into his side. Her soft sobs are muffled against his suit jacket. He doesn't move to help me. Nor does he move an inch when I struggle to climb out of the vehicle. His icy blue eyes say everything he wouldn't dare vocalize with this many people milling around us.

Hurry.

Get your act together.

Stop being such an embarrassment.

You're the reason we're here.

You pathetic fool.

He moves his foot slightly, and I hear my crutches clink together when he connects with them, telling me without words that will be the only help I'll be getting from him.

My muscles ache with every movement. They complain when I push myself out and scream in agony when I pull myself to stand next to the open door. The arm I used to shove my body off the seat sends searing pain to my bruised ribs. Each movement steals the breath straight from my lungs.

And the sharp intake of breath I force when the pain becomes too much causes my father's eyes to harden even further.

God, please help me. Take this all away. Everything.

When I've finally made it to my feet—well, foot—he starts marching forward. Ivy's small body pulled tight to his side and not one backward glance to make sure I'm following. The uneven earth under the wet grass makes my trek more challenging, but I'm determined not to give him another reason to be unhappy with me. I make sure my footing is solid, and I swing my body forward carefully.

I make it to his side well after they've been seated and move to take my seat next to him rather cumbersomely. I don't look up. Seeing the look of pity mixed with grief on everyone's faces around us would cause me to crumble, but I know if anyone were to look at me with the same blame my own father does … my heart would be forever ruined.

Instead, my eyes lock on the mahogany wood that holds the only person I know loved me in this life.

I will wear this mark of responsibility for the rest of my days. This burden of death will never be erased. After all, I was the one driving the car that night.

It doesn't matter that a drunk driver was the cause of our wreck. I wasn't able to prevent the crash that took my own mother's life. I wasn't able to stop her from dying.

As the final moments of my mother's funeral play out around me, all I can focus on are those last memories I have of youthful happiness. When my father's hate for me wasn't something so tangible because it was shielded by a mother's love. My sister's contempt wasn't thickly choking me. When I didn't hate myself for being alive.

I had everything in one second, and in the next … I had nothing. A void so dark it's killing me.

And now … now, all I can remember is how my father's booming voice berated me from the foot of my hospital bed. His words, laced with the venom of hate, telling me I should have been the one who died that night. That my mother's life was worth more to this world than that of her bastard daughter.

He made it clear he will *never* be able to look at me the same after taking his perfect wife away from him. I looked over, seeing my beautiful sister wrapped in his arms, before looking back down at my lap. The narrow seat I'm sitting on pinches my thighs when I shift, and with a deep sigh, I realize that when I took his perfect wife, his perfect life, and killed it in the crunched remains of my mother's car, I tainted the future with nothing but imperfection. After all, he was right ... I came into this world as a bastard and the world would probably be better off if I went out the same way.

CHAPTER ONE

WILLOW

SELF-LOATHING IS A DISEASE.

Okay, so maybe not a *real* disease, but it should be classified as such.

When you wake up in the morning and hate the skin you're stuck in. Or maybe when you look in the mirror and see round cheeks where perfect contours used to be and immediately want to shove your finger down your throat to *help*.

Worse yet, being married to a man who tells you day in and day out what an ugly fat-ass cow you are. Or to quote what seems to be his go-to in verbal lashings, 'your disgusting fat body.'

Ugh.

Self-loathing is a disease I've been fighting to *cure* for more years than I can remember. It didn't help that, until recently, I had been married to a man who fed that disease daily. His comments, his look of disgust at the person his wife had become, his infidelity—all of it had been the fuel needed for that disease to burn wild. And, worse yet, I let it. I became a product of my own mind's games.

But today, I get to try and focus on my future. The end of one hellish journey where I can finally, hopefully, take all the hard work I've accomplished in the months since my marriage ended and become the *me* I was meant to be. Today will mark the day it will be officially behind me.

Throwing back the covers, I look down at my thick dimpled thighs long enough to take an invisible slap to my waning self-esteem. *You're better than that, Willow. You see what your mind wants you to see. Remember that.*

It isn't that I'm a weak person. I'm a product of self-destruction, or so my therapist tells me. I'm a battlefield of strength versus weakness and reality versus my own mind. I don't look in the mirror and hate myself because I'm weak. No, I hate myself because even though my clothes and the scale tell me one thing, I *can't see it*. It takes all the strength a person can muster to continue fighting his or her own self-image. Fighting to find their way back from the damage they've done to themselves physically and mentally.

I don't think I was always like this. My childhood, I think, was the building blocks of where I am now in my life. My mother loved me as fiercely as any mother loves her children. But that's where the love ended. My father, or I should say the man who raised me since I was a wee toddler, has never liked me. I came into his life as an inconvenience that just so happened to be attached to the woman he fell in love with. Even after all these years, I don't know why I still crave his love and yearn to be accepted as his 'real' daughter. And don't even get me started on Ivy. His love all went to his true daughter, my half-sister. Even when she was a baby, she didn't like me. She would start crying the second I walked into the room. But the dislike they shared turned to hate the day my mother died.

The depression that started with my mother's death continued to compound with other issues over the years, as did my body, because I binge ate every single one of those issues. Looking back now, I'm confident that I only married my soon-to-be ex because he was the first man to ever pay any attention to me. Attention, in the positive light, was something I had struggled to find after her death. For almost a decade, I simmered in a vat of hate around me, so when I met him, I took everything he had to offer and grasped on tight. It didn't take long for that affection to turn into a nightmare of verbal abuse that I put up with for years. According to my therapist, I was my own martyr. I stayed because, in a sense, I believed I deserved it.

Until the day that it was over, when I realized I was worth more.

But at that time, married to a life of verbal lashings, I lost myself more than I could have gained back from his shadow of hate dissipating.

I went from being a healthy woman with a perfectly flat stomach, perky boobs, size four waist, and the best ass in town – to someone I didn't even recognize anymore.

And it was at that moment that I used all the hate others had toward me and turned it into the biggest cheerleader ever. I struggled. I continue to struggle. But I'm getting better, and that's all I can focus on right now.

With a deep sigh, I make my way to the bathroom and start getting ready for my appointment with my divorce attorney. The last appointment and the most important one because it means I'll finally be free of my cheating, verbally abusive ex-husband.

Like I said … today is the day when everything I have been working toward comes to fruition. Today, I choose to be a better me. One who doesn't hate herself. One who isn't so self-conscious of everyone around her.

Today, I choose strength.

I just pray the daily battle warring inside of me makes that choice possible.

CHAPTER TWO

WILLOW

I DRUM MY FINGERS AGAINST MY crossed legs as the cab takes me closer to my attorney's office. The fabric of my black slacks leaves me uncomfortably warm in the shockingly warm weather of late spring in New York City. We have been stuck in such cool weather for so long that I had forgotten what it felt like to be sweaty. Of course, that could also have a lot to do with where I'm going and not the actual weather.

Pulling out my phone, I flip the camera to look at my reflection. I cringe when I see how pale I look. My dark brown hair hangs like a flat curtain against my pasty skin. My eyes, having lost the sparkle of mischief a long time ago, look dead and scared. Actually, more accurately, they look like crap. Dead, brown crap.

To be fair, my eyes aren't the problem. *I* look like crap.

So much for that pep talk before you left the apartment, Will. Great job.

Locking my phone, I shove it back into my purse and press my head against the seat.

This morning started out so well. Until I walked out the door and a series of unfortunate events kept knocking me down like well-placed checkers.

First, my only pair of attractive heels snapped the second I slipped my foot inside them, forcing me to wear an old, worn pair that look more like something my grandmother would have worn. Then, the elegant chignon I had worked so hard to put my hair into lasted about two seconds before rejecting the bobby pins and falling back down to thick waves. Naturally, since I had been running late, I was stuck with my hair down around my face, which I feared would make me look weak ... as if I was hiding. And to add to my already dwindling confidence, the button on my dress pants—the ones that actually make me look good because they're a size too big—was missing. My carefully planned 'power outfit' instantly died, and now, I'm stuck in the only other pair I had, the ones that are a size too small and cut circulation off to my legs.

It was one thing after the next until I was a frazzled mess hailing a cab and rushing to my meeting.

Despite all that earlier confidence, knowing that I'm about to come face-to-face with Brad after not seeing him for six months is starting to wear me thin. The last time I saw his stupidly attractive face had been while he was in the throes of pleasure as my sister rode his naked and grunting body.

But ready or not, it's time for me to put another gloomy chapter behind me and continue to pick up the pieces of my jacked-up life.

My palms are sweaty and my hands shake just as much as my

legs tremble as I walk into the office of Buchanan and Buchanan. Taking a timid side-glance around the swanky office, I take a deep breath when I don't see Brad. Thank God.

I've always hated waiting in this lobby. The firm offers a wide array of services, so finding the lobby empty like it is today is uncommon. Regardless of that fact, it still feels like an expensively decorated holding cell.

Stepping up to the receptionist's desk, I softly say, "Ms. Tate for Randy Buchanan, please." She doesn't look up from her computer; she raises one thin, perfectly manicured finger, which I'm guessing is a signal to wait, before she points over at the seating area to my left.

Right. Dismissed.

My nerves do nothing but jump up the charts as I sit there and wring my fingers together. My earlier determination to be confident and strong dies with each second that ticks by. Once again, I'm that weak, little girl I've hated for the last decade. My purse strap digs into my shoulders as I sit there, rigid and full of fear. I loathe feeling like this. I've worked hard *not* to feel like this. Constantly nervous. Afraid of what others think about me. So unsure of myself. I know why I feel like this. And I hate that even after all these months apart, months I've worked hard to change, knowing Brad will be here has me reverting instantly. He was the catalyst for all my problems spiraling out of control, so it makes sense that just the mention of seeing him again has me regressing to *that* person. Years of being his verbal whipping post, making it a struggle to enjoy the simplest of tasks without fear, are piling thick on my shoulders.

And naturally, during my inner panic is when Brad walks in

… no, struts in is more like it. Not a hair out of place. His suit tailored impeccably to project his normal look of perfection and his whole air of arrogant affluence. Of course, when *he* walks up to the receptionist, she smiles and bats her thick lashes and—gag—giggles. They look like Barbie and Ken up there. Permanent faces of perfect happiness etched in their expressions.

"Excuse me, but could you stop your pathetic flirting with my man?"

My jaw drops at the voice that interrupts my musings. Probably dropped to the same place my heart just landed.

At my feet.

I'm going to vomit.

There isn't a thing I can do but sit here like an idiot and gape as my sister walks to Brad's side, swaying her thin, narrow hips seductively. She threads her arm around his waist before placing one perfectly manicured hand on his chest. The sight of them together holds my gaze hostage as she looks around his body. If looks could kill, I would be dead the second her eyes connected with mine.

I'm going to be sick. It's official.

I hear the receptionist say something. I assume she's talking to Brad because, with a nod, he turns and walks to the other side of the room, pulling my sister with him. Her eyes never leave mine, but *he* completely ignores me.

No shocker there.

It's been years since Brad has been able to stand to look at me.

After ten terribly nauseating minutes of studying my hands to avoid looking at Brad and Ivy, our attorneys step out. Mine, the first Buchanan in Buchanan and Buchanan, walks over with a sympathetic smile and offers his hand. Randy was an old college friend of my mother's, so when I needed an attorney in a rush, I didn't falter in contacting him, even if I can just barely afford his rates. But, true to my unlucky nature, his brother just so happens to have connections with Brad's family and didn't have any issues being his counsel, even if family law isn't his focus.

Rushing to stand, I fumble with my heavy purse, but in my haste to keep my eyes away from the duo of doom, I gravely miscalculate every inch in my rush to stand. Mutely, I watch in horror as the strap to my purse snaps. The heavy bag drops in an embarrassingly slow-motion display, and with a slap against the marble floor, every content inside my overstuffed bag spills and scatters around me.

Lip gloss, pens, notepad, cell phone, wallet, probably every spare coin ever made and—oh, God—tampons and maxi pads. Because, naturally, it's completely normal for someone to be a walking dispenser for any menstrual issue needs.

"Oh, God," I gasp and twist to bend so that I can collect all my spilled crap. But before I even have a chance to blink, I'm flat on my back when my ankle gives out and twists on whatever I manage to hook on my stupid granny heel.

This day couldn't get any worse than right here at this moment as I lay sprawled out on the floor with my personal belongings scattered around me. What did I say? Just like checkers, the final piece—me—has finally fallen.

I can't breathe, and it has nothing to do with the fact I'm pretty sure all air I had in my lungs just got knocked straight out of my body with the force of my landing. This would have been embarrassing enough without anyone to witness it, but knowing the two people who would love nothing more than to see me stoned got a front row seat.

Yeah, I'm going to vomit.

"What a mess, Brad. Aren't you thrilled you're finally going to be rid of … well, that?" My sister's hurtful words bring a heated blush to my face and my nose pricks with tears. Tears that I'm determined not to shed while they can see me. Tonight, alone in my small apartment, I'll drown in them, but here … no.

"Willow? Are you okay?" I hear at the same time as the receptionist calls out my attorney's name and frantically waves at the phone.

"It's Mr. Logan with the Logan Agency. He says it's imperative he speaks to you before your meeting with the Tates."

"Kill me now," I wheeze when I hear my father's name. Rolling to my side, I make the always-awkward attempt to climb to my feet. It feels like every eye in the room is watching me. Judging me.

"I'm sorry, Willow. I have to take this," Randy explains and moves to help me stand.

"Allow me," I hear spoken from my other side, stopping me before I can move from my position seated on my bottom with my hands ready to push off the ground. The smooth rasp of his voice wraps around me. Those two words were said low, but with sympathy, and cause me to snap my eyes from the horrified ones of Mr. Buchanan and over to where that sinfully deep voice came from.

I hadn't noticed anyone else in the room, let alone someone who must have been sitting just a few chairs down from where I had been before my crash to rock bottom. Literally. He moves to stand before I can see his face, but his denim-clad legs hit my vision. All I can see is two muscular thighs molded in dark-wash denim as if they were made for the man. As he moves closer to my body, I feel something like electricity lightly zapping my skin.

If his face matches what I can see, I can only imagine how good looking he is. God, I really am surrounded by perfect people. Even Randy Buchanan at his ripe age of sixty-two has a body I'm sure he spends hours a day in the gym to keep looking that way. I don't even need to see this stranger's face; with a body like that, he could be a troll and still be closer to perfection than I'll ever see in myself. Is it too much to ask to see someone, anyone, who doesn't look like they were made from a mold?

Great, just what I need; another witness to this repulsive scene my checkers of a day fated to suck created.

"It's all right, Mr. Masters. I have it. Won't take but a second, right, Willow?" Mr. Buchanan asks, bending to assist me from the floor. Where I still haven't moved.

"That might be, Rand, but it looks like you're needed elsewhere," the man, Mr. Masters, continues. He raises one hand from the side of his body and points over toward where the receptionist is still trying to get my attorney's attention and then bends at the waist to offer me his hand.

I get my first glimpse of the man behind that voice.

The foreign feeling of pure lust coils so tightly that it steals the breath straight from my lungs.

My cheeks flame once again as goosebumps fire across my skin when I realize just who has been witness to my living nightmare. Oh. My. God. Mr. Masters?! The one and only, Mr. *Kane* Masters. Sexiest Man Alive, most wanted actor around, the object of lust for maybe every woman in the whole entire WORLD! Good God! It can't be. There's no way that ... no ... oh, crap. I was wrong; this day could and did get worse.

"I … please … I'm so sorry," I whisper meekly. Please, God, open the ground up and swallow me whole. Just end it now. "Please, don't worry about me … oh, God."

"Willow, was it?" he asks, reaching out and pulling me off the floor with his hands hooked under my armpits. *Am I sweating there too? I feel like I am. Holy crap, is he touching my pit sweat?* "Are you okay?" he questions, continuing to assess me. Did I nod? I might have … or maybe I'm just gaping at him like the freaking idiot I am. "Do you need medical assistance?" he continues when I don't say a word.

"I—I'm—crap, I'm okay. Only what was left of my pride was damaged." I don't say anything else, but duck my head to avoid his penetrating gaze and kneel on the floor to start grabbing whatever I can within reach, stuffing everything hastily back into my purse.

"Kane, if you would follow me, I can take you back to Steven's office while he's busy," I hear the receptionist say, closer this time. I'm sure if I were to look, she would be right next to us.

I don't look, but I can tell he doesn't move. His presence isn't something I can ignore, and it just makes me gather my things a little quicker. What is wrong with me? Or a better question is what is *he* doing to my body? Every inch of my skin feels his presence like a physical touch. *Please, just leave. Don't stay. God, please don't stay.*

"Are you okay, Willow?" The concern is evident in his tone, and it's the only reason I pause long enough to look up and meet his eyes. That and the way my name sounds so sinful and erotic from his lips. His blue eyes, the color of the Caribbean Sea, don't hold an ounce of sympathy. They're imploring me with unasked questions, but the concern written all over his face is exposed. For me. That look, something I haven't seen in a long time from anyone other than my two best friends, stops me still.

"I'm ... I'll—thank you for asking, but I'll be fine." I have no clue how I managed to get that out, but if I was hoping it would appease him, I was wrong.

"Right. I've no doubt about that, Willow. But it would ease my mind if you would at least allow me to offer some assistance."

Oh, God. I need to get away. I don't know how to even begin processing the way he's making me feel. My feelings surmount the embarrassment I have over this situation. "That's okay, Mr. Masters. I'm sure you have more important things to do. Thank you, though." *Right. That wasn't too hard. At least, I made complete sentences this time. Well done, Willow.*

"Nothing that can't wait for me to help a beautiful woman out," he says, and I snap my head back, knocking it against the wooden table behind where I'm crouched on the floor. "Shit," he gruffs. Then, as if it couldn't get worse, he crouches down and his long, thick fingers dive into my hair and rub against the spot I just banged. The second he touches my scalp, a fire shoots from the pads of his fingers and pings around my body like lava.

"It's fine. *I'm* fine. Please ..." I plead and look up through the foggy haze created by my unshed tears.

I watch his eyes fire, something working quickly over his expression before he wipes it clean. Before I can give it much thought, relief washes over me. Whatever he sees in the gaze he's holding prisoner must be enough. A deep breath of air rushes from his full lips and warms my already burning face before he nods once and moves away from me. He doesn't speak again; instead, he gathers the rest of my personal belongings and places them back in my broken purse. I pull myself from the floor carefully to avoid look-ing like the weakling that I am, and when Kane stands, I take my broken bag from his fingers. He doesn't speak, just nods when I clutch it to my chest as if it was a shield.

"Thank you," I murmur, not looking up from his chest.

"It was nothing." He sighs softly.

"Well, thank you nonetheless. I'm sorry for interrupting your morning."

"At the risk of sounding like a jerk, the interruption was my pleasure."

My eyes flit to his quickly, and my mouth opens. I blink … slowly … a few times as his full lips turn up into a smile that makes my already racing heart pick up speed.

"Good luck in there, beautiful Willow."

Another slow blink. *Did Kane Masters just call* me *beautiful? Surely, not.*

"Until next time," he continues his deep rumbles.

Do what?

With that, he turns and walks over to the receptionist. With one more glance back, he follows her out of the lobby.

I take a few more minutes to collect myself before I grab the rest of my things and head to the doorway the others went through earlier. As hard as it is going to be to forget any of the last ten min-utes happened, I do my best to shove that embarrassing scene into my box of shame deep within and collect the last shred of my pride before heading off to end this terrible chapter of my life.

An hour later, my divorce from Brad finally becomes offi-cial. It was easy enough; I asked for nothing knowing damn well it wouldn't be given without a fight I couldn't afford. I spent the whole time inside the conference room staring at my hands while my headache intensified. When I managed to pull my pride up like a proverbial big tug of my britches earlier and walk through the door, the first thing my eyes met were the hate-filled gaze of Brad Tate, my now ex-husband. When I sat down across the table from my perfectly tailored ex-husband, all I could do was wonder, and not for the first time, how we ever made it through four years of marriage. He sat there with a tight lip and narrow eyes, never wavering in his directed probing, as I tried my hardest to remember if we ever even liked each other.

No, I take that back. I liked him. But I can admit now it wasn't love. I loved the *idea* of him, but it was only ever an unhealthy way for me to feel like I was desired by someone. I was alone and miserable, grasping at anything I could find to feel. But I can honestly say now it was *never* love.

He sat there as the mirror image of perfection. His body, one of his better qualities, looked nothing short of impeccable in his dark suit. His hair styled flawlessly and his face–the one I used to find so handsome—couldn't even hide his attractiveness with the twisted look of abhorrence he directed across the table at *me*.

And next to him sat my sister, Ivy. His way of making sure this day was even more painful for me, and she most likely was all for making sure that was the case. We have never gotten along. Not even as children. She is the only person, besides Brad and my father, that is, who I might hate the most.

And sadly, I've played into her hand far too often. When I look over at my sister, I see everything I'm not. Everything she's made sure to remind me that I never will be.

We may be sisters, but we're also complete opposites in looks and personality.

Ivy, like me, is tall, but Ivy is also a product of the utmost beauty money can buy. Beauty she has no problem spending one hell of a pretty penny to maintain. It's really a shame she couldn't pay someone to fix her evil, black soul.

"Well, Mrs. Tate," my lawyer starts while shuffling some of the papers around in front of him. "It looks as if everything is in order." He hands his thick stack over to his partner and together they make sure everything is, in fact, in order.

I don't speak.

My sister makes a noise deep in her throat that has me wondering if she's choking on her tongue.

"Don't you mean *Ms.*?" Brad retorts, venom dripping from each word.

My attorney clears his throat and looks at me with pity before addressing Brad. "Yes, my apologies, Mr. Tate. Slip of the tongue."

"How long until we can take care of that issue?" Brad strangely requests, looking over at the other Mr. Buchanan.

"Take care of what issue exactly, Mr. Tate?" my attorney interjects.

My eyes move from my lawyer to Brad. His eyes flash in anger before he slams his fist on the polished wood causing my headache to pierce through my skull.

"How long until that woman can be rid of my name?"

That woman? Jesus. You would think I was some stranger and not the woman he married and pledged forever to.

"Excuse me?" I whisper harshly, trying not to vomit from the pressure of pain my head is bringing me.

"You heard me, Willow. You have no business with my name

now that we are no longer married. I'll be damned if I allow you to tarnish my family's good name any longer. Especially now that I'm finally rid of you."

Ivy snickers, and my gaze moves over to hers. Her thick black hair is pulled back so harshly in a tight bun that it looks like her scalp is about to peel right away at her hairline. There isn't a single part of her that isn't made up right now. But even with the amount of Botox she shoots into her face, I can still see the hate burning brightly in her gaze.

"Why exactly are you even here, Ivy?" I snap. God, it feels good to let out some of my anger.

Her evil little smirk, or at least I think it was a smirk, slips. Maybe she has gas. Her eyes twitch and I guess that's her only way to narrow them since she can't actually change her expression.

"You stupid little cow. I'm here because, unlike *you*, I belong on the arm of my Bradie-poo."

Bradie-poo?

I hear, without focusing on my attorney, him explaining to Brad that *if* I should desire to return to my maiden name, then it would be my decision and mine alone. I'm too busy holding Ivy's gaze to pay attention. Brad grunts a few times, and I see both Mr. Buchanans move toward the door.

When the door final clicks shut, my eyes move from hers and I look at my ex.

"Do you really think you're any match for Ivy, Willow? You need to see to that name correction so that the Tate family name can go to the right sister this time."

I gasp and my eyes snap from his back to Ivy, who is doing her best Vanna impression to wave a giant—a lot bigger than my ring ever was—rock sitting pretty on her left ring finger.

"How long?" I question, not removing my gaze.

"You stupid girl," Ivy snaps. "I was fucking your husband the day he realized he married the wrong sister. We might be related, but when you started to balloon up like a whale, he realized his mistake real quick."

I don't react. I refuse to give them anything else. Not a second more of my pain and damn sure none of my tears. I'm better than this.

"Feels good to have someone ride me without taking all the air from my body." Brad snidely laughs.

My eyes connect with his, but I hold it in. I draw on the inner strength I have left and keep my face passive.

"Have a nice life, sister dear."

I watch as they gather their things. Brad places the official paperwork copy of our divorce neatly in his briefcase, and his arm wraps—easily—around Ivy's waist as they go to leave the room.

"Take care of it, Willow. I no longer desire to have any part of *me* touching *you* any longer than necessary. The Tate's reputation upholds a level of perfection that you no longer manifest."

He doesn't wait for me to respond—not that I would have. Instead, he ushers my witch of a sister right out the door … slamming it for good measure.

I look back down, my belly rolling over the button of my black slacks, and sigh. He's right. I'm about as far from perfect as it gets. I'm sure when the evil queen looks into her enchanted mirror and asks who the fairest of them all is, my image never pops up.

I reach up and swipe at the one tear that slips past my hard-built shell and vow right then and there that no one will ever make me feel like this again.

Worthless.

Ugly.

Undeserving.

No matter what it takes; from this moment on, I will never allow this feeling to define me. Hell, it hadn't been one I'd entertained in months. With the help of my friends and my therapist, I had come so far, and just like that—he easily knocked me right back down.

When I leave the lawyer's office, the lunch crowd is starting to rush through the busy streets. My body is craving some food—not just because it's well past my normal lunch hour, but also to help me emotionally cocoon myself. The desire to fall back on old coping methods is strong, but I push it away as I remember my vow back in the conference room. I walk past all the establishments I would normally jump right in line at; I rush past my favorite little Italian restaurant and keep going until I'm all but running down the busy New York streets. Bumping into people in my madness, I'm getting yelled at left and right. I don't slow one bit; I just power walk through my gasps for breath. Finally, when I see my building ahead, I allow myself to slow.

The Logan Agency, my father's pride and joy, is all the way on the fifty-seventh floor. Even through the long elevator ride up, stopping every few floors to let more people off, my breathing doesn't return to normal.

It takes me a good ten minutes *after* sitting down at my desk before I'm able to breath without the tightness and stinging in my lungs.

"Willow, my coffee, *now*," my father barks through the intercom. I look down at my phone and wonder, not for the first time, what would happen if I threw it at the floor-to-ceiling 'wall' that separates his office from where my desk sits outside his door. "And don't forget, only three sugars this time," he orders before slamming down the phone—severing the connection to my own intercom system.

This ends today, Willow, I think to myself as I mix in his sugar—just three packs—with the stirring stick. With each turn of my wrist, I solidify the vow I made earlier.

I will never, ever allow someone to get close enough to hurt me again. I will do everything possible to claw out of this heavy shell I've grown around myself.

I let the strength and motivation today's events have given me sink in. The push I've needed to take the final steps toward making myself someone better. Someone I could like. But even with that determination coursing through my veins, all I feel is more and more hate. Hate for those around me. Hate for the way I allowed Brad and Ivy to make me feel one inch tall again. Hate for being so freaking weak I let myself fall down. Back to the person I used to be. A person I hate down to my very core.

No more.

I have nothing left to lose.

Nowhere else to go but up.

It's time to finally be the Willow I can love.

Even if no one else can.

CHAPTER THREE

WILLOW

Six months later

"**W**ILL, GET IN HERE, BABY!"

I roll my eyes as I continue to gather the nail polish and remover we'll need and tossing them into the basket by my side.

"Willow Elizabeth! You don't want to miss this fine-ass man!"

There really is no telling who my lust-sick best friend is talking about. Truth be told, there really isn't a man Edward Hart doesn't find bed worthy. I love Eddie, God do I, but I swear that man is incapable of thinking about anything other than sex.

"What are you watching?" I ask before setting down the large basket full of multiple nail polishes, cotton balls, and just about every other mani/pedi tool you could ever need.

"Oh! I like this color," Eddie says in a whimsical tone.

"Honey, focus." I laugh, patting his thick, muscular thigh.

Eddie stops painting his thumbnail—light pink, I should add—and darts his deep brown eyes toward the television before returning his focus to the task at hand. "Just you wait for it," he mumbles, sticking his lip between his teeth and attempting to swipe his thumbnail with the pale pink polish.

"Kirk, are the rumors to be believed?" I hear an impossibly fake, breathy voice say from the corner of the room. Turning my head, I look over at the television and wait for the entertainment reporter to continue. "Surely, Mr. Hollywood royalty, Sexiest Man Alive at that, isn't off the market for good?"

"If the rumors are to be believed, then yes, Kennedy, he most definitely is. Being spotted leaving a doctor's office known for its specialty in high-risk pregnancies with none other than his ru-mored on-again, off-again girlfriend, Mia Post. Not even a week after the pair was seen relaxing on the sunny tropical shores of Tahiti, I might add."

I watch in rapt fascination while they go on yammering about Kane Masters' supposed 'baby mama drama.' My eyes widening and my ears sucking up every word. I've been obsessed with this man and any information I can find out about him since our run-in six months ago. Just thinking about how he made me feel on a day I thought could be nothing but horrendous causes my body to heat. He's been a running fantasy. The star of all my self-induced ecstasy. My obsession.

"Rumors aren't exactly solid truth, Kirk. Take for example how just earlier this year there was one flying around that his oldest brother, Kyle, had apparently separated from his supermodel wife, the stunning Jessica Deen."

"Yes, well ... I suppose that sometimes they aren't exactly confirmed, are they?" Kirk laughs. The screen changes to an image of Kane with his two older brothers, Kole and Kyle. Just seeing them together is a reminder of the good genes that run in the Masters family. They're a triple smack-down force for any woman.

Including me.

All well over six feet tall, dark brown hair that looks black in most of the tabloids magazines, and the bluest eyes you've ever seen. You would have to be dead or blind not to have any one of them affect you. Kole, like Kane, decided to take the path of fame and fortune, and both of them went on to become hugely popular actors. The oldest, Kyle, wasn't famous in his own right, but rather was well known because of his brothers—and the fact he married one of Victoria's Secret's top models. But even with all three of them rocking impossible good looks, it's always been the youngest Masters brother who's caught my eye.

In the days that followed our run-in, I've spent more days than I care to admit grabbing any tabloid magazine, entertainment report, or online article I could find about Kane Masters. His image and the scene forever burned in my memory have been the gasoline to my already burning fire of determination to become the Willow I am today.

I used him. Sure, it started out as fantasy and dreams ... but it turned into me using him and everything he represents to drive myself toward the change I am today.

The picture of the Masters brothers changes and an image of Kane flashes on the screen, drawing me from my thoughts. I lean forward slightly, sucking in every single inch of his face. The same feelings I had when I was face-to-face with him resurface like a slap to my hibernating libido; same as every time I see his image.

His lightly tanned skin is darkened with an even more golden version of the tan he always carries. They continue to sift through various pictures of him on a sunny beach, his swim trunks hanging low on his hips, that sexy V on display, and those abs … good God, don't get me started there. When they've displayed a million different poses of him just walking out of the surf, they settle on one of him taken at his last red carpet event. His burning blue gaze causes me to shift uncomfortably on the couch, knocking into Eddie's knee. I hardly hear his hushed expletive because Kane's penetrating gaze has me completely transfixed.

As if he's looking right into my very soul, his eyes never waver from their connection with the camera. The lopsided grin that probably results in panties being dropped nationwide is in full force. I watch with bated breath as he runs one hand through his thick hair.

Could he be any more perfect?

"Yeah, maybe. If he turned that sinfully sexy scruff he's rocking into a beard. That would probably throw his hotness levels over the edge and cancel out any negative traits he might have … therefore, perfection would be mastered."

"Huh?" I question, not moving my eyes from the television.

"Sweetheart, has he rendered you stupid? You've been mumbling under your breath since beach picture four, which I might add was definitely fry your brain worthy, but you don't see me over here acting like a moron. Well, I might have forgotten my name for just a brief second when that image appeared. There was no hiding the eggplant in his swim trunks. Bet he's hung like a damn stallion."

I roll my eyes, and with one last wistful sigh, I move my eyes from Kane's image back over to Eddie—narrowing them instantly when I see him smirking.

"You aren't funny."

"Sure, I am."

"No, you really aren't. How are you not even a little impressed by everything that is Kane Masters?"

"Because he is one hundred percent unattainable dick for me, Will."

"Yeah, well, he's one hundred and fifty percent unattainable dick for me too, Eddie, but you don't see that simmering down any of my hormones. God, how pathetic can I get." His eyes get hard, but that doesn't stop me. "Even if he was just some normal guy, could you ever see someone like him with someone like … me?"

"Willow," he snaps in warning.

"Eddie," I fire back. "Be serious." I flap my arm out in the air but quickly drop it when I remember I'm wearing a tank top … the number one enemy of a chubby girl is the skin under her arms. I always feel like it's just jiggling like crazy. No matter how hard I work out, I still feel like it grows daily.

"I saw that," Eddie grunts, narrowing his eyes. The issues I have toward my body have been an ongoing sore spot for Eddie.

"You saw nothing."

"You look beautiful, Willow. I wish you could see what I see when I look at you. Any man, Kane included, but yours truly excluded because you know … you have the wrong equipment, would be lucky to have you on his arm."

I snort, pick up the remote, and turn the television off, saying good-bye to Kane's handsome smirk and all the tingly feelings his face gives me. Why do I feel so upset about the news that he and his supposed girlfriend are expecting? I mean, it's not as if I had a chance.

Sighing, I look over at my handsome best friend. "Eddie, people like me don't get the handsome ones. We get the short, bald, pot bellied ones."

He opens his mouth to respond, and I know from experience this is just the beginning of a fight; one I'm not interested in having with him tonight at all. I could only imagine how this conversation would be going if he knew about my run-in with Kane just months before. Tonight is about relaxing and celebrating his promotion out of my father's company. He's finally going to be living his dream. He's grown such a reputation for excellence in his work that his demand has outgrown my father's reach.

"When is Kirby getting here?" I ask, effectively letting him know the subject is closed. Conversation over. Done.

"Soon." He sighs. "Something about Rob needed her to take Alli to soccer practice because he would be working late and she would be over as soon as she got Alli home and settled."

"Right, well, let's get started." I pick up the pink polish he made a complete mess of his nails with and recap it. "Where's the remover? You look ridiculous."

Smirk back in place, Eddie and I resume our pampering and forget all thoughts of Kane Masters.

Well, kind of.

Not really.

An hour later, Eddie pops bottle number three of the most delicious Moscato d'Asti. Maybe it was our overly buzzed minds, or the fact we had covered both our faces in a mud mask, but when the door snaps open with a loud bang, we both scream. Hilariously, Eddie sounds more girlish than I do, causing me to double over in laughter.

Kirby walks in and stops dead in her tracks. "You two bitches started without me?"

I look over at Eddie, his lips moving in a weird pucker-like pout as his mask cracks around his lips. Each visible crack makes his pucker grow until he looks absolutely ridiculous. I'm sure my own mask is well beyond ready for me to wash off. Just seeing him make that face makes my lips twitch until I'm copying him. Both of us start laughing again when we see our faces contort as the mask cracks around our movements.

Clearly, we had started without her, but I stupidly look back over at my other best friend, still laughing. "Uh … no?"

Her violet blue eyes narrow more until they're just tiny slivers. "Uh … yes! And you've so obviously gotten a head start on drinking since you two are drunker than a skunk. It's a good thing I brought dinner," she grumbles and finishes walking into my apartment, kicking the door closed with her booted foot. "I got Stanzo's, Will. I know how much you love their eggplant parm."

Well, isn't that sobering.

I don't let my inner cringing show; I give her a smile and walk over to give her a hug. "Awesome. Let me just go wash this off," I tell her, walking to my bathroom. I'm going to need to run myself into the ground tonight to burn off Stanzo's.

I closed and turned the lock before walking over to my vanity to stare into the mirror. With a quick twist of the tap, I continue to look into my eyes as the water warms and the mouthwatering scents of the best Italian mom and pop restaurant around fills my nose.

My breathing speeds up, and I do everything I can to mentally talk myself back up. Every Friday night, it's the same. We have the best time during our 'girls' night' fun of beautification, but it always ends with me having to talk myself into playing the part of carefree Willow. The one who hasn't had to give up just about all the foods I used to love and replace them with salad just to shed some pounds. It's so easy to hide this part of myself when we're together at work, but here … it isn't as easy to sweep things under the rug. They notice too much.

Just get in there, eat slowly, and wait for the wine to continue to flow. You can go to the gym when they leave and work it off.

I continue to repeat those words to myself as I bring a warm, wet washcloth to my face and start rubbing off the overly dry mud from my skin.

Small bites. Move the fork around, a lot. Small bites. Make sure their glasses stay full. Then move the food around some more. Gym later.

Tonight is one of the more challenging meals. Most of my favorite meal is easy to make disappear with a few calculated shifts of my fork, but because it's basically one lump of food, it's harder to make it look … eaten.

But if they've remained clueless this long, I doubt tonight will be any different.

Keep the wine flowing. Eat slowly. Small bites. Fork shifts. More wine. You've got this, Willow. It's only one night a week of pretending. Tomorrow, it's back to salad and water.

I take a few cleansing breaths, and with a small nod, I make my way out of the bathroom toward where my two best friends are laughing around the kitchen table.

God, that food smells like heaven. But I know better. Nothing good ever comes from indulging. It might smell like heaven, but it's a package sent straight from hell. A package that has been my greatest weakness. But I'm in charge now. I've worked too hard to lose the weight I have to allow old habits to bring it all back.

"I grabbed you a plate, Will," Eddie says, looking at me a little too long for my liking.

Slow bites, Willow. Just take it slow. Keep the wine flowing. You could probably last four hours at the gym and still be able to function tomorrow at work. Who needs sleep?

"Thanks, honey." I sit in my seat and look over at Kirby, starting the first dance of my fork against the devil's temptation sitting in front of me. "How was soccer practice?" I question, picking a small sliver of my dinner and placing it between my lips. It takes everything in me not to moan at the explosion of flavors that hit my neglected taste buds.

"Good, good. Alli is a rockstar, like always." She brags about her eight-year-old daughter.

"When's her next game? I missed the first couple. Work's kicking my ass," Eddie complains.

"Yeah, Mister Hotshot Photographer. If you would stop shooting all those gorgeous men for two seconds, then maybe we would see you more often." Kirby laughs, taking another huge bite of her food and making my mouth water a little more.

"It's been insane, Kirb. I'm so glad we finally finished up with that campaign. I never thought I would be happy to have half-naked women back in front of my lens. Those men are the biggest divas of all."

They continue to talk about work while I work on moving my

food around and keeping their glasses filled. Of course, as I was concentrating so hard on making sure I put the minimum number of bites between my lips, I miss Eddie's next question.

"I hear your sister is trying to get her job back. Know anything about that, Will?"

My fork drops, flinging the piece of food I had been shifting last in the air before it lands with a wet slap on the table.

"Excuse me?" I implore, ignoring the mess I just made.

"How did you not hear about this? Jesus, you sit outside your father's office every day, Will! Have you been living under a rock?"

"Tell me?" I whisper. God, I know my father couldn't care less about me, but I really thought we had been turning a corner when Ivy quit. Well, that's a lie. But it felt better to be at work when I had just one person's hate to deal with instead of two.

Eddie's concerned gaze rolls over my face as he assesses the damage he knows this turn in the conversation is causing me.

"Just tell her, Eddie. She deserves to know so she can be prepared."

"Right, well … it's all rumors, of course. But I heard from Pam, who heard it from Stacy, who heard it from Janelle when she was filling in for you last week while you were on vacation, that your sister had a meeting with your dad. Apparently, when they finished, he said he would look forward to seeing her around the office next week. Which I'm assuming means tomorrow. Shit, I'm sorry, Willow. I thought for sure he would tell you."

"Yeah? Because we have such a close relationship," I snap, pushing my plate away. At least they won't question my lack of appetite now.

Eddie looks at my plate before looking over at Kirby. They

continue to have some silent conversation while I let my mind drift to what it would mean if Ivy were to come back to work.

We all work together at my father's agency. He's been a driving force in the modeling world for the last three decades. His offices, one of many, are headquartered in New York City, and he handles everything from models to photographers and everyone between.

Kirby, being one of those inbetweeners, works for my father as a well-sought-after makeup artist who he hires for various events such as on-location photo shoots, fashion shows, and here lately, television and movies. Luckily for my father, she's happy to remain in New York and has no dreams of moving on to work on her own, like Eddie.

Eddie had been working for the Logan Agency as one of his top photographers, but because of his superior work and in-demand status, he's recently branched out on his own. Thus, our little celebration of his 'promotion' and leaving the Logan Agency. I couldn't be more thrilled for him and his new path in life. Even if I'm sad that when he leaves for some commitments he has in Europe, our girls' nights will never be the same.

And me? I'm a glorified secretary for the owner, my father, but all that boils down to is I'm his gofer, coffee maker, and overall little bitch. Ivy had been working as his personal assistant, right hand, and general face of the Logan Agency before leaving to 'start her life with Brad.' Apparently, if rumors are true, her life got started and she's ready to torment me a little more while getting all the gratification she can from being fawned over constantly at the agency.

And here I am, the stupid little girl who believed she could make her father love her during my quest for healing. If it weren't for Kirby still being there, I would have left when Eddie did last week and never looked back. But I've sunk the better part of my twenties into working for a man who hated me just so I could attempt to earn his love. Stupidly believing the impossible possible. And now, well … who would hire a twenty-nine-year-old woman with a dusty degree in business administration and the only experience under her belt being making coffee and answering the phone?

"Will? You okay, honey?" Kirby asks.

Giving myself a mental slap, I look over at her and give her my best smile.

"Yeah, just lost my appetite thinking about what that might mean for me."

She looks over at Eddie and then down at my plate before looking back into my eyes. "You sure? You didn't eat much," she states; obviously, since I probably had maybe four full bites.

"Yeah. Ivy tends to do that to me. I'm going to go clean up." I don't wait for them to ask any more questions; I gather my plate and walk into the kitchen, scraping the food into the trash before washing off the plate.

Well … at least I didn't have to pretend to actually eat it any longer.

CHAPTER FOUR

WILLOW

THE NEXT DAY, WHEN MY alarm starts blaring, I wake up with a sense of dread over the news that Ivy might just be back in the office today. It doesn't matter that I've changed mentally and physically since the last time I saw her. It doesn't matter that in that time, I've gained some of my confidence back. I've been stronger. At that moment, the feeling of hate and fear instantly pushes me back once again. Hate for her, but even that is overshadowed by the hate I feel toward myself for being so weak that I forget every step I've made to better myself over the last six months. And fear that being around her again is going to cause me to slip and forget the strength I've earned.

Physically, I've worked hard to shed some weight and have dropped a solid fifty pounds from my body. I no longer look in the mirror and hate who I see looking back. I don't love it, but I'm getting there. I had been a size twenty for so long that sometimes I still struggle to see the size fourteen I've earned through basically starving myself of the food I crave and maintaining daily—sometimes twice a day—trips to the gym. Getting ready this morning, though, no matter how hard I try, I see the old me. I feel the same helpless self-loathing I had for so long. Just because of Ivy and what her return could mean.

I know the problem. I know *why* I see the old me. It's taken months of deep theory to understand that it is a trick my mind plays on me. I have a preoccupation with finding my flaws. All of this stems from suffering from what my doctor calls body dysmorphia. I've made the vision I see for myself a product of the imagined flaw. Even realizing this and working daily to overcome it, I still find that it's easier said than done. A week after my divorce was final, she started me on anti-depressants, and with the help of our sessions, my journaling, and a lot of extensive therapy I had been able to put it behind me … for the most part.

To be honest, I'm mad at myself for allowing Ivy to bring me back down to my lowest of lows with just a thought.

You're better than this, Willow. You've come so far. Don't let her take everything you've earned from you. You aren't weak anymore. No one has that power over you but yourself.

I dress with care, picking one of my more flattering black dresses and black pumps. The dress hugs my ample chest, covers my arms to the elbow, but more importantly pleats at the skirt to hide the slight roundness of my stomach I can't seem to rid. Even I feel pretty in this, so hopefully, it will add some much-needed confidence to my mentality going forth today.

The ride to work, like always, is uneventful. The ascent to the floor of Logan Agency's offices has my pulse spiking. I try to mentally prepare myself, but when I step off the elevator and into the glamorous lobby, I lose every ounce of careful preparation. Like a sixth sense, I just know she's here. As if Ivy's very being has left her twisted vines of evil behind with every step she takes.

Why would he bring her back? God, really, I can be so stupid. Why *wouldn't* he bring her back? She's his pride and joy.

"Hey." I jump when Kirby's voice calls out to me from behind Mary's desk, the floor's main receptionist. Mary, an older woman who has been with the agency from conception, gives me a kind smile and wave before lifting the ringing phone from the cradle.

"What's up?" I ask, shifting the weight of my purse and giving Kirby a small smile.

"You look pretty, Will," she praises.

"Thanks."

"You know, don't you?"

"That she's here?" I ask. Kirby's eyes soften before she nods. "I know. It's okay, Kirb. I'm not worried about it."

Lie. Big freaking lie.

"What can I do? I can start a small fire in the break room? We could be out of here before you ever saw her face. Run off to Mexico? Drink those yummy tropical drinks until we pass out in a drunken stupor?"

Despite my unease, I laugh. "Nothing you can do. I just need to get it over with. Rip off the Band-Aid. Who knows, maybe she's going to be happy to see me." I laugh; the sound hitting my ears is as fake as it feels coming out.

"We could quit," she continues. "I wouldn't mind being a kept woman and staying at home all day," she jokes, trying to lighten the dark mood that has settled over me.

"You would be bored out of your mind, and *I* wouldn't be able to pay my bills."

"Right, well ... it's a suggestion. If you want to run, just pull the fire alarm or something ... I'll follow your lead."

"I love you, Kirby Quinn."

"I know. And I love you back, Willow Elizabeth."

Might as well get this over with. I give Kirby a hug and walk around the corner to begin my walk down the west wing of our offices. This side, the whole west end of the floor, belongs to my father. One long, narrow hallway full of pictures of the popular signed models he's had over the course of the agency, no doors, and dim lighting with little spotlights on each picture. The other wing of our floor, being the meat of operations, is full of offices, studios, and chatter from all angles. But not here ... nope, this hallway is long and silent.

That is until I hear her high-pitched giggles carrying down from the open door of my father's office. I reach the end of the hallway and walk around to my desk tucked in the corner. I always thought its placement was my father's way of placing me away without actually losing sight of me. Keeping me close, but far away at the same time—which really makes no sense because, from the way his eyes go hard every time he's within a few feet of me, I'm not sure why he would even want to have me around. Hell, I'm not really sure why he even gave me a job to begin with.

My area is basically just the outer room to his huge office. I have no windows and the only natural light is from the glow of his office of glass. All the lighting around me is dim. What isn't coming from a few strategically placed lamps comes wholly from his office's walls—even when set to the fog privacy setting. His whole office takes up the back half of the room, paneled in floor-to-ceiling glass on my end and the one inside his office. But like now, when he has the fog-like setting turned on, those glass walls make this room almost dungeon like. My desk takes up the right side of his outer sanctum. The other side of the room has two chairs, one leather loveseat, a sleek glass coffee table, and one longer console table against the far wall. A huge television flashes pictures of the talent he's held or holds under the Logan Agency's name. The room my desk is in is used only for clients to sit while they wait for him to call them in.

That calling always being done by Ivy when she worked here. In recent months, since Ivy hasn't been around, he's actually let me take more of an active role as his secretary. But I'm sure that now that she's around, I'm going to be back to being a wallflower, stuck answering phones and gathering his coffee and meals.

Cinderella probably had it better than I do.

Storing my purse in my desk, I sit down and power up my computer. I can hear them laughing as I sort through the emails from overnight and make note of all pressing issues. Checking the calendar for today's scheduled meetings, I frown when I see a huge blank spot on the lunch hour with a notation I'm to have lunch catered and arriving no later than noon for three people.

"Willow!" My father bellows through the intercom, spiking my already frayed nerves.

"Yes, sir?"

"Get me my coffee," he demands before severing the connection. I hear him through the opening in his office door as he slams the receiver down, grumbling his complaints.

After a few deep breaths, I stand and walk through the doorway behind me and into the small kitchen area housed in our wing for him and his clients' needs. How hard would it be for him to just walk to his door and speak to me like a human and not some robot slave?

I plop the K-cup in the machine and wait while the water heats before it starts spitting coffee into his mug. Making sure I measure out the correct amount of sugar—no cream—I walk back through the doorway, careful not to spill the hot liquid.

With my focus on my feet and my concentration on avoiding burning myself, I don't even see the person standing in my path until it's too late.

"Watch where you're going, dumbass." And with those venomous words, my sister twists her body and knocks into my arm with her elbow, sloshing the coffee over the edges and all over my hand.

"Crap," I hiss and jerk my arm to attempt to ease the pain, completely forgetting the mug itself is attached to my burning skin. And like most of the things in my life that Ivy touches, disaster hits in the form of a frontal attack of caffeine as the coffee hits my body, soaking through my dress in a liquid fire burn.

"Nice to see some things haven't changed, *sister*." Ivy laughs before turning again and slapping me in the face with her long, sleek ponytail. I watch as she walks down the hallway and away from the office.

"Willow! My coffee!" My father's voice comes booming through his partially opened door, making me jump slightly.

Crap. God, that is hot.

"One second," I call out.

I turn, ignoring that my sister just effectively ruined my morning, and make my way back to the kitchen. Dabbing my body with a towel the best I can, I wash my hands and fix his coffee once again. I need some Excedrin and quick.

I add the right amount of sugar packets—three—and grab one of the stirring sticks from its tidy bin next to the sugar.

I'm more careful this time, and when I walk into the main office, I make a mental note to avoid looking into his eyes until I'm done with my task. He would flip if I spilled just a drop on his desk. Placing his coffee down, I take a few steps away from his desk before I look up.

His eyes, so much like Ivy's, look at me.

"Your sister is back, Willow," he tells me, not looking up from the papers he's shuffling. Uh, yeah Captain Obvious, I noticed.

"Yes, sir," I reply evenly.

"I'm going to need you to finish out the work day by getting Ivy up to speed on where we are with upcoming shoots and new model acquisitions, but then I would appreciate it if you cleared out all your personal shit and left by the end of the day."

Wait. What? "Excuse me?"

His head tilts slightly, and I hold my gaze with my father, Dominic Logan, and pray this is some sort of a joke.

"Really, Willow. You didn't think I would keep you on after your split with Bradley, did you? I did him a favor by employing you while you were married, and I did Ivy a favor by keeping you while she and Bradley enjoyed some time together as newlyweds. But now she's back from her honeymoon and ready to take her rightful spot, so there is no need for you here."

"Excuse me?" I repeat a little more forcefully.

My father's eyes narrow, and his meaty fist slams down on his desk. The coffee I had so carefully prepared sloshes at the force of his fist and splashes over the edge, causing him to curse.

"Fucking hell!" he booms. "How much more clear would you like me to be? Catch Ivy up and then get out. I gave you a job out of respect for your mother, Willow, but even that duty has come to a long-awaited end. You were no use to me when I married her, the bastard daughter always attached to her hip, and you damn sure aren't now. We have certain standards here at Logan. Standards *you* never have and never will be able to excel at."

"Excuse me!" I yell and lean forward to slam my own hands on his desk. Surprising us both, his coffee tips over from the coaster it was resting on and rains brown liquid over his desk, soaking everything in its path. "You can't fire me! I'm your daughter!"

"*Step*daughter, Willow. Let's not forget that. And I believe I just did, little girl," he seethes.

Feeling the carefully constructed control over my emotions snap after years of mastery, I finally ask him the one question that has been burning in my mind since I realized my father … no, stepfather hated me. "Why does my very presence bother you so much, *father*? Do you have no concern you're essentially taking away my livelihood? My income? The fact you're throwing your own *step*daughter away doesn't concern you at all?"

He doesn't move, doesn't give a single emotion away with his cold stare. But his words, those do all the damage of a thousand knives piercing my body at once.

"You, Willow, will never be a daughter of mine. I have an image to withhold here, and for the last five years you've worked here, that image has been tarnished. The Logan Agency is about perfection and that, Willow, is just not something you have. You've been nothing but a waste of space since you started to let yourself go."

"Let myself go?"

"That's what I said."

"You freaking bastard! I didn't let myself go. Maybe if you acted like you actually cared about me for one second since Mom died, I wouldn't have *let myself go!*"

"Do *not* mention your mother."

"Why? Because I'm right? You stopped caring about me the second you walked into the hospital to find out Mom had died and I lived. Is that it? You hate me because I lived?"

Floodgates open. I can't and won't stop now. Everything I wished I could say to him for years is finally coming to an ugly head at our confrontation.

His face gets beet red and I watch as his nostrils flare a few times before he responds through thin lips. "Yes, Willow. Are you happy now? The wrong woman died that day, and every time I have to look into your eyes, the same eyes of your mother, I hate you more and more. So do what I fucking said. After today, do me a favor and don't turn back up. It would be nice not to have to see you again. Then maybe I could pretend it was *you* and not *her* who died!"

I hear a shocked gasp from the doorway and spin around; my anger dies instantly when I see Kirby's tear-streaked face. But where that anger was before, burning mortification has now replaced it. When I look behind Kirby, I see the pissed-off face of none other than Kane Masters himself.

Of course. That makes sense. Fantasy meeting nightmare.

CHAPTER FIVE

WILLOW

"**A**RE YOU OKAY?" KANE ASKS, his eyes not leaving my father. "Uh …" I stammer, my anger dying with the shock of seeing him here.

"Right." He smiles slightly, his gaze colliding with mine, and I watch in fascination as his softens just a breath before looking over my shoulder and becoming a mask of anger. *What is that about?* He doesn't lose the hard look of anger until he looks back at me. His eyes roamed over my face before moving down my body. I shift, uncomfortable, and pull my dress at the waist, hoping it isn't sticking too tightly to my body. Those cerulean orbs narrow at my movement and only cause me to pull a little more. *God, this is embarrassing.* "Stop that," he commands harshly, and I instantly drop my arms.

I hear my father clear his throat before addressing the witnesses to our heated fight. "Kane, you'll have to forgive me. I thought our appointment was later today. Willow was just leaving."

Dismissed.

Again.

By the man who I have called my father for my whole life. The only one I've ever known, even if he wasn't the one who helped give me life. Instead, he's always been the one who has resented the fact I existed. *Hello, Daddy issues anyone?*

Kirby moves into the room and clasps her hand in mine, giving my father a clear f-you by making her stance at my side known. I try to pull my hand from hers, knowing my father won't hesitate to reprimand her for butting in. She digs her fingers in, grasping hold of my hand until the strength of her hold is bruising and her nails are biting in warning.

"Kirby, stop," I plead.

"No. Not this time, Willow."

I try, once again, to remove my hand, but she holds strong.

"Is this how you treat your own family, Dominic? I would hate to see how you treat someone outside that bond."

My eyes widen as Kane speaks. His voice is strong and true as it rumbles around us like thunder. I watch in rapt fascination as he stands up to my father. For me. I haven't had someone other than Eddie and Kirby go to bat for me in close to ten years. In fact, the only person I remember ever doing it before was my mother.

Why is he doing this? He doesn't even know me.

My relief that he obviously didn't hear everything is short-lived when my father speaks.

"I'm sorry you had to witness that, Kane. It's unfortunate, but it seems like my stepdaughter needed a firm hand. You'll understand one day when you have kids of your own. It's necessary to be hard. Please sit. I'll have Ivy set up the conference room." He clears his throat before continuing. "Willow?"

I move my eyes from the detailed study of Kane's body and glance over at my father. Maybe he's changed his mind. Perhaps this was all just a daydream … yes, I'm sure it's all a big misunderstanding. "Sir?"

"A word?" He walks around his desk and flicks his hand toward the doorway. I'm sure this is when he's going to admit it was a big prank—admittedly, not funny in the least, but I'm sure there's a reason. However, I'm not sure that would matter now that the verbal damage is done.

Kane doesn't move as my father attempts to get through the door. Not surprisingly, he radiates a dominating presence that leaves no room for argument. He slips his gaze from mine to look down at where my father is standing in front of him before looking back just as quickly.

Not many people can look down at Dominic Logan. At six-foot-one, he's always been one of the taller males who floats around the agency. Most of our male models sit somewhere around five-foot-ten; the females, though, most of them are right about level with him. Not Kane though. It's hard to tell someone's height from magazines, television, and movies, but Kane has to be pushing closer to six and a half feet.

His eyes are holding mine over the top of my father's head, and I feel Kirby's hand tighten. *What is he doing?*

"Oh, Kane, sweetheart! It's been ages." All four of us look into the outer sanctum as Ivy comes strutting back down the hall, her voice breaking the silence around us. I look over at my father to see a beaming smile in place before moving my gaze to Kane. His eyes are no longer on mine but assessing Ivy. Perfect. Freaking. Ivy.

Well, I'm certainly not going to stick around for this. I would prefer to keep the fantasy I've built around the image of Kane Masters on my pedestal of 'the perfect man,' and I know anything he might do right now would ruin that. Or actually, what Ivy might do, and his subsequent reaction to her.

I've yet to meet a man who could see Poison Ivy for the evil human being that she is. Kane will just be like the rest stuck in her spell.

"Come on, Kirb," I whisper and tug her forward. I have to suck in to make it through the doorway Kane occupies, but no amount of air forced through my panicked lungs would make me a smaller person. Nope; instead, my large breasts rub against his chest, and I hold back a shiver with the friction of his touch. I cringe when I think about what he must think. Someone like Ivy would have no trouble slipping through. I turn to look at Kirby, avoiding his penetrating gaze at all costs, and my shoulders drop when I see her move past him with no trouble at all. Her slim build makes it easy to walk through the narrow opening provided with little effort.

"I brought you a trash bag, Wills," Ivy says with a slither.

"For what, Ivy?" I say with rancorous sarcasm dripping from my tone.

"For all your shit, sister dear." She laughs, her face not moving from her tight-lipped sneer.

"You bitch," Kirby fumes.

"You have ten minutes, Willow," she continues. "Make sure you turn in your keycard to the offices as well as any other property of Logan Agency you might *think* you have rights to. Ten minutes, Willow, to remove all your shit and don't let me see you back here again."

Perhaps, it was years of verbal abuse from my father, sister, and Brad. Maybe it was years of self-hatred finally boiling over the tipping point. Coming to a head between who I was and who I have worked so hard to become. Or maybe I just finally had enough. Recognizing when you hit the ground of rock bottom and it turns into quicksand puts into perspective that you really don't have anything left to lose. They've taken it all, but they will *not* get my pride. Whatever the driving force behind it—I snap. And I don't snap in a pretty, ladylike fashion where I whip off a metaphorical white glove and slap some faces.

No. Not me.

In typical Willow fashion, I go big when my crazy surfaces.

"I hate you!" I scream. "For years, I've been your punching bag. For YEARS, I've put up with everything you've thrown at me verbally. I've been nothing but a glorified human pile of crap for the two of you to step in whenever you need to feel better about yourself. You want me gone? Every piece of *me*? Fine!"

I look over at Kane. The instant reminder of our first encounter has me ripping my hand from Kirby's and bending to snatch my shoes off my feet, tossing them at Kirby. Not this time, heels, not this time. She catches them easily despite her shock. Moving toward Ivy, I grab the bag before marching over to my desk. I throw in anything that isn't '*Logan Agency*' property. I'm a tornado of mental torment chanting *mine* over and over again as I snatch whatever I can. Pencils, pens—mine. Tape—mine. Notepad— mine. Little pillow for back support—mine. Mug with a cute little kitten on it—*mine*. All freaking *MINE!*

I stomp from my desk to the coffee table in the sitting area, grab all the magazines I had been in charge of buying each week from the little vendor on the corner of our building, and throw them in too. The fake flowers sitting on the small table near the hallway mouth are thrown in the bag too since I was the one who purchased them in the hopes of adding some happiness around here. Happiness! Ha, what a joke.

In my hysteria, I throw open the kitchen door and start to dump sugar packets and coffee stirring sticks into my bag. Because I'll be damned if I let him make his demanded coffee with ease. Have fun finding three sugars now, jerk!

By the time I've grabbed anything I could deem general property, my trash bag was full to the point of straining the lining. I huff back to Kirby and thrust the bag at her, making her fumble a little to keep hold of my shoes and grab the balled up end.

I puff a piece of hair that had come loose from my bun so that it is no longer in front of my face. With one last look at my boiling-mad father, I grab my iMac desktop. With a strength I never thought possible, I pull it from its connecting cords before I heave it forward and watch in satisfaction as Ivy scampers out of the way. My eyes leave Ivy's weird dance to watch as the computer slams through one of the panels of glass that make up my father's office walls before it crashes to the floor in a rain shower of glass at the foot of his desk.

"There, *Dominic*," I pant angrily. "There is the rest of your stupid property. Thank you for reminding me that I luckily share none of your blood. If I never see you again, it will be a day too soon."

I look over toward Kane, wondering again why he was even here to begin with, but when I see Ivy in his arms, I stop caring enough to ask. I know for a fact she doesn't know him. She looked as shocked as I did that day in the lawyer's office. But leave it to her to hook her claws into another man who's spoken for. Let's hope his relationship fares better than the one Ivy has already succeeded in ruining.

Just as well.

"Be careful with that one. Her bite is deadly," I mumble heatedly toward him.

His eyes fire at mine before looking down at the woman in his arms. Apparently, he's just noticing for the first time that she is wrapped around him like a little monkey. No, monkeys are cute. Snake. That's it. Like the deadly snake she is.

I don't give any of them another second of my time. I can feel the tears coming, but I refuse to let one drop in this room. I vaguely hear Ivy say something as I walk through the room and down the hallway. My silent, shoeless footsteps pad quickly and the tapping of Kirby's heels follow right behind me.

Without a backward glance, I leave behind another part of my life that was slowly drowning me.

CHAPTER SIX

KANE

Six months earlier

The offices of Buchanan and Buchanan

I'M NOT EASILY ENAMORED WITH someone. In my line of work, a beautiful face is a dime a dozen, and usually, those beautiful faces hold nothing but vapor between their ears. It's made the simplest of relationships all but impossible. The intrigue was missing. Nothing there was compelling enough to keep my attention past a quick glance.

I wouldn't say I'm a saint, but I'm losing interest in meager exchanges of sweaty bodies and awkward good-byes. That dreaded period of holding my breath and waiting to see if our shared encounter would make it into the rags. Meeting someone when you're a celebrity of my status has also been a big consternation for the last few years. Women want Kane Masters the icon and not Kane Masters the man. They couldn't care less what makes me tick, what makes me happy, what goals I desire for my future. They want the status and money that comes with being on my side. The only future they can see is one I would have to pay for.

It's been fifteen long years since I starred in my first lead role. Fifteen years of nothing but success that has no chance of slowing down anytime soon. I could stop making movies tomorrow and that success would never die. It used to be the only thing I wanted in life. Acting was my one and only aspiration. It was never a question of *if* I would become one of the most demanded names in Hollywood—it was always *when*. Two years after my first major motion picture role, I won my first Oscar. The year after that, another. Multiple awards followed. SAGs, Golden Globes, BAFTA—British Academy of Film and Television Awards—you name it; I hold it in a shiny case in the media room of my Malibu beach house.

But in all of that success, it's become painfully obvious to me in the last couple of years that I was missing something in my life. The meaningless affairs dwindled down to nothing. The attraction to the women in my normal circles disappeared. I began to see them for what they were, and I've been struggling significantly with that.

I want companionship. I want a partner I can build a life with outside the insanity of my celebrity status. I want more for my future than bright lights around me.

Aside from my brothers, my few closest friends, and my parents, there really wasn't anything left for me. I've begun to believe I would never find someone to fill the emptiness haunting me.

Bottom line—I'm lonely. Surrounded by millions and still the loneliest motherfucker around.

But I will never be lonely enough to settle for one of the vapid, fake women who surround my lifestyle. I want someone real. I need a challenge. I want to feel that *connection* to someone I've never been able to find. That one you read about. The one that makes you feel alive. Awakens you with just a glance. I know it's out there because I felt it once before; a fleeting feeling gone just as quickly as it hit, but it's out there ... otherwise, the movies they pay me millions to create wouldn't be instant blockbusters. Everyone dreams of finding that feeling. And until I find it, I'm afraid I'll spend the rest of my days wandering around like a lost puppy.

Even my agent has noticed a change in my normally full throttled drive. I've slowed down on the circuit; taking fewer offered roles, I'm focusing more on producing and directing. If I'm quite honest, I'm not even sure acting is something I want to do anymore. The industry has lost its glamor; I know if I have any hopes of finding that life partner I crave and a chance at making my dreams a reality, being in the spotlight will blind me from the path to find those things.

Who would guess that the real Kane Masters is a lonely little boy wandering around in a thirty-five-year-old's skin second-guessing every decision he's made up to this point? If I had just followed my brother, Kyle, in his footsteps outside this life of fame, would I be married now, too? Have kids? Be able to walk the streets without paparazzi swarming me? I'm sure, at the very least, I would be able to form lasting relationships with the absence of the lie-riddled tabloids. Kyle still struggles because of Jessica, his wife's own fame, but they've been able to carve out a life for themselves that seems to work.

"Drop me off here, Cam," I tell my driver, bodyguard, and

friend when he pulls up to my attorney's office at Buchanan and Buchanan. "I'll just be a second. I need to see if Steven looked over the contract I had dropped off yesterday and I'll be right back. Just wait here and I'll be quick." He gives me a hard look, and I know damn well it's because he hates that I brush off the potential dangers my celebrity status brings. "Seriously, Cam. No one has ever caused a scene here before, and I'm just going to be in and out."

Cam begrudgingly nods but doesn't reply. I hear him turn up the book he had been listening to before I jumped in the car earlier this morning. Normally, I don't give a shit what he's listening to, but he's been on a romance kick lately and he knows I'll get pissed if I start getting into a book only to have to stop. Those romance books get me hooked every time.

Call me a pussy—but there's nothing wrong with a man who enjoys a good romance book. My dad always said the best way to learn what a woman wants is to pick up some of the smut they love to read so much. Written by a woman, it might as well be a road map to instant pleasure.

I laugh to myself as I take the elevator up and step into the immaculate offices of Buchanan and Buchanan. I look over at the couple standing off to the side and give them a nod. I see recognition flash in the man's eyes, but the woman next to him catches my gaze.

She's beautiful—I'll give her that, even with the shocked recognition written over her features. But her beauty isn't something that causes me to take a second look. I will never understand why women feel the need to erase everything that makes them soft and feminine to turn themselves into one of those masks you pick up at Halloween. You know, the ones you put on and you could be screaming and carrying on within, but there wouldn't be a flinch in your facial features.

Fake.

Unattractive.

I move my gaze from her frozen face and look down at her thin body. Don't get me wrong; I'm sure there are men who love the sleekness of a smaller woman, but not me. I've always been attracted to women with curves. Because the women within my inner circle favor—like this woman—to pay for their beauty, the better part of my adult relationships have been with women like her by my side, even though my preferences run differently.

My best friend, Mia, was the voice of reason when my last serious relationship ended ten years ago. Jenn had left me claiming she couldn't keep up with the expectations of being by my side. I still don't understand it completely, but according to Mia, the media will rip anyone who isn't society's idea of perfect to shreds—something Jenn had been subject to for the vast duration of our relationship. Naïve enough to believe that 'love' was strong enough to protect anyone; no one was more shocked than I was when she didn't last long after we publicly came out as a couple.

Since that day, it's been nothing but women like the one before me. Women who I hold back with—not just emotionally, but also physically. Yeah, I love my women to have curves because I find them mouth-wateringly attractive, but also because when they lacked those curves I crave, I always feared I would break them if I fucked how I love to fuck.

Hard.

Bruising.

Rough.

Nothing but meaningless hookups followed the departure of Jenn. Hookups that I learned very quickly were a waste of my time and a headache of attachment issues from the women when you were done.

I turn the second her eyes flash with recognition, shaking me out of my thoughts as I walk over to Stacy, another insipid woman. Fake tits, annoying laugh, and a self-centered air seeping from her pores. I ignore her flirting and let her know I need to speak with Steven, turning before she can speak again and walking over to take a seat while I wait.

That's when I see her.

A flash of something familiar hits me as I study her. I've seen this woman before. Somewhere, our paths have crossed. She looks miserable, but even that can't disguise her beauty. A cloak of anxiety and fear wrap her body tightly as she shakes slightly while twisting her fingers together in her lap nervously. Her legs bounce and the movement makes her chest quiver. Moves that, even with them covered in fabric, I can tell are her natural tits.

Huge, larger-than-a-handful tits.

Fuck, I want to see her face. I've felt this before. A jolt to my senses I've experienced before followed by a protectiveness I've never felt before … not even with Jenn.

I sit in the chair to her left, just out of her eyesight, and wait for her to move. The way she has her head tilted now, I can't see her face through her long thick brown hair. I take the time to study the rest of her, trying to place her body. Her thighs look like the kind that would cushion my hips as I powered into her body. Her body—ripe, full, and all woman—has my groin tightening.

Not much could take the attraction away from this timid little mouse. God, when was the last time I saw a woman who caught my attention at a glance? I glance back over at the couple in the corner, the man, and I remember. Except, if I'm right, it wasn't the woman at his side that time but the one sitting full of fear to my right.

I was lost in thought when the Buchanan brothers walked into the lobby. Because they're used to seeing my face when I come to see my attorney, Steven, I get a nod of acknowledgment, but they wisely don't make a scene that greeting me would cause. My mystery woman fumbles to stand, and I watch as her bag snaps and crashes to the floor.

"Oh, God." I hear her whispered words, but they're so low, had I not been studying her so fiercely, I would have missed them. I feel her anxiety soar through the roof as she moves to collect the items scattered around her.

The desire to protect this woman—this familiar stranger—is so fierce. There's a roar in my ears from my blood pumping so rapidly through my veins. I don't even know this woman and watching her obvious struggle both physically and mentally is making my chest hurt.

And the moment I watch in horror as her heel catches on her broken strap, knocking her from her feet to her back in seconds, I feel like I'm being stabbed right in the chest.

What in the hell is wrong with me?

"What a mess, Brad. Aren't you thrilled you're finally going to be rid of ... well, that?" My contemplation snaps from the woman prone on the floor over to the couple from earlier. What the hell? That explains some of the anxiety and visibly shaken demeanor from the mystery woman.

"Willow? Are you okay?" Randy questions, stepping forward

at the same time Stacy starts squawking from her desk about some call he *must* take. Right, I'm sure.

Willow. I test her name out, repeating it a few times. Beautiful. Then it hits me, confirmation that this is someone I have met before. Brad Tate. His arrogance is something I'm shocked I didn't place before, but seeing this woman—Willow—I remember with clarity exactly when the last time a woman instantly caught my attention. However, now I have a name to place with the face I've thought about too many times to count. A stranger who had once again captured me in her web without even uttering a single word. That connection. I felt it simmer before, but now, now, it's a raging fire. I had ignored it before because it was clear she was spoken for then, but now … now, I'm not sure. I know damn well that Randy Buchanan is in family law, so why else would they be meeting with him?

"Kill me now." I hear the gasped words thick with pain, but even that can't hide the velvet tones that roll over my overheated senses. God, she even sounds like a dream come true. Husky voice made for sex.

"I'm sorry, Willow. I have to take this," Randy explains and offers his hand to help her up, but I move quickly from my position and stand next to her before addressing Randy.

"Allow me." My voice is thick with desire. Desire for a woman whose face I haven't even seen in years. I clear my throat and wait for Randy to move so I can help her … help Willow.

"It's all right, Mr. Masters. I have it. Won't take but a second, right, Willow?" he states before bending once again to offer his assistance. Assistance I don't want him to give her. *I* should be the one to help her. It should be *my* hands to touch her. No one else.

56

Fucking hell, what is going on with me? I feel like I'm seconds away from beating my chest and pissing on the floor. I don't even know if this is the same woman. Yet I'm acting like an animal just at the memory of what I felt only once before when I was sucker punched with just a gaze from across the room. Surely, this isn't her. I just need a vacation. To slow down. Right?

Thinking quickly, I take a small step forward and stop Randy before his hands can touch her. "That might be, Rand, but it looks like you're needed elsewhere." I lift my hand, mentally making sure my fists are relaxed, and point over to a very vocal Stacy while she continues to huff in annoyance. I'm sure it's because she's not the center of attention. Randy nods once and moves away. I wait for a beat before bending down and balancing my weight on the balls of my feet before offering my hand to her.

That's when I finally see her face.

She's stunning. She possesses the kind of beauty that even her demeanor tense in pain and panic can't hide. Her eyes widen when she looks into mine and I give her what I hope is a reassuring smile. Clearly, I need to work on my acting skills because I watch as her face heats and a light blush covers her neck and face.

Exquisite.

Just like she was the first time I saw her briefly, years before. She was there one second, lighting my skin on fire with one look into those brown eyes, and then she was gone. I had thought I imagined it, even after I asked about her, but seeing those eyes up close— yeah, I didn't imagine shit. That connection I had been hunting was indeed right in front of my face. I let her slip away with excuses of too many drinks and a long dry spell. Not this time.

"I ... please ... I'm so sorry," she mutters meekly. "Please, don't worry about me … oh, God."

"Willow, was it?" I ask, feigning the ignorance I should have at a 'first meeting.' Unable to resist any longer, I slide my hands under her arms and I help her stand. My body hums with arousal when her scent hits me. Peaches. Fuck, she smells like peaches? I bet she tastes like them too. Mentally slapping my undersexed mind, I look into her eyes, imploring. "Are you okay?" She doesn't speak. Her eyes just continue to roam over my face, drinking me in as hard as I am to her. Shit, maybe she hit her head when she fell. "Do you need medical assistance?"

"I—I'm—crap, I'm okay. Only what was left of my pride was damaged." She ducks her head, and I hate that I've lost her eyes. She moves to a crouch to start collecting her personal belongings, hurriedly cramming them into her broken bag.

"Kane, if you would follow me, I can take you back to Steven's office while he's busy," Stacy purrs from where she's now standing next to us. Her hands propped on her trim hips don't hide the clear annoyance on her face. Can she not fucking see the woman struggling right under her nose? What a bitch.

"Are you okay, Willow?" I try again desperate to see those brown eyes again. I'm at a loss as to how to help her—how to protect her. This feeling of not being able to control the situation is doing nothing but amping up the adrenaline-fueled desire pumping through my system.

Her eyes move back up to mine. Is she shocked I'm still here? Or shocked that I care?

"I'm … I'll—thank you for asking, but I'll be fine." Her words are reassuring, but her eyes show me how close she is to breaking.

With the need to protect her riding me, I attempt again to get her to allow me to help. "Right. I've no doubt about that, Willow. But it would ease my mind if you would at least allow me to offer some assistance."

"That's okay, Mr. Masters. I'm sure you have more important things to do. Thank you, though."

She couldn't be further from the truth. "Nothing that can't wait for me to help a beautiful woman out," I reply, trying to lighten the mood, but the second the words leave my mouth, I realize how gravely I miscalculated this beauty before me. She snaps her head back at my words, and before I can reach her, she cracks her head against the wood table she had been crouched in front of while collecting her belongings. "Shit," I say under my breath pissed at myself for jumping her like an overeager hunter, spooking the doe-eyed fawn before I could even get close enough.

My body moves on autopilot, and before I know what I'm doing, the protective instincts she incites roar higher to a life of their own. My fingers thread into her thick hair, and I rub the spot she knocked with my fingertips. Her eyes dilate, and I know I'm not the only one who feels this connection between us.

"It's fine. *I'm* fine. Please ..." I watch her eyes shimmer, and I curse myself again when the feeling of failure hits me.

Not wanting to be the reason for her tears, I release my hold with a deep exhale. Losing the link to her warm skin has me clenching my hands again. Looking for something to keep busy so I don't scare her again, I move to help gather the rest of her stuff, placing them slowly back into her bag. When the last pen is dropped inside, she grabs it and slams the bag against her chest.

A move of protection.

From *me*.

Fucking hell.

"Thank you," she softly mumbles, her eyes once again refusing to meet mine.

"It was nothing." It was everything.

"Well, thank you nonetheless. I'm sorry for interrupting your morning."

I smile at the spark I hear in her tone. There's the girl behind that fear. "At the risk of sounding like a jerk, the interruption was my pleasure."

Her eyes snap to mine, and she just blinks at me. Her long lashes fan against her porcelain skin with every downward blink.

Stunning.

"Good luck in there, beautiful Willow." Don't leave. "Until next time," I vow, mentally promising myself this will not be the last time I have my hands on her.

It takes herculean strength to move away from the hold she has on me. Each step feels as if an invisible cord is tugging at my chest.

Step—tighter. Another step—the cord jerks, and I turn to look back at her shocked face. Those beautiful wide eyes round with questions.

Soon, little doe … soon.

CHAPTER SEVEN

KANE

Present

UNFORTUNATE TIMING PUT ME OUT of the country on location filming for longer than I had wanted. Making it back to my little doe-eyed beauty was stalled even longer when I had to deal with some issues that had arisen back in LA. Add to that the obligations I had for press junkets for my next film's release, and then I was finally able to come back to New York City.

Just as determined as I was the day I left.

Only this time, I have to deal with rumors floating around me that could potentially fuck up my chances with my doe. Stupid rumors I'm powerless to do anything about until it's safe. Christ, when will I learn? One phone call two months ago was all it took for me to forget reporters are everywhere. They see everything.

"Did you get me the appointment?" I demand before shifting

my phone to my other ear.

"Yeah, Kane. Not sure I understand your motivation in approaching the Logan Agency, but your appointment is set. You do realize that the cast has been set for *Impenetrable*? Extras were cast a long time ago. Hell, you're in final stages of production, Kane. You don't *need* anyone else. And … why the hell are you off on a scouting mission when you pay people to do that for you?"

I move around my penthouse apartment to the floor-to-ceiling windows overlooking the city and mentally remind myself why I don't want to kill my best friend and overall confidant in all aspects of my life.

"Seriously, Mia?"

"Okay, I mean, I kind of understand your plan, but I don't think I can see what the end game is here? We both know this façade of finding models to act as extras is a bunch of bullshit. So, tell me. After you get in, how will you get the girl?"

I laugh. Leave it to Mia to see right through me. We've been close since high school drama class and that hasn't changed since we both hit the big screen running. Most of the media assume that because of our closeness, we're hiding a relationship, but they couldn't be further from the truth. Mia and I will never have anything past friendship. We tried it, briefly, and thankfully, it didn't ruin our friendship.

"I figured I would handle it like I do most things in my life, Mia. Wing it."

Her lyrical laughter comes through the line, causing me to smile. "Yeah, Mr. Big Badass … not sure this is one of those times. From what I hear, Dominic Logan is a real hard ass. If you aren't genuine in your interest, he's going to see right through you."

"You would be right, but lucky for me, he has a lot to gain here. From all the research I've done on the Logan Agency in the past six months, it's a dying company. He's overextended himself and his money, and fortunately for me, he's grasping at straws to stay afloat. He's lost more than fifty percent of his models this year alone when they refused to renew their contract. His lead photographer is leaving the agency, and there are rumors that more under his command are planning their exit as well. Best I can tell, I'm his savior."

Turning from my view, I move from my sunken living room and into the kitchen to grab a package of Tim Tams from my stockpile in the butler's pantry. They've become one of my biggest weaknesses since I discovered them while on location in Australia a few years back.

"How are you feeling? Mia, we really need to talk about things now that I finally have this plan of mine coming to fruition."

She lets out a deep sigh. "Yeah, I know. Just not now. When you come back to California, maybe. When you figure out if there is even anything between you and this chick, sure. But no need to rock the boat right now."

Grabbing one of the Tim Tams, I take a bite, swallowing half of the small cookie. I could polish off a few packages in one sitting. Those damn things are addictive.

"You're eating those nasty cookie biscuit things, aren't you?" Mia asks in my ear, letting me know the subject is closed. I don't like it, but I'll give her that play. She's under enough stress; the last thing she needs is for me to add more to it.

"Nasty? You're insane," I huff around a mouthful.

"Yeah … they are. They melt in your mouth, Kane. That just

isn't natural."

"That's the best part," I quip, knowing my favorite snack grosses her out.

"Anyway, Logan Agency … the girl—the mystery girl behind this ridiculous quest. You have told me next to nothing about her, Kane. That isn't like you."

And there's a reason for that. "Nothing to tell, Mia. I don't want to jinx anything." Which isn't a complete lie. I *don't* want to jinx anything, but I also don't want Mia to shoot this down before I even have a chance to explore it. I'm not a person driven by lust anymore; I'm a man who knows a real solid connection when it smacks you in the face. "I felt it, Mia." I sigh. "I felt that zap. That feeling of being kicked right in the chest. All it took was for her eyes to meet mine."

"Good God, you sound like a Lifetime movie," she groans.

I laugh but don't respond. Instead, I think about the last time I saw those beautiful doe eyes.

Willow Tate. Daughter of Dominic Logan.

It took only five minutes of my charm to get her full name out of Stacy on that fateful day, and it's taken me six months of planning to get where I am now.

Today is the day I put all my wheels in motion and find out if what I felt in her presence was as powerful as I remember and not a figment of my imagination. Surely, my mind didn't make something like that up.

"As much as I would love to chat, Mia, I have to run if I plan to make that appointment."

"Just promise me that you won't do anything foolish that has your PR team running crazy?"

"Not sure that's a promise I can make in good faith," I joke with a smile that matches the one I hear in her voice. "I'll call you later. You make sure and rest, okay?"

"I will. Be good," she warns.

"Aren't I always?"

I disconnect the call at her laughter and finish the package of Tim Tams before paging Cam and letting him know I'm ready to hit the road.

Five minutes later, we head out and I'm a few miles away from what will hopefully be the beginning of what I promised all those months before.

The Logan Agency looks just as pompous on the inside as the reputation it has built around its name is. Every overly decorated inch of the fifty-seventh floor screams success. If only they knew what my people had been able to unearth about the company most still think is so powerful in the industry.

The glamor hides its failings.

Failings I'm hoping to capitalize on today with my meeting under the guise of finding extras. I wasn't completely lying to Mia when I hatched this plan and had her put the wheels in motion— getting a few extras for the movie I'm directing and producing is just the stepping-stone to the office. If I happen to find some, great, but I wouldn't be losing sleep over not having some extra bodies we don't really need. We're in the homestretch of production, the final weeks before I'm finished directing my first film one hundred percent.

But really, the motivation behind today is just about getting back face-to-face with Willow, and hopefully, the rest will fall into place.

"Mr. Masters for an appointment with Mr. Logan, please," I tell the older woman at the front desk. I'll give her credit; if she recognizes my name or me, she doesn't give anything away.

"I've got it, Mary. I was headed that way," I hear and turn to look at the smiling face at the other end of Mary's desk. Her eyes twinkle with mirth, and I know *she* recognizes me and has no issues letting me know she knows exactly who I am.

Ah, what is this one up to? Trying to get me alone? I'm sure she's going to pass her number and a whispered fantasy she has about sex with *the* Kane Masters. She extends her hand, and I look down to see a substantial rock on her wedding finger. Christ, not another married woman.

"Kirby Evans, makeup artist extraordinaire here at Logan."

"Kane Masters," I deadpan and take her outstretched hand in greeting.

I watch in fascination as she closes her other hand around our combined ones and throws her head back with a deep throaty laugh. "Oh, calm down, Kane Masters, Hollywood hotshot, you're at no risk of exploding these ovaries. They're spoken for and happily so."

She lets go of my hand, and I manage to keep a straight face despite the shock I feel from her bizarre outburst. Seems that I pegged this one wrong.

"I've been married for ten years to my high school sweetheart, Mr. Masters. It would take a lot more than some big bad actor to knock that down. Come on, I was headed back there anyway to check on a friend, so I'll show you the way."

"Call me Kane," I shock myself by saying. Something about this woman, she could probably cause a monk to open up.

"Right. Well, Kane, follow me."

She takes off down a hallway I hadn't noticed, and with a smile to Mary, I trail behind her. Her slow, leisurely stride picks up speed at the yelling that can be heard when we're about halfway down the long hallway.

"Oh, God. Willow!" she cries out weakly before looking back at me in shock. Without wasting a second, she turns her focus and begins running the rest of the way. My senses pick up at the hostile tones echoing around us, and I hurry to follow behind her. When I walk through the end of the hallway and into what must be the outer seating area to Dominic Logan's office, I see Kirby standing stock-still in the opening of the office labeled with his name in neat gold script against one of the glass panel walls.

If it hadn't been for Kirby speaking her name just seconds before, I might not have known it was Willow who stood before us facing off with Dominic Logan. She's much slimmer than the last time I saw her. Her curves are still prevalent, but much less abundant than before. Just seeing her causes that connection we shared before to spark to life. Clearly, that isn't lacking in the least. Even without seeing those beautiful eyes, I would know her anywhere—as crazy as that sounds even to me.

I was too busy perusing Willow's lush body that I had zoned out until Kirby's whimper caused my ears to perk up again.

"Yes, Willow. Are you happy now? The wrong woman died that day and every time I have to look into your eyes, the same eyes of your mother, I hate you more and more. So, do what I fucking said. After today, do me a favor and don't turn back up. It would be nice not to have to see you again. Then maybe I could pretend it was *you* and not *her* who died!"

At Dominic's words, I can feel my temper spiking. My anger soars through my bloodstream at the vile tone with which he's speaking to his daughter. Before I can interject, Kirby's harsh gasp has both of the office's occupants swinging their heated gazes toward the doorway. I watch as the hurt soothes from Willow's features when she sees Kirby; obviously, this is whom she had been heading to check on, and based on what we just walked in on, I would say she was just in time.

When those doe eyes move to lock with mine, embarrassment replaces her heartbreak, and I want to kick myself for being the cause, yet again, for added shame.

Shame that has no business ever crossing her face.

Shame that, despite not even knowing this woman, I would love to wipe from her features.

Those protective feelings once again confuse me. Not because they're there, but because the intensity of them, so much stronger at this meeting, shocks me to my core. I know nothing about her, yet I would do anything I could at this moment to fix whatever is harming her.

Not able to stand the silence any longer, I speak, trying to ease her pain the only way I can right now. With my words. "Are you okay?"

"Uh …" she stutters. Fuck, she's adorable. Even her pain can't mask her appeal.

"Right," I reply with a small smile, reminding me of her stumbled words at our first meeting. Moving my gaze from hers, I lock eyes with her bastard father. Or stepfather, according to my investigation into their backgrounds. Any chance he had of getting me to help his company crawl from their looming home in the forgotten bowels of the industry is long forgotten. Willow makes a startled noise, and I move my angry focus from her father and back to her. Willing myself to calm so she feels safe with me.

I hold her eyes just a beat before allowing myself a quick glance at the body haunting my dreams since I first saw her. Fuck, those tits still make my mouth water, but the rest of her causes my body to harden with desire, despite the hostile environment we're standing in.

Her black dress isn't tight by any means, but it also doesn't hide the stunning, luscious body underneath it. A body I would love to get my hands on and my body over. My cock tightens at the thought of my fingers digging into the soft skin around her hips.

She shifts uncomfortably under my scrutiny, and her hands come up to pull the fabric away from her frame. What the hell? I can feel my eyes narrow, and her hands start to pull more of her dress. No way? No fucking way. What reasons could she possibly have to make a self-conscious move like that? Does she have no clue how beautiful she is?

"Stop it," I demand, and I'm instantly rewarded when her hands drop.

Before I can return my eyes to hers, Dominic's voice interrupts. "Kane, you'll have to forgive me. I thought our appointment was later today. Willow was just leaving."

My heated, anger-filled gaze flits to his, and once again, I can feel my anger burning like an out of control wildfire. I'm vaguely aware of Kirby moving toward Willow. Out of the corner of my eye, I watch her stand at her side and take Willow's hand, but I don't move my focus from the man before me. He's around my parents' age, but where they have a presence that is open, accepting, and loving, this man holds none of that. I can hear the two women whispering to each other, but I don't move. Fuck, I'm not even sure I'm breathing as I refuse to back down from Dominic's cold stare. He won't dominate *me*.

"Is this how you treat your own family, Dominic? I would hate to see how you treat someone outside of that bond."

He narrows his eyes, but at the risk of pissing me off, I can tell he's measuring his response. God forbid he show his true colors, that we had the displeasure of already witnessing, to someone like me. Someone with the power *I* wield.

"I'm sorry you had to witness that, Kane. It's unfortunate, but it seems like my stepdaughter needed a firm hand. You'll understand one day when you have kids of your own. It's necessary to be hard. Please sit, I'll have Ivy set up the conference room." His cold, calculating eyes leave mine and focus on the woman of the hour. "Willow?"

Apparently, he thinks the fact she isn't his own flesh and blood gives him the right to talk to her as if she's nothing. I know damn well he has been the only father she's known. I look over at Willow quickly enough to catch her gaze on its way up from my chest before she looks back over at Dominic.

"Sir?" she asks weakly.

"A word?" he questions, and before giving her a second to respond, he starts to move around his desk.

I lose her eyes, but her shoulders drop in what looks like relief for just a second before she catches her slip and straightens her posture, showing her strength in an impossible situation.

When I look back at Dominic, he's standing in front of me, obviously hoping I'll move. Fat chance of that, asshole. Standing to my full height, I look down into his eyes and don't hold back the fact I find this whole scene disgusting. I give him a few beats before looking back at Willow, giving her the lead, the power Dominic is doing his best to wipe from her bones.

I can see the wheels moving behind her shocked eyes. Her mouth moves, but before she can speak, a new voice interrupts.

"Oh, Kane, sweetheart! It's been ages," the voice speaks.

What the fuck? I remember her instantly as the woman from the law firm's offices. While I'm trying to figure out what the hell she's doing here, I hear Willow's whispers before she's pulling Kirby behind toward the door. My shock holds me still as she moves past me, but my body fires to life when her body brushes against mine. Those tits I've imagined bouncing in my face as she rides my cock rub against my chest, and I exhale a breath to try to feel more of her.

"I brought you a trash bag, Wills." I hear the other woman speak, but I don't move my eyes from Willow. I watch helplessly as the shame and embarrassment are back.

"For what, Ivy?" she snaps, the sarcasm dousing the heat of her embarrassment and making way for anger to take its place.

Ivy. Now, I can put a face to the name I know belongs to her sister.

"For all your shit, sister dear." Her laugh makes me cringe.

"You bitch," Kirby sneers.

"You have ten minutes, Willow," her sister continues. "Make

sure and turn in your keycard to the offices as well as any other property of Logan Agency that you might *think* you have rights to. Ten minutes, Willow, to remove all your shit and don't let me see you back here again."

I open my mouth to interject, not really sure what I'm going to say, but the animalistic snarl that comes from deep in Willow's throat stops me dead. I'm not even sure she was aware she made a noise, but in seconds, she's like a bull in a china shop. I'm positive nothing could stop her at this point.

"I hate you!" she screams shrilly. "For years, I've been your punching bag. For YEARS, I've put up with everything you've thrown at me verbally. I've been nothing but a glorified human pile of crap for the two of you to step in whenever you need to feel better about yourself. You want me gone? Every piece of *me*? Fine!"

She moves with clipped movements. Her shoes are pulled from her feet and thrust into Kirby's arms. Then in what I could only explain as a woman who has reached her breaking point, she snatches the bag and starts to pile in anything and everything she can.

I stand immobile and let her have this. Clearly, this is a moment she needs, and after everything I've witnessed, I'm sure my interference would do more harm than good. I lean with my back against the glass wall to the right of Dominic's open office door and cross my arms over my chest. Waiting. Ready to catch her if she needs me. That is until she picks up the computer off her desk, and with a scream, Ivy jumps into my arms, forcing me to catch her.

"There, Dominic," she pants angrily. "There is the rest of your stupid property. Thank you for reminding me that I *luckily* share none of your blood. If I never see you again, it will be a day too soon."

Before I can push Ivy off me, Willow's eyes turn to where I'm standing. She takes in her sister in my arms with her limbs wrapped around me, and even with her ire, that wounded look is back deep in her scrutiny. "Be careful with that one. Her bite is deadly."

I try to tell her to stop. Working my mind to think of anything that would abate this feeling of helplessness, but my words fail me. And the next thing I know, she's gone.

"Oh, my God, Kane? Are you okay? She's certifiable. I swear, Daddy should have put her ass out a long time ago."

I look down at Ivy and push her away. Judging by the fact she had to struggle to stay upright in her pencil thin heels, I didn't quite hold back the rage in my forcefulness.

Movement behind Ivy catches my attention and I flash my eyes to see Dominic pinching the bridge of his nose. His face is red, and I have no doubt it's with anger and not embarrassment. Something tells me it takes a lot to embarrass a man like him—if anything. A man with no morals and absolutely no issues stepping on whoever he needs to.

Including a woman who appears to carry a world of pain on her shoulders.

"You disgust me," I seethe, earning his calculated stare. "How a man—any man—could treat a woman that way is beyond me. How a father—regardless of the step in front of that title—could treat his *daughter* in a way so despicable only shows your true character, Dominic. Anyone who has no qualms in spewing the malevolence that you just did deserves all the hell karma could bring you. I'm sure that will happen sooner than expected considering you had planned on me being your savior—the financial life raft to your drowning company."

I take a few measured steps forward, stopping when my body is crowding his personal space. Even though he's in good shape for an older man, he has nothing on me. My body, shaped and honed by years of strict dietary limitations and physical training, is solid muscle. Add to the fact I'm a solid six or so inches taller, and my intimidation factor isn't just with my words.

I could crush him. Physically, easy, but the hellfire I could rain upon him within the industry would be more damaging than any verbal cockfight I could ever have with this asshole. And he knows it.

"You," I emphasize with a sharp check to his shoulder, "could have reaped the just deserts of me walking in your doors today. *You* could have picked up the pieces of shit you've managed to let this company of yours become just by signing a contract with *me* after our meeting. I had come here to discuss the use of a good number of your clients and employees. Do you understand that, Dominic?"

"What's he talking about, Daddy?" Ivy whines behind me, but neither of us is willing to break from the heated battle of domination we're warring.

His eyes narrow and his brow furrows. "Now, wait just a goddamn second here, son," he fumes.

"One thing you should get straight, old man—do not ever call me son. It would be an embarrassment to me to even imply that we had the kind of relationship that calls upon that sort of familiarity."

I can tell he wants to say more, but he doesn't. His chest is puffing up in defiance of my words, betraying the power he's desperately trying to hold on to. He's used to being in control of everything and everyone around him. I can only imagine what it's costing him to shut the fuck up to avoid pissing someone as powerful as I am off.

I hold all the cards here.

And fuck if I understand it, but I'm willing to go to bat for a woman who I know nothing about just based on a feeling.

All because with one look into those wounded doe eyes, I was willing to give her anything at just a chance to explore the connection between us.

I've lost my mind, but even if it weren't for Willow, hearing a man talk to a woman like that would have been enough for me to step in.

"Word on the street is you're so far in the red you're fucking bleeding out." I step a little closer and look down my nose at him; the arrogance he held earlier vanishes with the panic. I know more about him than he bargained. "How's it feel to know that with your actions today, you kissed any chance of aligning yourself with my name away. Lucky for me, I believe you just threw the best part of Logan Agency out the door like trash. I'm going to enjoy picking her up. My guess, she knows more about your own remaining clients than you do."

He sucks in a deep breath, and I know I've hit the nail on the head. Willow might just have been a secretary in his eyes, but you don't work that close to someone like Dominic Logan without soaking up everything you can.

"Good luck ending out this quarter with the Logan Agency's doors still open, Dominic."

My smile is nothing short of satanic when I turn and assess Ivy. "You were wrong, Ivy. The only certifiable people I see here are the two of you."

Stomping my way toward the hallway that will lead me out of here, I turn, addressing the two Logans with cold calculations. "I think what Willow forgot earlier was a good fuck you to the both of you pathetic idiots. I'll see myself out."

By the time I walk past a nervous-looking Mary at the front reception, my adrenaline is spiking so high I know I need to find a way to burn off my aggression. Unfortunately, how I would like to do that isn't an available option. Sure, I could pick any one of my old New York 'friends' and spend a day fucking this out, but fuck me—until I have a taste of the one who tempts me, no other pussy will do.

With no other options, I have Cam take me back to the penthouse, and I spend the next four hours working my body to the point of exhaustion in my home gym. It's time for a new plan, but fuck if I know how to get what I want now. Willow is clearly more fragile than I had counted on and challenging doesn't even come close to scraping the top layer.

A woman like her isn't going to give a shit about the public Kane. If anything, that might be the biggest hurdle I have to overcome.

Fuck.

The way Willow, a complete stranger, can completely unman me makes me feel like the biggest fucking pussy. I'm protective to the point of madness over someone who has mumbled a handful of words to me. That's it. I know nothing about her besides what I've learned the two times I've been stuck watching her fight and struggle through impossible situations.

Pussy or not, I would be a fool to give up on what I feel shooting straight down my spine when my eyes locked with hers. Stupid man, I'm not.

Willow will be mine. I just have to make sure I don't harm her further just by being me and everything that comes with being by my side. It takes a strong woman to be able to handle being in the public eye. Most of the fiercest women I know couldn't even hack it when the media started to have a field day picking apart every single fiber of their life. I don't even have to know Willow to see that she is as far from fierce in nature as it gets.

I sigh deeply with the direction of my thoughts. Fuck. *Fuck!* For the first time since I decided she would be mine, I'm unsure if capturing my scared little doe would be the best thing for her or the most selfish thing I could ever do.

CHAPTER EIGHT

WILLOW

'M JUST IN DENIAL ... right? Surely, that's why I haven't broken down after everything that happened yesterday. I'm not losing my shit further than I did in the office yesterday. I mean, it's not the end of the world that I've lost my job and what was left of my dysfunctional family. I'm better off. I know that. I shouldn't be embarrassed at all that a mega movie star watched me go insane and toss a computer through a glass wall. Okay, well ... maybe I should be slightly embarrassed with that.

Crap.

I squeeze my eyes shut and try to block out the memories of yesterday that have been assaulting my mind. Everything keeps playing over and over in one heck of a humiliating display of my madness.

The clamoring of my phone vibrations on my nightstand pulls me from the mortification replay. Reaching a blind hand out, I keep my belly on the mattress and my head buried in my pillow. Knocking a few things to the ground in my refusal to just roll over and grab my cell phone only adds to my frustrations.

"Hello," I mumble into the receiver after successfully tagging the annoying device off my nightstand and looking at the screen long enough to see Eddie's name on the display.

"Well, aren't you Sally Sunshine this afternoon," he quips.

"I love you, Eddie, but right now, I'm really not in the mood for your ridiculously happy disposition."

He huffs out a breath. "Sweetheart, everyone needs a little of Eddie's happy disposition."

"Not me," I declare.

"Pfft."

He's silent for a moment. Long enough for me to wonder if he's been disconnected. Quiet and Eddie just aren't two things that go together.

"Why didn't you call me last night, Will?"

Ah. Looks as though Kirby's been busy today.

"Willow," he warns.

"Look, it wasn't a big deal. Kirby brought me home and supervised while I polished off the rest of that bottle of Jack Daniel's you left here last month. I just needed to forget. I forgot, and now, I'm over it."

"You aren't over it, honey," he softly says.

He's right. I'm not. I had to call on all my therapeutic tricks not to revert to the old Willow, who would have plopped her butt on the floor of my pantry closet and ate everything within reach. Getting drunk isn't any healthier in terms of a coping mechanism, but considering my past of binge eating, it was a better choice for me.

Another sign that despite the crushing disappointment around me, I'm stronger. It also helped that Kirby stayed by my side until she helped me stumble to bed.

She must have left afterward because she wasn't here when I woke up at eight this morning puking.

"Willow? You there?"

"I'm here," I respond quietly. Holding the phone to my ear, I roll over to my back and look up at my ceiling. "I'll be okay. You can't lose anyone who you never had, and Eddie, I never had him or her. Before Mom died, Dominic Logan wasn't the type of 'father' who showed me much love. I was okay with that, taking what I could, but I realize now that I'm better off. And even though Ivy is ... well, Ivy, I gave up the hopes of having a normal sister relationship with her long before she slept with Brad. I guess in a way they did me a favor. I wouldn't have left Logan without being pushed out. Being there reminded me of when I would go to work and spend the day under my mom's desk, my old desk. It was an unhealthy way of keeping her alive."

Eddie hums in agreement. "You're loved, Will. Just because that bastard and his evil spawn aren't capable of being decent humans isn't a reflection on you. You *do* know that, right?"

Smiling, I respond. "Yeah, I do. I would be miserable without you and Kirb."

"Yeah, you would." He laughs, the somber mood lifting slightly.

"Did Kirby tell you *everything* about yesterday?" I question, wondering just how much Eddie heard.

"I think she hit all the highlights. I got a playback of what she heard and then an even better playback of your imitation of those little 'mine' seagulls from *Finding Nemo* while you grabbed everything that wasn't nailed down. I've always loved those little seagulls. Let's see, then we went over your impression of its raining men with your computer against the glass wall." He pauses and just when I think maybe Kirby left out the fact that Kane Masters had yet again been witness to my misfortune, he continues. "And she ended her play-by-play with Kane sexy-as-hell Masters."

I sigh. "Yeah … that about sums it up."

"So, Willow, the good friend in me would wait for Kirby to fill you in on what you've missed while you slept off your hangover, but you do know how I love a good juicy story full of dramatic flair."

Sitting up, I swing my legs out from under the covers and shiver with the chill in my bedroom. "What are you going on about, Eddie? I swear you have the worst ADD."

"No, no. It's all related and flows with the topic at hand. And that hand is pointing straight toward Kane Masters."

"There is no way I'm awake enough to deal with this. Let me shower off this hangover and you can come over and gossip until your head falls off."

I don't give him a chance to continue. I quickly pull the phone from my ear and press the red circle to disconnect the call while his deep voice rumbles through the earpiece. I smile, despite the unease settling in my gut, and make my way to shower and wake up. Knowing Eddie, he'll be walking through my door before I've had a chance to rinse out my shampoo.

Shockingly, I was able to rinse my shampoo and conditioner before I heard my bathroom door open and Eddie's muffled greeting over the shower spray.

"Do you even care that I'm in here naked right now?" I ask, bringing my body wash-lathered loofah up my left arm and around my shoulder. "I mean most friends would give someone the privacy they deserve when they're bathing."

I hear a grunted laugh and the sounds of him rummaging around in my cabinets.

"What are you looking for?"

The curtain jerks and I squeal when his head pokes into the steamy confines of my solitude. His eyes light with mirth when I hastily cover my breasts with one arm and my crotch with the loofah.

"Relax, Will! It's not as if you're working with the right stuff to stir little Eddie from his nap. Where's that hemorrhoid cream you had from that one time you—" I cut him off by picking up the closest thing I could find—my shampoo bottle—and throw it at his head. He squeals, like a girl, and jumps back. "What the hell was that for?"

"You know damn well I've never had hemorrhoids, Edward!"

He laughs and sticks his head back into the stall.

"Nice tits, Will." He smirks. "If I didn't love a good dick so much, you might be able to convince me to give a woman a run."

"Get. Out!" I scream.

"Right, well, since you asked nicely, I will. But only because I don't want it to go to your head that I'm so impressed by your girls. First, where's that cream?"

"You're such a jerk. It's in the bottom of the facial mask basket in the right side of the cabinet directly under the sink. Now, go!"

I make quick work of rinsing off and wrapping a towel around my body. Eddie isn't one for personal boundaries so it wouldn't surprise me if he barged back in.

Throwing on some sweatpants and an old college sweater, I grab my brush and pull it through my long tresses as I make my way into my living room slash kitchen slash dining room.

Stopping dead in my tracks, I openly gape at Eddie. "What in the world are you doing?"

He doesn't look at me, his focus directed at my toaster pulled to the edge of the bar that separates my kitchen area from the rest of the room, while he coats the skin under his eyes with none other than hemorrhoid cream.

"What does it look like I'm doing? I'm fixing the luggage I've been carrying around under my eyes. It's not easy being this hot, Willow."

I laugh. "Yeah, I'm sure it isn't. Care to explain why you're using up all my cream? I'm going to take it out on you when my period acne hits and all of that powerful stuff is gone."

"Pfft." He grunts and continues to dab more and more cream under his eyes.

"I bet you would go blind if you slipped and got that in your eye."

"Everyone does it, Willow. You act like I'm the only person who uses a little ass cream on my face." He stops what he's doing when he realized what he said, a slight frown between his brows. "Don't—"

"Don't what? Point out the fact you're probably used to butt cream in other places?"

"Don't be disgusting, Willow," he complains with a slight blush, which only causes me to laugh harder. "Fine. I was going to wait until I finished." He pauses to recap the cream then wipes his finger on the towel next to his makeshift mirror and turns from the toaster to focus on me. "Let's finish talking about Kane Masters."

Well, that's sobering.

"Word has it that things got heated *after* you lost your marbles yesterday, marbles I will stress you were justified in spilling, but that wasn't even the good part. I heard from Mary who heard it from Amanda who heard it from Stephanie that Kane gave both Dominic *and* Ivy one hell of a verbal slap before storming out of the office. Not only that, but Kirby had to stuff her resignation under his door this morning seeing as he refused to open it once. She said there was a big, ugly piece of plywood blocking that hole you so gracefully created too. I bet he loves that."

"What?" I gasp.

"Yup. And it gets better."

"I'm not sure it ever started getting better, Eddie. God, how humiliating."

"Whatever, Will! You had the hottest man alive—aside from yours truly, obviously—taking your back yesterday. How is that not a good thing?"

"Eddie …"

"Don't *Eddie* me. I let it go when you got all red faced the first time you crossed paths with him. *After* you finally told me the whole story, that is. I didn't point out the fact he was clearly trying to flirt, but you were too blind to see it. I kept my mouth shut. But I won't let this go. He stuck up *for* you to a man who most wouldn't dream of crossing. You know what that means?"

I shake my head. Not in affirmation of his comments, but because I'm not sure I want him to continue talking. The fear of knowing where he's going with this is overtaking my false calm.

"Kane Masters was staking a claim. On you. Willow, you might have been able to brush off the first meeting with him, but he obviously wasn't. You don't act like a big bad white knight over someone you know nothing about unless you plan to make it a point to learn more."

I continue to shake my head, this time in denial. "Don't be ridiculous, Eddie. He was just being a gentleman in the unfortunate situation in which he found himself."

"You're wrong, again. What do you think the tabloids would do with the story of him all but throwing a punch at Dominic Logan? No way he would risk that, not to be a gentleman about one fucked-up situation. No, if that is the case, he would have made his *gentlemanly* move silently to keep that risk down."

"You're being absurd. He knows nothing about me. There isn't some grand serendipitous force in place here, Eddie. End of story."

His eyes light up, highlighted by the white cream under his tawny eyes. "That, sweetheart, is where you're dead wrong. But the rest can wait for Kirby to get here. She's on the way."

"What? Why isn't she at work?"

He looks at me as if I've lost my mind. "Did you miss the whole 'Kirby pushed her resignation under Dominic's door' part of my story?"

"What?"

"Good Lord, did you lose your brain in that bottle of Jack last night?"

"Why would she quit?" I implore.

He opens his mouth, but closes it when my front door opens and Kirby walks in. She's left her blond hair pulled back into a sloppy bun, and her face is free of makeup. She enters the living room area and pulls her sweater over her head, leaving her in form-fitting yoga pants and a tank top.

"I swear, it's getting cooler than normal out there for October." She plops down on the couch and looks over at Eddie. "Hemorrhoid cream bag treatment?" she questions him.

"What? Seriously! How am I the only one who didn't know about this?"

She laughs. "It's my job to know all the tricks I can about improving the face. Half the models I get stuck with need all the help they can get when makeup isn't applied and Photoshop isn't working wonders."

Who would have thought? Making a mental note to remember that tip, I look from Eddie's face to Kirby. "What are you doing here? Shouldn't you be in the middle of a workday?"

"You suck at playing dumb, Will. I'm sure Chatty Cathy here filled you in. I quit. No way would I stay working at Logan Agency after yesterday. Rob was one hundred percent behind me when I told him what happened."

"You can't just quit, Kirb! You loved working there."

She leans forward on the couch and gives me a soft look. "No, I loved working with my two best friends while I did something I enjoyed. With Eddie gone and after the way you were treated and fired, there was no way I could have stayed another day. Plus, we already have a new job."

"Get ready for it," Eddie whispers loudly.

"Ready for what? *We?* What do you mean *we* have a new job? You two are exhausting."

"Did you tell her everything?" Kirby questions Eddie with a devious smirk.

"Nope. I saved the best part for you."

"I got a call late last night from none other than Kane Masters' personal assistant. He was very nice and forthcoming about the current conditions on set for the film Kane is directing. Apparently, a few unfortunate situations have him reevaluating his current crew. One of them being the lead makeup artist for the whole cast. Something about her sexually harassing Kane, which, by the way, I find hilarious."

Kirby's pause gives my mind a second to process all of this and a big smile to form. This is huge for Kirby. I know she never planned to leave the Logan Agency, but something like this falling into her lap is a large stepping-stone for her career.

"That's great, Kirb! Holy crap! You're going to do makeup for a major motion picture?"

"It's a huge deal, but because of the magnitude of this project, Kane has requested I bring an assistant who can help me keep up the pace of such a demanding role."

"Well, that shouldn't be hard. You know a ton of people in the industry, Kirby. Anyone would be ecstatic to have that chance. I'm so proud of you."

"That's nice that you think so since you're coming with me and all."

"Uh, what?"

"Kane requested that *you* be my assistant."

"Very funny." I laugh, pulling my wet hair back and tying it in a bun to prevent a frizzy mess. I walk away from Kirby and into the kitchen for a glass of water, pulling my sweatpants up as they start to sag. When did these get so loose? "You had me going for a second there."

"I'm not joking, Willow."

"You expect me to believe that Kane Masters asked for *me* to come?"

"I do, but I knew you would have issues believing me, so I told the PA, Sam, to call back and leave me a message with the offer. That was after I told him we would be on a plane to Georgia first thing next Monday."

"What?!" I scream and drop my full cup of water, shattering the fragile glass. "Crap."

Eddie, laughing under his breath, moves from his perch on my barstool and walks past me to get the broom and dustpan. Shock holds me immobile while I lock eyes with Kirby. She smirks and brings her phone out. After fiddling with it for a few moments, a voice I would recognize anywhere fills the room.

"Kirby, this is Kane. Sam told me that you requested a little verification to further aid in your assistant hopefully joining our team. First, let me express my gratitude that you have decided to accept the job offer. I'm sure you will fit in with the cast of *Impenetrable* and find this new career venture to your liking. Secondly, Sam expressed your need to be home as much as the filming schedule would allow, and you have my assurance that we will do everything we can so you're not away from your home and family more than necessary."

The deep rumble of his disembodied voice pauses, and I imagine him taking a long sip from the glass you can hear ice clinking in before his sexy, gravelly tones are making love to my senses again. I bet he would even sound unbelievable with that smoky voice gruffly speaking the alphabet.

Ignoring the tightness coiling in my gut, I focus back on his voice. "—my understanding is that you believe Willow wouldn't believe you when you told her that her presence was personally requested. By me. So, Willow, it would be my utmost pleasure if you were on that plane to Georgia as well. And so there isn't anything misconstrued here, yes, I hope you're able to come so Kirby is less overwhelmed with the magnitude of what's expected of her, but I also hope you'll come because I want you here. I imagine at this point you either are shocked or rolling those gorgeous brown eyes, but be sure, Willow, I most definitely have ulterior motives. Kirby, Sam will email you the travel instructions and all the other information you'll need. Thank you for getting the contract back to me so quickly. I look forward to seeing you. Both of you."

"Close your mouth, Willow," Eddie rumbles from his crouched position on the floor as he sweeps up the shattered glass.

My wide eyes follow Kirby's movements as she moves her phone from where she had been holding it in the air. With my mouth still slack with shock, I meet her confident regard. Of course, the woman has the most devious smirk on her face.

"Now, do you believe me?"

I nod.

"Are you shocked stupid?" Her smirk grows to a full-blown smile.

I nod.

"Planning on freaking out?" Her smile goes wonky.

I nod.

"Okay, I'll give you that. But can we freak out while we talk about what you'll be packing? I'm already halfway packed, and since Alli is on fall break next week, she and Rob will be coming down to spend the week and weekend with us while we settle in."

I shake my head.

"What are you protesting to? The packing or my family joining us?"

"I love your family," I tell her honestly.

"Ah, so it's the packing."

I nod.

"You're going to turn into a bobble head if you keep that up," Eddie smarts.

"I can't go to Georgia," I tell her, ignoring Eddie.

"Yes, you can, and you will," he snaps. "You have nothing keeping you here, Willow. I'm about to leave for London, and Kirby's going to need you. I'm not even going to touch that whole sexual fantasy come to life that Kane just delivered, but I swear to God, Will, if you ignore this, then you're one stupid woman."

"Hey!" I object. "I can't just leave! I need to find a job. Sure, I have enough savings for a while, but I can't just run off. Plus, I have … uh, I have plants?"

"You don't have plants, Willow. Nice try. You killed the last one a month ago. Anyway, I'm glad you mentioned that. I'm going to need your account information. It's in my contract for my assistant to be paid. So, your job slash income slash whatever the next excuse will be in that aspect is null and void. I'll be back in the city every chance I get, and we can have Rob keep an eye on your place too. Come on, Willow. I need you."

Knowing she has me with that, I pick a different line of protesting.

"What did he even mean?" I whisper, hearing the words crack with my lack of confidence and honest fear for what his message to me meant. "He doesn't even know me. Why on earth would he make those demands?"

"I think it's pretty clear what he means. He wants you."

I drop to the couch next to Kirby and roll my neck against the back of the cushion to look at her. "There's no way," I demand with conviction. "There's just no way."

"What is it that shocks you so much about Kane Masters wanting you?" Eddie questions as he comes to sit on my other side. "What is so damn shocking that a beautiful man wouldn't want an equally beautiful woman?"

I snort. Full-out graceless snort. Like a pig.

Eddie's eyes narrow and Kirby sighs.

"Don't you think it's a little bizarre he would want *me*? I mean, come on! You see his image in every tabloid magazine each week. There is always a stunning Amazon of perfection at his side. Eddie, you were watching the television with me when that damn entertainment reporter said he was in a relationship! Spotted leaving a baby doctor! A man in a relationship that serious wouldn't act like that."

"You can't believe everything you read in those papers, Willow. We know this. Hell, I see it often enough with the models in and out of my chair. They claim this about someone he's gone on record, numerous times I should add, saying she is just a close friend of his."

"You don't know if it's a lie made up by the tabloids or not, Eddie."

He looks at me then over to Kirby and back at me. "So, ask him."

"Yeah, right. Ignoring all of that, why me?"

"Why not you, Will?" Eddie snaps. "Do you even see how attractive you are? No, I guess you don't, seeing as you keep hiding under clothes that are too big for your body and you go out of your way to downplay your beauty. *You*, Willow, are stunning, and if I have to drag you down South myself just so that Kane can help you realize that, I will, dammit!"

"Well said, Eddie!" Kirby exclaims and reaches out to slap his outreached palm in a high-five.

"This can't be real. I can't be … I can't do … I can't be that person he thinks I am." I wheeze in panic.

"What exactly do you think he wants you to be?"

"Some sort of play toy? He's known to be a playboy, Kirby. Whatever weird fascination he has with me will pass and I'll be left to pick up the pieces. I'm not one of those perfect women who belong at his side. Oh God, maybe he wants me to be the other woman!"

"Just shut up!" Eddie snaps. "I'm so sick of you thinking you aren't worthy. Honey, I get it. Kirby gets it. I used to be overweight too. You know I struggled with my self-perception for years, but Willow, you need to stop. I am so sick of watching you destroy yourself because you aren't willing to see your worth. You're stronger than that. You've come so far since that douchebag Brad."

"He's right," Kirby interjects. "I might not have to deal with the body issues like you two do and have, but being on the smallest side of skinny, I've always had to deal with people laughing at me because I was so small. There isn't just one way for a body to be for someone to have confidence issues, Willow. You don't see how beautiful you are because you're too busy hiding to avoid more pain."

I wipe the tears that have begun burning down my cheeks and take in my two best friends. They're right. I know they are. But I've also had years of behavior that is hard to shake just because I know they have a point. I've been in this position before when an attractive man paid attention to me, and I've been picking up the pieces since. It's hard to trust the strength I've worked so hard to obtain and take a chance when it could cause me much more pain than Brad did. I have a feeling a man like Kane Masters would leave an emotional scar more painful than any physical marking if it went the same way as my last relationship.

"He's met me twice, guys. Twice when I've been at some of my lowest of lows. How do you expect me to believe he saw something sexy enough to pursue during those times?"

Kirby smiles sadly. "Because, like us, he can see past all the bullshit and just see you. The Willow who is stunning inside and out. Let me ask you something. Can you honestly sit here and tell me that if you turn this opportunity down, you won't regret it?"

No, I can't, and she knows it.

"This whole situation is so far out of my comfort zone that I'm terrified down to my bones. *He. Is. Terrifying.*"

"Sweet Willow." Eddie laughs. "Didn't anyone ever tell you that life starts at the end of your comfort zone? When you break free of the fears that have held you back, you're going to be free to fly, and that, honey, is when you're going to find the happiness you deserve. But you have to start somewhere. You have to push that fear aside and just wing it—trusting you will never be alone should you fall."

With a deep breath, I do just as Eddie suggested. Despite the fear clawing at my insides, I look at Kirby and tell her that I'll be on that flight with her Monday. This is my chance to prove to myself that I'm not the weak Willow of my past. *Take a chance*, they say. Well, maybe they're right. It's time I take the last remnants of the old me and be the strong person I know I can be.

"Willow?" Eddie questions softly.

Turning, I look into his eyes. "Yeah?"

"You've come so far, honey. Promise me that you'll try and look over those walls you've trapped yourself inside."

I nod, not trusting my voice. Eddie reaches up and brushes the lone tear that trails down my cheeks. "I'm ready, Eddie. As scary as that is … I promise to go into this adventure with an open mind."

"Even if that adventure takes you to Kane?" he asks softly.

I take a fortifying breath before speaking, a small smile playing across my lips. "Even if," I promise.

I'm going to be sick with worry all week wondering if I've made a huge mistake, but they're right. I would regret this if I said no, and maybe, just maybe, this is what I need to find some happiness.

CHAPTER NINE

WILLOW

'M GOING TO BE SICK.

My nerves are going haywire, and ever since our plane took off from JFK, I've been a jittery mess. By the time we touched down in Atlanta, I would have been a certifiable mess had it not been for Alli, Kirby's daughter. Her excitement has been a blessing of distraction. Keeping me company during our short flight, we gossiped and talked every minute that the plane was in the air. Watching her enthusiasm over this 'vacation' has worked to ease some of my nerves, but not all of them. At this rate, by the time we land and make it to our temporary housing courtesy of Masters Entertainment, I'll have no nails left on any of my fingers.

Following Kirby's lead, I went with jeans and a simple tee shirt with a light jacket. Both of us being born and raised in New York, we weren't sure what to expect from early fall in Georgia. From what we could tell, weather there was in the low seventies, but from what Kirby's husband said, add the humidity and you never know what you'll get. The weather in the South is a crapshoot.

I had never been to the airport here in Atlanta. From the second we debarked the plane, it's been insanity. Their transit system used to travel from point A to B within their massive airport was a rush of tired bodies. And the escalators toward the baggage claim seem to be sending us to the heavens. Add that to the feeling of hundreds of people pushing their way out of the airport and I couldn't help but feel a little out of place. I'm used to crowds—we're no stranger to them in New York City—but here, with all of us being carted up to the mysterious top level of these never-ending stairs to heaven, it's taken to a whole new level. I'm pretty sure the older businessman behind me just sniffed my hair, and Alli's Barbie backpack is digging uncomfortably into my stomach.

I hate escalators. I swear they're just a step above some sort of barbaric torture device.

What a great way to start this little adventure.

"This way, Will," Kirby tells me loud enough to be heard over the people swarming around us like bees.

I follow the finger she's pointing toward the long line of people waiting behind some weird barricade and see the group of bad suit wearing men holding iPads with names displayed on their screens.

"There, on the end," I hear Alli's melodious voice exclaim, pointing just like her mother.

How they can see around all these bodies is beyond me. I can't even say it's because Kirby is a few inches taller than my five-foot-seven. If Alli can see whatever it is, then I'm just lacking brain function today.

We walk around a few hugging couples and groups of families welcoming home their loved ones. I feel a twinge in my chest knowing I won't ever have something like that, but really, if having the two most negative people out of my life means I won't have a crying family to welcome me home, then I consider that a win on my end.

I almost run Kirby over when she abruptly stops walking. I look up and catch her smile at the tall man before her. He's like a human wall of muscle and intimidation. But, if judging by his all-black clothing, he and I could be good friends.

The man before us, despite being indoors, has dark glasses shielding his eyes.

"Are you from the *Men in Black*?" Alli asks in awe, her tiny body almost tipping over to look up at this giant man.

His head dips down and a ghost of a smile tickles his lips before he shakes his head. "Nope."

"You should be. You're huge! I bet you could kick some serious alien butt."

"Alli, language," Kirby scolds.

"Seriously, Mom? I said butt not a-s-s."

Even with all my nerves, Alli's sass brings a bubble of laughter up and through my lips, followed by one loud snort. And, as simple as that, all eyes in our little group are on me.

Giant Man in Black looks over briefly and smirks before addressing Kirby. "Mrs. Evans ... and family," he nods toward Rob and Alli before looking back at me, "Ms. Tate, if you'll follow me. Name's Cam and we're to meet Sam back at the house."

"Right-o, hulk ... lead the way," Kirby jokes.

His lips stay curled in a barely-there smile while we walk through the baggage claim area and make our way to the carousel that holds our flight's luggage. It doesn't take long before we have two carts full of bags. Because Rob and Alli are staying for the week, we have a considerable amount of luggage.

"Could you have packed any more, Kirb?" I joke, heaving her fifth suitcase up and onto the cart.

"Hey, you could have waited for hulk to lift that one. I think that's all shoes."

"One suitcase, Kirb. That's all I have with me. All I need. How the heck do you really think you're going to need eight of these suckers when you'll be flying back and forth from here to New York? You can just get new stuff when you go home." I pull my hair tie out and readjust what was a sleek ponytail into a knot on the top of my head. "I'm sweating," I complain. "I bet I smell. Oh, crap. We're going to the house first, right?"

"Yes, Ms. Tate. The house is where we're headed next."

"Okay, good. I can shower. Then what, Kirby?"

"Calm down, babe." She laughs. "From what Sam said in our correspondence over the week, today is our day to get settled, but he would be by at some point to make formal introductions."

"To whom?" I ask stupidly knowing darn well what the answer will be.

Kirby annoyingly just shrugs her shoulders and with a smirk, pulls her sunglasses from her large purse before turning and following Cam's lead.

So, this is how she's going to play it.

"Do we have time to stop and grab some fast food real quick?" Kirby inquires, and I cringe.

Fast food is on the long list of foods I avoid at all costs. Covered in oversaturated sodium, usually deep fried, and always bad for me. Hopefully, Kirby wasn't paying attention during our short flight, and I can pass on food without raising any of her red flags.

Hiding how little I eat is becoming a full-time job. I eat; I don't think my regimen would be considered an eating disorder, but it's far from healthy. I skip breakfast, lunch is usually a protein bar or something equally light, and since I'm alone at dinner, I usually just nibble on a salad and carrot sticks. I keep telling myself that after the next ten pounds I lose, I'll start eating more. But that's been going on for the last twenty I've shed ... so I'll stick to what I know for a little longer while I get down to my goal weight.

"Right this way," Cam says and points to the two sleek black SUVs right outside the door. "Ms. Evans, if you would, you and your family can go ahead and get settled." He directs Kirby, Rob, and Alli to the first big black vehicle before guiding me to the one behind it. "Mrs. Evans was nice enough to warn us that she would have a considerable amount of luggage with her, and with this many bags, it's necessary that we have two. If you'll follow me, you'll meet back up with Mrs. Evans when we arrive at your house."

"Kirb?" I call, twisting my fingers together in my lap.

"It's time to start that life, my little creature of comfort. Just jump right out of that zone you've been stuck in." She winks, and I want to throttle her for throwing Eddie's words back in my face.

I look back and forth between the two cars and take a deep, steadying breath. *Okay, enough of this scared Willow. It's time to live your life and live it for yourself. It's time to stop worrying about what others think of you. Time to stop living in the fear of upsetting someone because you're your own person and to hell with what anyone thinks.*

One step in front of the other.

I give Cam a smile, one I actually feel with the lightness in my step, and move toward the second vehicle. He follows behind and opens the back door, offering his hand to help me step up onto the shiny metal step before I place my bottom down and move to swing my legs inside.

"Thank you, Ca— oh, crap." The smile I had dies and the calm I had been feeling packs up and says to heck with this.

"Hello, Willow."

I close my eyes. Crap. Crap. Crap.

He laughs, the sound deep and rough. I feel that sinfully dangerous sound all the way between my legs, causing me to push my knees together and bite the inside of my cheek.

"Do I make you nervous, Willow?"

"Yup," I answer, the end making a loud pop in the silence around us.

"I promise I won't bite," he jokes then adds almost as an afterthought, "That is, unless you ask me to."

My eyes snap open, and I look into the crystal blue eyes of Kane Masters. The dark stubble dancing across the sharp planes of his jaw don't mask the laugh lines around his thick lips or the small, almost inconspicuous dimple in his left cheek. His thick hair is unruly, as if he's run his fingers through it a few dozen times.

He's utterly perfect.

And I'm sitting in front of him rumpled from travel, sweaty from hustling through the busy Atlanta airport, and just a big, hot mess.

I'm the imperfect to his perfect.

"Crap," I grumble.

CHAPTER TEN

KANE

SHE'S STUNNING. I STUDY HER as we travel down the interstate and leave her to her silence for the moment.

That familiar spark started zapping between us the second her eyes connected with mine. Hell, it started before then. When I watched her walk through the sliding doors and toward the vehicle I was forced to wait in, I felt it. Everything I had once again started to wonder if I made up with the hopefulness of finally finding someone who I felt was worth pursuing was confirmed the second she pulled her body into the truck. Her scent, sweet … *peaches* … wraps around me like a drug I feel in the tightening of my pants.

Exquisite.

And she has no clue.

"Willow?" I question, hoping I can get her eyes back on me.

I watch as her shoulders straighten and her gaze leaves its

study of the busy traffic on I-85. She visibly collects herself before turning and *finally* giving me those eyes.

"Kane," I tell her and hold my hand out toward her.

She jumps, looking back and forth between my hand and my face for a few beats before timidly placing her palm against mine with a small laugh.

"Will—" Pausing, she clears her throat before continuing. "Willow. As you obviously already know." She offers a little sass I wasn't expecting, betraying her unease.

"Yeah, that I do." My fingers rub the inside of her wrist and a fire-like whisper burns up my arm just from that small contact. Not unaffected herself, I watch her body shudder slightly.

Nice, Kane.

We don't speak, and I don't make any moves to release her hand. It doesn't take long for her pale cheeks to start turning pink and for those eyes to drift from mine. Embarrassing her again is the last thing I want to do, the very last. I release her hand, feeling the loss of her touch instantly.

"I apologize for not being able to meet you in the airport. It would have been a disaster had I stepped out of the truck."

I get her eyes quickly before she looks down at her hands now resting in her lap. "I understand. It wouldn't be good to be seen with me … I mean us," she softly says.

What was that?

"I'm afraid you have the wrong impression of me, Willow. It's me not wanting to start a madhouse when I'm recognized. It has nothing to do with being seen with anyone. Have no doubts that being seen with *you* wouldn't cause me the least bit of unease. We should probably clear that up right now. You're going to see a lot of me, Willow," I tell her. Unwilling to be bereft of her touch, I reach out to pull one of her worrying hands from her lap and grasp it between mine again. I notice the difference as I turn her hand over to study how delicate her tiny hands look between my rough, long fingers. "I can tell you're nervous, but at the risk of making you more uncomfortable, I'll just lay it out there. I want you, Willow. And I intend to have you, so you should probably get the thought that I don't want to be seen with you right out of your head. I *will* be seen with you."

She gasps and moves to pull her hand from mine, but I don't let go.

"I can tell you are either not used to men being so blunt or you are genuinely unaware of the spell you've cast on me. I know you feel it too, Willow. A connection that strong can't be a fluke, nor can it be one-sided."

"I don't know what you're talking about," she evades.

"Your eyes," I tell her.

"Excuse me?"

"Your eyes. They don't lie. The last two times we've been in the same room, your pupils dilate until they almost completely cover all that deep brown color that's haunted me since the first time I saw them *years ago*." I watch shock color her face at my words. Choosing to ignore the question in her eyes at the mention I've seen her before, I continue. "You know that feeling you get that causes your skin to dance with goosebumps? You can't sit here and tell me that feeling is a lie. The rush of pink to your skin, the way your breathing speeds up—all of it, Willow. I see it all now just as I did then and trust me when I tell you, I felt it too and it's been on my mind since."

"Years ago?" she questions.

"Yes."

"When? I would have remembered that."

"Perhaps," I evade.

Her eyes narrow when I don't answer. "You don't even know me, Kane."

"I don't need to know you for my body to want yours. Getting to know who you are on the inside will just be the added bonus."

Her expression hardens slightly and that light pink blush turns a shade darker. Anger? At me?

"So you just want sex?"

How did we get here? I decided going into this that honesty would be my best path with her. Well, as honest as I can be.

"I would be lying to you if I said I haven't thought about it, often, but I'm not after cheap thrills here, Willow. I'm not that guy."

"According to just about every tabloid and member of the media, that's exactly the type of guy you are. You don't do relationships, or at least you haven't publicly had one during the span of your career, until recently. Or so they say. You aren't seen with anyone who isn't the picture of perfection and that includes your *girlfriend*. So forgive me, Kane, if I don't buy this for one second. Did someone put you up to this? Some sort of sick job at my expense? Does your girlfriend know? I bet they all got a good laugh." She trails off, and I watch as a look of horror takes over her features. "Oh God, did you even really have a job for Kirby? Is that part of this prank? There's no way she knew. She would never do that to me."

Her breathing starts to pick up and that overwhelming feeling to protect her starts forcing its way out. My mind races to keep up with her rushed words. She's right about most of it. I haven't been a relationship man, but that wasn't a choice made out of playboy ways. She thinks this is some joke at her expense? How could this beautiful woman even think that about herself? Can't she even see what I see?

And then it hits me. Each second of our prior meetings. The way she would fold into herself, the pulling at her clothing, the way she tried to move past me when I blocked the doorway in Logan's office.

She really *can't* see it.

And if I'm right, she probably really believes that bullshit she just spewed out of her mouth.

"Fuck it," I growl, cutting off her muttered panic. Her eyes snap to mine just seconds before I push from my side of the bench seat. My hands frame her face, my fingers curl around the soft hair on the nape of her neck, and I crush my lips against hers.

She gasps, and I use that to my advantage, dipping my tongue into her mouth and caressing against hers. Fuck, her taste is just as addictive as the rest of her. Her scent wraps around me, and just like that, I'm a starved man feasting like it's the first meal I've had in years. I move my mouth to take her bottom lip and bite it softly causing her to let out a moan.

That's right. Pretend all you want, my timid doe. Throw some bullshit lies at me. I'll make it my mission to prove to you that this feeling is damn sure real and not some sick joke.

She's immobile just a second longer before she gives me another moan that causes my cock to harden even more, pressing against my jeans uncomfortably, and then her hands are fisting the cotton of my shirt for seconds.

Our kiss deepens, and when I know she's just as lost in me as

I am in her, I move my hands from her face, use one to unsnap her seat belt before placing them on either side of her hips. She tenses when her belt clangs against the side of the door, but I nibble on her lip again, keeping her focus on me.

The sounds of our breathing echo around us, and unable to wait, I grasp her before pulling her toward my body. One leg goes to either side of my thighs and I use my hold on her body to press her center tightly against my rock hard cock.

Let's let her try to explain that as disingenuous.

Fuck, the heat from her pussy hits me a second later, and with a brutal groan, I rock her slightly on my erection. Her hands dig into my hair and tug, giving my scalp a sting before her hips start rocking on their own. Taking what she wants. What I'll happily give her.

Jesus, Kane. You're doing nothing but proving her right.

Logically, I know I should pull back before I'm past the point of stopping, but having her body moving against mine and her moans being swallowed by my mouth takes my desire for her to levels I've never felt before.

Pulling back is the hardest thing I've ever done. But if I want to prove to her that I'm not some playboy out for cheap thrills, I need to shut this down now.

"God, Willow," I pant against her lips, swiping my tongue out for one more taste.

She stiffens when the haze of desire from our kiss lifts and I watch her eyes open and shock begin to etch in her features.

She's bracing herself. For what, I'm not sure, but I'm going to work my ass off to make sure this look never washes over her features again.

This connection between us is even more powerful than I could have imagined, and now that I have her in my arms, nothing will stop me from making her mine.

CHAPTER ELEVEN

WILLOW

"**Y**OU HAVE A GIRLFRIEND," I gasp. "A pregnant girlfriend, at that."

Of all the things I could have said at that moment, that's what I go with. It seems safer than asking him what the heck he's trying to prove here. Or better yet, safer than to acknowledge the fact his erection is pressing firmly against my wet core. Good God, I don't know what's come over me. I have never acted so brazenly.

"I don't," he insists, allowing me to climb off his lap.

My eyes narrow, and anger fires my blood. "You most certainly do. I might be naïve in a lot of things, but pictures don't lie, Mr. Masters. I would have to be blind to miss the headlines that have been all over the place for the last few weeks."

"It's Kane," he forces through tight lips before the silence returns around us. He shakes his head and opens his mouth to speak before closing it and shaking his head again. I can tell by his body language that he's uncomfortable. I'm assuming that's because he just tried to cheat on his pregnant girlfriend. Oh God, he *did* cheat on her. I'm going to be sick. I've turned into my sister!

His voice breaks the silence of my inner thoughts. "You can't believe everything you read in those fucking magazines, Willow. They print what will sell. What will cause people to stop and throw down a few bucks on what really equates to a handful of pages full of bullshit."

"So you're saying that every single one of them, plus the online media outlets and television reports, are lies? Just like that?"

My body hums with anger. I'm angry he had the nerve to kiss me. And the tipping point of my anger is the fact my body loved every second of it, girlfriend or not.

He wasn't wrong. I feel it too; I'm just not sure what I'm supposed to do with it. I felt his reaction to our kiss against my soaking wet core. There is no way he could have faked a reaction like that. I'm just having a hard time understanding how he could feel that way about me. Each time I've been face-to-face with him has been during the most humiliating of situations. I've been at my worst. Those magazines he claims prints lies can't make up the kind of woman he usually has at his side and they're nothing like me.

"You're right. They couldn't hold a candle to you," he says, breaking into my thoughts with a smooth purr of hypnotizing tones.

I snort out a laugh and throw my hand over my mouth, my eyes widening. Well, that's just lovely; apparently, my thoughts slipped through my lips yet again. I really need to work on that.

His distressed gaze falters at my unladylike display. Those full lips curling. The way he looks at me is so unnerving.

Well, Eddie—what was it he said? Life begins at the end of your comfort zone? I'm so far outside of my safe zone of comfort; I might as well be on another planet.

"I don't have the slightest clue what I'm doing here," I tell him honestly. "Things like this don't happen to girls like me."

Those crystal eyes slight, and he cocks his head adorably. "That's not the first time you've referred to yourself negatively, Willow."

I laugh again, his eyes narrowing further. "Yeah, well, one thing you should know about me, Kane, is that I'm not exactly the most positive person."

"And why's that?"

Yeah, right. As if I'm going to open the floodgates of the cesspool of my many issues.

"Willow? I asked you a question."

"Has anyone ever told you that you're a very intimidating person?" I hedge.

"Wouldn't be the first time. But you don't get to where I am by not taking what you want."

"Look," I start. *Hike up those big girl panties, Willow.* "I'm really not sure what I'm supposed to say here. I don't understand why I'm here … with you … and I'm really not sure I trust you and whatever is motivating this situation."

His features smooth out and he reaches out, again, to take my hand. I try to resist, but his determination is something I can't match. I shift uncomfortably and swallow the lump in my throat.

"You don't know me, Willow, but I don't lie. You're here because *I* want you here. Sure, I went about it unconventionally, but

I live a life that isn't conventional in the least. I'm the kind of man who takes what he wants with no apologies. So I won't give you any. Just like you don't know me, I don't know you, but what I've *felt* by just being around you makes me believe it's a feeling worth some drastic measures to explore further. I took what drastic measures I needed in order to rectify the situation at hand."

"And that situation being me?"

He laughs. "The situation has everything to do with you. I haven't felt a bond like I feel with you toward anyone in a damn long time, if ever, and I would be a stupid man not to use all my cards to explore that."

"And your girlfriend?" I question, my voice coming a heck of a lot more steady than the rapid beating of my heart.

"I told you, I don't lie. I don't have a girlfriend, Willow."

I sigh, shifting again before pulling at my top when I feel it tighten against my belly. I don't miss the way that his eyes move to follow my hands movements.

Crap.

"I'm going to be honest," I warn him, shifting *again*. My body betraying the calm I'm trying to present outwardly.

"Please do." He nods, the hand still holding mine and giving me a squeeze before his dexterous fingers sweep across my wrist, spiking my already pounding heart to dangerous levels.

"Okay," I squeak, clearing my throat. I look down at our connected hands and take a deep breath. "You ... the things you talk about ... *crap*."

"Willow, you can speak your mind," he assures, his voice calm and low.

"This has never happened to me. I'm not sure I can be the person you want me to be." Spit it out, dang it. "You've seen me twice before, that I know of, and both of those times could probably sum up the downward spiral of my life. I've been a roller coaster of dips and turns that have made me a skeptical person who doesn't have the type of ... confidence that you seem to exude. I've learned it's easier to tighten my buckle and take the safer rides in life. Ones that don't set me up to fall on my tail."

He's quiet for a moment when I finish speaking, but his eyes are telling me everything his silence isn't. Kane is a smart man, so I'm sure he's reading between the lines with no difficulties at all.

"Three times," he says confusing me for a second before I remember his claim to have seen me years before.

"So you say," I respond.

"We'll come back to that," he promises with purpose. "You say it's easier to take the safer rides in life, so I guess that means I just need to show you that life is a lot more fun when you learn how to enjoy the ride. Look, I'm not asking you for forever, Willow, but at least give me a chance to show you the fall is worth taking off your seat belt and saying to hell with it, regardless of what your mind is telling you." His eyes look over to where my seat belt is hanging, unconnected, next to the door. "I think you've already seen what fun it can be when you decide to unbuckle."

"Not that I had much of a choice," I mumble.

"That's right. But can you tell me you didn't enjoy the fuck out of it? Feeling the rush when you stopped thinking and just rolled with it. Each and every hard inch created by that rush?"

I gasp, catching his meaning.

"All I'm asking is that you give me a chance to find out what makes you ... you. Explore all those things I know you felt before and confirmed just now when you were in my arms. I have no hidden agenda here, Willow. I'm just asking you to take a chance. What you see through those skeptical eyes isn't me exuding confidence, but rather me trusting my gut when it has never steered me wrong before."

"That's what I'm afraid of," I whisper and pull my hand from his when I feel the SUV stop. I ignore his sigh and look out the window to see we've parked next to a large home. "I don't want to be the girl who's stuck on the kiddie rides in life anymore, Kane, but I'm warning you this won't be easy for me. It won't be easy for me to just let go and trust this isn't some cruel joke fate has tucked up her sleeve." I turn my attention back to his while reaching my hand out to the door handle. "Everything you make me feel scares the crap out of me, but you're right. Regret is an ugly thing, and I'm sick of being the girl who has a closet stockpiled with it."

His face, which has been the picture of apprehension since I started speaking, relaxes, and the smile he's famous for knocks the wind right out of my sails.

"A chance. My head says no, but for once, I'm going to follow your lead and trust what my gut is telling me. My mind has proven lately that I don't always know what's best for me." I take a breath and hold my hand up when he opens his mouth to respond. "Please, just don't make me add another regret to my already stuffed full closet."

I don't give him a chance to respond; instead, I pull the handle and step out into the comfortable Georgia fall weather. Kirby is standing nervously outside of the vehicle that brought her and her family here.

"Are you okay?" she questions obviously noting my appearance and frazzled nerves.

I sigh. "Honestly, Kirb? I'm not really sure."

I look back at the black windows that close Kane to us and wonder what in the hell I'm thinking by allowing myself to potentially be crushed by that man. I wasn't lying; I don't trust him. I would be a fool to blindly trust someone I don't know, let alone someone who is so publicly scrutinized.

I've wanted a change, and this is about as big of one as it could possibly get.

It's time to put the new Willow out in the world and finally be the strong woman I've been building myself to be. Fear is no longer a ride I wish to travel.

CHAPTER TWELVE

WILLOW

WE SPEND THE REST OF our afternoon enjoying the house we've been put up in. I'm not sure how Kirby managed to swing this, but we might as well be staying in a mini mansion. With seven bedrooms—SEVEN—four bathrooms, the largest gourmet kitchen I've ever seen in my life, two living rooms—both formal and informal—and probably every upgrade known to man, this place is far beyond something that a regular member of the production team would ever have. Kane's entertainment company sure did roll out the red carpet for Kirby.

Alli and Rob have been playing PlayStation in the media room—yeah, actually, it's more like a mini movie theater that takes up the entire third floor. Complete with a candy vending machine, soda dispenser, and popcorn maker. Last I saw Kirby, she had been enjoying it just as much as her family, but if I know her, she's dying to hunt me down and question me about what happened on the way here.

I've been in the kitchen baking things I have no intention of eating. Taking full advantage of the fully stocked fridge and pantry, I replay every second of my encounter with Kane. Cooking out my thoughts and trying to convince myself that I haven't lost my ever-loving mind when I agreed to explore this ... bond Kane and I seem to have linking us together.

My stomach rumbles when I place the last of the chocolate chip cookies on the cooling rack. I look down, and with a sigh, I stuff one of the warm cookies into my mouth. I let out a deep moan around the sweetness that explodes in my mouth and start to lick the chocolate off my fingers.

Heaven.

"Fuck me," I hear mumbled harshly and snap my head over to the doorway and the intruding voice.

"Crap," I muffle through a full mouth of sugary heaven. I had been so lost in the first taste of sweets I've had in a long time that I didn't even notice I wasn't alone anymore. Finishing the bite too quickly to enjoy and wiping my mouth with a discarded towel, I look over at the man filling the room with the thickness his heated gaze is causing. "You're going to give me a heart attack," I snap, more embarrassed at being caught mouth raping a cookie than I am at the man himself.

He reaches down and I watch in shock as he presses his hand against the crotch of his jeans before adjusting himself. Does this man have no shame?

"That noise. Shit, Willow, that noise."

"Yes, well ... I'm sorry, but it was a really good cookie," I lamely tell him.

"Yeah, I'm sure it was," he purrs and moves toward me.

"How did you get in here?" I question, my mind clearing long enough to form some sort of coherency.

"With my key," he answers with a devilish smile.

"You have a key? To our house?"

"I would hope so since I own it."

Do what? "You own this house?" Well, that would explain the grandeur around me. "So why are we here and you aren't?" I evade his advancement and back up a step when he takes another toward me.

"Because." He doesn't continue, but his smile widens.

"Because ...?" I implore. Crap, I can smell him—that delicious cologne he wears—and I swear my body hums with arousal.

"Why are you in here cooking?" he asks, ignoring me when I back up again, butting into the counter behind me.

"Because," I smart, and even with my nerves spiking by just being near him, I'm enjoying this little game.

"Fair enough, Ms. Tate, fair enough."

"You're a confusing man."

His eyes twinkle with mischief as he walks further into my personal space. His eyes study my face, my body, and then my face some more. I resist the urge to pull at my top when his eyes travel the length of me.

Barely.

"You missed some," he oddly says, but before I can comprehend what his words mean, his head is lowering and his mouth is on mine.

Teasing.

Exploring.

Feasting.

Oh. My. God.

The shock of his lips against mine, soft and warm, holds me still, but my heart picks up and panic starts to invade.

He pulls back, licking his lips, and the fire in his eyes burn into mine.

"Delicious," he whispers, then turns to grab a cookie off the cooling rack and leans against the counter.

"Is this you trying?" I ask, giving in to the urge to lick my lips, tasting him again on my tongue.

"No, this is me taking," he retorts, and with a smirk, he takes a huge bite of the cookie. When I don't respond, he continues to study me … study my reaction to his kiss.

Okay, Willow. You want this. You promised yourself you would be better, honest, and try. So … do it.

"You're terrifying." *There … that wasn't so bad.*

His smirk dies. He drops what's left of his cookie on the island, and he opens his mouth.

"Willow?" I hear Kirby call, cutting off his response. I look around the room frantically as her footfalls get closer.

Crap.

"I don't want to scare you," he tells me honestly, ignoring Kirby's advancement.

"Wills?" Kirby's calls out again, her voice closer this time, and my eyes widen. My shocked and somewhat panicked brown eyes meet his calm and assessing ice blue ones.

Searching and questioning me with just a glance.

God, he confuses me.

"Trying to find somewhere to stuff me?" He laughs. Stepping

away from me slightly, he grabs his discarded cookie and swallows the rest in one bite.

I shift, trying to ease the throbbing between my legs as his tongue comes out to lick his lips.

"No," I deny. "Okay, maybe."

He throws his head back and laughs. The heavy energy flooding the room just seconds before starts to dissipate some. I watch his throat work as his hilarity reverberates around us. God, he's beautiful.

"Oh," Kirby says, faltering as she walks into the room. Her eyes move from Kane's smiling face to my shocked one before she quickly recovers. "Mr. Masters, nice to see you again." She walks forward and reaches out to shake his hand, looking over at me with an expression that tells me she'll demand answers as soon as possible.

He ignores her hand and pulls her into a friendly hug. "Kirby, it's a pleasure. Thank you for getting here so quickly. I apologize for not coming in earlier. I had some things on set that needed my attention."

"Earlier?" she asks, knowing dang well what he's talking about.

"Yes, I should have had Willow pass on my regards, but we were busy," he pauses and looks over at me wickedly, "discussing other things."

"I'm sure you were, Mr. Masters." Her words say one thing, but what I hear is '*We'll be discussing this in more detail later, Willow.*'

"Kane, Kirby. I've told you already, please call me Kane."

"Kane it is, then," she smirks. "Busy day exploding ovaries?"

I gasp at her audacity, which really shouldn't surprise me with Kirby, but Kane just laughs.

"I only care about one set of those, Kirby. Glad to see you haven't lost that sense of humor."

She smiles, and I look back and forth between the two of them, my brow crinkling in confusion. "You two are so strange."

They both look over with matching smiles, and I roll my eyes.

"I see you and Willow have made up for lost time?" she asks.

"Yes," he answers at the same time I snap out a no. His smile grows, and Kirby laughs.

"Right-o. Well, I'll leave you two while you're not making up for lost time. Alli smelled cookies, so I was on a mission. By the way, Willow?"

I meet her eyes. "Yeah?"

"Your lip gloss looks great on Kane."

My eyes shoot over to his lips—those full, delicious lips—and I feel my cheeks heat when I notice the glossy shine coating his. How did I miss that? Oh, that's right, you were too busy succumbing to his charm and falling into the desire that his touch ignites. How is it that he makes it so easy to forget any misgivings I could have about him … or whatever *this* is between us?

He smiles but doesn't move to wipe his mouth, just dips his tongue out and—slowly—licks over the shiny coat. And God help me, I moan, not even the least bit ashamed he's brought that reaction out of me. What is this man doing to me? I've never reacted like this toward a man before, and Kane, a man I hardly know, knocks down all my insecurities in one fell swoop. Or better yet, a few kisses.

Kirby and Kane continue to talk about her schedule for tomorrow—going over the call sheet for the day and how early the leading actress needs to be ready for her first scene. I tune them out and move to clean up the mess I made during the last batch of cookies. Alli comes running in a few times, completely ignorant to the movie star before her, and scrambles off with as many cookies as her little hands can carry.

"Willow? Did you catch that?" Kirby questions, and I move my attention from the mixing bowl I had been scrubbing.

"Catch what?" I ask, rinsing my hands and turning off the tap.

"Kane said he needs you to help him with some things tomorrow. It will be a light day for me since only Alessandra and two other actresses are in my chair, and then I'm just sitting on the sidelines waiting for touch-ups, so it won't be a problem for me."

"Uh … isn't the point of me being here to help you?"

Kirby looks at Kane, and they seem to communicate briefly without words before she looks back over and shrugs.

"It was the point, Willow, but I've decided things are going to be a little different now. We're at the tail end of production, so there aren't as many demands on Kirby's plate. And per her contract, she does have one other makeup artist at her disposal. Unfortunately for me, my PA, Sam, was called away for some business he needs to tend to back in LA, so I need a little help until he can return."

"Help?" I look back at Kirby for some direction, but she's avoiding my probing gaze. "What exactly do you mean by that? I'm sure I'm not qualified for anything you could need help with."

Kane chuckles. "You couldn't be further from the truth. I think you'll find you have all the qualifications I desire."

Kirby clears her throat, but I don't move my eyes from Kane. It's obvious he isn't talking about anything work related at this point.

"I'm sure your desires are not something I would be able to

meet, Kane." Actually, I would love nothing more than to meet his *desires,* but just the thought of taking things further than the few kisses we've shared has me hitting panic level DEFCON 5.

"Yes, well ... that's the beauty of *trying,* Willow. You'll find I would never lead you down a path you couldn't handle while enjoying every second of it."

"You two ..." Kirby pauses and pulls at the collar of her tee shirt while fanning her face with her other hand. "You could light a fire with the amount of heat you two are sparking."

My eyes narrow when Kane winks at me.

"Take a chance," he tells me, his voice a low rumble for my ears only.

I study his eyes. Their blue depths pleading.

I nod, and his relief is evident when he lets out a deep exhale.

"If you'll excuse me," I tell them and walk around them both and through the house until I reach the bedroom I had claimed.

Yes ... if you'll excuse me, I'm going to go silently freak out where no one can see me.

CHAPTER THIRTEEN

WILLOW

'M NOT SURE WHAT I expected when we pulled onto the set of *Impenetrable*, but what I got definitely wasn't it. Kane had literally taken over a good portion of one of the local high schools. Kirby explained on the way over that the school was on break for the next week, and they will be filming all of the scenes they need at this location in seven days. Seven days that she would be on set for almost eighteen hours, but because she wouldn't be needed during every second of those eighteen hours, she would be taking breaks to see Rob and Alli. They would be coming to visit her on the set as well.

"There's Kane," Kirby tells me, snapping me out of the shock over seeing my first movie set. "Watch your step," she adds, but naturally, I miss what step I should be watching because I still had my eyes glued to where she said Kane was.

"Crap!" I gasp when my foot hooks on a power cord that had

bunched up despite the tape placed around it to keep it from … well, tripping someone. I'm sure if someone had a slow-motion camera on me right now, this would be hilarious to replay. But true to my history of run-ins with Kane, it wouldn't make sense for me to just glide into the building without a mishap.

My hands hit the ground at the same time my knees painfully collide with the unforgiving flooring. Heat warms my face and my vision blurs with the tears that rush forth from the pain from my hands and knees.

"Shit, Will. Are you okay?"

I don't look up at Kirby. I just nod my head and pray that the earth swallows me up. Even with the hum of activity around us—the rush of the production team, camera crew, extras and all milling around—I know that my little spill didn't go unmissed.

I see Kirby drop her kit next to me then her rolling bag full of supplies next to it, and her face fills my vision. "Are you okay?" she asks again, this time low enough that I hope no one else hears her.

"Tell me he didn't see that?" Seriously, is there ever going to be a time when I'm not completely making a fool out of myself in front of this man?

"Yeah, I can't do that," she responds. "Come on. Let me help you up," she continues, and I shake her off.

"I've got it."

"Jesus, Willow, are you okay?" Kane rushes to my side, helping me the rest of the way off the floor. "Zander," he snaps at the young man standing off in the shadows. "Get some electrical tape and make sure this shit is taken care of." He points down at the ripple that caused my spill before taking my hand.

"I'm okay," I tell him, but he only sharpens his gaze at Zander.

"Seriously, Kane."

He finally looks away from Zander and focuses on me. "You hit the ground hard, Willow."

"Uh, yeah. I know, seeing as I was there. Nothing is damaged but a little bit of my pride."

"Smartass," he mumbles under his breath, shaking his head again. "You sure?"

"Positive."

"Right then." He holds my gaze a beat longer before turning to Kirby. "Good morning, Kirby. Follow me and I'll show you where your trailer is. I made sure that all your supplies were stocked, but if you need anything, just let me know."

"Don't you mean to let me know?" I ask remembering that I'm supposed to be helping him in his PA's absence.

He looks confused for a second before he seems to remember himself. "Right, let Willow know."

"I see you, Kane," I tell him, seeing this as some sort of ruse to keep me close while I *try*.

It came to me last night as I replayed every second of our talks from the day. He clearly capitalized on the situation he found me in and wasn't joking when he said he took matters into his own hands when he wanted something.

We walk into the makeup trailer, and I'm sure now that Kirby's job offer was one made in genuine need. This place is a mess of chaos and destruction.

"As you know, we had a quick departure of the old makeup lead. She, uh, didn't go quietly."

Kirby laughs and places her things next to the wall of brightly lit mirrors. "Yeah, well, I imagine when she threw herself at the boss, rejection wasn't something she had planned on."

Kane laughs. "You would be right."

"And the others?" she questions.

"Grant, your other artist, was grabbing breakfast from the catering trailer when I headed this way. I'm sure he'll be right over when he's done."

Ah. Yes. The helper not mentioned when Kirby said her job needed an assistant. Assistant, my butt.

"Grant?" I question with a raise in my brow at Kane.

He coughs and at least has the decency to look a little ashamed.

"Someone call?" I hear and look over at the open doorway where a thin man pushes through carrying two plates of food.

Kane looks at me and smiles slightly before introducing Grant to us. I ignore Kirby's chatter and continue to look at Kane. He shrugs one shoulder, and I give him a smile. I might not understand exactly what my place is here, but I'll figure it out. It took me all night, but I know without a shadow of doubt that if I ignore what's in front of me, then I would definitely be adding another regret to my growing pile.

Hello, adventure.

His motives might be a little foggy right now, but I meant it when I told him I would ride it out. Throw caution to the wind and get off the safe kiddie rides of life. If he doesn't need me here, then I go back to New York with fond memories of this little jaunt of exploration.

"Ready?" Kane asks and gestures to the door.

"Yeah, I think I am." I smile and turn to tell Kirby bye.

She walks over to me and gives me a hug, turning her head to whisper in my ear. "Don't be mad," she says.

I could laugh. But I don't. So I got played to get me here, so be it. I know Kirby, and she wouldn't have led me here if she wasn't sure it was worth it.

"I'm not, Kirb, but later, we're going to talk."

She releases me from her hold and gives me a nod followed by a wink. "I have a bottle of wine with our names on it."

"Make it two and we've got a date."

I turn to Kane, and clearly, he wants to say something, but he just holds his arm out and waits for me to exit before following.

He doesn't speak but settles his palm against the small of my back, leading me without words toward the madness set up around us. I watch people scurrying around with not a clue as to what they're doing, and we walk around them until we settle in behind where the crew is busy setting up what I can only assume is the set where today's shoot will be.

"Are you hungry?"

I sit when he points at one of the two chairs set up in front of a bank of monitors and settle in. "I'm okay."

He takes the seat next to me and doesn't question me further. A few people come up to question him about the lighting and whatnot, but I tune them out and watch the action around me. I'm clueless as to what each of these monitors mean, but given they each display a different angle of the classroom in front of us, it doesn't take much to figure things out. Kane continues to talk to a few people, directing them to change some of the angles.

"What do you need me to do?" I ask when the last person walks away.

"Have you heard about this movie?" he asks, not answering my question.

"*Impenetrable.* That's the title and about as much as I know."

He smiles, his dimple winking deeply in his cheek. "It's been my pet project for years. An idea I had a few years ago when the bullying stories seemed to be the highlight of every news channel. I wanted to paint light on it with a different take."

"Meaning?"

"It seemed to me everything we had heard about led us in one direction, which was obviously the negative. Nothing showed us what it was like for someone to go through such a terrible situation, and instead of drowning, they overcome and become someone better. They take the hate, the viciousness around them, and become, well … impenetrable to the harm others wish to cause."

"So what you're saying is instead of the bullied being influenced by those doing the bullying, they are closed off from their influence?"

He studies me. "Yes and no."

"Well, that clears it up." I laugh.

"Yes, they are influenced by it, at first, but the point is to show the audience that instead of tainting their future negatively, they thrive and become a better person *because* of it. I want to give hope to those who need to know life isn't what others want for you, but what you want for yourself. Strength in the face of weakness."

I frown, dissecting his words. "I'm guessing by the location that we're dealing with high school age people here?"

"You would be right."

"And you think someone at that age, without a wealth of maturity on their side, is capable of seeing past the hate that such an influential time in their lives would cause them and be strong instead of crumble?"

"The point is to show that someone, regardless of their age, can make the decision for themselves and thrive instead of fail when faced with adversity."

"You're hoping to change the way society as a whole looks at the challenges they're faced in life?"

"Yeah. And give hope to those who need it."

"Hope is a fickle word, Kane."

"How so?"

I study him, thinking about the best way to explain something I know all too well about. "Hope isn't always something people can understand, regardless of the picture you paint. More often than not, the promise of something better is more terrifying than the horrible situations life can throw your way. Sometimes, they just aren't strong enough to believe in something so unpredictable. They aren't capable of being or becoming impenetrable against life."

He leans back in his chair and studies me in a way that makes me think he can see right through me. "You're right, Willow, but I believe that by showing the audience you can overcome something as huge as this, it would give someone struggling a little bit of that so-called fickle hope and plant a seed of doubt that can grow into the knowledge that their future is their own. The influence of others only holds as much power as you let it."

"That's easy for someone to say when they probably haven't had to struggle with a bully once in their lives," I return. "How will you show that the hope is worth taking a chance on? Make the audience believe in something that isn't always so easy to take a leap of faith on."

"What is the one thing someone at rock bottom needs, Willow?" he asks; the seriousness in his tone makes me wonder if we're even talking about his movie anymore.

"That depends. If they *want* to change, they would need a reason to climb up and rise above. If they aren't at the point in their lives where they can see that a change is possible, well, then even the most impenetrable soul would be stomped further into the ground."

He nods. "And if the path to change is something that is forced on them?"

I ponder his question. "Well, then, I guess they wouldn't be past the influence of others, now would they?"

"Okay, that's true, but just because someone makes the choice to be stronger doesn't mean they have to do it alone, Willow. Our protagonist here is someone who has forever thought of herself as weak. The bullying *did* get to her, but the difference here, what makes her impenetrable to those trying to influence her future, is that she chose to take the hand reaching out to help her thrive. Using it as a shield, she made all their negativity into something that couldn't influence her further. It protected her and, in turn, showed her what it's like to live without fear and flourish instead of drown. In a way, I guess they *are* influenced by that hate, but instead of it turning into something that shapes their future in a negative light, they're able to use it as motivation to be stronger."

"Not everyone has that person, Kane. You know that, right? You're painting a picture that to some isn't always achievable."

God, if he only knew.

"And therein lies the beauty, Willow. Everyone has that person. And what *Impenetrable* will hopefully show is that person is most often themselves."

I lean back, not taking my eyes off his, and let his words sink in. He's right. I know he is. I've lived that life—where the bullies around you want nothing more than to watch you drown. It doesn't take a physical person to be your shield, but you turning into someone new. Being reborn in a sense as someone stronger. What did he say? Thriving in the face of the fall.

"In order for it to be believable, the protagonist has to want to be someone stronger, which in turn allows her not to be influenced when it comes to the distress in life and the doubt others wish to cause her. She has to be able to show others that the hope they need is within themselves and you are stronger than fear tries to trick your mind into believing."

He stops talking, and I look over, understanding what he's creating here and hoping that he's right; it does give others the hope I didn't have at that age. Hope to make the change.

"You're giving people the hope they need to *be* impenetrable?"

"No," he says. "I'm giving them the power to believe."

"In the one person they view as the weakest really being the strongest?"

"Exactly." He smiles, and when I feel his hand squeeze mine, I realize that during our conversation *I* had reached out to *him*.

CHAPTER FOURTEEN

WILLOW

"**C**UT," KANE CALLS OUT, SNAPPING my attention from the scene I had been held captive watching. "That's a wrap," Kane continues letting everyone know we're breaking for lunch while the next scene is set up. I'm still so enamored at everything I just witnessed that I can't bear to take my eyes from the action around me.

After we had sat down earlier, he caught me up to speed on everything they had filmed so far. Allison, played by Alessandra Hall, was playing a senior in high school. She had been raised in foster care, didn't have many friends, and didn't date. That is until the very popular Mark had turned his eyes on her. They had already filmed the majority of the movie; the parts where she had struggled with believing his interest, the contention he had faced in making her believe he was genuine in his interest, and most importantly, how he didn't care what others thought about him. He was who he was, and he made no apologies for that.

At the beginning of their budding relationship, others around them—his friends and others in his crowd—did their best to ruin things. Allison had verbally and physically been attacked because of their relationship. The 'popular' crew was not too happy that their shining star was bringing someone they felt unworthy into their ranks.

The scene shot today was one when Allison finally realizes she is worthy of Mark and the love they share. She emerges from a physical battle against Mark's ex-girlfriend bruised and beaten on the outside, but finally fighting for herself and not against herself. She decides to make the change and take the higher road, past the forces that want nothing more than to knock her down. *She* becomes her own shield.

Kane explains to me, through my tears, that this scene is going to be toward the end of the movie. Everything they had shot before had led up to this moment. This mental break where she becomes impenetrable to the hate of others. The point Allison becomes free to soar and becomes stronger.

Alessandra is a brilliant young and up-and-coming actress, but shockingly, she nails the fears and insecurities flawlessly. Her acting is so convincing I'm moved to tears. It's like seeing my own life—well, not exactly what Allison has gone through—being played out before me. I watch the same emotions I've felt in the past choking me strangle her, and then as the scene breaks, I watch in awe as she finally makes the climb to become strong.

"That was beautiful," I whisper, not wanting to break the magic that is floating around the set after Alessandra walks off. We had been sitting here for so long that I actually felt like what I was watching was reality, even with all the cameras around us. It felt so real.

Kane doesn't speak, so I finally tear my eyes away from the monitor I had been watching in rapt fascination and meet his penetrating gaze. I don't say another word, but I can tell by how he's watching me that he sees right through me. It's as if he can see inside my mind and the bits of Allison that I carry around. Or did, until I was able to find the strength inside myself to reach my own breaking point.

His phone rings right when he opens his mouth to speak. Looking down at the display, he gives me a sigh. "I need to take this."

"Of course. What can I do?"

"Just wait here?"

I nod, and he climbs to his feet before walking away slightly. But not before I hear him address his caller.

"Hey, Mia," he says softly.

Mia. Mia Post. If rumors are to be believed, his pregnant girlfriend. I turn my eyes to where Kane is standing, his head bowed and free hand holding the back of his neck—he looks like he has the weight of the world on his shoulders. I need to trust that if whatever this is we're doing has any—what did he say? Hope? Yeah, if exploring what's between us is going to have the hope for more, then I have to trust that he'll tell me what's going on when he's ready. Reluctantly, I stop watching Kane, giving him his privacy, and direct my attention toward the monitor that had just before played the most beautiful scene I had ever witnessed.

I want to believe him. He said he wouldn't lie to me. I think back to our exchange earlier about the movie and his words to me.

She has to be able to show others the hope they need is within themselves and that you are stronger than fear tries to trick you into believing.

If I allow my fears to continue to rule me, I would take the safe route and ignore all caution. I know there's more to his relationship with Mia Post than he's told me, but I want to believe he's right. A person can be stronger than fear tries to trick them into believing. My past makes me want to automatically take the safe, fear-free path—but I don't want to be ruled by that anymore. I'm ready, fear be darned, to trust the unknown.

I look back over at him and sigh. It's time to take that leap and be what he believes is something achievable. Finally shed the weakness old Willow wore as a cloak of protection and allow my determination to be stronger and to be all the armor I need to protect myself.

I'm choosing to take that seed of hope, the promise of something bigger, and grow with the knowledge that the future really is whatever I make of it.

Kane was pulled away the second his call with Mia ended. He looked at me with an apology clear in his expression before following one of the lighting techs toward the next filming location. They had been busy breaking down the equipment around me in order to move to another area within the school.

"How are you doing? Pretty exciting, huh?" Kirby asks, reaching down to fiddle with some of my hair. Her smile is cautious but animated enough that I know she's having the time of her life.

"Insane is more like it. God, Kirb, the makeup job you did on Alessandra really made it look like she had been in a fight."

I smile when Kirby actually blushes. "That was so much fun. It's been a while since I was able to really get creative with makeup. It's been the same stagnant palate for so long, I forgot how much I loved this." She points and waves her finger around. "I know it sounds corny as hell, but I know I wouldn't be here if it weren't for fate. How stupid does that sound?"

I nod, reaching over to wrap my arm around her shoulders. "Yeah, I think I know what you mean, Kirb."

"I hate everything you went through in order for this opportunity to literally fall into my lap, but I can't thank you enough, Willow."

Letting my arm drop, I turn to Kirby. "What do you mean? I didn't do anything." I laugh.

Kirby smiles, this one much different from the one she had before. This one is more sly … as if she holds a secret I will never know. "Oh, Willow. You did it all, honey."

"You're being weird," I jest.

"Do you really think Kane would have offered me a job had he not wanted to ensure a certain someone who captured his attention was able to come along? As I said—fate. He just happened to be in the right place during a crappy situation, but everything that followed opened it up so that … well, here we are."

I laugh, finding her theory hilarious. "Be serious, Kirb. He probably knew exactly who you were before he went to Logan last week. Getting me here was nothing more than him making sure you weren't overwhelmed."

Her brow raises, "Yeah? If that's the case, then why aren't you in there," she points in the direction of the trailers, "with me doing just that?"

My silence is enough for her. She knows I can't answer that. Sure, that was the reason I was *told* I was needed, but we both know—especially after everything that's happened since I got on set—she's most likely right.

"Okay. I'll admit, I think you're right about the motivation."

"Yeah, I know I am. The question is, what are *you* going to do about it?" Her voice is soft, questioning without being overbearing about it. She wants to know because she's worried about me, not because she wants to gossip.

"Honestly, I have no idea what I'm doing here, Kirb. I just know it's time to let go of my fears and take a chance. Kane's been very … blunt with his feelings so far." Ha, blunt. That's one way of putting it.

We both stop talking when the intern—Zander—from earlier comes over to collect the chairs Kane and I had been sitting in. He mentions that everyone is still finishing lunch, but filming will be starting at the end of the hour.

"Willow?" Kirby asks when Zander walks away.

"Yeah?"

"Promise me something, okay?"

I nod.

"Be honest with him. Open up *to him* and let him know what's going on in your head. Don't close yourself off. I know you have your reasons for that, but you've come so far that I want you to know you're not alone. I'm here. Eddie is just a call away. And Kane, well, you won't know if you don't try, but he could be one of those people too."

My throat feels thick with emotion. I squeeze my hands together, balling both hands into a fist for a few moments before taking a cleansing breath. Kirby knows me better than most, so it shouldn't surprise me that she has just the right words when I need them the most.

"It scares the ever-loving crap out of me, Kirb, but I promise I'm not going to close myself off to this. It might not happen right away, but I can do baby steps."

She smiles, nodding her head in agreement. "Baby steps are good, but if what I witnessed yesterday is any indication, Kane might be ready to sprint and skip those little baby steps altogether. Damn, Willow, but those were some intense vibes you two had sparked all over the place. Just make sure, when you talk to him, that you let him know you need to learn to walk before you can run. You know what I mean?"

Just thinking about *sprinting* with Kane makes my heart pick up speed. Not in fear of *him*. Well, maybe a little of that. He makes me feel things I've never experienced before and only after a few days of really knowing each other. You add in those kisses, and I'm way beyond anything I've ever experienced.

The way he makes me feel … I know that when things progress past a few steamy kisses, I might not be able to let him in all the way. Thinking about Kane—every sinfully flawless inch of Kane—seeing *me*—every flawed inch of me—intimately might be the hardest chip to knock off my shield of self-preservation.

Am I ready to be intimate with someone again? Brad was my first, and last, lover. Being intimate with him was never an enjoyable experience. It was always about him. Instead of giving me heated words meant for pleasure, his always meant to hurt.

Will I be able to *be* with Kane without letting those memories get the best of me?

"Jeez, Kirby, if I wasn't a ball of nerves already, you have successfully planted the thought in my mind that makes me turn into a supernova of anxieties."

She laughs. "Well, I have an easy cure for that."

Judging by her expression, I'm not sure why I ask, but I do. "That being?"

"Just think about how big his cock is. I mean, really Wills, have you seen his shoes?"

My mouth drops, and I turn to her in shock. She did not just say that. Here. Anyone could have overheard her. *Kane* could have heard her. Oh crap, here he comes.

"Hey, Kirby. Settling in just fine, I see. Alessandra looked flawless during her last takes. Even I had a hard time remembering she was just staged to look beaten."

Kirby responds, but me? My eyes are locked on Kane's leather clad feet.

Good. God.

CHAPTER FIFTEEN

WILLOW

"WILLOW?" KANE CALLS OUT ACROSS the parking lot that separates the school's main building from the make-shift camp of trailers set around the front parking area.

I had been making my way to Kirby's trailer to grab her small kit so she could touch up some of the shine on the actors behind the camera for the final shot of the day. She had run out of powder during the last take, and unfortunately, Grant left their backup kit behind.

"Yeah?" I ask, turning from the door of the makeup trailer. "Aren't you supposed to be directing, Mr. Masters?" I smart.

He jogs over and smiles down at me. Even standing two steps off the ground, he's still taller than I am. "That's the beauty of being in charge. I call the shots."

Hmm. His tone makes me think we aren't just talking about things on set. Going for broke, I ask, "Do you have an affliction for being in charge in all aspects?"

His eyes crinkle, and his smile widens. "Oh, Willow, I think you'll find that I can be flexible when needed, but if I remember correctly, you enjoy when I call the shots."

To anyone walking by, one would think we were just discussing the day's filming, but I know exactly to what he's eluding. I give him a small smile even though I can feel my cheeks heat as a blush warms my skin. "Perhaps."

He laughs, the low and gritty rumble vibrating from his chest. "We're almost done today," he states.

"That we are. It's been a long day. I'm sure you're tired."

He steps closer, up one step so our bodies almost touch. One hand comes up to whisper against my cheek. "Have dinner with me?"

"Dinner? It's almost nine o'clock at night, Kane."

"Okay. Look, I'll be honest here, the meal is an excuse, but I would love to show you around the rest of the filming locations we have set up for the week. I asked catering to have something light prepared for us, and I figured we could enjoy a glass of wine and some conversation before you head back to the house for the night."

"We have an early day tomorrow, Kane."

He leans in, smile widening. "I know—I believe I was the one who handed you tomorrow's call sheet requests to hand out."

"Wine and conversation?"

He nods. "I just want to get to know you better, Willow. Today was a heavy day of emotional filming, and I can tell it affected you. It will be nice to relax and have someone to talk about the film with who seems to get how important this is to me."

"All right, Mr. Director. You call the shots." I laugh. "Wine and conversation sounds good to me." It actually sounds terrifying considering my earlier promise to Kirby to let him in, but I can't deny the buzz of excitement I feel at the thought of spending some time with him one on one.

"It's a date," he utters, leaning down and placing a light caress against my lips with his own.

When he turns and walks back toward the building, my hand comes up to press against my lips. "A date," I whisper against my fingers. "*Holy crap.*"

The rest of filming went by in a blur. I could hardly focus on the actors, Alessandra and Logan—Allison and Mark—as they filmed one of the final scenes of the whole movie. It was weird, seeing things filmed in weird orders, but Kane had told me earlier in the day that it was just the way things were done in order to best utilize the time they had. Because the school was only available to them for the week, they had to break things up and film all the scenes that would take place at the school location in one sweep of well-planned filming.

You would never know that what we were witnessing wasn't real life. Alessandra and Logan were brilliantly talented, their chemistry off the charts, but bottom line—their performances were breathtakingly beautiful.

Kirby left shortly after Kane had wrapped filming for the day. She gave me a wink across the room as her and Grant packed up their gear and headed to the trailer to clean up and prepare for the morning. I had told her when I returned from grabbing her stuff earlier that Kane would be taking me home later. She didn't ask questions, just gave me a smile and continued to powder the nose of one of the extras.

Now, I'm waiting in Kane's trailer for him to make sure the rest of the crew closes the set before heading off. I take a hearty gulp from the glass of wine Kane poured me before walking out the door ten minutes earlier with the promise of returning quickly.

Fortitude of strength in the form of liquid courage.

I reach out to the bottle of wine chilling on the table and refill my already empty glass. Looking around, I notice how homey it looks for being his temporary home away from home.

It's not large, but it's inviting. There's a small kitchen area; however, after peeking in the fridge, it's clear he's never used it. Behind the kitchen is a doorway that leads into a bedroom. I looked, but quickly closed the door when I saw some of his shoes neatly lined in the corner. All of Kirby's earlier comments came rushing back. I slammed the door so hard that I startled myself when the noise rang out around me. The other side is a worn couch and television set up. And the middle of the room, where I've determined is the safest spot to be, holds a small four-person table and chairs.

Middle ground. Away from the bed … and those shoes. Not on the couch where things would feel a little too intimate for me. Safe.

Ugh. There's that word again. I'm starting to *hate* that word.

I look over at the couch again. It would be safer than the bed, but not something I would have picked because it wasn't the stupid safe choice.

Screw it.

Grabbing the bucket holding the wine and ice in one hand and my glass in the other, I walk over to the couch and place the bucket on the coffee table. Then I spend a ridiculous amount of time trying to find a position I can feel good about. When I relax and lean back, I feel like my pants are too tight and my gut has some sort of neon sign saying 'hey, look at me.' Scooting to the edge makes me look about as nervous as I feel.

Dang it.

Finally, after draining my second glass, I settle on the couch and make a mental note to keep my back straight so my pants don't get so tight around my middle.

I was just about to reach out and refill my glass—again—when the door clicks and Kane climbs in. His eyes roam from the kitchen to the table, and when he sees that I'm settled on the couch, his eyes go soft. Clearly, he thought I would have picked the table too.

"Get started without me?" he asks with a nod to the bottle in my hand.

"Hey, you're the one who poured the first glass," I tell him, a little too loudly, and then—to my horror— I giggle.

Giggle.

I don't giggle.

He shakes his head, and his smile grows slightly.

"You make me feel so weird." Uh. Hello? Filter … did you decide to just take a hike and leave me?

He laughs softly but doesn't move toward me.

"Like really weird."

"Good weird?" he questions, that darn smile not dimming at all.

"Even your teeth are handsome." His left brow arches. My eyes follow the movement and all thoughts about his impeccable teeth are abandoned. "Do you pluck your eyebrows?" God, Willow, *shut up.*

"No, Willow."

"Well, they're really nice eyebrows."

"Thank you." He laughs. He looks at the bottle, over halfway empty, and then back at my face. "Are you drunk?"

"I didn't think so five minutes ago, but I think I'm well past tipsy."

He lets out a low, but deep, laugh and finally moves toward me. "Let's get some of that food you didn't think we would need."

I follow his movements when he walks over to the table and leans down to collect a cooler placed near the back wall. My eyes move down from his face, and I watch the fabric of his black tee shirt pull against his muscles. His forearms flex when he lifts the cooler, and before he turns, I note how good his butt looks in his denim jeans.

"Is it hot in here?" I ask and lean back to fan my face. "It feels hot."

"It's not hot, Willow," he responds, bringing the cooler over and sitting next to me on the couch.

Right next to me.

Not a few spaces down to leave plenty of space between us. Nope, right next to me, so close that his thick thigh presses against mine. The heat his touch brings feels like a scorching burn through the fabric of our pants.

"Hey," he says, his hypnotic voice soft like smooth velvet.

"Hi," I squeak.

"Are you nervous?"

I nod. "Uh, clearly. I just sucked back the majority of this bottle trying to calm myself down."

His laugh is low. His eyes are shining brightly. "What makes you so nervous around me?" He turns his attention to the cooler and pulls out some grapes and cheese slices.

Pulling a plate from inside, he arranges a few slices before passing it over to me. I look at the plate as if it's a snake about to bite me. I hate eating in front of people. I always wonder if they can hear each bite and then swallow as it settles in my stomach.

Reaching out, I take the offering and pick up one of the grapes, plopping it in my mouth and chewing, not taking my eyes from his.

"Willow, talk to me."

I grab a slice of the cheese and swallow it down before I speak. "You're really intimidating."

His brow furrows. He doesn't speak, but nods, waiting for me to continue.

"And ... okay, well, you make me feel things that I have no idea how to process."

He nods. "Yeah, Willow, likewise."

"What?"

"Honesty, right?" he asks and waits for my confirmation before continuing. "A few years ago, I was at a charity function in New York for one of the local hospitals. They were opening a new cancer treatment center, and Kane Entertainment was one of the majority donors. That, Willow, was the first time in my life I felt something burn my senses into awareness. I couldn't understand it. The spark against my skin, the tingles down my spine—none of it made sense. It wasn't until about an hour into the event that I found out why ... or I should say who had caused it."

"What?" I gasp, knowing exactly what event to which he was referring.

He doesn't speak, but when my eyes widen, he nods, letting out a soft laugh.

"Yeah. You. I didn't know anything about you. I went to leave the table as soon as dinner was over, but that was when you stood from your table and left with someone else. I brushed it off because it was clear that you were spoken for, but I didn't feel it again until that day at Buchanan's firm. Thirty-five years and not once has someone made me feel like that, Willow. I still knew nothing about you, but there was no way I was going to ignore what my body was telling me. It confused the hell out of me. I felt protective of you. A stranger to me in every sense of the word, but it wasn't just that foreign protectiveness that confused me. I felt as if I had finally found something I hadn't even realized I had been searching for."

"But ... Jesus, Kane, I was a mess."

"No, Willow, you weren't."

I look down at my now empty plate before leaning forward and placing it on the table. The buzz I had felt earlier ebbed, and I'm pretty sure it had nothing to do with getting something in my stomach and everything to do with the shock his words caused.

"That day ..." I pause, looking down at my hands. "Kane, I was without a doubt a mess that day. Emotional and a ball of nerves because I was having to deal with my jerk of an ex and my sister—two people who loved to see me suffer."

"I remember, Willow, but I also remember seeing someone who, even though she was suffering through something hard,

147

pushed herself through it."

"I think we're going to have to agree to disagree. I was there, Kane. Sprawled on the floor and seconds away from breaking."

"I told you before that your eyes are like a window to your thoughts, Willow. I didn't have to know you to be able to see the strength in those beautiful eyes. You just hadn't realized it yet."

I shake my head.

"Yeah," he continues softly.

"You—" I start but have no clue what to say. He's right, but he's also wrong.

"Tell me, what did you feel when I helped you up that day?"

My skin heats when I think back to how that day played out.

"You were stuck in a situation I have no doubt was hard, Willow. I know enough from watching those two around you that it was painful. But when we touched … you forgot it all, didn't you?"

I take a deep breath and nod. I hadn't looked at it that way. I had always looked back on that day with great humiliation because he had witnessed so much of the torment I had lived with for too long.

"You looked at me, and when you forgot what was happening around you, *that* is when I got a glimpse of the strong woman you are. You forgot to be scared. You forgot you were hurting. You didn't know it then, and hell, you might not realize it now because it took me a while to place it, but when we touched … your body recognized the bond we share."

"Maybe I was just star struck?"

"No, Willow … I live that daily, women who are enamored by my celebrity status don't come to life with one touch. They act like savage animals, but you, Willow, you tried to get away from me even though I know damn well you felt the same pull I did."

"Kane," I start but again can't find the right words. It's as if they're all just floating around in my head, unable to form a coherent thought.

"Honesty, Willow. With me and with yourself."

"How can you possibly say you were attracted to someone like *me?*"

His eyes flash. The crystal blue darkening and his full lips thin. "Why do you do that?"

"Do what?"

"Talk down your beauty."

I laugh, the sound coming out shrill and almost animalistic. "You have no idea what my life was like leading up to this moment. When I saw you the first time, I couldn't see one appealing thing about myself. It's been a momentous struggle to get to the point I am at now, and I still struggle. But I also know the type of woman you have been linked to in the past, Kane, and they are nothing like me."

He sighs deeply, looking away, and his jaw ticks as he measures his response.

"Even now, after working as hard as I could, I still don't see it."

"Then I guess I'll just have to show you."

My eyes widen wondering what he's going to do next.

"Christ, Willow, I'm not going to attack you."

"I think it's safe to say that even though I'm here, ready to take the steps toward something unknown, I'm still scared. I hate that I am, I do, but I don't know how to flip that switch and turn it off."

He had just lifted his wine glass to his lips when I started speaking. His eyes don't leave mine as he takes a sip. Lowering the glass, he sets it on the table and takes one of my hands in his. The warmth of his skin against mine seeps into my chilled fingers, and a feeling of peace settles inside me when just seconds before my senses were fighting in overdrive.

Shifting, he moves so his face is closer, his breath dancing on my face, as he takes deep, calm, and measured breaths. "Trust me," he whispers. "Trust what you feel when you're around me. I meant what I told you yesterday, Willow. I just want a chance. A chance to prove what I feel is something genuine. Give me a chance to show you why I'm so bewitched. So I'm asking you, are you ready to let go and trust my lead?"

"What do you want from me?"

"I just want you."

My grip tightens around his hold.

"Willow," he says tenderly. "Talk to me."

Pulling my body away slightly, I lean back against the couch again and close my eyes. "You have no idea what you're asking of me."

"Then tell me."

I take a lungful of air until I feel the burn in my chest, letting it out slowly. "After my mother's death, I floundered through depression until I became someone I didn't even recognize anymore. I lived through a verbally abusive marriage for four long years because I thought that was all I was worth. I was weak, Kane. Heck, I wasn't just weak—I was living and breathing, but felt no life. I put up with so much—from Brad, my ex, my own family—and I let it define who I was. Since the end of my marriage, I've worked so hard to become stronger, to believe my own worth, but it's moments like this when I have a hard time believing that I shouldn't run. I don't even know if I can be who you want me to be. I feel it, everything that you said, but I'm so scared, Kane. Scared of what you make me feel, but I'm scared to trust that hope you seem to believe in so strongly."

He leans forward and places his glass on the table. I follow his movements so I was a second behind him when he shifted again and wrapped his arms around me, pulling me into his embrace. My back settles against his hard chest and my head rests against his shoulder. I'm stiff for just a second before I allow myself to relax. He notices instantly when I open myself up to his touch. His head drops, and his forehead lands softly on my shoulder. His arms, wrapped tightly around me, leave his hands gripping my biceps lightly before I feel his thumbs rubbing soothing circles.

"I want you." He breathes against my skin, turning his head so his lips move against the skin on my neck. "God, Willow, do I want you. You're stronger than you realize, but until you see what I see, just lean on me and let me be strong enough for both of us."

I don't allow myself to overthink. It's time to believe in hope. It's time for me to believe I'm worth something. It's time to give myself to someone blindly and trust.

"Okay." I sigh, and the second that one word leaves my lips, I feel his relief seep into my skin. I actually believe at that moment this remarkable man means every word he's promising.

CHAPTER SIXTEEN

WILLOW

AFTER THE HEAVINESS OF OUR chat, we stuck to safer topics. Kane told me about his childhood and his parents, whom he clearly respected deeply. Their relationship had always been something he wanted for himself, but because of his career, he had never been able to find someone who sincerely wanted him for *him*. He had all but given up on that dream. I could tell he wanted to say more, but he changed the subject to his brothers.

The way he spoke of Kole, it was obvious they're close. Even with them both busy with demanding careers, they have a bond that is clear with the fondness in which he speaks of him.

It wasn't until his comments about Kyle, the oldest Masters brother, that a different picture was painted. The fondness was gone, and in its place was a bitterness he visibly struggled with in order to say something positive about him. I don't press him about it. When he's ready, it's something he can tell me.

I tell him about my mom, the accident, and what it was like to lose her. He nods and offers his support while I talk about one of the hardest times in my life. Listening to him talk and open up about his life gave me the confidence I needed to strip away the lingering fear and let him in. I opened up about my marriage more, and by the end, he knew everything there was to know about my past.

"What about Mia?" I ask as we're collecting the trash and cleaning up his trailer before he takes me back to the house.

He hesitates slightly but then quickly masks his features.

"Kane?"

Hesitation is a dangerous thing. It hints that something is hiding when you take that pause.

Trust him, Willow.

"Mia's been my best friend since we were maybe fifteen. She's the sister I never had and I would do just about anything for her."

Well. Okay.

"Yeah?"

He stops his task. The cooler drops from his grasp and hits the table harshly. The calm I'm so used to seeing in Kane is nowhere to be found. My mind starts to doubt everything I've felt, but as quickly as the thought pops into my head, I beat it down. No. I'm not going to allow my mind to overcome what has been such a powerful night between us. I'm not going to let *myself* ruin this before it even starts.

"This is when I'm going to ask you to trust me with that blind faith, Willow. Trust me when I tell you that Mia is just a friend and leave it at that."

His eyes scorch their pleading gaze into mine. Searching and begging me with the force of his stare. Beseeching without words to believe in him and the fragile relationship we've started to build.

"Okay, Kane."

His shoulders drop, and I realize just how tightly he had been holding his body while he waited for my assurance. While he waited for me to give him my trust completely knowing how much that gesture of blind faith means to me. If I hadn't witnessed him sag with relief, I might have doubts. The fact I would allow him to keep something obviously troublesome enough that he is visibly struggling with the enormity of it is an immense relief to him. But this man is holding something back, and I have a feeling he wishes he could tell me.

"I promise, Willow, I promise I will tell you everything, but right now ... right now, I can't. Too many people's lives are going to be affected, and I gave my word. My word, you'll find, means everything to me. I'm giving it to you and with that promise, know that I care too much about you already that keeping anything from you isn't something I'm doing lightly."

I walk over to him. I wrap my arms around his torso and press my cheek into his chest. His heart beats frantically under my ear as his strong arms come around me. It isn't lost on me that when I would normally tuck my tail and run as fast as I could away from him and the uncertainty of his words, that instead ... instead, I run *to* him. For the first time since this dreamlike reality started to be my life ... I'm the one who initiated things and it was *me* giving him the strength this time.

CHAPTER SEVENTEEN

KANE

DON'T WANT TO LET HER go.

The intensity of my feelings has grown to insurmountable levels.

And after tonight's talk … shit.

I look over at her, sitting quietly in the passenger seat; I smile to myself before looking down at our joined hands. For the second time tonight, *she* was the one who reached out and connected our bodies. She didn't even flinch, as if just being apart from each other for one second is unbearable.

I'm beyond thrilled I was able to talk Cam into heading out without me earlier. I know he hates it. If anyone takes his job more seriously than I do, it's Cam. I'm still not sure what it was that finally convinced him to leave the set without me, but thank fuck he did. I wasn't ready to share Willow with anyone else right now. Just the thought of leaving her at the house tonight has my skin feeling as if it's a size too small.

I flex my hand before circling my thumb against her silky skin.

I can't even explain it to myself, and truth be told, I don't need to know why I feel so strongly about someone I really just met. I just know without a shadow of doubt that this—right here at this moment—is where I'm meant to be.

This feeling of bone-deep contentment, the connection to someone that feels physical even without a tangible touch, *that* is what I've been missing. What I've been looking for. Every second I'm around her, that feeling only grows, and if it continues to flourish like this, then I know everything I've been hoping I could have for my future could finally be mine.

She ... *fuck* ... she will be mine. I can't even entertain the thought I won't feel like this every day.

"You're looking awfully serious over there."

I take my eyes off the road and look over at her when her voice fills the comfortable silence around us. My hand flexes against our connection, reassuring me that she's here ... with me.

"Yeah."

"What's going through your head?" This time she gives me a squeeze.

"I don't want to let you go."

She shifts, and for a second, I think she's about to pull her hand from mine, but she just turns her body so she can focus on me. "I know the feeling."

I nod, but choose not to speak.

We're close to the house that she and Kirby are staying in this week while we film. My house. The house I decided *not* to stay in because I liked the idea she was in my space, even if I wasn't there with her.

Jesus fucking Christ.

"Kane?"

"Hmm?"

"You want me to trust you so I need you to give me the same in return. What's going through your mind?"

Checking the rearview mirror and seeing that we're all alone on this back road, I pull the SUV off the road and push the gearshift into park. The only sound around us is my harsh breathing.

"Kane?" she questions, and I turn toward her, not letting go of her hand.

"Do you have any idea how badly I want to feel your body next to mine? I'm going insane over here, and all I'm doing is bringing you to the house, knowing damn well I'm going to see you in the morning. But instead of enjoying the ride, I'm over here feeling as if I'm coming out of my skin. You give me a calm I haven't felt in years, Willow. At the same time I feel that peace, my whole body is coming apart because of how strong my want for you is. I'm a starved man, and you're the meal I've been fantasizing about."

"Why?" She clears her throat. "Why do you feel like you're coming out of your skin?"

Her innocence is beyond attractive.

"Fuck if I know. I can't even explain it to myself. It's been two days, Willow. Two days since I've finally gotten you where I've craved to have you for months. Hell, years if you count a fleeting glance across a crowded ballroom. I know all too well that we've just started something here, but I'm greedy. I want more. More of you. I want it all." I throw my head back against the headrest and let out a burst of air, more frustrated than I care to admit.

She lets go of my hand, and for a second, my heart picks up speed so fiercely, I can feel the blood pounding through my veins.

Until her soft fingers reach up and cup my cheek.

"You have no idea what hearing you say all of that does to me, do you?"

"Fuck," I bit out harshly and reach up to pull her hand from my face, pressing it against my rapidly beating heart. "You make me feel alive, Willow Tate. I feel alive after years of nothing but loneliness. Knowing I'm just miles from dropping you off has that loneliness closing back in on me."

"You aren't the only one who feels alive after years of feeling like you were walking around dead." She takes a deep breath, one I feel as if it were my own. "I would be lying if I didn't admit I'm apprehensive about the things you can't tell me, but in order to trust you, well, I have to start somewhere."

God, she's stronger than she even realizes.

"I'm a selfish man, Willow. I want you with an intensity that's quickly becoming a living, breathing need."

I study her face before she shocks the shit out of me and leans over to press her lips to mine. Soft and brief, but if you asked me if I could stop a train with my pinky finger right now, I would probably run to the nearest tracks and prove I could.

She settles back in her seat and with a small smile, nods her head toward the road. "Take me home before Mama Kirby grounds me for breaking curfew."

Five minutes later, I'm punching in the code to the front gate and pulling the SUV down the driveway. I should be embarrassed that I lost my shit back there, but I feel better than I did before leaving the set that she isn't upset I couldn't tell her more about Mia.

I have no doubt that the feeling of dread I felt when she asked about her and the situation I find myself in is what sparked the growing ache the closer we got to the house. For the first time since I started out on this quest to conquer Willow, I was unsure if I would be able to win her over. Not being able to tell her the truth about Mia when I have been begging her to trust me … well, if that isn't being a hypocrite, I don't know what is.

It's time I called Mia and figured out how we can fix this, and quick, because I'll be fucking damned if that's what tears Willow from my grasp.

I park in the middle of the circular drive so I'm next to the front door. I put the SUV in park and make myself move to climb from my seat. I keep my eyes on Willow as I walk around the hood, not wanting to look away from her before I have to. Not wanting to lose the feeling having her near does to me.

When I open her door, she grabs her bag and slides from the seat until she's standing before me. I don't back up, so when she straightens, our bodies are just a hair away from touching.

"You have no idea how hard it is not to take you right here, Willow," I groan in complaint. The warmth of her body is causing mine to come alive just knowing how close she is for me to take. I have to tighten my grip on the car door I'm holding open so I don't reach out and pull her body into mine. "I want you. So fucking badly."

She blushes and reaches out her hands to timidly run them up my chest before curling her hands around the back of my neck. I close my eyes and savor her touch. I can still feel the heated burn left behind from the path of her hands. She moves her feet forward the inch needed to press her body against mine. There's no way I can keep my hands off her now.

With my eyes still closed, I let go of the door and allow my hands to grab her hips and pull her roughly against my body, fusing us together. She lets out a small gasp before it turns into a low moan.

Her breathing speeds up and she whispers, "I think I have a pretty good idea just how hard it is, Kane."

My eyes snap open, and I look down into her eyes. With the soft glow of the lights within the house burning out into the darkness around us, I can make out the slight blush against her pale skin. But it's her eyes, always those expressive doe eyes, that tell me what I need to know.

She wants me just as furiously as I want her.

"Kiss me," she pleads.

"Fuck, yeah," I snarl and crash my lips to hers.

CHAPTER EIGHTEEN

WILLOW

HOLY CRAP.

That kiss.

I didn't think it was possible for him to beat the kisses I've had from him so far, but each one seems to grow in intensity.

And that kiss was … wow.

After reluctantly pulling ourselves apart, he gave me one more slow kiss before walking me to the door. I understood what he meant when he told me that he didn't want to let me go. I felt the same way as I watched him walk heavy footed away from the porch. Each step he took away from me felt as if some imaginary livewire was violently pulling me.

I haven't been able to pull myself from the closed front door since walking in and reluctantly shutting it behind me. The cool glass soothes my feverish skin as I rest my forehead against it.

"Shit, Willow. That was hot."

I spin around and gape at Kirby. She holds up a bottle of wine and two glasses, signaling for me to follow her with a nod. I drop my purse on one of the two chairs to the side of the entryway and follow behind her.

She takes a seat on the couch and I move to the large chair next to the side she settled in. Leaning back, I take a deep breath.

"So? That kiss?"

I look over at Kirby and burst out into a deep laugh, letting the heaviness of the evening and every other overwhelming feeling I've felt since this morning rush out of me as I let go of the tightly wound tension in my body.

Kirby smiles, and before you know it, we've already polished off the whole bottle and started on the next.

"Tell me again," she demands, her voice high with excitement.

"Which part?"

"The part about the charity dinner."

I sigh, remembering how powerful his words were. "He said he felt like he had finally found something he didn't even know he had been searching for. God, Kirby, how crazy is that?"

She lifts her head from where it had been resting against the couch and looks over at me. Stars dance in her eyes and her expression is just shy of dreamy. "That's so romantic, Wills! Holy shit! I mean, who would have thought … all this time."

"I had no idea. I'm still shocked."

"Tell me what happened next again." She flips onto her belly, reaches out for her glass, and downs the rest of her wine in one gulp, wiping her mouth with the back of her hand when she finishes. "The part when he said you were a witch." Her brows crinkle together trying to remember my words.

"He said ... he said I had bewitched him. What does that even mean?" I pull myself from my crouched position and reach my hands behind me to unsnap my bra and pull it off without removing my shirt, sighing in relief when that torture device hit the ground—away from my breasts.

"That man has it bad, Wills. So bad. Did he really tell you to lean on him and let him be the power?"

I shake my head. "No, he told me to let him be the strength when I can't be ... or something like that."

She sighs.

"Am I crazy?"

"No. Well, yes. Crazy that you didn't molest him right there in the front drive, but I wouldn't say crazy in general."

My eyes widen.

"You thought about it," she smugly states.

She isn't wrong. I ignore her and take another sip of my wine. I can feel my buzz crossing over toward drunk at this point.

"He said it felt like he was coming out of his skin when he thought about dropping me off tonight. Kirb, I felt it too. I didn't want to leave him. I don't know what to do with the way he makes me feel. Isn't it too quick to be feeling something this ... powerful for someone I literally just met?" She sighs again, and I narrow my eyes at her. "You aren't helping," I snap.

"Willow," she starts, the serious tone making me lean forward in my chair so I can focus on her and not the spinning ceiling from moments before. "What you're explaining to me is something that some people never find in their lives. You have a connection to him way beyond the definition of time. It transcends that and has a power of its own. I can't tell you what to do, but if you want my advice, I would tell you to hold on to that and do everything you can never to let go. No matter how scary the enormity of those feelings can be. If he said let him be strong for you, then let him, but Willow, *do not let this go.*"

"And what about Mia?"

She flops back down and waves her hand in the air. "What about her? He said trust him, and as hard and daunting as that is, do it. I don't know him that well, but Willow, he wouldn't be working this hard if he just wanted a cheap thrill. A man like Kane Masters could have any woman in the world. He's not going anywhere. But more importantly, he's in the public eye. Do you really think he would start something with you if he was already in a relationship, or whatever the hell?"

"I don't know, Kirby. I'm completely new at this!"

"I know, honey," she says and turns her head to meet my eyes. "And it's so beautiful to watch him bring you to life."

I hold her gaze and let her words permeate my mind. Let them take hold of my doubts and squeeze them right out of my head.

She's right. He's bringing me to life.

"I need to let go of my fear once and for all, Kirb. It's time, and you know what? I think I'm ready. Ready for Kane."

I smile, big and toothy. She returns my smile, and with a nod, she sits up and refills our glasses.

I stumble up the stairs and squint my eyes in the darkness. Stupid dark. Stupid stairs. Stupid, weird house I don't know.

Kirby left to head toward the other end of the house a few giggles and thumps ago, leaving me behind to fumble my way toward my temporary bedroom.

Why is this stupid, weird house so big?

It takes me three doorways to finally find the large bedroom where my stuff had been placed. If I hadn't seen the size of Kirby's room earlier, I would feel guilty for taking the master. But now I wish I just had a cot in one of the closets. Then maybe I would be able to find the stupid bed in this big house.

Why is this place so big?

Who needs this much space?

I kick my shoes off and pull my shirt over my head. My nipples tighten when their warmth feels this cool air around me. My pants become a problem when I can't figure out how to get the button through the little hole. My struggles and wiggles make my phone—which I had tucked into my back pocket—drop loudly onto the hardwood floors.

"Stupid phone," I mumble, bending over and picking it up.

Giving up on my pants, I drop down on the mattress and sigh when the softness of the down comforter acts like a warm hug.

I love warm hugs.

I would love to give Kane a big warm hug.

Right now.

I bet my nipples would love that.

My phone scares the crap out of me when it lights up and vibrates in my hand. I let out a gasp followed quickly by a little scream and toss it away from me on the other side of the bed.

My phone lets out a soft hum and my eyes narrow at the evil little device. The third time it goes off, I reach out and squirm against the mattress until I'm able to get my hands on it. Bringing it close to my face, I squint at the offensive brightness that rapes my eyes. It takes me a second, but I finally make out the words on the screen.

Kane: I can still feel your lips.
Kane: I wish you were here.
Kirby: Got ask. Dod yous chk his shoe siz?

The first two steal my breath, but it's Kirby's message that makes me bark out a loud laugh. I'm drunk, but clearly, she's a lot drunker than I am.

Unlocking the phone, I bring up my messages and quickly type out a response to Kane before I chicken out. Kirby can wait. She's probably asleep now anyway since it took me a million years just to get to my room in this stupid big house.

Willow: I can feel your lips too, and I wish I could feel them again. Now.

I smile, feeling proud of myself for flirting back with him. Riding my high, I respond to Kirby. At least she will be able to understand *me*. Even drunk, I can still work this stupid phone to message her back.

Willow: I didn't look in his shoes, but I felt his big, huge dick when he kissed me good night. You were right. Shoe size means A LOT! ;) I wonder if his big, huge

dick tastes as good as his lips?

My smile widens, and I lock my phone before crawling off the bed, almost falling to the floor, and attempting the button on my pants again. It only takes me four times to peel the denim from my legs and kick them off to some dark corner of my room. I should go find something to sleep in, but that would require way too much effort.

I pull my hair back from my face and secure it with the hair tie I had on my wrist. Pulling back the covers and climbing in, I let out a deep sigh when the bed's warm hug once again envelops me.

I had just closed my eyes when I feel my phone vibrate somewhere around my feet. Crap. I forgot about that thing.

Lifting myself away from the warm hug, I fumble around like a blind woman before finally closing my hands around the phone. Why did I want this thing again? I shrug and reach down the side of the bed to connect the charger before lying back down.

"Hello, warm hug bed," I mumble into the darkness.

I was almost asleep when I hear my phone hum again.

"Ugh."

I roll over, fumble with the phone, and almost drop it. When I pick it up, I have to try a ridiculous number of times to unlock it before I finally get the sucker to work. Bringing up my text screen, I click on Kirby's name.

But when I read her message, I feel nothing but confusion. What the heck is she going on about? Why would I want to kiss her?

Oh. My. God.

"No, no, no," I slur and close out of her screen before looking at the only other bold message.

The one from Kane.

The one responding to what I sent him thinking I was responding to Kirby.

I drop my head without opening his message, but it doesn't take long for curiosity to get the best of me. Worrying my lip between my teeth, I press my finger against his message and gasp when it opens.

Kane: Fuck, Willow. You can't say shit like that to me and not have my 'big, huge dick' begging you to take a taste. Goddamn.

Holy crap! How am I supposed to respond to that? Do I tell him it was a mistake? That I'm well beyond drunk?

No.

He liked it. He wasn't mad. Maybe a little shocked, but *he liked it.* I read back his response and throw caution to the wind. I respond quickly before I can let reason win over my drunken mind.

Willow: I bet you taste delicious. Can I taste you?

I add a little eggplant emoji and the big tongue one before clicking send. Good job, Willow! I bet he'll like that. I smile, letting the rush mix with the alcohol and wait for him to respond. This is fun.

I see the little bubbles that indicate he's typing and wait. The anticipation spiking my newfound courage even higher. I hold my thumbs hovering just above the keypad and get ready for his response so I can be ready to type back.

> **Kane: Fucking hell. You have no idea how hard I am right now. This is Willow, right?**
> **Willow: Yup.**
> **Kane: Goddamn.**
> **Willow: You didn't tell me I could taste you. I really want to taste you.**
> **Kane: Willow …**
> **Willow: Kane …**
> **Kane: I can't decide if it's a good thing I can't get to you or not.**

I frown. What does that mean? I might not have a lot of recent practice at tasting a dick, but how hard could it be. It's probably like riding a bike. I should probably let him know that. Then he won't be wondering if I would be any good. He said he was hard, so he must have liked what I asked. Right?

> **Willow: If you were here, I could taste you. I bet you would like it. It's like riding a bike. I could ride a bike for a long, long time.**

I smile and turn to my side, pulling the covers over my shoulder.

Kane: I'm two seconds from driving over there. What would I find, Willow?

I read his message back a few times. What would he find? Well, uh ... duh, me. *Oh!*

Willow: I'm in bed. Are you in bed? I want to see your bed.
Kane: You're in my bed.
Willow: Uh, no, I'm not. I think I would know if I was in your bed.
Kane: Fuck, you're adorable.
Willow: You're really, really hot. Do you have your shoes on?

I wonder if he's wearing panties too. Just panties. No. Kane wouldn't wear panties. Boxers. No, boxer briefs. Wait. Maybe he doesn't wear anything at all. That would explain why I felt him so well when he dropped me off. It was almost like I could picture exactly what he looked like just by feeling his erection against my body.

Willow: Do you wear panties?

The dots start. Stop. And start again. He doesn't respond for a solid minute, making me wonder if he went to bed. It's not late, but maybe he's sleepy. I'm so sleepy.

Kane: No, baby, I don't wear panties. LOL.

Do you?

Willow: Right now that's all I'm wearing.

Kane: Fuck.

Willow: That would be nice. I really want to taste you, but that would be nice too. I mean, I'm not sure I'm ready for THAT, but I really, really think it would be really nice.

Kane: Nice isn't the word I would use. You might not be ready for that, but Willow, I really, really want to sink my cock inside you.

Willow: Oh, boy.

Kane: Go to sleep, sweetness. I'm going to take care of the 'big, huge' issue I have pressing against my stomach now. Tomorrow, after we're done filming, you're mine, and this 'big, huge' cock will be waiting.

Holy ... wow. Well. Does he mean what I think he means? What do I say to that? Looking at my phone, I reread his message and figure I'll just play it safe.

Willow: I think I'm already yours.

I drop the phone on the nightstand and roll over. I don't hear a responding buzz from my phone, so I slip off to dreamland with a smile on my face and arousal burning through my veins. I spend the rest of the night in a restless sleep with dreams about bikes, shoes falling from the sky, and bizarrely enough, Kane in my panties.

CHAPTER NINETEEN

WILLOW

WHY DID I DRINK SO much last night? To be fair, I'm not even sure we realized we had put away so much wine. We normally have Eddie there, so the bottle goes quicker—we drink less—but Kirby and I were clearly so lost in our chat that we didn't even question why the bottles were piling up.

I finished my hair, blowing it dry and running my straightener through my long locks, before walking into the bedroom and dropping my towel to get dressed. My head is pounding, but hopefully, with something light in my stomach, that will pass. I'm not sure I could get through a long day on set with this hangover. I haven't had one like this since college.

I pull on one of my favorite pairs of jeans; the dark denim always makes me feel like my legs are longer and slimmer than I know they are. I grab a white long sleeve shirt from the closet, and after settling it on my body and tucking it in, I grab my gray three-button vest and push my arms through. I had forgotten all about this outfit until Kirby had mentioned it when we were unpacking. I had brushed her off, initially thinking I wouldn't be caught dead wearing it, even as she assured me that it made me look phenomenal. Her words, not mine.

I admire the way the vest fits while looking in the floor-length mirror set in the corner; it gives my figure an hourglass shape, disguising what I normally see as too round of hips and more fuller than flat stomach. Instead, the two buttons give spotlight to the narrow sides of my torso and put my large chest as the accent. Matched with my jeans, the whole look makes me feel pretty. I don't see what I normally see. I'm not sure if it's because, through Kane, I'm now seeing myself in a different light, or because I can actually—finally—see a change in my body.

I never would have been caught dead wearing this a year ago, when my marriage was at the tail end of its destruction, but something about the way Kane looks at me makes me take a longer look at myself. Instead of seeing what I hate, I look for what he finds attractive.

And ... dare I say ... I think I like what I see.

My cheeks have a slight blush to them that I know just the thought of him induces. My normally dull eyes are bright and shining. Bottom line, I look happy and carefree.

I twist around, grab my knee-high boots, and sit on the long bench at the end of the bed to pull them on. One last look in the mirror leaves me satisfied with my look and I'm walking down the long hallway to the back staircase that will take me to the kitchen. I hear Kirby chatting with Rob, and Alli laughing at the cartoons playing softly in the background. I smile.

Today's going to be a good day.

Even with a hangover from hell, I know it will be. I'm excited to see Kane today. I don't know what it was about our chat last night, but when I woke up this morning—even through the hangover—I felt as if a calm had settled over my soul. Sounds ridiculous, corny even, but I'm at peace with my decision to go forward and not look back. I'm not saying it's going to be easy, but I'm ready and eager to see what every future second holds.

"Good morning," I tell Kirby and Rob when I walk into the room.

Rob gives me a nod and looks back down at his iPad. I know he was able to get vacation from work to come here this week, but I'm sure he's going insane not being able to keep up with the demands of his law firm.

He's been expanding his firm for the last five years, and even in New York, a town saturated with the who's who, he's managed to make a name for himself in entertainment law. A part of me hopes he might have even more clients knocking on his door with Kirby's new job.

I move around the island, but before I can get a few steps, Kirby grabs my face between her hands and smacks her lips on mine. Full-on contact, closed mouth, eyes open. Surprise holds me still and confusion captures me dumb.

As quickly as she grabs and attacks, she pulls back, standing in front of me with the oddest expression on her face.

"What the heck, Kirb?"

She cocks her head to the side, that curious expression getting even more inquisitive as one sharply sculpted brow rises before falling again. Her blue eyes, wide and vivid, dance with mirth deep within their depths. She stands there a beat studying my stunned face before quirking one shoulder and turning to walk back to her bagel.

"You're so peculiar," I tell her, my surprise making way for a very unladylike, snort-type laugh.

Rob looks up at his wife and just shakes his head. Her shoulder comes up again to shrug me off while taking a big bite of her breakfast.

Brushing off Kirby's odd behavior, I finish making my way around the island and pop my own bagel into the toaster. We finish our breakfast, making small talk while we wait for our ride. I know now that the special treatment we seem to be getting has everything to do with Kane's interest in me. I'm not sure if I would have been bothered by this a few days ago or maybe a little scared at the control he wields, but now—knowing whatever is between us is a lot stronger than I could have ever dreamt—it just brings a smile to my face.

Yes. Today is going to be a good day.

Cam was quiet, for the most part, during our drive. When we first opened the doors to climb in, I caught the tail end of a book playing through the speakers before he powered off the sound. Judging by what I heard, I was stunned to hear something that clearly had some romance in it. Cam, to me, seems like a man who would prefer action, guns, and death. Oh well, I guess that just goes to show you shouldn't judge a book by its cover.

Things are insane when we make it to the set a mere fifteen minutes later. Kirby had been going over the call sheet I handed her yesterday afternoon, making notes about when she needed to have each actor in her chair in order to have them camera ready in time for their scenes. She didn't have anything too intense like Alessandra's battle wounds yesterday, but today, the bulk of scenes filmed would involve the supporting actors. Kirby and Grant were in charge of three or more heads for each scene. I could tell she was nervous when we finally parked behind the trailers. Yesterday was easy for her; she loved it, but today would really put her to the test.

"You're going to be fine, Kirb."

She nods, her silence betraying her calm and showing just how nervous she is.

"Hey," I say. "I'm going to go tell Kane that I'm sticking with you today. He might have been full of crap when he said I was your assistant, but you need me. Let me help you out."

Her shoulders visibly sag when she lets out the tension that had been growing. "You think he'll be good with that?"

"Why wouldn't he?" I challenge.

"Umm, maybe because he clearly likes having you close."

My snort-like laugh comes out before I stifle it. "He'll be fine. Plus, I'll be close enough. If I stick too close, he's bound to get sick of me."

"I doubt that. What are you really thinking? That he won't have the same crazy yearning to be near you that he displayed yesterday if you spend too much time together or something?"

"It's crossed my mind," I respond honestly.

"Ha! Fat chance of that, Wills. That man is so enchanted by you that he might as well be hypnotized."

"Whatever," I huff. Yeah … funny thing, I feel the same way. The feelings he gives me when we're together are like a drug—and I feel the withdrawals of its loss when we're apart.

Insane.

Crazy.

Extreme.

All-consuming.

"I'm going to let Kane know you're stuck with me today, but I just want to make sure he doesn't need anything. He seemed to be fine yesterday, but I can tell he definitely needs some help when the cameras are rolling. He goes into a trance, and he would probably not even notice if a tornado came blowing through. I'm sure Zander is around here somewhere and can pick up the slack. Plus, I wouldn't feel right being paid for nothing, and so far … I've done nothing. You're stuck with me."

She nods and walks over to the makeup trailer. My attention is diverted for a brief second when I see the amount of people with cameras trained in my direction. They're standing on the other side of a barricade that the local police had set up. I know they can't actually get in here, but seeing them with their cameras snapping away toward me is a little unnerving.

A vision of my face being on one of the tabloid magazines that Kane's always a front-page star of fills my mind. Crap. I don't know why the thought didn't cross my mind before. Being with Kane is a guarantee I will be put out there and judged. I'm not sure what I would do if they were to print what I've thought myself. I'm not good enough to be at his side. Pick me apart for the world to see.

I calm myself down but make a mental note to talk to Kane about that. Maybe he doesn't want to deal with what would follow if we were to be seen together. That would explain why he hasn't mentioned anything past our time in Georgia. The old Willow would have let this fear consume her, but I'm determined to change, and I really need to trust I'm strong enough to handle more than I believe. Be the change I wish for myself. That's what I need to do.

I open the front doors and enter the high school. The front office area of the school is massive with a long hallway that leads into the classroom sections within. This had become a central hub of sorts. There are tables set up with different types of equipment, and a few other areas around them acting as a ground zero of sorts.

I see Kane talking to Zander and another man. When I reach Kane, he dismisses them. With a hand pressed against my lower back, he leads me over to where a table of refreshments is set up. He looks around to see if we have privacy before turning his attention toward me. His eyes look like the clearest sapphires.

"Are you ready for tonight?" he strangely questions. His tone is light, but I don't miss the demand within his words.

"Tonight?" I probe.

His eyes linger on mine, brows slightly raised and a slow smile twitches his lips. A second later, he shifts closer toward me, closing what little space separated us.

"Yeah, baby, tonight. Fuck, I haven't been able to get the thought of tonight off my mind yet."

I swallow thickly and have to clear my throat. Frowning, I ask, "Kane, what—?"

His mouth opens and I stop talking; his smile dims slightly and he runs one of his hands through his thick hair. He seems to be sitting on the edge of confusion and uneasiness, but why? Didn't we leave things in a great way last night?

"I meant every word I typed last night, Willow, but the question is, did you?"

With an uncertain tone, I open my mouth and lamely say, "Huh?"

He offers me a bemused smile, surprise dances across his handsome face before he looks at me with a question of disbelief. Clearly, he knows something I don't.

"How about you check your phone and get back to me." He leans down, presses his lips against mine, and breathes deeply before leaning back. He takes a few steps backward, his head shaking with silent laughter. "I'll be waiting," he says oddly and turns.

What in the world?

I reach behind me and pull my phone from my back pocket. I stuffed it there before I left my room, but in my rush and after Kirby's weird lesbian act this morning, I don't think I even looked at it once.

I don't have any notifications. The screen just displays the date and time. I slide my finger across the glass and unlock the phone. No emails. No missed calls. No little red dots on any of my other apps. I open my email folder first and frown when I don't see anything new *or* from Kane. My call log doesn't show any voicemails. My brow pulls in slightly when I click on my messages app and see Kane's name as one of the last received text.

When did this happen?

Pressing my thumb to his text line, I almost drop my phone when I see what takes over the screen. I know I let out a loud gasp.

Oh, holy *shit!* I don't even hesitate to curse when I usually avoid it at all costs. Holy. Shit. Indeed.

My shocked eyes snap up from the evidence that my drunken

self clearly had some fun last night when I hear Kane's booming laugh from where he's standing with one of the techs I didn't recall meeting yesterday. His eyes capture mine, and when I see him wink, I feel like I might melt into a puddle of aroused embarrassment right here in the hallways of some middle of nowhere Georgia high school.

CHAPTER TWENTY

WILLOW

TODAY HAS BEEN ... INTERESTING.

After the shocking revelation that drunk Willow is like a hooker in heat, I've been avoiding Kane at all costs. Or, I should say, I know it's more like Kane *letting* me avoid him than me actually succeeding in keeping him at a distance. If Kane wanted me, he would make it happen. I get the feeling this is more about him putting the ball back in my court, so to speak. The ball I all but threw into his lap with my hussy messages last night.

I need to make the next move. I know this. Otherwise, he's going to wonder if I meant what I said last night. What I agreed to. And as terrifying as the thought of being *with* him is, the thought of him thinking I have doubts is more daunting.

I wring my hands together and flop down on the chair Alessandra just vacated. Kirby is busy washing her brushes, and Grant has been cleaning the same spot for the last five minutes.

Heck, he doesn't even know me, and he can tell my mood is all over the place.

"When are you going to tell me what crawled up your ass and died?" Kirby's voice breaking the silence makes me stop fidgeting. She doesn't turn from her task, just waits.

I look over at Grant, who stops his cleaning and looks at me with a smile. "I'm just going to go … uh, check on … hell, I'm leaving." Looking flustered, he grabs his kit and walks out the door.

"I have ten minutes before I need to be on set. Ten minutes, Willow. Give it to me." She puts the last brush away, grabs her kit she will need when she leaves to go stand by for touch-ups, and snaps it closed. Finally, she turns and crosses her arms over her chest. The perfect picture of stubborn compassion.

"Ten minutes might not be enough to touch this one," I deadpan.

"So start at the beginning and see where we end up."

I nod, unsmiling. "I drunk texted Kane last night."

Her eyes go round, and she visibly struggles to find her words. "Uh, okay. Clarify that."

I stand, walk over to the couch where I had thrown stuff earlier, and dig my phone out of my purse. After unlocking it and finding Kane's messages, I scroll to the beginning and hand it over to Kirby.

She looks from my eyes to the phone, and then back again, before she reaches out her hand and grabs it from me. I keep my eyes trained on her face as she reads the messages. Her mouth opening slightly when she starts, and by the time I know she's read the last message, it's hanging open widely.

"Holy shit! Well done, Wills!" The hand that isn't holding my phone comes up and she waits with a big smile for me to give her a slap. Seriously? She wants to congratulate me and not talk about what he said? "Come on! This is brilliant. I'm so proud of you."

I weakly tap her palm with mine and smile. Not a big smile, but more like a reaction to *her* reaction. I should have known she would look at this as a positive.

"Kirby, serious. Did you read the same thing I did? I pretty much had text sex with Kane."

"Sext. You sexted him. That's what it's called. Sure, you were a little rusty, but we can work on that."

I gape. "Rusty? I told him I wanted to taste his big, huge dick."

"And bravo with that." Her smile widens, and she looks back at my phone, her finger moving across the screen to bring the text back to the beginning. I watch her face light up this time.

"I asked him if he was wearing *panties*! Panties, Kirby! Oh, my God, I'm so embarrassed." My cheeks flame and I bring my hands up to press them against my burning skin. The chill in my hands is useless against my fevered skin. "I … heck, I'm not even sure what I was talking about for a second there, but I basically begged him to let me taste him."

She continues to look at the phone, her smirk not even having the decency to dim a little. When her gaze flits to mine, I can tell she most definitely doesn't see this in the same horrifyingly awkward light as I do.

"Stop freaking out. Clearly, he enjoyed it, even if we need to work on your execution some."

"My execution? Jesus, Kirb. That performance was ridiculous. He most likely thinks I'm the lamest person around. He's probably used to women who have no problem telling and *doing* exactly what he wants. With all the right words."

Her eyes narrow. Locking the phone, she hands it over and her arms go right back over her chest. "Far as I can tell, you had all the right words, Willow. Did you read the same thing I read? Sure, part of it was pretty funny, but did you even read his responses back? He liked it. No, he *loved* it."

I snort.

"You're so infuriating." She sighs. Reaching out, she grabs my phone out of my hands, and after pressing my code, she continues. "He said, and I quote, 'I'm going to take care of the big, huge issue I have pressing against my stomach now.' Still don't think you had the right words?"

"Maybe he was just saying that so I didn't feel embarrassed."

"And maybe you're acting like an idiot." I gasp, and she sighs. "I'm not being mean, Wills. But I don't even understand you right now. He said you were his. Tonight, after filming, you. Would. Be. His."

Shifting in my spot, I meet her searching eyes.

"That's it," she says softly. "Strip away all the adorably cute sexting and the bottom line is you, my love, are nervous. Why?"

I drop down on the chair next to where she's standing and look up at her. "It's obvious, isn't it? I have no idea what I'm doing. Even more, I'm not sure, when it comes down to it, I'll be able to be … that." I motion toward my phone. "I feel like a fool. An imposter. I'm not that person, Kirby, and you know it. I don't say things like that, and we both know I'll most likely clam up when it comes to taking things further than the kisses we've already shared."

"Oh, Willow." She moves and bends at the waist. Her arms come around me, and she pulls me into a fierce hug. "You're so much braver than you give yourself credit." She laughs when I start shaking my head. "You are. You don't know it now, but you are. Kane brings out a side of you that I don't even think you understand. You forget to be afraid of what he thinks *about* you when he's around because he makes it so easy. Yesterday, when I was watching you, you smiled so much, Willow. You enjoyed being with him, watching him create something that is so personal to your own life, and with each scene you witnessed, those smiles came more often."

"We don't even know each other."

She laughs. "I bet you know more about him in this small time that you've had together than most. You spent four hours with the man after I left. Can you tell me in that time you didn't get to know each other better?"

I don't answer because she's right. We both opened up, and I do feel like I know so much about him regardless of the time in which we've been around each other.

"You're ready, Willow. It's time to stop overthinking things and take that chance. Stumble. Fall. Hell, trip over your ass and make a fool of yourself with drunken messages. Who cares? Enjoy yourself and let go of the rest of your worries and fears." Her hands come up and frame my face. For a split second, I wonder if she's about to kiss me again. "I'm not going to say this again, Willow. That man out there could have anyone, and he wants you. You have to open your eyes and realize he wouldn't be making this much of an effort if he wasn't all in, so it's time to do him a favor and do the same."

"All in," I echo.

She nods and steps away. I watch her move around the room while she keeps bringing her eyes back to mine periodically. I know her time is running short, and as much as I would love to keep beating a dead horse, I let her words sink in. The confidence I felt in pursuing this with Kane last night comes back. Sure, it was embarrassing to see what I texted him, but she's right, it didn't turn him off in the least.

"And what do I do if it turns out that I'm not ready … for … crap."

"You won't know until you try. Look, I get it, that jerk of an ex did a number on you … did a number on what already slipping confidence you had. It isn't going to be easy for you after that to just strip naked and scream take me. Take it slow. And, most importantly, Willow, communicate with him. Make him understand where your head is, and the rest will fall into place. I have a feeling, though, he's going to surprise you and knock all that doubt right out of your beautiful little head."

I can do that. He made opening up to him effortless. The normal trepidation I would have had is gone. All because of the way he makes me feel when I'm around him. Safe. A word I had started to hate now taking on a whole new meaning. No longer the easy route, it's beginning to feel more like my salvation.

It's time to believe in myself completely. Fear can stay because I know he will help me knock it back. And if he can't, well, hopefully, I'm ready to do it myself.

I nod, and Kirby smiles. Lifting my phone up, I unlock it and look down at the still open text screen. An idea pops into my mind, and before I can stop to question it, my thumbs fly across the screen. I know I was right earlier when I thought about how I needed to make the next move so he is clear I'm serious and, as Kirby says, all in.

Locking my phone, I take a solidifying breath before standing and giving Kirby a smile of my own, this one feeling as light as I do at this moment.

It's time to be the change I wish for myself.

It's time to let go.

When I catch my reflection in the mirror across from where I stand, I take a moment to really *see* me. Like earlier this morning before leaving the house, I stop looking for what I don't like and see the Willow that Kane sees.

My whole body seems to glow. My eyes are bright, cheeks flushed, and even my posture seems to exude the confidence I've been fighting for my whole life. For the first time in as long as I can remember, the fear of the unknown doesn't consume me. It doesn't define me.

I look like the Willow I deserve to be.

I look like the Willow who's ready to get the man.

And I'm ready to enjoy wherever the ride takes me.

With a nod, I pocket my phone and follow Kirby to take our spots on set for the next few hours of nonstop filming.

CHAPTER TWENTY-ONE

KANE

I TURN AWAY FROM THE MONITOR and run my hands through my hair. Nothing today is falling into place. That's a fucking lie. The actors are flawless. They've hit their stride and every take seems to get better and better. I should be thrilled, but my head isn't in the game.

Which makes no sense.

I'm finally behind the camera, directing and producing a film I've been working on for the better part of five years. A film I've put my own blood, sweat, and frustrations into beginning with the screenplay. This is my moment. This film is my baby. I should be fucking thrilled.

Instead, I can't get one stunning brown-eyed woman off my mind. I can't stop seeing the same fear Alessandra eludes to in Willow's eyes. I know she's been through shit, but I'm beyond frustrated I can't just fix it, and I have a feeling that until she's ready, I might be doing more harm than good by coming on as strong as I have.

"Fuck," I expel.

I know this isn't going to be easy. Thrusting her into my insane life seems to be the least of my issues. Mia and everything that comes with her are another reason I'm about to come apart. They go hand in hand with the spotlight of my life. I'm floundering, and the only time I feel sane is when that woman, *my* fucking woman, is looking at me as if I hold all life's answers when I can't even seem to answer my own.

Last night, I knew she wasn't herself. It took a few messages from her to realize that my little doe was drunk off her ass. Adorably so. I spent the rest of the night fucking my hand over the image of her lips around me. Then this morning it was as if she didn't have a clue. The look on her face, even though it didn't do fuck all to dim the erection I've been sporting since, has had me a mess all day.

I crave her.

And honestly, I'm not sure how to handle it if she were to walk away now.

My phone vibrates in my pocket, and after calling out for everyone to take five, I look down at the screen.

Willow: Okay. Clearly, I was a lush last night. But, yes, I meant every word. I'm nervous, slightly embarrassed, and not entirely sure I will be able to go THERE without a few little freak-outs, but Kane … you make me feel safe at the same time

you burn me alive with how much I want you. So, yes. I meant it. Just hold my hand and help me get there.

I don't respond, but fuck if my smile doesn't hurt it's so big. Yeah, baby, I'll hold your hand. Fuck yeah, I will.

Tonight, I'm going to show this woman just how much I want her, and I'm going to make sure she enjoys every second of me holding her hand.

CHAPTER TWENTY-TWO

WILLOW

"**R**EMEMBER WHAT I SAID, OKAY?"

I give Kirby a nod and the reassuring smile she needs to see I'm ready and feeling the weightlessness of my decision to give myself to someone who makes me feel *safe*.

Her own expression shines with so much happiness it's infectious. Before I know it, we're both laughing and the few crewmembers left milling around are giving us a wide berth. We probably look manically insane, but God, does this lightness inside me feel euphoric. She walks away to the waiting Cam and car that will take her back to her family.

Turning around before she climbs inside, she calls out toward where I'm standing. Ignoring the few photographers I can see through the darkness around us just a few yards away, she screams, "I won't wait up! Enjoy getting back on the bike again!"

God, she has no shame. I chuckle and turn, but halt in my

steps. Kane laughs softly and smiles in Kirby's direction before looking over at the photographers who are now snapping away. His expression hardens slightly before it washes just as quickly as it came.

"Come on, Willow," he tells me, and his hand hits my back, a place I've begun to love having his touch, before guiding me toward his trailer. "I know it's late, but I just need to grab a few things and then we can head out when Cam gets back."

"Out being?"

He doesn't answer, but I can see his eyes smile from my view of his profile.

I step inside, the scent of all that is Kane permeating the air around me, assaulting my senses in a rush of woodsy-like freshness. The pure rush of it causes my body to physically shudder. I take a deep breath and close my eyes, savoring the alluring scent.

When I open my eyes again, he's staring at me with an expression of pure rapture. Me, Willow Tate—as if I'm a meal he can't wait to devour. A drink he's been craving after years lost in the desert. Like I'm the only thing he can see, and at this moment, I believe him.

"You all right over there?" His voice vibrates through my body, and I gesture with a nod of affirmation. "Do you want to talk before we leave?"

"We probably should. Or we can talk wherever we're going. Which is where?"

"I'm staying at a friend's house while we're filming here. Not too far from my own house, the one you're in, but it will allow us the privacy we need."

He turns away with a wink and grabs some paperwork off the

table, his phone, and tablet, and places them in a messenger-type bag.

"Hey," I call, and he turns to give me his attention. "Why are we staying in your house, and you're staying somewhere else? Wouldn't it be easier for you to have just put us up somewhere? A hotel even?"

His eyes shine brightly. At this moment, his handsome face looks less roughly rugged and more youthful in his enjoyment. "Because, Willow, I love knowing that you're in my bed." He bends down, his full lips firing the nerves in my own when they press against me briefly before lifting away just enough for his lips to dance over mine as he continues to speak. "Easier it might have been, but I wouldn't have been able to stop thinking about you no matter where you called your home away from home here. I can't even tell you what it does to me when I think about your body wrapped in *my* sheets. How you walk across my room in the morning to get into *my* shower. And the image of your body, naked, in that shower while water runs over every inch of your skin … *that* definitely didn't make it easier, but fuck if I don't love knowing you're there."

"Oh … wow." My breathy words come out quickly, and with his face so close to mine, I'm rewarded with watching his pupils dilate. He's as turned on as I feel right now. I swallow thickly, the sound seeming to echo around us. "Wouldn't … don't … do you not want to be there with me … doing those things?"

His pupils grow even more until the bright blue of his eyes is almost completely covered. "Fuck, you can't say that kind of stuff to me, Willow. I'm hanging on by a thread right now."

"I know the feeling," I tell him honestly.

"Don't doubt that I wouldn't rather be there with you, not for a second, but I know you wouldn't have been ready for that without trusting me. I didn't, and still don't, want to push you for things you aren't ready for. I guess, to answer your question, I was selfishly pleasuring myself while I waited for you to make the move and let me know you're ready."

"Kane?"

"Yeah, baby?"

"You make me crazy nervous." The desire in his eyes dims slightly, and his head cocks slightly to the side in question, spurring me to continue. "Well, *you* don't, but I'm … God, this is embarrassing."

His hands come up and frame my face, moving in closer, but not touching me past his two warm hands. Comforting. Strong. Reassuring. But most importantly, *not* judging me.

"You know I have a lot of issues with how I see myself. It's taken me a long while to get to where I am right now, standing in front of you and even telling you all of this. Bottom line, intimacy and fear run hand in hand with me. I'm so afraid, Kane, that deep down when you see me, all of me, you will be so unsatisfied because I'm not even close to the women you're used to." I rush the last of that out in a breath of words, and I would question whether he understood me except for the rapidness of his breathing and the slight flare of his nostrils.

"I won't tell you again, Willow," he starts, his voice a deadly calm. "Those women hold nothing to you. They aren't the ones I want. You are. If I have to knock each and every one of those fears out of your mind, I'll gladly do it if it means you understand, without a shadow of doubt, that when I look at you, I fucking love what I see."

"And that, Kane, is what scares me the most. I'm not sure I'm going to be able to let it all go to get there, no matter how hard I want to."

His eyes go soft. "Give me your hand then, Willow, and let me take you there."

I follow Kane through the doorway and look around the entryway. What the heck am I doing? I can hear Kirby and her family laughing somewhere in the back of the house. I turn to look at Kane as he walks in behind me and give him a shaky smile.

When Cam came back to get us, I know it was his intention to take us to the house he's staying at, but Kane's words about why he has me in his space had me speaking up and telling Cam to take us here. If Kane was shocked, he didn't show it. Instead, he gave Cam a small nod and turned to look out his window, but not before I saw the smile that took over his face.

And not once during our short drive here did he let go of my hand.

Even when we arrived, he only let go long enough for me to climb out behind him, but the second I was out of the SUV, his hand was back in mine. He's taken my words to heart, and he is showing me that he understands my needs by taking my hand and literally helping me get there.

"I'm going to let Kirby know we're here so she doesn't freak out if she wanders over to my end of the house."

He doesn't respond; instead, he starts walking deeper into the house, his hand still holding mine. When we round the corner that brings us into the large family room, each of the three Evans family members look over at us in shock.

"Willow!" Alli jumps up and runs to give me a hug. She smiles one of her adorable innocent smiles and looks over at Kane. "Hi!"

"Alli," Rob starts. "Come on, little one, it's way past your bed-time."

She continues to stare up at Kane but defiantly rolls her eyes at her father. "But Dad! Mr. Masters is here, and I heard Mommy tell you that he is going to melt Willow's pants off her. I gotta tell him that's not okay."

"Oh, my God," I rush out.

"Allison Marie!" Kirby gasps.

Rob just shakes his head before bending down and playfully throwing his daughter over his shoulders. "Sorry about that." He shrugs and takes Alli laughing toward the kitchen, and I'm assuming the back stairs that will lead to their end of the house.

When they've cleared the room, I look over and narrow my eyes at Kirby. She holds her hands out and laughs. "Oh, whatever. I could say something to defend what I said, but both of you know it's true, so just shut it."

Kane laughs and I look over at him. He isn't embarrassed; if anything, he loves this.

"What are you doing here? Didn't you have plans?" Kirby asks.

"We still do," I tell her and try to tell her to shut up and leave with my eyes.

"Ah. I see. Well, carry on, children. I'm going to go up and spend some time with my crazy kid and husband. Have fun and all that." She grabs the television remote and clicks the power off, moving to leave the room. "Hey, Wills, I saw a few bikes in the garage earlier." She doesn't give me a chance to respond, which I'm sure was intentional since she was giving a not so subtle reminder to me to buck up before she leaves the room laughing.

"She's interesting," Kane tells me, his mouth near my ear and his breath making my whole body tremble.

"Yeah," I breathe.

This time, I reach out and fold my hand around his, walking back the way we just came and pulling him toward the stairs leading to my end of the house. Each step I take has my heart beating more and more erratic. Even though I feel like I'm about to swallow my tongue, I'm positive I need to make this move, especially since he knows how nervous I am. I want him to know that even with that, I have no doubts about where this is headed.

"Willow?" he asks when we step through the threshold and into the bedroom. His bedroom.

I turn to him, dropping his hand and trying not to pass out with how quickly my breaths are coming now. The violent pounding of my heart takes over my body until I feel like I can hear the blood roaring through my veins. He takes a step forward, the warmth of his nearness bathing the front of me. We aren't touching, but it feels like he's consuming every inch of my body.

"Are you nervous right now?"

I nod.

"Tell me why." His demand, steady and calm, gives me the courage I need to tell him. To open a vein and bleed my insecurities.

"I'm not perfect," I whisper.

"And neither am I, Willow. I don't want perfect. What so many see as perfect, to me, is fake. Perfect isn't achievable naturally. No one, and I mean no one, is perfect."

I'm shaking my head before he's even done speaking, but one long finger comes up and presses against my lips before I can speak.

"No, let me finish. There isn't beauty in perfection. It's as fake as the image the word projects. Beauty is found in imperfection, Willow, because to admit you're not perfect means you're admitting you're not whole and absolute. When I think of myself, I see someone willing to admit he's as far from complete as it gets because, in order to get to that perfection, I need to find the other part of *me* who will make my life better. To take all the faults I have and fill them, and only then will I be there. You see, the way I see it, the only way to become perfect is to find that perfectly imperfect person who brings it out of you."

When he stops, I swear I might have stopped breathing. How am I supposed to respond to that?

"Do you trust me?" he asks, his voice strong and sure.

"Yes, Kane. Nerves or not, I do."

"Then let me show you what I see when I look at you."

He brings his hands up, framing my face once again in a way I'm quickly becoming addicted to the feeling of. His warm eyes implore, begging me without words to let him continue. I do not intend to stop him, regardless of the butterflies currently taking over my system. I'm all in.

When his lips touch mine, my whole body comes alive. My hands fist the soft cotton of his shirt, and I breathe him in. Our mouths move together, and when I feel his tongue sweep against my own, I moan deeply into his mouth. Each kiss we've shared before now feels like child's play compared to the way he's indulging in the taste of me—the same I am him.

It's a slow build of power. Our desire rises with every twist and slide of our tongues. My hands release their hold of his shirt, and I slowly press them down, gliding against his cotton-covered muscles, desperate to feel the heat of his skin against my palms. My fingers tingle with each drag against his body.

Before I can move the hem and touch him the way I'm itching to, he spins me around and pulls my back to his front. His mouth returns to my body, and he presses softly against the sensitive skin just below my ear. My neck, branded in the heat of his wet kisses, has the tension of arousal coiling tighter and tighter with each slow drag.

"Your taste makes me feel like a drunk man, Willow," he hums against the soft skin where my neck meets my shoulder. "I'm never going to get enough of it. Open your eyes, baby."

I obey his command and gasp when I see he's managed to move us in front of the mirror. The image of his large body behind mine makes it look as if he surrounds every inch of me. The heat combined with his kisses and hands makes me incapable of looking away from the image before me.

"Don't you dare take your eyes off that mirror. Do you understand?"

I watch his lips move against my neck, my eyes moving from the erotic image up to his eyes, burning brightly, daring me to look away. I nod, but gasp only seconds later when the hands he had resting on my hips come up and start to unbutton my vest.

"This, this is so sexy. When I saw you earlier, all I could think about was what it would look like if you had just this on. The way your breasts would be on display for me to feast on. And I would feast until you were begging me, Willow. You would tell me how much you want me to move my mouth down your body as I pop each of these buttons open."

His words end when he pulls the last of the three buttons open; he drags the garment from my body and drops it to the ground. His hands come up and cup each of my full and aching breasts.

"And then I turn those pleas into prayers when I deny you what you want until you're as desperate for my touch as I am for yours." He presses his hips into my back, his erection thick and heavy against me. "Only once I had you at the very edge would I dig my fingers in these hips I've been dreaming about and turn my mouth to the rest of you. I've been dreaming about having your thighs hugging my head for months, Willow. Months of wondering what you'll taste like, how you're going to scream my name when you come against my tongue, how you're going to cry and plead for me to fill you."

I gasp when his hands move from my hips and around to the button of my jeans. My eyes widen—not in fear or from nerves, but in anticipation. He laughs a wicked one full of promise, leaves my jeans, and before I can think of protesting, he pulls my shirt up and over my head, leaving me standing there in a barely-there black lace bra.

"Fuck me," he rasps. "Beautiful."

"Touch me," I whisper huskily. Every word he's spoken has created a web of confidence that wraps around me.

"I will."

"Yes," I pant.

"No." His word is definite, but before I can let disappointment consume me, *he* does instead.

His deft fingers work quickly to snap the button and pull the zipper down, and then I feel his hand press into my jeans, cupping my core and rocking his hand against the wet material of my lace panties.

"You're dripping for me, aren't you?" he asks, his eyes half-mast and full of lust. The hand not currently wreaking havoc to my senses moves from my hips and he cups my heavy breast, his thumb and finger pinching my erect nipple through the material of my bra. "Do you feel how badly I want you?" he questions, rocking against my body.

I nod and my head falls back to his shoulder, watching him through the mirror as his lip goes between his teeth, then I feel his own moan vibrating against my back.

"You're stunning, Willow, but when I see you like … *fuck.*" His breath comes out in a harsh hiss, and I shudder against his hold. "When I look at you, I see a woman who could bring me to my knees in a second, but like this, you have me begging to stay there."

I moan shamelessly when he slips my panties to the side and one long finger pushes into my heat, curling and pushing against the tight walls inside me. A rush of wetness follows when his thumb presses and rolls against my clit, and I cry out as the coil inside me wraps so tightly its pleasure is consuming every inch of my body. I'm so close to shattering into a million blissful pieces that my trembling body would fall to the floor if he weren't holding me captive against his strong hold.

My eyes start to grow heavy and his protest rumbles against my back, the noise coming from deep within him. "Don't you dare close your eyes, Willow. See what I see. Watch your body responding to my touch. See how beautiful you are to me."

He adds another finger, pressing them both deep into my body, stretching while he thrusts them in time with the hips rocking against my back. His free hand comes up and presses just under my stomach. I tense for just a second, but that second was all he needed. He makes a noise of protest before those wicked fingers plunge in deep, the hand against me pulling me tightly to his body.

"Every sinful curve on your body makes my mouth water. I want to run my tongue over every inch of you, tasting and biting until you have no doubt that what makes you tense with apprehension makes my cock hard to the point of insanity. Your body is meant for mine, and there is no place in your mind for you to doubt that."

"Please," I plead, not even sure what I'm asking him.

His eyes fire and his hand travels up my stomach; the rough pads of his fingers against my soft skin until his fingers hook the cup of my bra and pull it down, freeing my breast to his eyes and touch. Seconds later, his groan of satisfaction is filling the air as one hand pinches and teases my nipple while his fingers continue to build me up on a crest of pleasure.

"Kane." I gasp his name, my hand coming up to hold his wrist. He gives me a hard look assuming I'm going to pull him back, but I press against his arm and push him deeper into my body, finally losing the ability to hold myself up when he hits that spot deep inside me that has me crying out. This time his name isn't a soft gasp of air, but a loud burst of noise that matches the power firing through my body.

I come, my wetness soaking his hand, and I watch, unable to look away, as he closes his eyes and lets out a moan of his own. His fingers continue to move and the waves upon waves of ecstasy rush over me until my lungs are straining for air.

When the last stream of pleasure leaves my body, his eyes burn into mine, and he tells me again in a command that leaves no room for bending, "Watch."

His fingers give one more thrust before he pulls them from my heat. I watch with wide eyes as he brings them up and closes his lips around them. His eyes close and his moan is loud and sure.

"Fucking delicious," he grinds out in a thick voice after licking the last of *me* off himself.

CHAPTER
TWENTY-THREE

WILLOW

MY CHEST IS BURNING. EACH puff of air expelled is sucked back just as rapidly as I watch Kane's eyes fire to a brilliant hue of the brightest blue. His lids, heavy with arousal, make his expression one of pure indulgence.

I pull my eyes from his and look into my own reflected in front of me in the mirror. My pants hang open, one hip completely exposed, and the denim loose around my waist. I can see just a hint of my black panties, but they're roughly shifted so that my bare sex is more uncovered than not. My eyes roam the rest of my body; bra still pushed under one of my breasts, my nipple still hard from his touch. My skin is a pale pink from the treatment of his firm hands.

Kane doesn't speak and neither do I. I flit my eyes to his long enough to see him assessing me as I evaluate my body. When I look back at my own eyes, I don't see any of the nerves or the apprehension I would normally feel standing almost naked and completely exposed. The way he's expressed his desire for me has left no doubt in my mind of his genuine nature.

I see, through his words, what I've never before been able to see. Even with Kirby and Eddie always by my side while I worked hard to better myself through therapy and working out, I haven't been able to see the change until Kane opened my eyes. I see a woman who pushed herself to the point of starvation for months because I never thought this body was enough. I mentally battled with what I believed was wrong and what I'm not seeing, through his words and actions, as beauty.

I feel beautiful.

I *look* beautiful.

I didn't even realize it, but in just the last week, I've let go of almost every one of those negative habits. I eat normally. I don't exercise myself to the brink of exhaustion, and I actually feel as if I could love the skin that I'm in.

My body, flush from his ministrations, has captured this man, and with his words, I see something I had never realized before. Where I've seen areas I hated, he's seen ones that entice. I didn't think that was possible—for what I now see as well-placed curves to seduce a man such as Kane.

A smile curves my lips, and I turn to Kane, his hungry gaze watching me. Waiting for me to make the next move, testing the waters with his silence to see how I'll receive his words.

The old Willow, the one who let fear and insecurities rule her world, would have broken down at the first hint of intimacy. But now, with the confidence his actions have birthed in my mind, the last shreds of my haunting past fall to the wayside.

Reaching out, I place my hand on his chest, feeling the rapid thump of his heart. He doesn't move, his eyes inviting me as they lure me. I take the step needed to bring me close enough so I can feel his warmth again. My hand on his chest slowly presses against his body as I trail south.

Keeping our eyes connected as my hand travels the length of his torso, I let the thrill of excitement fill my system when his jaw ticks and his head rolls back, and I finally lose sight of those cerulean orbs.

My other hand joins the seduction, and I wrap my fingers in the hem of his shirt, bringing it up and over his body. He lifts his arms and helps me remove the material, and when they fall back down, he places them on either side of my hips. His fingers dig in and a noise of pleasure echoes from his chest, tickling my breasts as they crush against his body.

"You're awfully quiet for a man who had so much to say a few minutes ago," I purr, the sultry sound of my voice making me want to high five myself. *Way to go, Willow.*

He pulls his lips in and rolls them together, his expression betraying the control he's exhibiting. Witnessing what my touch does to him encourages me to continue. The way he pulled me to his body placed my hands against his chest and I use that as leverage to push myself away.

"Willow," he bites out with a harsh breath, his eyes flashing with what looks like panic. Panic?

I quicken my pace, not only to reassure him, but also because I would be lying if I didn't admit I'm slightly worried my newfound confidence is going to vanish at any second.

Reaching behind my body, I unhook my bra and pull it from my body. His fingers flex against my hips, his strength almost to a point of pain, but the touch showing me just how close he is to losing his control. He looks down, seeing my naked chest fully for the first time, and his tongue comes out to lick his lips.

There is no way his reaction isn't honest. Talented actor or not, you can't fake a body's response like this.

My hands come back to his fevered tan skin, just above his pecs. I dig my fingers in, massaging up to his neck, and finally lace my fingers through the soft hair just past due for a cut at his nape.

Our eyes communicate our combined need for each other, and with our bare torsos pressed together, I lean up while pushing against his neck and bringing him toward my lips to kiss him with the consuming hunger I feel.

Our moans meet in a powerful rush. His hands move from my hips, inside my undone pants and down around to my ass. His fingers dig in roughly and grab hold as he thrusts his hips against me. It only takes seconds before the sounds of our excitement drown out the wet sounds of our kiss.

"I need to feel you, Willow." He pulls away from my lips and presses his forehead against mine. "I will never take more than you can give me, but I'm ready to beg if that's what it takes for you to let me feel the body I crave against mine."

I feel the unforgiving hardness of each coiled muscle in his body pressing against the softness of my own. He forces my body even closer as he flexes his hips and thrusts against me. For a small second, I'm slightly nervous again, until I see just how tense his desire, for me, is making him. His whole body locked while his eyes plead with me.

"Trust me, God, trust me. Feel how much I want you."

His hips rock again, the hard bulge of his erection hitting my stomach. My mind wanders, wondering what he feels when all his hard meets my soft. My breasts jiggle as my breathing speeds up. That panic I had been worried about slapping me in the face.

Can I do this? Can I allow myself to be stripped bare not just physically, but emotionally for this man? Let him see me *completely*? More importantly, do I trust myself and the fragile strength I've just gained? Am I ready to really, truly let him all the way in?

He holds his silence, but his hands tense against my butt, and I feel his heart speed up.

It's as if he's just as nervous that I'll say no as I am that I'll say yes.

His vulnerability meeting my own, and in a rush of clarity, it washes me clean when I see just how much my answer means to him.

Stepping back and dropping my eyes, I hear his sigh when he assumes I'm denying his request. I take one more step away from him before looking back up and locking my eyes with his. His brow, slightly furrowed, questions my movements.

But when I lift my hands and pull my jeans and panties down in one fluid movement, I hear his rushed expletive seconds before my feet are freed and then he's right there. His hands grab my hips, roughly digging in and lifting me effortlessly up his body. I gasp, my hands coming out and grabbing his shoulders frantic to take the weight of my body from his strain. Only, he isn't straining because of his hold … I can see it in his eyes that he's struggling because his control has snapped, and he's lost in a battle of need.

Need for me.

"Thank Christ," he growls and crushes his mouth to mine.

I meet the powerful desire the roughness of his touch brings and open my mouth to kiss him deeply. My legs wrap around his hips, and when his erection nestles against my bare sex, my whole body jolts in pleasure.

We're a mixture of harsh breathing and the dominating want we share for each other. His body moves, and I feel myself lowered until the softness of his bed is at my back. His mouth doesn't leave mine, but his hands release me from their hold. I feel them come between our bodies and his knuckles brush over my wetness as he starts to remove his pants. I want so badly to pull away so I can witness this, but when he rumbles out a deep moan, I swallow it and press my lips harder against his. We continue to kiss as he kicks off his pants and then his hands are on my hips, lifting my body and shifting me back further onto the bed.

Only when he seems satisfied with our movements does he allow his hips to fall between my open legs and I feel every hot inch of him on top of me. When his length settles against the wetness between my legs, I feel him start to rock and our moans grow as his dick hits my oversensitive clit.

"Willow," he gasps when I feel another rush of wetness between my legs. Lifting my hips and pulling my thighs to the side, I open myself for him to slide against, hugging his steel like flesh as he quickens his pace.

My need for him, to have him fill me, hits so violently that I feel as if I'm on the verge of breaking down in tears.

He studies my expression, not once slowing down his thrusts against my body. He's not penetrating, but rather creating a burn in which I feel I'll forever be scarred from. We continue to watch each other, neither of us in a hurry, but at the same time, our need to take this further is consuming us to the point of insanity.

"I need you," I beg on a sob. "I feel like I'm going mad if I don't, Kane. What are you doing to me?" My words hitch when he presses himself more firmly against me. The tip of him causing sparks of ecstasy to zap from my center and all over my body. Tingles firing from every direction until I'm overcome with a demand to make him understand what I need. My hand reaches down and wraps around his thickness, trying desperately to feel more of him and not to lose the feelings he's bringing out in me.

"It's never felt like this for me, Willow. I have to know you won't regret this. I have to know you understand I want more from you than just a rushed fuck. I want it all. Tonight, tonight is about you, baby."

I whimper when he lifts his hips and I lose my hold on him. His hands reach up to grab my wrists, and he pulls my hands over my head. Holding me captive as he settles back in to rock against my slickness. His eyes lock on mine as he moves.

We aren't even having sex, and I feel as if we're making love at this moment. He's building me up and showing me that my needs are more important than his own are. By denying himself, he's proving he doesn't just want me as an easy lay. True to his words— his vow—he's making me understand his need is for more than my body.

My legs wrap around and tighten, bringing his friction against me to a fever pitch just before I tip over and come long and loud. His rocking thrusts against my soaked flesh pick up speed. The head of his dick hits my clit with so much force as he powers against me that it sparks another orgasm just on the heel of the other. I cry out, my head flying back and my chest pushing into his.

His steady movements falter as my gaze comes back to his,

those eyes of his so bright and open as he tenses against me and I feel a rush of heat burst from him as he comes on my stomach.

I've never felt so close to someone as I do at this moment. The honest intimacy we just shared was more powerful than words could have ever expressed. He's managed to break down every wall, insecurity, and doubt I've ever had in myself in such a short time; there's no doubt in my mind that this man is worth the trust he asks of me. The way he makes me feel, only a promise of what could be, reassures me that I have the strength I need to give myself completely to him. I give him a wobbly smile, and through the blur of tears filling my eyes, I watch his handsome face transform with the knowledge that I've handed myself over to him.

"Thank you," he breathes, his mouth peppering the lightest of kisses against my temples. As the tears spill over my lids, he takes my tears of acceptance on his lips before licking his tongue over them.

"For what?" I utter.

"For giving me your trust. I'm not letting you go now, Willow. I'm not making cheap promises. I'm going to do everything in my power to ensure you never doubt that."

His lips take mine, and after a heated kiss, he lifts from my body and walks into the bathroom. I hesitate for just a second as old insecurities try to knock back in, but then I remember the way he looked at me and I settle my tense muscles to relax against the bed. When he walks back from the bathroom, towel in hand and not even attempting to cover his body from my eyes, I give in to my urge to ogle him.

Every golden, hard, and toned inch of Kane Masters.

He lets out a low chuckle as my eyes widen when I see his hard and heavy erection bob with his movements. I give him a smile—not from nerves, but to let him see I'm loving every second.

He makes quick work of cleaning himself off my stomach before tossing the towel over his shoulder. Turning off the lights and pulling back the covers, he climbs in and holds his arms out for me to move on him. After we adjust our bodies, pulling the covers over us, his arms tighten until my whole body presses against his. My head rests on his chest, and our legs tangle as we wrap ourselves together.

The rest of the night, we lie in the darkness and spend hours just enjoying our closeness as we continue to nurture the bond between us into something that feels unbreakable.

Strong, solid, and sure.

Safe.

CHAPTER TWENTY-FOUR

KANE

One Month later

I'M JUST BARELY HOLDING MY temper back right now.

As I stare down this defiant woman in front of me, her posture is equally as annoyed as mine seeing as we've been having the same argument for the last thirty minutes.

"I'm not backing down from this, Kane."

"Why the fuck not? I don't understand what the big deal is."

Her temper flares again, and I have to fight my cock when her tits press against her shirt. She isn't wearing anything revealing; the long sleeve black shirt covers her completely, but I know what's under there. When she's mad, those tits heave, and I'm seconds away from coming in my pants like a little teenage shit.

"The big deal is that I feel like a whore!" she shouts.

My head snaps back at her heated scream, and I can feel my

control slipping. A whore? How in the fuck she got that impression is beyond me.

For the last month, we've spent every second we weren't filming—and a few stolen while on set—getting to know each other. We've grown from testing the waters to what I had hoped she saw as a relationship. Sure, I haven't come right out and said the words, but how could she be clueless to how I feel?

She knows everything about me … well, not *everything*, but this woman knows more about me than my own mother does. I've given a hundred percent of myself to her while I watch her become more and more confident. Left no word unsaid that wouldn't reassure her of my feelings. Fuck, did I ever straight up tell her I wanted a future with her? Now that she's standing in front of me claiming she feels like a whore, I doubt it.

After that night a few weeks ago, she's had no trouble letting me in. Just as I've shared all with her, she's done the same with me. We've managed to even sneak away for a few carefully executed dates without the media catching wind of our relationship, which I know is only a matter of time.

Which brings us to where we are now.

"A whore?" I repeat through thin lips.

She nods, crossing her arms over her chest and making her tits strain even more against their confinement.

"A whore!" She jumps at my outburst, but I ignore it. She knows I won't hurt her. "A fucking whore, Willow? When have I ever treated you like that?"

Heat rises to her cheeks, and for a fleeting second, she looks a little embarrassed. Something I haven't seen on her beautiful face since I broke through the last of her lingering fears about my intentions.

"Well, *you* haven't, but if I continue to be paid for a job I am most definitely not really needed for, well… then I'm going to be no better than a whore."

Is she fucking serious? "Because I'm paying you for a job that you're doing, you feel like a whore? How is there any logic in that?"

"You're exasperating!"

"I am?" Fuming now, I try to calm down before continuing. "You started freaking out the second I mentioned you coming to California *with* me when we finish here. Looking for a reason to run. I'm the exasperating one? Should I remind you that I'm not the one insinuating her boyfriend is making her feel like a whore!"

She had her mouth open to interrupt me before I stopped talking, but the protest she had been ready to throw back dies on her lips. With the color still high on her cheeks, her eyes are wide with shock. She stands before me now looking unable to form another word when for the last half an hour she's had no issues with that whatsoever.

"What is it now?" I ask with the anger still present in my tone. I ready myself for whatever ridiculous bullshit she's going to throw in my direction next and try to think of what could possibly be her next excuse for why she can't come to California when we wrap at the end of the week for our Georgia filming. Why is she trying to leave me?

I brought this up when we finished the filming at the school two weeks ago, but she easily brushed it off. She said we would talk when filming was over at the next few locations here in Georgia, which just so happens to be now.

"What did you just say?" she timidly asks.

I move from the kitchen counter I had been resting on and stalk toward her. She doesn't move, and her shocked expression doesn't dim.

If I didn't want her so desperately, I would throttle her right here.

"Which part? About you trying to think of anything you can to run?"

Her eyes heat. "I'm not running!" she yells.

"Then what do you call this bullshit about you going back to New York to 'find a job' and not coming to California like I asked when I offered you a *job*?"

"It's not bull, Kane! Let me paint a picture for you. I was brought here under the ruse of a job. One that you and I both know I really wasn't needed for. You did what you needed to do to be able to explore what you felt when you met me. I get that, and now, I'm thankful that you did, but you know Kirby doesn't need me. She might have had a demanding schedule, but between Grant and the other two artists you had come in last week, she doesn't need me. And, hello! I know nothing about makeup."

I move to explain myself, but she stops me. Her eyes still hold a little of that anger when she continues. "I'm here, Kane, but besides a few comments when you ask my opinion about a scene and helping out whenever I can find a place *to* help so I can pull my weight, the only thing I actually seem to be doing is sucking your dick and begging you to have sex with me! Which, I might add, you keep refusing me. So how do you figure that *isn't* me being a glorified whore when the paychecks *you* sign hit my bank?"

My anger drains from my body instantly when the real reason for her resistance becomes clear. "Willow," I breathe. "Come here, baby."

She lets out a loud sigh before she walks around the island she's been using as a physical barrier and stops in front of me. I reach out and lightly hold her biceps, holding her gaze so she can hopefully see the honesty I feel for her.

"First and foremost, you've been invaluable, Willow. You've spent every day for the almost whole month running between helping Kirby maintain her schedule and helping me keep my shit together. Don't you dare undervalue yourself and make light of just how much work you've put into this. You might not see the enormous help you are, but trust me, others do. Myself included."

"Kane, be reasonable."

I tighten my grasp, making her shut her mouth and see how serious I am.

"Let me paint *you* a picture now, Willow. You've been running the call sheet schedule, catering orders, production schedules, and at the same time you're doing all of that, you also make the time to see if Kirby *needs* help, and if she does, you do everything in your power to make it happen. When Alessandra was struggling to find the emotion she needed to hit the big breakthrough scene, the most important scene in the whole film, who helped her work through it? When we couldn't figure out what was missing in the scene from yesterday, who offered the one piece of advice that actually helped? You do a lot more than you can even imagine. Don't insult yourself and say you don't. I saw early on that you were effortlessly, and without direction, making my life easier. Why do you think I've been having you chat with Sam, syncing up with him and learning all you could? I had done that way before I offered you his job."

"If Sam's mother wasn't sick, then you wouldn't need me to do all of that. He would be here doing it for you," she weakly protests. I can tell she is finally starting to understand that her claims are ludicrous.

"Baby, Sam isn't coming back. I told you that a half-hour ago when I offered *you* his job. Those little phone chats and FaceTime calls have one hundred percent been about him slowly giving you the reins. I hadn't planned on bringing up the job offer quite yet. I wanted to wait for filming to officially wrap for *Impenetrable*, but clearly, your beautiful little mind is up to no good, which is why my offer came today. Not because we leave in two days, but because the second I asked you to come to California and not go back to New York, you started to panic."

I pull her closer to my body; her hands come up and rest on my chest, and I finish explaining myself. "Willow, I had a feeling back at the Logan Agency that you were much more powerful than just a secretary. My gut feeling is that Dominic was intimidated by you and put you in that position to make you feel the way you do now. Like you aren't capable of a job with huge responsibilities. But you also told me about your degree in business administration and how much fun you had when you interned during your final semester as a personal assistant. When Sam's situation made it clear I would need to find someone I *trust* to replace him, the only one I wanted was *you*. So, my love, you are most definitely not a whore. You're the woman who is becoming just as invaluable to my professional life as you have become to my personal life. You, Willow, have managed to weave yourself so firmly into my life that I don't really give a shit what excuse you come up with next. I'll fucking kidnap you if I have to."

"What did you just say?"

That shocked expression is back, and I play back my words, trying to figure out what tripped her up this time. I feel like I'm running in circles.

"Did you just say *my love*?" she says, awe apparent in not just her tone, but her expression as well.

I give her a smile I hope is reassuring, but I don't answer her question. I will, but not yet. "Willow, be honest with me. Do you not want to continue here? Have I given you reason to feel like you need to back off and run?"

"I'm not running, Kane! I'm just trying to figure out what's going on and at the same time letting you know how I feel. For the last month, I've had no official job title, yet a paycheck has hit my account twice. I help out around set because I want to feel like I'm earning the money. The only thing I can say with absolute certainty is that with no real job, I'm being paid to pleasure the man who pays me. Just like a whore."

"You aren't a fucking whore, Willow! I won't say it again."

"You're serious about the job?"

"Fuck yes, I am!"

She sighs and drops her head to my chest.

"Think about it, Willow, and you will see exactly what I'm saying and why I know you would be the best PA I've ever had. Not just because you're beyond capable of it, but also because I know you care about me. And trust me, that's important. You haven't been getting paid for nothing. You've been working your ass off. Twelve to fifteen hours *a day* while you make sure everything not nailed down got another slam from your efficient hammer. One mention from me in passing about our delayed schedule—time I couldn't afford to add to an already stretched budget—and you managed to find the solution. You not only took two days off production time, but in doing so, you saved me a couple million I had already been prepared to sink into this film. Now, we're finishing ahead of schedule and under budget. Things are running so smoothly, I don't know how I managed without you."

She starts shaking her head against my chest. I wrap my arms around her; I pull her toward me and give her no choice but to return my embrace.

"Willow, baby, look at me." I wait until she gives me her eyes—those always-expressive eyes—to show me that regardless of what she's saying, she scared. "I know I wasn't completely honest about why I brought you with Kirby. I won't apologize for that because, in the end, you came and I was able to confirm what my mind already knew. You belong with me. The fact that Sam's mother got sick and pulled him away, resulting in his resignation, was just more confirmation that I was on the right path. I have no hidden agenda here. I wanted to wait for *Impenetrable* to wrap so you could finish with the stride in which you've flourished, but now that you actually doubt things, I can't allow that."

"Kane, I know nothing about being your PA. My degree didn't set me up to be a mega hunk movie star's employee."

"Mega hunk movie star?" I smile. "Baby, you know everything about it. You know me better than anyone does, and for the last few weeks, you've seemed to understand more about my world than people who have lived it their whole lives. Think back, and I mean really think about everything we've gone through on the set. Everything that almost slipped and spilled into a massive pile of shit until *you* caught it and fixed everything."

She continues to look into my eyes, and I relax the tension from my body and open myself up so she can see my sincerity.

"Outside of that, Willow, the time we've spent learning each other's bodies, what makes the other person tick, the late-night chats while I feel your body naked against mine … none of that was fake, and it damn sure doesn't deserve you trying to cheapen it by calling yourself a whore."

"Kane, honestly, I feel like I'm struggling right now. Where do we go from here? It just seems so big to pack up my whole life and move to California, and I don't want to have any doubts about why. I'm sorry for acting like a brat, but I'm not sorry I got that off my chest. I feel like, had I not, it would have become a bigger issue down the road."

"What's really bothering you, Willow?" Surely, this is bigger than I can see. I don't think she would have made such a big deal, grasping at straws, if there wasn't a bigger concern—doubt—on her mind. "Is it me, us, that you're questioning?"

She shakes her head. "No. Maybe. Heck, I don't know. I feel silly now." She looks away and worries her lip between her teeth. "Aside from the job, which I'm not sure I feel qualified for, I'll admit I've had so much fun stepping up and helping make sure you're taken care of, easing your stress. I know there isn't anything left in New York but Kirby and her family, and even she will be back and forth with her career starting with you. Eddie isn't there anymore with his travel and clients keeping him constantly jetting all over the globe. So I guess, deep down, I'm freaking out because I have no idea where we're going from here. Am I about to move across the country just for a job, or more?"

"So it *is* us that you're questioning. Have I not made it clear about where this is going?"

She looks up at me, and I can see that apparently, I have not.

"Baby, I'm too old to play games. I've spent thirty-five years looking for something I've felt was missing. Three times, I felt I had found it when I looked into the timid eyes of a beautiful woman I knew nothing about. That was enough for me to do what I needed to take a chance, and in order to do that, I had to be underhanded. But now we've had a chance to explore it, and I now look at those three times in the past as a missed opportunity. Because I know *you* are the something I've been missing." I reach up and swipe at the moisture that spills over her lid. "A month later and because my life makes dating challenging, we've spent more time together than normal couples just getting to know each other. That might seem early for the vast majority, but to me, it feels like I've known you for years. I wouldn't be weaving you tightly into my life if it wasn't where I wanted to have you for a long time coming."

She nods her head, and her arms wrap around me, embracing me before speaking. "I don't doubt you when it comes to us, but I guess I needed to hear it. When you look at it in time, it does seem quick, so it is a little daunting. I guess I was falling back on some old habits of doubt."

"You said you trusted me, Willow. I don't just mean with your body, I meant with all of you. I want you ... this, us. But our relationship will never be normal. We went at the speed of light because honestly, that is just how things are done in my life."

Her eyes continue to gaze into mine, the love I've felt coming from her in the last few days not even masked in the least. "And, to the public, will I be your employee or more?"

God, I want to kiss her. Just by her asking me that is a testament to how far she's come in the last few weeks. Going from be-ing scared of me, her feelings, and whether she could open herself enough to give herself to me to the stunning woman standing up and asking for what she desires. She shows me daily that she's be-yond brave. Overcoming the issues she had with herself was a huge hurdle. Everything else has just fallen into place since. She hasn't held back, not once all month, until today. And I know that with the enormity of what I'm asking of her, I should have expected it. I pull her closer; my lips brush against hers and then wrap my arms around her tight and reassuring. I allow the silence in order to make sure I can word my response in a way that leaves her no more fucking doubts about us.

I'm asking her to leave the life she had been living. One where years of verbal abuse had made her afraid to really live because of the fear she had of others' judgment. She let that fear rule her completely. Their judgment had made her hate herself. I know she started to heal a year ago when her husband cheated and she left, but that healing didn't compound into completion until she started to let go of those fears, insecurities, and doubts. She was almost there before I came into the picture, but she crossed the finish line with me at her side. I know that. But I know my mention of not only a job, but also a future together is why some of that is trying to rear its ugly head.

And now, now I'm asking her to take a chance on a life that will thrust her into the public eye. Into a life full of nothing *but* the kind judgment that beat her down in the past. I'm asking her not to just be with me, but to face her fears head-on.

"I'm asking you to be mine. I'm too old for titles and shit, but if you need them, baby, then that's what you'll get. If you want to be boyfriend and girlfriend, having that title to our relationship so you understand that what I'm building here is a future and not a fling, then it's yours. But, bottom line, I'm asking you to be mine and not to end what we're starting. I'm going to ask you to be strong, but if you can't or need help along the way, know I will never be far. I will not hide someone I care about from the world. I would notify the media right now if that's what it took for you to see I don't just want you as my employee, but my lover as well, but I want you to feel comfortable with our relationship before we let in the vultures."

Her silence is unnerving. I keep studying her face, trying to find a clue in her expression. My chest feels tight, my throat thick, while I wait.

"Lover?" Her lips tip, her smile widening until her eyes crinkle. She gives me a nod, and I watch her eyes water. "That's the second time you've hinted that word."

"It is."

"You said 'my love' earlier." Her already full smile gets a little bigger. "Kane?"

I let my face show her what I'm feeling right now; I open myself and make sure she not only sees, but also hears. "I fucking love you, Willow Tate. Come to California. Be mine for the world to see."

The satisfaction in her enchanting smile is so powerful that I swallow thickly at the emotion clawing its way up my throat. "I love you, too, Kane. God, do I."

Fuck, she's beautiful and all mine. Everything else will just have to fall into place because I'm not ever letting this woman go.

CHAPTER TWENTY-FIVE

WILLOW

IT TOOK US ANOTHER WEEK to finish filming in Georgia. The weather had turned cold and dreary. Unfortunately for Kane's filming schedule and all that time I had managed to save him, the bad weather put us way beyond saving the budget. We had to film all of the outdoor scenes during that unlucky time, and because of the scenes calling for bright and sunny weather, we had to improvise. Which put us five days over schedule.

Kirby had flown home six times in the time we were in Georgia. Forty plus days away from her family was too much for her, and I'm shocked that she only went home six times. Kane's been so understanding and even helpful in making sure she was able to get away—hence the reason he brought in the extra help for her a week into filming. The second we wrapped last night; she hightailed it off the set and caught the redeye home. She has a four-day break to spend with her family before she's needed in California, so I know she was eager not to waste a second of that time.

There are another three weeks to a month left of filming *Impenetrable* and I've been busy studying each and every call sheet I drew up for that timeframe, but also looking for ways we can turn a few filming locations into longer takes to cover more ground. I'm attempting to find a way to consolidate some of that time to make up for the budget slips in Georgia. So far, I've only been able to take a few days off here and there, but I haven't been able to find a way to make up for all of the overages.

The last few days of filming before I flew back to New York were a whirlwind. I took over Sam's position officially two days ago. After I agreed to the position, it only took a few days to get the contract signed. Even though it's a little intimidating, I'm confident I know what I'm doing. I initially worried about the working relationship with Kane bleeding into our personal one, making up excuses that my fears had planted in my mind to pull back, but I know now it's *because* of our relationship that I'm positive he meant every word about me being the only person he trusts.

Placing the last of my clothes into the box I had been working on for the last hour, I turn my head and look for the packaging tape I swear was just right here. I've been trying to get as much packing done as possible before Kane arrives. He had to handle some interview promos for *Impenetrable* and provide a tour of the set for the companion book that will release side-by-side with the film. Now that's finished, he's finally on his way back to me and we can officially cross Georgia off our to-do list.

My phone rings, and I abandon the search for tape, rushing to the kitchen where I placed my phone earlier.

"Hey," I rush, trying to catch my breath after almost tripping over the stack of boxes in my path.

"You okay, baby?"

The rush of arousal from the deep rasp of Kane's voice hits me instantly, and I smile. "Yeah, just almost took my head off on the way to grab the phone. Are you on the way?" God, please let him almost be here. I feel like I'm about to come out of my skin in anticipation.

"Just left the airport. It was a mad house. No fucking clue how they knew I would be here. Cam fought through the endless amount of paparazzi, but we're mostly in one piece."

"Mostly?"

A rumble of laughter follows my question. "Yeah. There was just a small incident."

"Incident?"

"Not as bad as it sounds. However, I might not feel that way when TMZ repeats the clusterfuck that followed." He laughs again.

"I'm going to go out on a limb and guess that since you're laughing about it, there isn't a need for me to worry about your well-being. You didn't punch one of those paparazzi guys, right? I mean, I've seen it before when they don't back off and it never ends pretty."

He starts to laugh harder, and it's hard not to follow suit, even not knowing the situation.

"Kane, you're freaking me out with all the scenarios I'm imagining being painted all over the world right now."

He manages to get himself under control, but I still hear the smile in his voice. "It was nothing like that. A chick was a little too exuberant in her quest to get to me. I'm not even really sure what happened, but one second, I was trying to weave through blinding flashes and screaming fans, and the next, I had a bra on my face and Cam had a bloody lip. Apparently, in her rush, she bumped into Cam, who then stumbled into the reporter from TMZ. It was a mess of elbows, grunts, and one dirty undergarment."

By the time he finishes going over his airport insanity, I'm laughing just as hard as he was. "Should I be worried about flying bras?" I chuckle again just envisioning the scene described to me.

"Besides the fact that the only bras I want flying in my face are yours, no. It was just a normal day in the life of Kane Masters."

I move and sit down on my couch; the only piece of furniture not covered in things I still have to pack. "Normal day, huh?"

"Exaggerating. Well, slightly," he jokes.

"All right, all right. I'll ignore the female masses and their lingerie heaving. As long as you only enjoy it when they're mine."

"Are you ready for me?" he asks, changing the subject.

"God, yes," I breathe.

"Fuck, it's only been a day, and I miss you like crazy."

I smile, moving the phone to my other ear. "You have no idea, Kane. But if I get the kind of texts from you like I did last night, we might have to spend a little more time apart."

"Yeah, that's not going to happen. I'll be there soon, okay? Cam's got to make sure we're clear before we head that way. I don't want to bring the media right to your door."

"Okay, honey, see you in a little bit." I keep my voice even so he doesn't know I'm a little bothered by him easily brushing off my attempt at flirting.

"Love you, Willow."

My annoyance dims. Just like every other time he's told me that, my heart picks up and the butterflies turn into a tornado of activity in my stomach. "I love you, too."

I disconnect the call and drop the phone into my lap.

I shouldn't be annoyed right now, but for the last six weeks, I feel like we've been having this massive session of foreplay. I could understand it at first, even welcomed the slow pace of our intimacy. But now? Now, I'm about to come out of my skin with the fierceness in which I desire to take our relationship to the next level.

Over the course of our time in Georgia, not only did I start to come to life each time we were together, but in the end, I was so ready to take it to the next step I felt desperate with it. Kane always stopped us before we could *finally* go all the way. He wasn't shy about doing everything else, but he always put a stop to our bedroom activities. He never did it in a way that made me doubt he wanted the same thing I did. I could see it in the heated gaze he would burn my skin with, and I felt it in his heavy erection when he would pull me in his arms and we would spend the rest of the night tangled together as we talked.

Just the thought of sex with Kane is all it takes for my body to start to flush with heat and my panties to dampen with my arousal. My hands shake and my breath quickens. It's all I've been able to think about—well, outside of work—and I know if I don't have him soon I might just go insane.

It's hard to imagine anything else. I keep replaying the faces he makes when he would come in my mouth, the look of complete rapture as his body tenses and jerks with each jet that shoots down my throat. Knowing I was able to bring those reactions out of him makes my need to see that raw energy while bringing him *there* while he's inside me to dangerous levels.

My core clenches, and I drop my head back against the couch

with a groan. I bet if I pushed my hand into my pants right now, it would take only a second for me to take care of how hungry I am for him.

That's it. When Kane gets here, I'll let him get in the door, but if he doesn't give me what we both need, I'm going to have to look into natural ways to date rape him.

Forty-five minutes later, I still haven't been able to stop thinking about all things Kane. I finished packing the rest of my clothes, a few boxes worth of personal items, and my vast collection of romance novels. There was a lot I wasn't bringing. The house I would be staying in—Kane's house—was obviously fully furnished, so there wasn't a need for the majority of my things. My furniture and anything else I didn't need would either be dumped or given away. Eddie would be home for the next week and had assured me that he would take care of it before turning my keys over to the landlord, who shockingly didn't give me a hard time about breaking my lease.

At first, Kane had wanted me to move directly into his home. Sam had lived there while working for Kane—obviously, not in the same capacity in which Kane had hoped I would be—but when he had mentioned it to me, it was as natural a thought as breathing. Kane didn't agree with me when I denied the arrangement. As much as I would have loved to spend every night with him, once I explained to him that I needed to be able to carve out a place for myself, he hesitantly agreed. I say hesitantly, but the pouting he did after giving in to my request would rival Alli on a bad day. I assured him that we could revisit this subject in a few months and that seemed to appease him.

I did agree with him that being near my job would be easier, but with the quickness that our relationship has progressed, it's important for me to be able to have a place of my own. Not to get away from him, but rather to give us a little sense of normalcy in his abnormal world.

Maybe I'm being a little timid, pulling away without completely doing so to make sure he doesn't get sick of me being around, but when I really think about it I know I'm making the right decision. We will never be able to date normally. The long period of time when couples go out, get to know each other, and then enter a relationship of love happened in a month for us. Because of his celebrity status, we kept our dating to catered dinners, private screenings of movies not yet released, and hours upon hours of talking. We basically condensed six months of speed dating into just weeks. Because of that, I know I need this space—well, space without real space—to put a little reality into the mix.

The brisk knock on my door makes me jump and let out a little scream of surprise. I had been too busy daydreaming and had lost track of time.

Walking over to the door, I make quick work of the locks and swing the door open. I don't even get a second to enjoy the view of Kane filling my doorway before his arms are coming around me, lifting me with his hands on my rear, and pushing me into the closest wall. I hear the door slam just before his lips crash to mine.

"I missed you," he rasps against my lips before kissing a blazing path down my neck.

"You just saw me yesterday morning." I laugh, fisting his shirt in my hands when the warm heat of his mouth pulls at the bottom of my ear. "But if this is how you tell me hello, we can do this again."

He makes a rumbling sound of protest and bites my sensitive

lobe while rocking his hips into mine.

"Kane?"

He shakes his head and continues to assault my neck in kisses.

"Kane, please." My hoarse whisper comes out desperate and weak.

His head comes up; those brilliant blue eyes hit mine, and my whole body shudders with the force of his need. His thick hair, blackened with the dim lighting where we stand, looks like he's been running his fingers through it all day. The stubble on his jaw makes him look even more rugged than normal, but it highlights the sharpness of his features making him look even more handsome.

"I need you," I tell him. "I can't wait anymore, Kane, and if you push me away again, it might just kill me. I need you that badly."

I watch, with satisfaction, as his eyes darken and his jaw slacks with my forwardness. He starts to protest, but I push my hands from their resting place around his neck and slide my fingers into his hair, pulling him to my mouth.

Without letting our lips touch, I keep my eyes trained on his and demand, "I can feel how much you want me, Kane. Stop denying it and take me. All of me."

His throat works and rapid breaths fan from his thick lips. "I would never deny that I want you, Willow. I've wanted nothing more than to sink my cock into your body for weeks, but I have to know you want this just as much as I do. I wasn't denying you to be cruel, baby. That's the last thing I wanted to do. I was trying to go slow, give you time, and not rush you into something you might not be ready for."

"I've been ready, Kane. So ready I'm about to go mad."

"You aren't scared?"

I push my head back slightly so I can study his face better. The pieces of the puzzle I had lacked finally coming together. He hasn't been pushing me away; he's been making sure I wouldn't regret anything. Letting me learn to walk in this newfound confidence before I could run without abandon. He was letting me heal.

"I needed to know you were ready, and it wasn't something you were doing because you thought I wanted it, or because it was something I expected. I had to make sure you knew this wasn't just about a quick fuck, Willow. It's killed me, burned my gut to turn you away, but baby, I had to."

My eyes burn with emotion, but thankfully, no tears rush forward. "And I love you even more for that, but listen to me when I tell you I'm beyond that point. I'm so far past it that if you don't take me right now, I'm going to tie you up and take you myself."

His jaw moves, clenches, and his whole body trembles at my words. *Yes, thank God* is all I can think when his mouth crashes against mine. His head lifts and I see him look around, searching for the way to my bed. Before I can point, his mouth is plundering mine as he stomps toward the open doorway of my bedroom. The light, much brighter than the dim hallway by my front door, washes over us. For the first time, the thought of sex with the lights on doesn't terrify me. I don't care if my boobs bounce too much or the soft skin around my stomach jiggles as much as my butt does. I *want* the light because I wouldn't be able to see how much this man loves every single one of those things that I used to hate without it. I would miss the way his eyes burn in hunger when he follows the path of his hands down my curves. And most importantly, I would miss the look of rapture when he finally comes inside my body.

I welcome the light just as much as I welcome the body I used to hate, because not only does the man I love adore every inch, but through his eyes, I do too.

CHAPTER TWENTY-SIX

KANE

GOD, YES.

I look down and have to pause when I see how much Willow wants me. She isn't letting me doubt she's ready for this at all. Her skin is pink with arousal, and I see no embarrassment there at all. Her eyes are hooded and her kiss-bruised lips curved into a small smile.

This image alone is enough to test the confines that trap my already painfully hard cock. Hell, I'm so hard that it feels like I could just give one thrust and my cock would power through the thick denim. When her hands come up and push into my shirt, caressing the burning skin underneath, my head drops to her shoulder and my moan echoes around us.

Her head turns, and I feel the movement against the side of my head. Her lips brush my ear and then her tongue comes out and licks a blazing trail around the shell of my ear.

Then it happens. The moment that my control snaps and any thought of taking this slow goes flying to the fucking moon.

"Take me." She whispers the words so close to my ear that chills race over my skin.

She wants me to take her?

With pleasure.

She lets out a scream of surprise when I knife off the bed and jump to my feet. My shirt comes off in one quick movement. I grab a condom from my wallet while kicking off my shoes. My pants are shoved roughly down my hips. I leave my boxer briefs in place and pull my socks off while keeping my hungry eyes on her.

Throwing the condom on the bed next to where her body is, I reach my hands out and start to work the button at her waist. She lifts her upper body slightly before she pulls her shirt over her head and throws it somewhere behind her. She only loses her connection with my eyes when the material moves over her head.

I pause in my attempts to get the offending jeans from her legs at the sight of her hot pink lace bra. My mouth waters and I feel the tip of my cock strain against the elastic band holding my briefs up. Noticing my pause, she gives me a wink and reaches back. She unhooks the sinful garment and slowly moves the straps down her arms before letting it fall, freeing her full tits.

My fingers fumble with her jeans as whatever blood left in my brain drains straight to my cock. The button seems too small for my large fingers, and I let out a curse. I look down, breaking our connection, and attempt it again. She lets out a soft giggle and bats my hands away.

"Let me," she hums.

I step back, and she moves to stand. Her heavy tits sway with each of her movements, and my mouth waters at the sight. Suddenly, I don't give one shit about her pants; with those tits begging for my mouth, it takes a herculean effort to keep my feet planted in place. Her hands come up and have the button open before I can decide which one of her tits needs my mouth the most.

Probably the right one. It's closer. No, now the left one is. Fuck.

She bends and takes her magnificent chest away from my perusal. I hear her laugh when I groan my complaint and adjust my cock before dropping my hand and holding them both next to my body, my fists clenching as I mentally tell myself that I need to calm the hell down.

I drop my head and roll it on my shoulders as I try to ease some of the tension I'm feeling right now. I'm just seconds—no, less than that—away from coming out of my skin. My control is gone, and the ability to slow down and make sure this is good for Willow is quickly evaporating. At this rate, I'm starting to wonder if I'll even be able to slow my need for her down when the only layer keeping my cock caged is removed. The barbaric demands flowing through my veins are making me feel more animalistic in my primal instincts.

And then the choice is out of my hands. Completely and utterly gone.

My head snaps up when her hands slide into the waistband at my hips and push down. My cock, wet at the tip with a drop of pre-cum, springs forward and almost takes her eye out with its eagerness. Then those lips are wrapping around my thickness and the wet heat of her mouth is burning a trail down my shaft. Her brown eyes look up and meet my shocked gaze and the lust-filled enjoyment in them makes me groan. One hand comes up to circle my cock just below her lips and the other comes up to lift my heavy balls. The combined touch of her hands with the wet suction created by her mouth is making my knees weak.

I brush away the hair that falls next to her cheek and hold it against the side of her head as it bobs in my hold. When her teeth lightly scrape against me, I almost grab her head and start to fuck her mouth with vigor.

"Willow. Stop," I order her with thick authority in my voice.

She lets my cock fall from her mouth with a loud pop before she licks her lips.

"Get up, baby." She gives my cock a look of longing before standing at my command in front of me. She shields her body from my appraisal—something that she hasn't done in weeks—and I know it was because of the harshness of my order for her to get up. "Don't do that. I'm not mad. I didn't make you stop because I didn't like it. I *had* to make you stop or I was going to lose control, and I need to be inside you when I come."

Her hands drop, and she gives me the view I want. Stepping closer, I bring my hands to her cheeks and tip her head up. She holds my stare, and I'm rewarded when the uneasiness there just seconds ago disappears. "I love when you suck my cock, baby, fucking love it. You're so good that I almost come the second you take me in this talented mouth. But right now, it's time for me to finally make love to you, and I don't want that to be over anytime soon."

My erection presses into her stomach when I pull her body to mine and take her mouth in a deep kiss meant to devour. I spend my time deepening each swipe of my tongue until she lifts her leg and hooks it around my hip. I dig my fingers in and hold her to my body up as she tries to shift her hips to ease the ache building between her legs.

Breaking our kiss, I drop to my knees and press against her until she's sitting on the mattress. "Lean back and let me eat, Willow." I don't wait for her to obey. Instead, I grab each thigh and throw them over my shoulders. My mouth opens and I suck in, hollow my cheeks, and lick the wetness from her cunt. I eat her loudly, and when I feel her running down my chin, I start pulling away. Not to stop—oh, fuck no, not while the sweet taste of her is running down my face. I move slightly so I can adjust my hold on her hips and pull her voraciously against my mouth. Letting her fuck my face with each thrust of her hips, I ride wave upon wave when her climax bursts free. The legs caging my head tighten, and I look up through a haze of ecstasy and watch her come undone.

Her hands are clenching her tits, pinching the nipples, and then clenching them again. I had expected to find her head thrown back because I can still feel her pussy constricting against my tongue as the waves of her orgasm still hold her captive.

Giving her one last swipe, I swirl my tongue around her clit and give her a kiss, making her jerk her hips. Her thighs fall heavy against the mattress, and I stand, her legs open wide and that delicious pink pussy red from my attention.

She doesn't move, and I have to wonder if she's waiting for me to stop as I have ever other time, but unlike then, I know she's ready and on the same page with me. This step in our relationship was always more important in its meaning than just getting a quick fuck. I needed her to trust completely in me, but more importantly, I needed her to trust herself.

Seeing her lying open and vulnerable, letting me see every inch, and by not hiding, letting me know she wants me to see her.

I reach out, grab the condom, and make quick work of the annoying necessity. Her breath quickens, and she lets out a soft sigh when my body covers hers. One elbow hits the mattress and I push my hand under her head to bring her face closer to mine as I hover over her. Reaching down, I take my cock in hand and press the tip to her opening. She lets out a loud moan, and I follow the tear that leaks out of the corner of her eye.

"I love you," she gasps and pushes off the mattress with her feet, impaling herself on my length as much as she can. The second I enter her, we both let out a shaky breath.

The hand that had been attempting to slowly guide myself into her takes her hip, the full curve that I love so much, and holds on tight as my hips power into her. I keep my face an inch from hers. Swallow each one of her cries and give her my own as we move together in the perfect rhythm. When I push in, she grinds her hips up and rocks against my body. As I pull out of her tight heat, her inner walls clamp down in protest. I try to keep my movements at a slow pace until her nails come out and I feel the bite of them against my ass, trying to force me to go faster. Then I release her hip, bracing my weight with a palm to the mattress, and I let go and give her everything I had been holding back.

I lovingly fuck my woman, and when I feel her come rush against my balls, I let out a rumble-roar of completion and settle my hips to hers. I come so hard I struggle to breathe.

"I love you, too, baby," I tell her when the last tremor leaves my body. I watch two tears fall from each of her eyes, and I lean forward to finally take her mouth. I don't pull out—there's no fucking need because, even after the force my balls were just drained, I'm still hard and rocking against her.

It doesn't take long before we're gasping around each other's mouths. I pull back and reluctantly pull my cock out, rip off the full condom and reach out for my wallet to grab the only other one I have. I almost drop it twice, but I finally manage the pull it on and I push back into her slowly.

The rushed fever of our need isn't dominating us this time. I push into her slowly, dragging myself out before repeating. We're fused together in every way possible, and as our bodies climb higher, I feel the same overwhelming love I do every time I'm with her grow to something so immense in its power that I falter in my thrusts. The frantic beat of my heart picks up speed until I'm so overcome with my feelings that I can feel them clawing up my throat. I choke out some sort of sob-like noise before I whisper her name. We come together just seconds later, and not once do I take my eyes from hers.

I can see the same intensity I'm feeling reflected in her stare, and I know that what we're both feeling goes beyond the love we've developed. This is more than just coming together physically. This was our souls devouring any space left between them to become one. To fuse together in a bond that will never be broken.

At this moment, our love turned into something so much bigger than words can describe. It's only when I roll my back to the mattress, pull her body to mine, and feel her head rest gently against my chest that I realize tears of my own have fallen from my eyes.

CHAPTER TWENTY-SEVEN

WILLOW

I GASP, COMING OUT OF A deep sleep at the same moment my orgasm crashes over me. My head tilts back against the warmth of Kane's shoulder as he leans over me and continues to torture the deliciously sore spot between my legs. Two long fingers push deeper and curl inside of me right when I crest the peak of the first wave of ecstasy that washes over me.

"Kane!" I cry out and start to move my hips in tune with each pump of his hand. "Oh, God!"

My body arches, and my bottom presses against his body. I can feel the hardness of his erection as he rolls his hips against me to add some friction against the part of him that has kept me awake for long hours throughout the night.

"You're so tight my fingers can't even move, Willow," his husky voice tells me. I can hear the sleep still in his tone. "I woke up after what feels like a handful of minutes sleeping and felt like if I didn't get back inside you soon and feel you come on my cock that I wouldn't be able to take another breath. I'm desperate for you."

I shudder violently when his fingers hit a spot inside me that makes my oversensitive body jerk. His hand slips from between my legs, and I cry out when I lose the thickness of his two fingers.

I have to take a second to let my heart to slow down and then turn my body so I can look into his eyes.

"How can you still be hard?" I pant in question.

"Have you taken a good look at yourself, Willow? Your body is what wet dreams are made of, and after finally knowing what it feels like to have that lusciousness meeting my brutal thrusting—fuck, I'm not sure I'll ever get rid of my hard-on."

My face warms at his words, and I love the pride-like feeling that comes over me at his praise.

"I used to hate this lush body you seem not to be able to get enough of, but when you say those kinds of things to me, I really believe them." His face goes soft, and he loses some, but not all, of the harshness to his features that his desire has brought forward. "I never thought I would have this, Kane. Never. The way you look at me makes me feel like the most powerful woman in the world."

My legs open when he moves his body slightly, and he reaches for my leg to pull it over his waist. We're both on our sides, our faces sharing one pillow as our breathing comes out to dance between us. His dick settles between my center and he gives a few thrusts of his hips to coat himself with my wetness.

"Watch me," he tells me and then kisses me softly.

Reaching over to the side of the bed, he grabs a condom from the box he opened earlier after searching for it in one of the packed boxes and covers himself. When he comes back to me, he puts his back to the bed and pulls me to straddle his hips. My yelp of surprise is quickly followed by a moan when he helps me lift up and guides myself on him.

"Watch us," he continues on a moan when I seat myself completely on his length.

"Feel us," he groans, his eyes closing to slits and his hands giving my sides a squeeze.

I rock forward and slowly lift myself. He doesn't move, but his eyes roam over my face and down my body. I follow his lead and look down at myself. My breasts sway each time I circle my waist. Each one heavy as it shakes with not just my body's movements, but also with my rapid breathing.

"See us." His voice is not more than a harsh pant dripping with arousal. "Fuck," he continues. The erotic image of my body taking his seems to become too much, and he brings his eyes back to my face.

Arching my back and bending forward, my hands come to his chest and I use him as leverage to pick up speed. My hair fans out around our faces, and he looks at me through his mask of euphoria.

"Look. Down. And see," he puffs severely through his clenched jaw.

I lose his eyes when he looks at our joined bodies, and I bend my head down a little more to follow his gaze. My breasts are now heaving with the force as I'm sliding him in and out of my body, and the sight makes me pick up my speed. I bite my lip when they start to move together and the feeling of them rubbing against each other makes me moan. I look past them and when I see myself opening around his thick dick, I feel myself get wetter, and my breaths come in quicker bursts.

"Lean up," he grunts, and I comply with his demand. "See and feel, love."

My eyes watch his hands as he brings them up my torso; I follow his path and when his hands cup my breasts, I let out a long and loud moan, my hips jerking and his dick jerking inside me. I see my body through his eyes, the ones that feast on every inch of skin he touches when he drags those dexterous fingers back down. My stomach clenches and my body tightens around his length. He ends his exploration with one hand holding tightly to my side, his fingers holding me so tightly that they're white, and the pleasure I feel from the bite of pain of his grip makes me rock even quicker against him. His other hand moves down the center of my body until he hits the spot where our bodies are joined. My eyes leave his hand for just a second to look at his face, to witness what he sees with just one glance.

His face is flush, and his mouth is opened slightly. His rapid breathing is noisy through the opening, and he groans when his finger hits my clit and I jerk my hips roughly against him. His eyes are almost completely black from his dilated pupils when he moves his study from my body and meets my eyes.

"Now feel me," he commands, and in one rapid burst of energy, he has our positions flipped and I'm screaming his name as he thrusts into my body violently. My headboard slams against the wall, the wood audibly making a noise that tells me it's about to break.

He continues the forcefulness as his body powers into mine. Both arms locked tight, he's holding his body up from the mattress and giving me a view between us.

"Fuck, you were made for me," he rumbles. "Look at how you

take me, Willow. See how beautiful it is when I fuck you hard and each part of your soft body welcomes every powerful inch of my hard body. Goddamn, this body was made for mine. Made for me."

His voice is raw, the exertion of his movements bringing out the hunger we both feel. The frame of my bed continues to complain when his speed picks up and I'm unable to look away from the sight of him taking me deliciously hard. My body tightens harshly and my limbs lock as a tidal wave of feelings breaks over every inch. I hear him grunt, stutter in his thrust in, and my body locks even more.

My throat feels sore as I scream his name and a whole bunch of other incoherent gibberish as I splinter into a million pieces. When I hear his own roar of pleasure, blackness is edging around my vision and the last thing I remember is hearing how much he loves me.

I step out of the shower and run the towel over my sore body. A sore body that I hope always feels this way.

Well used and well loved.

I can hear Kane speaking on the other side of the bathroom door and shiver when the deep, rough tones hit my ears. We had spent the morning wrapped around each other, but after he made me pass out with the force of our coupling, we haven't made love again.

Made love. Yeah, that was without a doubt what we had shared earlier. The intensity of it was like nothing I've ever known possible. It was worth every day of foreplay that we had built toward that moment. We shared everything I had never known to dream of between us, and I'm still feeling the aftershocks of it.

Wrapping the towel around my body, I open the bathroom door and walk into the bedroom. Kane turns toward me and gives my body a long, leisurely inspection before I get his dimple and handsome smile. He's pulled his jeans back on, but besides that, he's still bare for my eyes.

He walks over and leans down to give me a kiss. I can hear the feminine voice through the phone pressed to his ear and wait to see whom he is speaking to. He seems off from his normal, calm self. He's moving like Kane, giving me the attention I have become used to, but something in the way his body is pulled tight has me on edge.

"No, Mia, we leave tomorrow. Late flight so we can finish getting Willow's things settled with the movers."

Ah, Mia.

I actually really like Mia, even though I tried hard not to in the beginning. We've been able to form a friendship over the last month and a half. The first time I spoke to her was weird. It was awkward because I know there is something Kane hasn't told me about her—about their relationship. I believed him when he told me that they were just friends, but it still bothered me that he held something back. But he asked me to trust him, so I have.

That first phone call was clipped and hesitant on my end until she laughed in my ear and gave me what I needed to let go of that hesitancy I felt toward her. Her words, and I quote, were, 'I can hear you worrying, but let me address the rumors that are out there about Kane and my relationship. He's always treated me like a little sister. He's always been protective and because of that, and our friendship, the media's always had it in their ass about us having something more.'

Hearing it from her, even though I believed Kane when he told me the same, helped to ease my mind. Sure, it wasn't an emphatic no, but it was a denial. Since then, we've talked on the phone a few times. I wouldn't say I'm going to start inviting her to girls' night, but I enjoy the chats we do have. She makes it hard not to like her.

"All right, I'll tell Willow, but I know we're going to be busy when we get in. There isn't much time between our arrival and our first day on set. There's more work than not at this point since Willow is still getting everything that Sam hadn't completed in order. Why don't you let us settle in for a day or two and then we can talk?"

He lets out a soft rumble of laughter, his eyes darting to mine before he rolls them dramatically. Something within his gaze makes a chill run down my spine. I can't put my finger on it, but just as quickly as it was there, it vanished.

"Yeah, I can guarantee that if you tried that shit, you wouldn't be successful. At all. Trust me, not even the promise of a lifetime supply of Tim Tams is going to get me to agree to dinner that early." He turns away from me, and I watch the muscles in his back tense. "A few days, Mia. There's just too much going on."

I turn from him and try to ignore the feeling and move about the room, grabbing my clothes and pulling them on. He starts to end his call and makes plans to call her in four days, Friday at the latest.

I ignore the little bit of nerves I have over seeing Mia for the first time in person in just a few days. What did he say? Friday at the latest? That gives me four days to prepare myself. We have today and some of tomorrow left here before I leave New York behind, and I know Kane meant every word about us being busy when we get to California. Not just because I have to get unpacked and all that comes with moving homes, but also to catch up on the work we're missing while we're here.

"What time are Kirby and Eddie coming?" Kane asks, his voice interrupting my mental checklist for his upcoming appearances and interviews. He pulls my back to his front, wrapping his arms around my body, and drops a kiss on my shoulder.

Just like that, everything that had been on my mind just seconds before drops from my thoughts and concerns. My mind only cares about Kane. Clearly, this is something I need to work on. I don't need to start slipping on the job because my infatuation with him consumes me.

My arms come up and I fold them over the corded muscles in his arms, just below my chest. "I think we have about an hour? I wasn't really sure when I talked to Eddie. He kept going on and on about someone he met in London, so it was hard to follow the conversation."

Kane chuckles. "He sounds like an interesting man. I'm looking forward to finally meeting him."

"You say that now." I snort with a laugh. "You have no idea what you're in for."

I swat his hands away when he tries to fondle my breasts, and when I turn to face him, I burst out with the hilarity of his pouting when I see his face. "Keep your hands to yourself, Mr. Masters. I'm sore, and my friends will be here soon. I need to get ready, and you need to prepare yourself for everything that comes with a girls' night with those two."

"I'm thinking, my love, that we need a new title for this night of shenanigans."

I smile and ignore him, walking into my living room. The mess I had left earlier when I got in the shower is completely gone. The boxes that the movers will come for tomorrow are neatly lined up behind the kitchen table, and everything else looks like my normal, tidy home, just void of all personal touches.

"I needed something to do to keep from barging into your bathroom. I figured I might as well get the packing finished so we have tomorrow free to do whatever you want before we fly out."

At the mention of tomorrow, my last day here, I remember I needed to talk to him about something that I've been thinking about a lot over the last couple of weeks. "Hey, can I run something by you?"

"Of course," he responds and takes a seat on my couch, reaching out and pulling me down into his lap.

"There's something I need to do tomorrow, and I'm not sure how you're going to take it. Well, not it, but what I need from you."

His brows furrow and a look of adorable confusion takes over his expression.

"Hear me out, okay?" I wait for his nod, the confusion taking on a hint of apprehension. I reach out and rub my finger over the tense pull of skin between his thick brows and smile when he relaxes. "I need to go to the Logan Agency."

"Fuck, no," he rushes out in a burst of anger. He looks as far from confused as he could get now.

Fury takes over him, and I rush to explain. "Stop, Kane. Please. I really need you to be able to put everything you're feeling aside and listen to me when I explain why I need to do this so badly."

He drops his head, his chin hitting his chest and I can just barely hear him softly counting. His breathing slows down slightly before looks up and gives me a brisk nod.

"I'm not sure I know the best way to explain this to you. I'm going to try the best I can, but I honestly don't know if I can put into words how important this step is for me." I shift my body so I can see him easier and rest my hands on his chest. His heart is rapidly hitting my palm and his breathing quickens slightly. Seeing how affected he is at just the thought of me going to see my step-father and Ivy fills my heart. I've never doubted the enormity of his feelings toward me since we became official, but visibly seeing the strength of that love fills me with the confidence I need to take this last step. The final transformation into the woman I've struggled to become for too many years coming to fruition in these few moments of pounding hearts and the mingled breaths that rush together in a rapid dance between our bodies.

"The day I left Logan was one of the hardest moments I had ever experienced. Aside from losing my mom, that is. I had been floundering through a life I hated for years, until my marriage ended and I started to try to change. I went about it as unhealthy as it gets. The quest to feel worthy of myself wasn't one I realized I was on until, through your love, I was able to really see. I starved myself in every way I could. Physically, to try to fit a mold I can now happily say I will never fit. But also mentally. I let myself put up with the verbal lashings that whipped me into a fearful life with my marriage. And I let it happen with Dominic and Ivy. I put myself through that because I was, I think, trying to prove that *someone* was what I needed to love myself. I so desperately wanted their love and attention that I let a man I had always thought of as my father verbally slap me over and over."

"Baby," he whispers, and I give him a smile. Not one of sadness, but one of understanding.

"It's okay, Kane. I've come to terms with all of that and accepted that it was a very painful lesson I can let either drown me or gain strength from it. I choose the strength. But in order for me move on and be able to be the woman I know I'm worthy of becoming, I have to let it go. I have to show them, *you,* and me that no matter how hard they tried, I win. But, most importantly, I need this closure in order to finally let it all go to *be* that woman."

He sighs and brings me closer as his arms come up and tighten around me. Shifting in order not to twist my body in a painful way, I return his embrace. He guides my head to his shoulder as I take a deep breath to inhale his scent.

Another deep sigh comes from him before he speaks.

"You're asking me to stand by and let you be put in harm's way, Willow, and I'm not sure that's something I'm going to be able to do. I might not have seen the way you struggled for years with my own eyes, but I did see the beautiful woman trapped inside, a woman terrified to live because of the way those people had made her feel. I've watched you win, and you don't have to prove that to anyone, baby."

God, I love this man. "It's not just anyone, Kane." I sigh. "It's me. I have to prove it to *me.*" I push off his hold and look at his face. "I need this, honey. I want to do this so I can get the closure I need and move on once and for all with no ties to the negative pain that was drowning me. I *have* to do this."

His features are tense with struggle as he tries to understand why I'm asking this of him. To fight against himself and his need to protect those who he loves. I know that what I'm asking of him goes against his character. To sit back and watch someone you have the basic instincts to protect willingly walk into a situation that you have the power to shield them from is unfathomable.

The painful fog that had been building, making his eyes look like the deep navy clouds of a brewing storm, ebbs slightly, and he lets out a noise of resignation.

"If you feel that you need to do this that badly, then I'll support you and this decision one hundred percent. I hate it though. I hate that you feel you have to put yourself through this, but I understand—or I'm trying to. But, Willow, you can't expect me to let you walk into hell without me. I will never be okay with not being there to hold your hand when you might need me. We're in this together."

"You have to let me do this alone. I have to do this alone." I hate that I can't find the right words, the words I need to make him see how it won't be the same if I don't do this on my own. "I'm not afraid of them." I exhale softly.

"I think it's time for you to realize you will never be alone again, Willow. Together, we go, but it's your show, and I promise you that I will let you lead. I won't take this away from you because I can tell you really believe you need it. I'm there to be silent strength if you need it. But I will not let harm come to the woman I love. I vow to you that I will only step in if I feel it's necessary for your safety. But please don't ask me to stay behind."

"Okay," I comply; leaning forward, I drop a soft, closed-mouth kiss to his lips. "Thank you. I know it isn't fair to you that I'm asking you to push aside every instinct you have to protect me, but I think a little part of me needs you to see I'm no longer afraid to actually live. I'm happy, and to be free of the fear and shame I had been trapped in, I have to be the one to fight it back."

"God, Willow. I see it every day. In every blinding smile you freely give. Present in each take-charge, confident sway of your hips. It's in every single breath you take."

His words ease the trepidation I had when I started this conversation. Not in the path that I felt I needed to take, but because I know and understand just how immeasurable it is that he's giving me something that will mentally pain him to allow. I'm ready for this, to shut the book of my past life and move on. Move on and be worthy of not just his love, but also my own.

CHAPTER TWENTY-EIGHT

WILLOW

KIRBY ARRIVED WHEN KANE AND I were enjoying a heated kiss. The kind that is just seconds away from turning into naked bodies and sweaty skin. Thank God, it wasn't Eddie. One look at Kane's naked torso and he would have gone insane. Completely insane.

Eddie's flight was delayed, so he would be joining us later. I can't wait to see him after being away for so long. We've talked on the phone plenty, but not enough. His time difference in Europe made the chats we did have too short for my liking.

One thing he's made perfectly clear though is that he's beyond thrilled with how things have turned out. I know a lot of that has to do with the change he's heard in my voice over the last almost two months, but I think a little part of Eddie's happiness is knowing that the one man we had claimed as unattainable has stolen my heart … just as I have his.

"Are you all packed?" Kirby asks and stuffs a handful of popcorn in her mouth.

I nod but keep my attention on the television we had been watching for almost two hours. True to form, girls' night is in full swing. The wine is flowing, nails have been painted, and our skin exfoliated. I decided to skip the mud masks that we would normally end the beauty portion of our night with because, let's face it, there is nothing sexy about being covered in drying mud as it cracks all over your skin.

Kane skipped our pampering but sat, drank, and laughed with us. Well, until we had a brilliant idea to turn on this movie. He hasn't been shy about his dislike for our feature film of the evening. I hear him grumble again, but I still don't look away. I blindly raise my wine glass to my mouth and take a hearty swig to ease the dryness in my throat.

"This acting is almost as bad as a porn," he criticizes.

Kirby laughs at Kane's complaint.

"You are not wrong, but I think it's safe to say that no one is actually watching this for the acting. I mean, look at the way Channing moves those hips," Kirby responds, making a clucking sound with her tongue. "Who is that hunk dancing with him?"

I clear my throat. Watching this scene between Channing and Twitch is making me way too hot and bothered. I imagine Kane doing the things I've been watching, and the thoughts of him spinning me around while grinding on top of me, in me—heck, all over me—is making my body heat to impossible levels.

"Twitch," I respond, my voice betraying the cool and calm I had been trying to fake.

"Who?"

Turning my eyes from the television before I attack Kane and beg him to strip for me, I look at Kirby before addressing her question.

"Twitch, I forget his real name. He was on *Dancing with the Stars*, no … the other one, what was that called?"

"*So You Think You Can Dance*," Kane offers, and I turn to look at him. He gives me a knowing smile, and I feel my face heat. "He actually was in a few movies before that show made him better known. I don't know a lot about him, but I think he's choreographed some of those dance movies too. Last I saw, he had been doing a lot on *Ellen*."

"What he said," I tell Kirby and smile when Kane throws his head back and laughs, reaching out to pull me to his side.

"Well, wherever he's from, he's just as delicious as Channing."

I ignore Kirby and settle into Kane's side, turning my head to look at him. "So…?"

He laughs even harder. "Don't even think about it. I'll get naked for you, baby, but there won't be any of that stupid dancing going on."

"I'll dance for you, Willow." Kirby giggles.

I open my mouth to send a sarcastic comment her way, but the lock clicks from the front door and the door opens with enough force to slam against the wall.

"Hello, my best friends! Eddie is here, and he wants some hugs from his best girls!"

"Eddie!" Kirby and I both scream at the same time and jump from the couch to run to him. There's a lot of talking after that—excited gabble of nonsense, giggles, and even some tears—before Eddie goes silent and openly gawks over our shoulders. Oh, my

God, I had completely forgotten that Kane was here.

"Holy shit," Eddie gasps.

I elbow him, and Kirby giggles.

"Eddie, I want you to meet my boyfriend, Kane. Kane, this is my other best friend, Eddie." I pull Eddie into the room and bring him to where Kane is standing, smile on his face, dimple out, and thankfully, for Eddie's sanity, fully dressed.

Kane reaches out a hand in greeting, but Eddie, for the first time I have ever witnessed, is completely star struck. I give him an elbow to the side, but he doesn't even register me.

"Seriously, Edward?" Kirby hoots. "I have never seen him like this, Kane. You should probably just ignore him. I bet he wouldn't even blink if the room fell down around him at this point. Hey, Willow?" She starts to laugh even harder now making me wonder where she's going with this.

"Yeah?"

"I bet we could snap him out of this trance. Come over here and let me give you another kiss. Bet that would shock him stupid enough to come to his senses." She's laughing so hard now that she falls down on the couch, tears leaking from her eyes.

I close my eyes and try to remember why I love her so much and why I would be sad if I killed her. Well, I would be sad tomorrow, but right now, I wouldn't be.

"Kiss again?" Eddie asks, finally turning away from Kane. "You two bitches kissed and no one told me?"

"Like you care! You just thought it was funny because it made me uncomfortable when you brought us to the club with you and someone asked if Kirby and I were a couple."

"Did you see this kiss?" Eddie questions Kane, all signs of his stupid star-struck trance gone. "Tell me someone caught this on tape. I've been waiting to have them drunk enough to get a black-mail kiss for years!"

"Sorry, man, I can't say I was around for that one," Kane responds and then lets out a loud belly laugh when I roll my eyes at him.

"Nice to meet you. Sorry about that." Eddie reaches out and I watch the two most important men in my life shake hands.

They start talking, and I look over at Kirby. "I'm going to strangle you," I tell her, unsmiling.

"Yeah, right. You told me we shouldn't tell him because he would never let it go. I didn't agree."

"Whatever. Now, he's going to try to get us to kiss again. You know he's been convinced we would have been the best lesbian couple ever."

"Well, we probably would have." Her giggles pick up speed, and I can't help but to join in.

Grabbing the wine bottle, I refill our empty glasses before picking up the one that had been waiting for Eddie and pouring him some.

We spend the next few hours talking and laughing. Having all the people who I love together in one place is one of the best feelings. I hate knowing I won't see Eddie much after tonight. Even if I weren't moving to California in a few days, I still wouldn't have moments like this often. He's living a transient lifestyle now that he is traveling full time for work. The plus side though is that he will often be on the West Coast, LA specifically, when he's on location.

"I still don't know how you two have managed to dodge reporters for this long." Eddie laughs. "I saw a few pictures of you guys together while you were down South, but none that show Willow clearly enough. Shockingly, there hasn't been any mention of Kane Masters and his new mystery woman."

"He kept her tied to the bed," Kirby jokes, pointing her finger and narrowing her eyes toward Kane. "I swear when we weren't on set I hardly ever saw her. Even when she was in the same house as I was. Those two would disappear for HOURS!"

"You didn't tell me that," Eddie whines at Kirby before turning back to where Kane and I are cuddled together on the couch. "So when you weren't locked away doing sordidly delicious things to our Willow, how exactly did you manage to keep your relationship locked tighter than the nation's secrets?"

Leave it to Eddie to throw that out there. Sure, it's something I've wondered myself, but I figured Kane had his reasons, and if I had doubted our relationship, then maybe it would bother me, but I just left it as it was.

"Just because I haven't gone out of my way to give them the pictures they want doesn't mean I'm trying to keep her or us a secret." Kane answers Eddie with a strong conviction in his voice. I smile at Eddie, hoping that is enough for him to lay off. I should have known better, though; Eddie seems to be on a mission.

"It doesn't have anything to do with all the rumors flying around about Mia Post, does it?"

Eddie's question makes me tense. I try not to, but Kane's still holding back when it comes to explaining more about Mia and his relationship—or better yet, explaining to me why he refuses to give me more when those rumors in question are thrown in my face.

I trust him, but it's hard to get upset when he just asks you to call upon that trust and drop it.

261

Kane shifts; the legs holding me between them flex with his movements. "No, Eddie. There isn't some nefarious reason for me to want to keep my private life out of the media. Mia and I are friends. Because of the closeness we've had through years of friendship, the media chooses to make it seem like more in order to sell their garbage."

I can tell Eddie wants to press him about Mia. Part of me wants him to, but I know if Kane won't tell me everything yet, there is no way he's going to tell Eddie. I just have to trust he will tell me when he's ready. I'm starting to think that maybe they did have a relationship at one point that was more than just friends, but it just didn't work. I could see why he wouldn't want to tell me about it; Mia is a beautiful woman, and I'm pretty sure she would intimidate anyone if they were faced with a friendship and old flame.

"I can get the whole keeping your private life to yourself, but surely, you know that it would be much easier to shut up the lies if you and Willow were seen, and the relationship brought to light, I don't know, denied the latest round of slander?"

"It's not that easy, Eddie. Not when you're dealing with people who will do whatever it takes to sell their shit. I do not intend to shield my relationship with Willow, not at all, but I also knew that building something with her was more important to me than trying to start that *and* have to fight off the media."

"So? Does that mean now that you two are officially a couple, oozing love every second you're around each other, and all kissy kissy, that you plan to take it public?" Eddie sighs, clearly exasperated, and waits for Kane's response.

"I haven't been keeping her or our relationship from going public. I just haven't been going out of my way to catch their attention while we were filming. I also didn't want to thrust that on her until she was ready to deal with that madness."

"Eddie." I interrupt Kane before he can continue to speak. "I know you're trying to be all big and bad here, looking out for me and all, but please just drop it. I know Kane's intentions are pure, and he's right. I wouldn't have handled it. A month ago, I wouldn't have been ready if I had to deal with so much public influence. He and Mia are friends and have been since they were teens. It's natural that the press would look at that as more, but Kane's asked me to trust him and I do. I need *you* to do the same."

Eddie has the decency to look slightly embarrassed before giving me a nod. "I'm sorry, Wills. I just worry about you."

"And I love you for that, but I'm okay. Really and truly okay."

He studies me, his handsome face letting me know just how anxious he's been about my relationship with Kane.

"He loves me, Eddie. Loves me so fiercely that I don't doubt it. I don't need him to turn that into some media frenzy or public stunt. I know it's as real as it comes. You don't need to worry about me. Not anymore. I'm so happy I'm almost floating. Not just with my relationship with Kane or my life, in general, but I'm so happy in my own skin that I feel like the lightest person in the world."

Kirby makes a choking noise that makes me think she's about to start crying and reaches out to grab her glass, taking a long sip. I know she gets it, but she's also witnessed me become the Willow I am today. Eddie hasn't, so I understand his questions.

"Eddie," I implore as I lean forward. Kane's arms drop from where they had been resting on my torso and rest at my hips when I reach out for Eddie's hands. "I'm ready to move on from my past, and I know you're worried about me because of everything you had to watch me suffer through, but you have to stop. It's taken me a while, but I'm free of that pain. I can see that I was trying to search for the feelings I felt lacking, but I didn't realize I was the one who held the key to them. I'm strong. I stepped out of that comfort zone I was stuck in, and just like you said it would, my life began."

His throat works, and his eyes mist. He works hard to control it, and I know if Kane weren't here, Eddie would have probably cried some very ladylike theatrics.

"What time's your flight tomorrow? Do we have time to fit some lunch in?" he asks, letting me know he's about two seconds away from a very unmanly emotional breakdown with what I just told him. God, I love him. He and Kirby are the only family I ever needed; I know that now, and he just proved why a million times over.

"If we didn't have to go to Logan tomorrow, we probably could," Kane answers for me, and Eddie's eyes jump from mine to Kane, over to Kirby, and then narrow back at me.

"Tell me you aren't going there willingly. And without a bomb or something," Eddie demands, his voice full of anger.

I feel Kane tense against my body, and I hate that I'm making him feel this way.

"I've already tried to talk her out of it, Eddie, but she isn't having it," Kirby snaps.

"And you?" Eddie asks Kane.

"And I understand why she needs to go. Do I like it? No, I fucking hate it. But it's important to her, so I will give her support. Even if she didn't want it, I would have given her that. I might not agree with her thinking she needs this, but I'm trying. If this is something Willow wants to do, then I'm there for her every step of the way."

"You're going, too?" Eddie gasps.

"Why does that shock you?" Kirby asks. "I told you, inseparable."

"Yeah, but going into Logan with him on her arm is going to make Ivy even more malicious than normal. You know that's going to set her off." Eddie looks over my head and addresses Kane. "I know you saw some of it, but let me clue you in on sister dear. She will not like it that Willow's moved on. Not only that, she's going to have a fit when she realizes that she didn't just move on, but also traded up. No offense, Willow. Throwing you in her face is going to make her unpredictable."

Kane's body jolts with small bouts of hilarity. "You know, I'm pretty sure anything Willow does is going to make Ivy go nuts. I know her type all too well. It wouldn't matter if Willow went in the same person she was six weeks ago. Ivy would still find something she wanted to strip from her, even when she didn't have anything left. I won't allow the possibility of someone, anyone, trying to take away one single shred of Willow's growth."

Kane's arms move and he pulls me tighter against his body. I reach down and give one of the legs framing my body between his spread thighs a squeeze. His head turns, and he places a small kiss against my temple.

"I love you," he whispers in my ear.

"Are you sure you know what you're doing?" Eddie waves his arm around, clearly at a loss since he knows he can't talk me out of it. I can tell he isn't going to try to persuade me out of going; he's asking out of concern that I'm not ready to face them.

"Yes. I have to do this, Eddie. I have to face them as the strong person I am now in order to let go of the pain. The ghosts of their past words can no longer haunt me. I need this not just to move on, but also to prove to myself that I can do something that just the thought of would have killed me before now. It's not as if I'm expecting them to welcome me with arms wide open. I *know* they're both going to be jerks, but I need them to see me and hear me when I tell them how I feel."

Kirby lets out a laugh void of humor. "I think if there is any time for you to let go of that stupid habit you have of not cussing, it would be now while we talk about those two evil assholes."

"Whatever." I chuckle. She's always made a joke out of trying to get me to turn into some foul-mouthed sailor. I'll never understand why she and Eddie get so much enjoyment out of this little game. I think I've gotten so good at not letting any curses pop out because I know it drives them nuts.

"I understand, sweets. I don't like it, but I understand. Plus, you have this strapping hunk to kick some serious ass if they step out of line." He gives Kane a few wags of his brow, his earlier concern and seriousness gone.

I snuggle in closer to Kane, but look at Kirby when I hear her struggling not to laugh. Following her gaze, I look behind my shoulder and see that Kane's cheeks are flush with embarrassment over Eddie's flirting. I look back over at Kirby, and we both burst out laughing.

The conversation moves on now that the heavy topics are over. We talk about our upcoming move and about what we plan to do in California.

By the time Kirby and Eddie go to leave, I'm about to fall

asleep on my feet. Kane and I walk them to the door.

All sleep is forgotten when Kirby grabs my head and gives me a long, closed-mouth kiss. She pulls back and shrugs. "What? It's kind of like our thing now."

Eddie is in stitches, and Kane is shaking with silent laughter.

"You're ridiculous." I smirk.

I give Eddie a hug, promising to call him and Kirby tomorrow. Kirby goes to open the door, but stops in shock when Eddie turns from me and grabs Kane's head, pulling his mouth to his. It's a brief kiss, over just as quickly as it started. I can't tell who is more shocked out of the three of us.

Eddie steps back to hook his arm through Kirby's. He gives Kane a wink and then turns to me. "What? It's like our thing now."

I burst out laughing. God, I love my friends.

CHAPTER TWENTY-NINE

WILLOW

OKAY, SO I WOULD BE lying if I didn't admit I was a little nervous about walking into the Logan Agency. Kane's been silent during our ride, but ever supportive with the hand that hasn't let go of mine since we left my apartment.

Cam's been quiet as he navigates the insanity that the streets of New York City bring. I didn't even realize he was still here until Kane called him twenty minutes ago to come pick us up. I should have realized he wouldn't have gone back to California ahead of Kane. Sometimes, I forget that Kane isn't a normal man. The time we spend alone makes his need for a bodyguard unnecessary. It's going to take a lot of getting used to when we're no longer able to have these long days of solitude.

"It's likely that when we leave, someone could tip off the media about where to find me," Kane says, and I look over from my window gazing to meet his eyes. He looks calm, but his eyes are appraising me in a way that makes me think he is still a little worried about how I'll handle being a potentially trending worldwide topic when our relationship news hits the masses.

I squeeze his hand, offering him, without words, a sign that I'm okay. Resting my head on the headrest, I think back to last night after Kirby and Eddie left. We talked a lot about Eddie's concerns, and I hadn't realized he was still nervous about it.

Kane's public image and the fact, like it or not because we haven't stepped out and announced our relationship, he's still linked to Mia. I understand where Eddie was coming from in asking, but I also see where Kane's justified in his hesitancy to go public. He's been burned in the past when he thought his relationship was ready to weather the media storm, and it wasn't. Given how afraid I was of my own shadow when we first met, I can see his protective nature wanting to shield me from the unknowns that come with his celebrity status and the media.

Most importantly, he explained that because of our schedule in Georgia, there just wasn't the opportunity for a big coming out of sorts, so even when I *was* ready, the opportunity just didn't present itself. Not to mention, because of the small town that we were filming in, Kane enjoyed the anonymity that he normally would never have if we were in California or heck, even here in New York. I keep waiting to turn around and have a million cameras in our faces.

"I know it's a possibility, Kane, and I'm not concerned. You shouldn't be either. Unless you don't want to have our relationship out there yet," I whisper remembering his promise to try to avoid the media better. "You can't just expect yourself to be okay with letting them invade your personal life overnight. Or openly let them into our relationship when you're used to not letting them know anything. You've had years of dealing with them picking apart everything you do, so I understand you like to keep your life as tight-lipped as possible."

He shakes his head. "It isn't that, baby. I just know how they can be, and I don't want *you* to have to deal with the negativity that will follow. I wish I could say it wouldn't, but I know better. The media loves to create drama where there shouldn't be any."

How can I make him understand I'm really okay with it? Sure, I don't think it will be easy, but I also know I have no fear of the things they could possibly say about me. Not anymore.

"If this was when we first met, I would have run for the hills," I say and rush to continue when he gets pale. "But it's been almost two months since then, and I can honestly say I have no doubt that I'm ready. I'm not worried about what they're going to say about me. Or about us. You made me realize I don't need to be afraid, so can you please trust me this time when I tell you it's going to be okay?"

He nods but doesn't look convinced. Sure, he has a lot more experience with the media than I do—which is none—but how bad could it possibly be?

"We'll deal with it when it happens, okay?"

His hand squeezes mine, and he nods, looking away and through the window when we slow.

"You ready for this?" he asks, and I follow his eyes to the building that houses the Logan Agency offices.

I study the entrance and wait for my nerves or fear to hit me, but they don't. The only thing I feel is a lightness I never knew was possible. Fearless. I feel fearless. And I know, given the fact that

Kane had no issues telling—and showing—me this morning, that I even look as powerful as I feel right now.

His hand releases mine, and I hear him open his door. I grab my compact from my purse and check my appearance before he gets to my side of the SUV. My blemish-free complexion no longer looks ghastly. Instead, it has a glow about it—still pale, but the rosiness in my cheeks gives me some color. My makeup is minimal, just some mascara and dusty pink lip gloss, understated and not overdone. I no longer hide behind a makeup-free face; instead, I accent the things I've started to love.

My eyes sweep down and over my features, and I smile when I don't feel the need to point out everything wrong because I see the positive in myself. The most prominent change I see is in my eyes. You can't miss the happiness that sparkles in them.

The door opens, and I tuck away my compact and take Kane's offered hand, my eyes appraising his body before I fold out of the backseat. He looks like he stepped off the pages of *GQ*'s Winter Casual edition. Dark denim jeans, blue long sleeve Henley top tucked in at his trim hips, and brown boots.

He looks delicious.

I chose my outfit with much more care than his obvious need for comfort. I feel a smirk lift my lips when I think about walking through the doors of Logan dressed as I never have before.

Where my makeup is done to subtly show beauty, my clothes are not. My black pants are tightly stretched against my thighs and butt, tapering out with a barely-there flare down to my four-inch red Louboutin heels. Even though the pants aren't showing any skin, the way they're tastefully painted on makes me feel as hot as Kane praised me to be this morning. An impulsive purchase from

Torrid that makes me wish I had found the plus-sized clothing store long before now. My top, like the shoes, is blood red. I might have gone a little overboard when I was told it was a power color, but now that I'm wearing it, I feel it. Powerful.

The chiffon tunic-style tank top is low cut, showing off a generous amount of my cleavage. It isn't tight anywhere else, but the way it flows from my breasts makes me look slimmer. And on top of that is a black blazer that, when buttoned, makes my chest look even larger than their double Ds.

It's subtle but designed to make every curvy part look amazing. When I looked in the mirror this morning, I felt stunning.

"Are you ready?" he asks when I stand next to him, taking my hand in his and giving Cam a nod.

"Yeah." I nod, smiling widely up into Kane's handsome face. "I really am."

Five minutes later, we're walking through the lobby of the Logan Agency. Mary looks up, and for a quick moment before her infectious smile hits, she looks confused. My eagerness to get this over with has me cutting our conversation short. As much as I would love to catch up, I know I have the advantage right now because they're not expecting me. The element of surprise allows me to hold all the power because they have no prep time.

Kane holds my hand as we walk around Mary's desk and make our way down the hallway. I look around at the images on the wall, taking in the dim lighting, and I don't feel an ounce of trepidation. None. I wondered if I would get this far and freak out, doing the opposite of what I set out to do today and just fall back on old habits. But being here around the images that used to make me feel even worse about myself drives home for me just how far I've come.

Looking over and up at Kane, we share a smirk, and I give him a wink, letting him know that I'm okay.

"I need you to let me go in there alone," I tell him, something I had left off last night when I was telling him about coming here today.

His eyes harden, and he instantly protests. "Not happening. I won't bend on that. I agreed to stay silent and let you drive today, but I will not let you go alone. Not fucking happening."

"Kane—" I start.

He stops walking, and I almost lose his hand when my body keeps going. Turning, I look at him in question.

"I'm this close," he says, holding his pointer finger and thumb just an inch apart. "This fucking close to throwing you over my shoulder. This showdown might not frighten you, but I'm going out of my mind worrying about what's going to happen when we walk through those doors. Those two held you captive in abuse-driven fear, Willow. You can't ask me not only to stay silent, but also to let you go alone. Not when I can *and will* protect you if it comes down to it. Please, don't ask me that."

His voice is just a whisper when he's finished, and he's not hiding the despair on his face. I knew he was against me coming, but I didn't realize just how much it was affecting him. I hate it. I would do anything to erase this expression from his face, but I also know I have to do this.

"Okay." I nod. "That wasn't fair of me and I'm sorry, but please, no matter what is said, let me get everything I have to out. Then you can burn the place down for all I care."

His shoulders fall, his relief instant. "Thank you." He sighs, dropping his head and giving me a light kiss. "Well, then let's go."

We start walking again, and I take a fortifying breath when we step into the outer waiting area of my father—no, Dominic's office. Luck is on my side because the transparent walls of his office are set to their foggy privacy setting. His door is open, and I can hear him inside laughing.

A few steps further and I hear my sister's hyena-like laugh and cringe. I don't think I realized just how annoying that noise she makes when she laughs was until this moment. It puts a smile on my face when I realize just how much I had built her up in my head to be flawless. No one with a laugh like that could be considered flawless.

I step into the open doorway and keep my smile in place with no effort when the occupants inside look over in surprise at the intruder.

"Looks like lady luck was even more generous than I had initially thought," I tell Kane with a laugh over my shoulder. "Everyone I wanted to see today just happens to be here together. I'm sure we can all agree to skip the polite 'how have you been' portion that usually comes when you haven't seen *family* in so long and all admit that we really don't care." I continue into the room, Kane's hand still holding mine, and let the powerful rush their surprise gives me spike my adrenaline a little more.

Looking over at a stunned Ivy, practically draped over an equally shocked Brad, makes me roll my eyes. They're both dressed impeccably, but I notice Ivy's face looks a little less Botox perfect now. Her skin, not having been kind to her as she ages, is dry from years of skin damage, and the bags under her eyes could probably count as a carry-on with most airlines. I'm now seeing the woman I had always thought got the better genes through the eyes of reality. She hides it well, but the way she's lived her life is clearly catching up with her. You can't expect money to buy everything, and Ivy is living proof. It can't buy happiness.

"Nice to see that you two are still together. I had worried, Ivy, that it wouldn't last. I mean, you worked so hard for him that it would be a shame for all of that to be in vain." Turning to Brad, I continue. "And Brad. Nice to see you. As you can see," I point at Kane over my shoulder, "I should be thanking *you*. After all, had I not been lucky enough to find you with my sister, I would be stuck married to you and I wouldn't have Kane. After years of thinking you were the best I would have, I can't even tell you how exhilarating it is to find out what I assumed was life's ten was more like a two. So thank you for pushing me out the door and right into the arms of a ten."

"Excuse me!" Dominic booms through the office.

Turning from Brad's incredulous eyes, I look at the man whose love I had always thought I needed.

"Dominic," I sweetly say in greeting. "You'll have to excuse my frankness, but I think you'll find I actually have no trouble speaking my mind these days. It really is a wonderful feeling."

"You'll keep in mind whom you're speaking to, Willow," he seethes.

I cock my head and look at him in confusion—well, fake confusion for his sake. "I'm sorry? And exactly who would that be, Dominic? Surely, you aren't implying that I should watch my mouth because there is someone I should be respecting in here?"

"You have a lot of nerve," he heatedly mumbles, moving to stand from his chair. "You have no right to be here!" he yells.

Kane's hand tightens, and I give him a squeeze.

"Perhaps, but I'm here, and I'm not leaving until I get a few things off my chest, so do me a favor and sit down, shut up, and for once in your life, listen."

He sputters but doesn't move around the desk. He also doesn't sit, but that's okay. Looking at each of them for a few seconds, I measure my next words—my reason for coming and everything that I hope to get off my chest. Short and sweet but everything I need to say in order to let go of my past. I couldn't care less if they agree; all that matters is how I feel at this moment.

"Dominic," I begin. "I want you to know that I forgive you." He sputters again, but this time it isn't anger driven. He's confused, clearly not expecting that. "I forgive you for being a terrible stepfather to me. I forgive you for treating me with nothing but hate and verbal abuse for years. I also forgive you for your inability to love because that is really just heartbreaking. I used to think I needed your love. For what reason, I'm not sure. I allowed you to beat me down because I felt the guilt of losing Mom, guilt I shouldn't have had to burden. It was a terrible accident I had no control over, and even though I'll miss her for the rest of my life, I know that the years I had with her were beautiful and even you can't take that away from me. I know now that if she were here, she would be as disgusted with your actions as I am. But most of all, I forgive you for being blinded by evil and not helping me heal after she was gone."

I ignore him and his beet-red face and turn to the duo of doom on the couch.

"Ivy." I smile at my sister. No. It's time I let go of the hope she would ever be a true sister. The half that had bonded us as together meaning more to me than her, so it's time I remember she will always be my half-sister. "I want you to know I forgive you as well. For different reasons, of course. I forgive you for being so unhappy with yourself that you projected that on me and spent your whole life building a relationship of hate toward me instead of one of love. You could have had the best relationship with me, but you were blind to that. I forgive you for whatever you lack in your heart to actually have the ability to care for another person, especially your own half-sister. It's okay because I see now that blood might bond us, but that connection is the only one we will share. And most of all, I thank you for being so driven by your hate toward me that you slept with Brad and saved me from the life I was drowning in. You didn't know it, but that was the best gift I had been given in a long time."

"You bitch," she screams, climbing to her feet.

"Be quiet," I snap, stopping her in her tracks before she can take more than two steps from the couch.

"Brad, I didn't know you would be here," I continue, fake enthusiasm dripping from my words. "I really didn't plan to have anything more to say to you, but it works out in my favor to have you here during this. So all I have to say is thank you for leaving me when you knew I was too afraid to do it myself. I forgive you for your part in the 'make Willow suffer' game. I'm not afraid anymore, and I can tell you with absolute honesty that you are the reason for that. I hope you're happy with my sister. I meant what I said. You two worked so hard for the common goal that it really would be a shame to waste all that malevolence."

Everyone is silent when I finish, and I look around at their faces. Each one shocked and bright red.

"Well …" I sigh cheerfully. "That's all I needed to say. If you'll excuse us, my boyfriend and I have a flight to catch."

I turn, but Ivy's silence has apparently found its endpoint. "You're with her? Why the fuck would you want her?"

I know her words are meant to lash me mentally, but she won't get that. Their words no longer have the power to hurt me. I know my worth.

I look up at Kane and give his angry expression a wink before turning back around. I stare at my half-sister and tell her the only thing I can to make her understand that she no longer holds any power to hurt me. "Why the *fuck* wouldn't he want me?" The curse word rolls off my tongue effortlessly, and it just makes my smile widen.

She doesn't respond, but I turn and ignore them. I said what I needed to in order to move on with my life. I no longer have any part of my painful past tying me down. I got the closure I needed, and it doesn't matter what they think.

The resistance in Kane's hold draws me up short, and I realize he didn't move from where he had been standing. He's staring at my half-sister, and if her trembling is anything to judge by, he looks terrifying.

"To answer your asinine question, it's because I fucking love her."

When he turns, he gives me a wink of his own and starts walking out the door, this time leading me. I'm too busy riding the high that my life's become to even notice what is being yelled at our retreating backs.

I don't care what they have to say because right now, I know when I leave this office, they're going to be dead to me. Not even the memory of them will haunt my mind.

I, Willow Tate, have won.

CHAPTER THIRTY

KANE

WILLOW DOESN'T STOP SMILING THE whole way out of the offices. She gives Mary a warm hug and promises to keep in touch. She turns toward me, and even though I know confronting her past wasn't easy, she looks happier than I have ever seen her. I had misjudged just how much this last tie to her past weighed on her. I have no doubt that she finally feels as strong as I knew she had become. Giving them her forgiveness wouldn't mean anything to anyone else, but to her it was the only way she could truly move on and be free from it.

The thought of letting her do this today had been filling me with unease all night and into the morning. I felt protective of her before we knew each other, so the thought of letting the woman I had come to love be in any pain I could prevent killed me. But when I stood by her side and watched her take charge of her future, I knew that moment was worth all the unsettling feelings I had.

Now, though, all of that is gone and the only thing I feel is pride. No, that's not true. Witnessing all of that turned me on so much; I could have fucked her right there in the middle of Dominic's office.

If watching her dominate the room wasn't enough to have my cock painfully hard, hearing her response to Ivy almost made me come unglued.

I've never heard her cuss. Not once. But now, all I can think of is hearing her beg me to *fuck* her.

When the elevator doors close and shut us in solitude, I turn to her and back her against the wall. My mouth comes down to hers in a hungry kiss. All of the pent-up frustration I felt at having to keep my mouth shut while she got what she needed back there came out in the brutal, savage kiss. All my worry and fear for her bleeding from my body as I let my hands roam all over her body and feast against her mouth. Her moans driving my need for her higher until I have to tear myself away before I really do fuck her right here.

"I'm so proud of you, Willow."

Her eyes open slowly, and I feel her fists uncoil around the fabric at my hips she had been fisting tightly.

"So fucking proud of you, baby."

The hazy gaze of lust is still floating over her expression, but her cheeks go pink at my praise.

Bending down so that my lips are just feathering her ear, I whisper, "And one day soon, I'm going to hear you say that word again. You know the one. You're going to say it when you're begging me to take you." I press my lips to the spot just under her ear that I know turns her on. I step back, just in time for the doors to slide open to the lobby.

Grabbing her hand, I lead us out and look around. Besides a few businessmen and women going about their day, there doesn't seem to be anyone paying us any attention. I was half expecting to have my presence noticed on the way out, but the front lobby is eerily quiet. I would have proudly marched through a sea of reporters if they had been tipped off, but I'm glad I have Willow alone after what happened up there. I know she's okay, but I still would feel better having her to myself just in case the enormity of cutting ties with her evil family hits her negatively.

Cam is standing outside the Range Rover when we walk into the crisp November air. He stands from his relaxed position leaning against the SUV and moves to open the back door. I allow Willow to slide in first and look around one more time, seeing nothing but the normal busyness of New York City. Shoppers, tourists, and locals going about their business without a care.

I climb in and ignore my belt, sliding across until my arm is over her shoulder. She's tucked into my side right where she belongs.

"I just talked to William. He said the jet is fueled and final prep is underway. They'll be ready to take off as soon as we get there."

"Thanks, Cam," I respond. Turning my attention from Cam's reflection in the rearview mirror, I look at Willow. The small smile still on her lips and her eyes closed while she relaxes against me.

"Are you ready to leave New York City and come home with me?" I ask, my words meaning a lot more than just asking if she's ready for her move. She's coming home, maybe not *in* my home just yet, but she is most definitely coming *home* where she belongs. By my side. And if I have my way, she will never be leaving.

She nods and leans her head back against the arm resting on her shoulder. "I am ready, so ready."

"The rest of your stuff will arrive Wednesday, but that should give us plenty of time to get you unpacked before filming picks back up. Are you sure you packed everything you'll need right away?"

"Yeah, Kane. I have everything I need right here." Her hand gives my thigh a squeeze, and I know she isn't talking about the three overflowing suitcases in the back of the SUV.

"Yeah, baby, likewise."

The rest of our ride is silent, and when we pull into the private airstrip, Willow climbs out and looks at the jet in awe. I should have known she wouldn't assume we would be flying privately, but it didn't even cross my mind. I'm starting to see my world in a new light. An excited infectiousness that has me looking forward to introducing her to much more.

We make small talk with my pilot, William. Usually, I would have had an attendant fly with me, but I wanted to have this time alone with Willow. Anything that we need, I can take care of myself. Cam, wearing many hats as usual, will be co-piloting during our trip home.

Willow climbs up the stairs and into the cabin of my plane, looking around with wide eyes. "This is yours?"

I nod. "Well, it's Kane Entertainment property, but yes, it's mine."

"Holy crap." She sighs.

I laugh and show her around the interior. There really isn't much. My other plane is larger, but when it's just me, I like to do my part in making my carbon footprint at least a little smaller.

There are two leather seats on either side of a small table against one wall, a couch on the other, and a refrigerated cooler against the back wall that holds wine, small snacks when stocked, and a handful of liquors.

"What's through there?" Willow asks with her hand pointing toward the rear of the plane.

I feel like the hunter stalking his prey when I move toward her without answering. Judging on how her brown eyes darken, she has a pretty good idea of what's behind that door.

"Let me show you." My voice sounds raspy to my ears, and I can feel the slight tremors of unsteady nerves running through my body.

I need her.

My body needs her.

Fuck.

Taking hold of her hand, I open the door that leads to the bedroom, walking past the small bathroom off this hallway. Since this is my private jet and not one I use for entertainment purposes, it's designed so I can rest between locations, but I also made sure I would be able to freshen up when needed. The seating area and bathroom being minimal, but back here it is pure luxury.

"Holy crap." She repeats her earlier shock.

"I think you said that already." I laugh.

"Yeah, well, excuse me for not being able to express in words how stunning this is. I never knew they even made aircrafts like this." She moves into the room and spins slowly around. "Kane, this is bigger than my old bedroom."

"It is not." She looks at me in shock, and I laugh harder. "It just looks bigger. It's the windows."

She turns around again, moving in a slow circle and looking over every inch. I wasn't lying, the windows do make it appear to be a larger space than it is, and the bed is just a double, so it gives the illusion of unlimited space. Just a bed, two leather chairs on either side of the door we just walked through, and both sides of the jet designed with windows that span the length of the room.

"It's beautiful." She sighs, her voice holding a dreamy tone.

Not taking my eyes off her, I respond, "Stunning."

I get her attention, knowing damn well I'm not talking about a stupid fucking jet I could give away tomorrow without a second thought. What I'm looking at right now, *that* expression on her face—I would do anything to keep this carefree happiness in place.

"Come on. Let's go have a seat and maybe a glass of wine before we take off."

More like give me some time to calm the fuck down so I can wait long enough for us to get airborne and for me to get Willow in that bed.

I wasn't kidding earlier when I said how much I wanted to hear her begging me to fuck her. It's going to happen. Soon.

It takes longer than normal for William and Cam to get up on the runway. Willow is all smiles as she relaxes in the living area; her face is pressed close to the window and she wears an open look of eagerness as we take off and leave New York behind. I can't tell if she's excited to be in my jet, if it's flying in general, or if the day's events are allowing her to move on carefree toward the future.

Or maybe she knows I'm about to come in my pants just watching her chest move with every breath she takes.

I bite back the groan that almost slips out when we hit a pocket of air and jolt slightly. The movement shifts my hips and pulls my pants tighter against my straining erection.

Fuck.

Lifting my glass, I take a slow pull of the bourbon, the burn down my throat just intensifying the one that had been blazing through my veins.

I crave her.

And I'm happily drowning in my obsession to own every part of her. All her smiles, laughs, moans, and screams.

"Are you okay?"

I open my eyes and look toward Willow. I hadn't realized I was clenching my lids tightly closed until Willow's voice broke through my thoughts.

"Kane?" she adds when I don't answer her. I continue to let my eyes roam over her face before I drift my gaze down. Her ample chest makes my mouth water, and I move to place my drink down when I feel my grasp tighten around the glass.

"Kane?" This time, her voice isn't inquisitive but worried. "Honey, are you okay? Do you not like flying?"

I shake my head. "I love flying." Rough air rushes out with my words.

"Then what's wrong?"

"Thank fucking Christ," I mumble when I look out the window and see clouds in every visible direction. I release the latch on my seat belt instantly and then stand, move around the table, and brace myself with a hand on each of Willow's armrests. My mouth crashes to hers, and her gasp gives me the opening I need to dip my tongue in and taste her.

The second my tongue licks against hers, she moans in my mouth. Her hands push into my hair and pull me closer. I don't waste a second freeing her from her belt before I grab hold of her hips and lift her into my arms. Our mouths stay fused as I walk toward the back of the plane. Her fingers alternating between running through my hair and gripping the strands tightly when she wants more of my mouth.

"I'm about to lose my fucking mind," I moan, pressing my hips against hers when I lower her back to the mattress. "All I can think of is hearing you beg me to fuck you. Beg me to take you. Scream my name when you come, begging me to keep fucking you. I'm going mad with the visions of the tits that have been teasing me all day bouncing in my face when you ride me. *Fuck*," I shout when her fingers scrape down my torso with enough pressure that, if I wasn't wearing a shirt, I know I would have red lines against my flesh.

"You want me to fuck you?" I ask, my teeth nipping at her neck and down her chest to the skin just above each swell of her breasts.

I feel the movement of her nod and smile against her skin. "Oh no, words only, Willow. You tell me what you want, and only then will I give it to you. But I promise you won't get my cock until I hear that word that's been driving me insane since we left Logan. Not one inch will you feel until you. Beg. Me."

"Oh, God. Please don't stop," she pleads with her hips thrusting and rolling up from the bed, pressing roughly against my own.

I lean up, my hands on either side of her hips, and I grab her roughly. She gasps at the force with which I'm holding her before a long moan slips through her swollen lips.

"Yes," she cries. "Please."

"Tell me," I command.

"Touch me." Her already blushing cheeks redden more.

I give her a smirk full of promise, but nothing more. I hold her body from moving against mine and continue to drive her to the same point of insanity as my need has filled me.

"Not good enough, Willow."

Her head moves against the mattress. I deny the friction she is desperate for even as I press myself harder against her.

"Please, Kane. I need you."

"You need me to what?" I rasp. Fuck, if I don't get inside of her soon, I'm going to come in my pants. I can feel her heat through both of our pants and the thin material of her top isn't doing shit to hide her erect nipples from me. I know what's under that top—the sinful lace that cups each of her heavy tits.

Licking my lips, I let go of her hips and slowly bring my hands to glide up her stomach. She used to flinch when I would touch her stomach, and it killed me each time, but now she doesn't even so much as blink. Every time I see how far she's come—from the woman who hated her body to this temptress in my hands now—pride as I've never known fills me.

"Yes," she moans. I shake my head and wait. Her expression flashes, and for a split second, I can see a spark of anger. Oh no, there is no place for that shit. She's mad that I'm pushing her, but not for long.

My hands grab each of her breasts, and I take the firm grasp I know she loves before letting go and removing my touch.

"Kane!" she snaps.

"Words, Willow. Give them to me and I'll give you whatever you want."

"Grab me, hard again," she begs, and I instantly comply.

My hands back on the tits I love, and I give her exactly what she wants. It doesn't take long before she's writhing and moaning my name. Knowing her tits are so sensitive she could come just from me playing for a few minutes, I regretfully let go. She starts to protest, but I take hold of her shoulders and lift her to sit on the edge. Her legs still spread, my hips planted firmly against her, and I help her remove the jacket before the top and bra are flying over my shoulder.

She leans back, her palms hitting the mattress and those fucking perfect tits begging for my mouth. She knows I love cupping the heavy mounds in my hand, rolling her nipple under my tongue and between my teeth. Yeah, I'm pretty sure with her arrogant expression, she knows just how badly I want her.

"Lick me," she commands in a voice that is calm despite the fact her breathing is coming so rapidly that her chest is shaking.

Fucking hell. She's so close. So close to the point where her desire for what I can give her takes over and her inhibitions disappear.

"Where?" I rasp, my head already moving toward the tits that tempt me.

"My … pussy," she whispers in a breathy voice with just the slightest hint of embarrassment.

The noise that comes from my throat makes her jump. A low groan that sounds almost animalistic.

"Fuck, baby." I continue toward the tit I was about to run my tongue over and bite her nipple with just enough pressure to make her cry out. "You have no clue what it does to me when I hear you tell me what to do. Where your body needs me. God, I've never been this hard. Touch your tits, baby. Keep your hands there and your fingers on your nipples. Let me see you."

"Oh, God," she moans, but instead of denying my command, she lies back and slowly cups herself and does just what I said.

Her cries fill the room as I work to remove the rest of her clothing. Her shoes, even though I would love to feel the bite of those heels on my back, go first. Her pants and panties are next. When I step back from the mattress, she is so lost in the pleasure she is giving herself that she doesn't notice until my shirt is off and my pants hit the ground with the jingle of my belt against the unforgiving flooring.

I stand there, harder than fucking hell, and palm my cock as her hands continue to roll each of her nipples. Her eyes widen, and her mouth drops open.

We continue to watch each other, but when it becomes too much for me, I drop to my knees and give her what she asked. My tongue swirls around her clit before I lick down the wetness and then push it inside her pussy. Her scream is shrill, and I look up her body to see her back bowed off the mattress.

Lifting one hand, I press down on her hips to keep her from bucking me off her delicious fucking pussy. My other hand continues to slowly stroke my aching cock, each time my thumb grazes over the tip I let out a hum against her that has her jerking each time.

Each press and lick against her clit has her crying out even louder until I'm sure she's just seconds away from one hell of a climax.

Then I deny her my mouth.

"Kane. God, Kane! Don't stop. Please don't stop!"

Leaning back, I lick my lips before I wipe the wetness from my mouth with the back of my hand. My eyes hold hers, and I wait for her to realize that I won't give her what she wants—what I crave—until she uses the words.

"I need you inside me," she moans, her hands still pinching her nipples, eyes begging.

Not good enough.

I shake my head, and she whimpers.

"Please, Kane. I need you."

I shake my head again, standing from the floor and reaching for the condoms I had stuffed in my jeans earlier.

"Kane, oh God, please."

"Give me the words." My command has her shaking her head slowly. "Beg. Me. To. Fuck. You." With each word I demand, her shaking intensifies. "Beg me to fuck you with the cock I know you want. Say it."

"Kane … please." She gulps when I finish rolling on the condom, and I move to press the tip of my cock against her opening. "Please fuck me," she whispers.

That word.

A word I've never heard from her lips before today, but one that has haunted my fantasies from that very second.

My cock is deep inside her before she even finished asking, and her whisper turns into a loud cry as her body stretches around mine.

I lean over her and take my time with my mouth on her tits. Each thrust of my hips matches with a deep pull of my mouth around her nipple. I take her body harder when her pleas for more hit my ears. Our skin slaps together with each movement.

"Fuck," I moan into her shoulder when the pleasure almost becomes too much. "So tight."

Her legs tighten around me, and I feel her nails in my back just when her pussy clamps tight on my cock. Lifting up, I look into her eyes as she climbs higher and higher. My own climax is just a few thrusts away, but not until I watch her come.

"I love you," she whispers then rolls her head back and moans a long, deep sound that melts into a high scream as she comes. I can't take my eyes off the beauty of it. In the middle of her scream, her hands grab her tits and her hips jolt against my thrusting as her orgasm seems to roll right into another.

"Fuck!" I shout, my head dropping to her shoulder. I fight to keep my weight from falling heavily on top of her as my own body comes so hard it steals the air from my lungs. "I love you, too, baby," I tell her, my voice hoarse and sore from the forceful shout.

When I finally am able to pull myself out of her body, feeling like it had been hours but knowing it was more like seconds, I look down to see one hell of a sated smile on her sleeping face.

Not wanting to disturb her, I make quick work of cleaning myself up and grab one of the extra blankets we keep onboard. I hate covering her body from my eyes, but I know she's had an emotionally hard day, and after how hard she just took me, she's worn the hell out.

I grab my jeans and pull them on before walking back to the living room area, grabbing my phone and forgotten bourbon before settling down on the couch. But the first message I see stops the glass from ever hitting my lips.

My publicist, Trace, had sent fifteen texts. All of them demanding to know why I wasn't picking up. But the last one is the only one I can focus on. I ignore his words and click the link.

Where's Mia? Meet Kane Masters' new play toy.

Fuck!

God-fucking-dammit. I knew it would turn into something like this when the media found out about us. I didn't lie when I told Willow that I did not intend to hide our relationship, but until recently, I knew she wasn't ready for the shit show that is sure to follow this news. Not only that but, as a fiercely private person, I hate seeing my personal life out there for all to rip apart with their lies. It's so hard to have anything for myself that I perversely loved I was able to keep Willow to myself for so long.

And now … now, we're outed as a couple—no, a goddamn fucking plaything—and all that privacy is going to fly out the window.

Fuck!

Worst of all, Willow has no idea just how bad it is going to get with the media. Not until I tell her everything. Everything I can't even tell her yet because I gave my fucking word.

Ignoring Trace, I pull up Mia's text screen.

Kane: We need to talk. I have to tell her, Mia. I know I promised you I wouldn't say anything, and at the time, I agreed it was best but not anymore. I won't lose her because of this.

Dropping my head back, I say a silent prayer that everything is going to work out and Willow won't leave me for keeping Mia's baby secret from her.

CHAPTER
THIRTY-ONE

WILLOW

I WOKE UP FROM ONE OF the deepest sleeps I had ever experienced when Kane came to gently let me know we would be landing soon and I needed to come and get my seatbelt on.

It took me a little while to shake the tiredness from my system. I'm sure a little of that had to do with Kane keeping me up for the last few nights, but I know emotionally today was just tiring.

"Hey," I tell Kane and press a light kiss to his lips before taking the seat on the other side of the table.

He looks up from his iPad and gives me a smile.

"Are you okay?" I question, cocking my head to the side and studying his expression.

His eyes flash, and I know, regardless of what he says, something is bothering him.

"I'm fine. I just have some things on my mind."

"Ohhhhhkay. And you don't feel like you can talk to me about those things?"

He places his iPad down and leans forward, reaching out and folding his hands over mine. "It's not that, Willow. I just wanted to be able to talk to you when we weren't rushed for time. When I can explain things without having to stop." He sighs. "I didn't want to worry you."

My skin flashes cold, and a little seed of dread starts to burrow in my gut. What on earth could have happened during the time we've been in that air that has him needing to explain things to me? Or better yet, what would make me have cause for worry?

And then, the cold flushes through me again when I realize what he could mean. Or more importantly, why he's worried about me.

"They found out about our relationship?"

He nods, his expression darkening.

"And that bothers you?" I continue, trying to field my way through the many things that could be wrong here. I'm not sure how I feel about him being bothered by our relationship becoming common knowledge now that we're being faced with it. He had assured me he wasn't ashamed or hiding our relationship, and I believed him. I know he's immensely private and not broadcasting us is a lot different from intentionally hiding it.

"That the media knows about our relationship? No. But I know how they work, Willow. They take a grain of truth, a sliver of the privacy I value, and splatter it with whatever lies they can in order to make their money. The truth doesn't pad their pockets, not when it doesn't hold anything sordid."

I lean back in my seat, my hands falling from his hold. Even though I didn't intentionally pull away from him, I can see the hurt in his eyes.

"What are they saying?"

He shakes his head, his shoulders dropping with a loud sigh. "The normal things. Speculating about how serious we are, where we meet, and who the woman in my life is."

I reach out to take his iPad from the table to see for myself what is being said, but when he notices my intent, he reaches out and grabs it from my grasp. The swiftness in his movements causes me to snap my hand back as if he had physically slapped it. That little seed of dread starting to sprout.

"Promise me, Willow, that you will just let me take care of this. Let's get to my house and we can sit down, but I don't want you to fill you head with that garbage until we can talk. We need to plan on how we want to address the media with our relationship officially and not just with hypothetical talk about what would happen if they found out. They know, and even though I would normally never address my private life with them, you know how I feel about hiding you. I won't do it. I just need you to let me explain a few things before we decide what to do."

"Why do I get the impression that there is more going on right now than you're telling me?"

He unbuckles and kneels down in front of me. "I love you, Willow. Trust in that and trust in me. You know there are things I haven't told you, but I haven't kept them from you for any other reason than I had made a promise to someone that I wouldn't talk about it."

"Not even to me," I add. I'm not mad about that. I know how important his word is to him, his integrity that his trust is worth something more than just a word. But it still unsettles me. That being said, I think it would be more unsettling if he had no issues breaking the trust he had asked someone to have in him when our relationship started out with me blindly giving him my trust.

"I'm sorry, baby. When I gave my word, it was before I ever imagined what we have would become a reality. The love we have is the best kind of unexpected, and you have to know how much I hate keeping this from you. I'm telling you, with absolute honesty, that I will tell you everything, but I have to do that without breaking my word. There are too many people who can get hurt, and I refuse to let you be one of them."

Taking a deep pull of air, I nod. "Okay, Kane. I trust you, and I know you wouldn't keep secrets from me that would hurt me. Before we leave this spot, though, I'm going to ask something of you that I had when we first started this. Please don't make me regret giving you my trust, Kane. I love you more than you'll ever know, but if you're keeping something from me that affects our lives, I deserve to know."

His jaw works, clenched in frustration, and he runs one hand through his thick hair. "I promise that it isn't anything that will affect us and our lives directly, regardless of what the media is saying."

The air between us ripples with uneasiness. I can see it in his eyes, the love that he has for me, but I also see the apprehension and worry written over his features.

"We're in this together, Kane. Just don't shut me out."

He sighs; one of acceptance and relief that I'm not fighting him on his request to let this be until we get back to his home. "I won't. Come on, love, let's go home."

Despite the uneasy feeling I had while we were landing, the ride to Kane's Malibu beach house was lovely. William had landed in a small, private airstrip just outside of Santa Monica that Kane owned. A Range Rover similar to the one we had been driving around in while in Georgia and New York was waiting for us, and after Cam and Kane had transferred over our luggage, we began the drive.

Kane pointed out different locations as we drove, and his hand was always in contact with my body somehow; as if he was worried that I would disappear if he didn't physically know I was with him. The conversation wasn't forced and neither was his affection.

I wasn't nervous about what was to come. I know that Kane is honorable in his trust and he isn't trying to hurt me. It's just the opposite; he's looking out for me and us. I can't be mad about that.

I settle into the soft leather under me and rest my head on his shoulder, my hand settling on his hard thigh, and I enjoy the ride. There's no need to consume myself with negativity.

It has no place today, the day we begin our lives together.

I must have dozed off because the next thing I hear is Kane cursing next to me.

"What?" I gasp and jerk to sit up, looking around us. Dusk had settled around us, the darkness of night starting to claw its way free, but the only thing I see is a brightly lit home, a few cars, and a whole lot of nothing.

Kane's house is set away from the beach. He had told me that in order to maintain his privacy, he had bought land that was high above the jutting rocks of one little butted-out piece of land. Enough area was fenced off between the cliff and trees; we were almost on a little island of our own.

He had also explained that he has enough security to give the White House a run for its money. So for the life of me, I can't understand what would have set him off. The expression on his face coupled with the curses that woke me had me expecting to wake with cameras and reporters in our face.

"We have company," he says through a clenched jaw.

"Company?"

"My family. All of them judging by the cars."

He points to his right, and I lean forward to look around his body.

"Okay? And that's a bad thing? I thought you were excited to see your parents."

I had spoken with Christian and Rebecca Masters a few times in the last few weeks and nothing in those conversations gave me the impression I should be worried about meeting them for the first time.

His father, just like Kane, has no problem expressing himself, and he's told me each time we've spoken how happy he is that his son is so happy. He's the father I had always wished I had. Open, affectionate, and supportive.

His mother was hilarious. She opened her heart and let me in as if I was one of her own. I knew from our last phone call that she was looking forward to meeting me as well.

So seeing Kane upset over his family being here is very unlike him.

"Kane? Why is this bad?"

He sighs, frustration and anger coming forward. "Fuck!" His outburst makes me jump, and he turns to me and offers his apologies. "Shit, I'm sorry. I'm not mad they're here ... well, most of them. I'm not upset that they finally get to meet the woman I love, even if I wish we had some time to ourselves. When I said they're all here, I meant *all* of my family, Willow."

"Your brothers?" He nods.

"Kyle?" Again, he gives me a nod. Well, that certainly explains things. I know he's close with his brother Kole, but he's made no secret that things with Kyle are strained. He didn't explain in detail. I could tell it wasn't something he liked to talk about, so I didn't push.

"I haven't seen him in almost five months, Willow. I have no idea why he's here other than the fact he's trying to play some part of good older brother to my parents, who as far as I know are blissfully unaware that their sons hate each other."

I scoot over and wrap my arms around him. "Then let's go in there and just ignore him."

His eyes hold mine, and he looks as if he is about to say something, but when he hears a high-pitched feminine call, his attention moves from me toward his front door.

I knew from seeing his mother accompany him one year to the Oscars that she was a beautiful woman. Kane favored his mother in looks. He had her same dark brown hair, blue eyes, and thick lips. But that was all he got from his mother. She was what I pictured when I thought of the quintessential mother figure. She was short, plump, and smiled in a way that almost looked unnatural. The love she had shone through her every movement. And right now, that love was rushing down the four stairs that led up to his front porch and right to the car parked in the front circle.

"My baby boy," she yells before pulling the door open. "Get out here and give me some love! It's been too long, and you've neglected your mother long enough."

He laughs against my body and slides out of the backseat, pulling me with him when he grabs my hand. I look up and see Cam laughing at Kane's mother as she bounces up and down on her feet waiting for her son to give her a hug, her arms wide and her expression full of excitement.

"Hey, Mom," he mumbles, letting go of my hand and bending down to wrap his arms around her.

"Oh, my big baby boy. Stop denying me the happiness of these hugs and come home more often."

Kane laughs and tries to pull back but fails when she refuses to let him go.

My own laughter joins Cam when I watch Kane pick his mother up off her feet. Her smile brightens, and he laughs even harder. Her feet dangling in the air as her 'baby boy' gives his mother the love she's been missing.

"Jesus, Becca! Let the man breathe," a deep voice laughs from the doorway.

I look over at the man I assume is Kane's father. He's just as tall, if not a little taller than Kane. And this would be where Kane got every other one of his striking features. Strong jaw, chiseled cheeks, thick brows, and that one dimple. They have the same powerful build. Impossibly thick muscles—the kind that shows they work hard to stay fit without turning into hulks—trim hips, and long legs.

"Isn't he handsome." Kane's mother laughs, and I look over from his father to see that he was no longer embracing her. She was now standing right in front of me with her beaming smile in place and this time directed at me.

I look from her to her son, now walking toward his father, and then back, nodding my head as my own beaming smile forms.

She throws her head back and laughs loud and long, pulling me to her in a hug that almost hurts. "Oh, I've been looking forward to meeting you, honey. I can't tell you how much I have been. I just knew you would be perfect."

Her words hit me, harder than her hug, and I feel myself getting slightly emotional. "It's great to finally meet you, Mrs. Masters."

"None of that, dear. Call me Becca … or Mom. Whatever works for you. No place for formalities with family."

Family.

God, she has no idea how much that means to me. I look up and meet Kane's eyes. He gives me a look full of love, and I give him a big toothy smile, relieved to see his mood has lifted when he returns it.

"Let's get inside and get you settled in. Kane told me you would be staying in the guesthouse, so I made sure the fridge was well stocked. Kole made sure that the sheets were changed, fresh, and dust-mite free since no one ever stays there."

Kane laughs at his mother's words as we walk through the doorway and into his home. "You made Kole do housework?"

"Well, who else was going to do it, young man? He knows better than to question his mother."

"More like I'm afraid of her when she's got a wooden spoon in her hand. That shit hurts."

"Kole Henry Masters! You watch that mouth of yours." Turning to me, she continues, "These boys seem to think that cussing makes them some big bad man, but I tried to teach them that it only makes them look too stupid to find a word worth expressing their feelings."

"Being that Willow doesn't curse, I believe you'll have an ally in that fight to clean us up, Mom." Kane laughs and I reach out playfully to slap his shoulder.

His brother walks toward the group, and he and Kane do that manly hand slap, body bump thing, and then he turns all of his attention to me.

"Well, well, if it isn't the woman who stole my baby brother's heart. Kole." He smiles while addressing me and holds his hand out. My eyes go wide, and I look from his offered hand to his face a few times, feeling my mouth drop with each repeated journey of my eyes.

"Willow?" Kane chuckles, and I feel my face heat.

"Sorry." I take his hand and give him a shake. "Willow, nice to meet you. I'm a huge fan."

"Seriously?" He looks over at Kane, and he winks. "Did she tell you she was a huge fan of yours too?"

I don't need to look at Kane to know he's shaking his head and probably struggling not to burst out laughing.

"Can't say she did. Guess you must be better at acting than I am," he surmises, hilarity mixing with the sultry roughness of his voice.

"I did too," I defend and look over at Kane. "I think?"

"No, baby, you didn't. That's okay. You just want me for my

good looks." He winks.

"Oh, you're impossible." I giggle and Kane reaches out to pull me to his body and away from his charming brother. "It's nice to meet you, Kole. Sorry about that. Well, maybe just a little sorry."

"Would you two stop picking on her," his mother interrupts with a laugh of her own. "My boys, talented and too good looking for their own good. They would probably make a nun lose her mind too. Too much hot male vibes and all."

"Mom, I'm not sure you should admit that about your own kids." Kole laughs.

Her eyes narrow playfully, and Kole holds his hands up in surrender. "Just because I'm your mother doesn't mean I can't appreciate how good looking my guys are."

We're all laughing as Kane's arm goes around my shoulders, and we follow his family as they lead the way deeper into his house. The front entryway didn't allow the view that I have now. Windows cover the whole back of his home. I'm sure when the sun is blazing, it gives you the most spectacular view of the Pacific.

A staircase to the right of the living room leads to a second floor. To the left of the open-floor plan is a large kitchen and dining area. The whole house is white walls, lots of glass, and deep gray and black accents. Instead of looking like a sterile bachelor pad, Kane's home holds warms despite its design to do the opposite. Family photos, old worn leather couch and loveseat, and quilts. I shouldn't have expected it to be different. Just like the man himself, his home makes you feel like you're welcome and invites you in a way that wraps around you like a physical touch.

I look up at Kane with a smile, but he's not looking at me. His focus is over my head and toward the kitchen.

Looking back in that direction, I see what I missed before.

The narrow, judgmental, and very angry eyes of Kyle Masters.

CHAPTER
THIRTY-TWO

WILLOW

INTRODUCTIONS TO KYLE WERE AS far opposite as it could get from the open friendliness I had gotten from Kole. The three Masters brothers look so alike that they might as well have been triplets. All had the same wavy, thick hair, dark in certain lights to give it a black appearance. With Kane and Kole, it was left to its own devices, usually a mess from many passes of their hands. It gave them a carefree look to their overall strong appearance of sharp angles and rough handsomeness. But Kyle's was styled with so much product that he not only tamed those waves, he also made his own appearance lose any trace of the relaxed and happy-go-lucky ease his younger brothers had.

All three had the bluest of blue eyes, something I now know they get from their father. But unlike the two younger Masters boys, Kyle's were hard, calculating, and so full of hate that you almost felt burned when his attention was on you.

There was no doubt in my mind that Kyle Masters was a troubled man.

He had spoken once in the two hours since we had arrived. And all it did was make the mood even darker. I had thought it was a simple question when Kane asked him why he was there, but when he ominously replied with a confusing 'you know why,' things just started to speed downhill quickly. Becca had gone overboard to try to defuse the intensity between her sons, but it only made things more awkward when Kyle refused to take the high road and respond to his mother if it had to do with Kane.

But, to my shock, the heated madness Kyle was showing his brother was nothing compared to the disgust he openly had with my presence. Something I couldn't for the life of me understand. I had never met this man. As far as I knew, he really shouldn't know anything about me since he and his brother weren't exactly on friendly terms. But regardless, he wasn't trying to hide his feelings, and it only made things more awkward.

Kane seemed to be seconds from snapping. His parents were attempting to keep things from turning into a war between the boys. Kole seemed just as uneasy as I did, but he did a better job of hiding it. Instead of silence, he attempted to placate the heavy mood with jokes, but they all fell flat.

"Kyle, dear, where is Jessica tonight?" his mother asks in an effort to pull her oldest son's sneer away from me.

My attention, however, is pulled from Kyle when I hear Kane bark back a laugh that holds absolutely no humor. His hand, which had been holding mine firmly but softly, tightens when Kyle looks over and they both lock heated, angry, matching blue eyes together.

Oh, boy.

If things had been awkward before, then they're painfully so now.

Kyle never answers, but he does take another healthy swallow of whatever dark brown liquor he had been keeping his glass full with for the last two hours. Actually, probably for a lot longer than that given the way his body keeps swaying to the side before he catches himself.

"Well, look at the time," Kane's father exclaims and makes the effort to yawn loudly. "Bec, honey, I think it's time that we head out."

"Great idea, honey," she whispers, and I notice just how much of a toll her son's behavior has had on her. The exuberant happiness that she had just hours before is now completely gone. Worry lines hold her expression captive as she takes the plates from in front of her and her husband. Christian takes the rest and follows his wife to the kitchen.

"Let's go, Kyle," Kole snaps and grabs his brother's arm.

"Don't fucking touch me," he seethes, jerking his arm free and almost falling to the ground in his inebriated state.

"Jesus Christ, Kyle. This is a new fucking low, even for you." Kane exhales and stands from the table.

Kyle opens his mouth; I'm sure to spew more nastiness, but stops when his parents return. His mother gives Kane another long hug before his father does the same. I let out a sigh of relief when Kyle moves to follow them out. I know there were three other cars in the drive when we arrived, but I'm assuming that with how drunk Kyle has become, he's going to be leaving with their parents or Kole.

"I'll call you tomorrow," Kane tells Kole as they say good-bye.

I get hugs from both his parents as well before we follow them out, smiling despite my unease as they make their exit and drive off. Just when Kole is about to tell me good-bye, Kyle finally speaks, obviously having waited for his parents to leave before he makes his move.

"How does is your new *plaything* feel about Mia and the baby, Kane," he slurs and steps closer to me. The blood drains from my face with his words, and my heart falls to my feet when Kane lets out a curse. "Oh, let me guess. You haven't told her about the baby yet," Kyle continues with an evil laugh, the sound so sinister to my ears that I shiver. "Guess you missed all the tabloid reports about how his affair is the reason Mia's pregnancy has been so touch and go with the stress. Tell me, how will you feel if she loses the much anticipated Post/Masters baby?"

"You son of a bitch," Kane bellows, and I jump at the furious sound I had never heard from him.

"Shit," Kole spits out and grabs me just as Kane lunges for his brother.

"You shut your fucking mouth, Kyle," Kane yells at his brother, slamming him against the side of his house with his hand clenched tight against his throat. "You, of all people, know just how fucked-up your behavior is!"

Kyle's eyes narrow and he shoves back at his brother, dislodging his hold. "Do I, Kane? Who was the fucked-up one who hasn't seen Mia in almost two months, huh? Have you been there for her once since the first doctor's appointment?"

"You have no right, Kyle. No fucking right to question where I've been."

Kyle turns his head, letting his heated ire focus on me as I tremble in Kole's arms. "Yeah, guess you're right since I can see just where you've been while Mia's been all alone."

"Motherfucker," Kane grunts, and his fist flies out to connect with his brother's face. The impact snaps Kyle's head back and added to how drunk he is, he falls in an unconscious heap in the middle of Kane's driveway.

I can't bring myself to look at Kane. Even though I can feel the heat of his stare on me, my eyes stay on Kyle's prone form. Kole doesn't loosen his hold on me. His arms stay looped around my upper body, holding me captive with my back to his front.

We stand there, silence thickening, until Kyle's words finally register completely, the force like a tidal wave. A sob pushes from my shocked body so violently that I almost fall from Kole's arms. My eyes finally move to where Kane is standing, his face the mask of pure agony as his rapid breathing heaves his chest.

He moves to walk toward me, but I hold my hand up to halt him. "No."

"Willow, please." He attempts to reach me again, but I push against Kole and force him to move with me as I step away.

"Do not come any closer."

Kane's whole body slumps as his desperation becomes paramount to the madness that had just been brewing.

"Do you deny his words?" I ask, pointing at where Kyle is still out cold.

"It's not that simple, baby," he responds, despondently.

"Then explain it to me," I demand, proud that my voice sounds a lot stronger than I feel right now. "Explain your relationship with Mia Post and your role in her child's life. Do it now, Kane. No more hiding."

"I can't," he weakly answers.

I nod and turn to Kole. "Can you please take me to a hotel," I ask, resolved in the knowledge that I can't stay if Kane isn't willing to tell me what I need to know. Not now. Not after his brother's admission. This isn't like him asking me to blindly trust in him with media lies. This came straight from his own family.

Kole looks past me and toward Kane. He doesn't speak, but when he looks back at me, he gives me a nod. Instantly, I feel relief that I'll be able to leave when I know I have nowhere to go.

"Willow. Fuck, don't leave." Kane reaches out and grabs my hand, but his arm falls to his side when I rip myself from his hold.

"Then tell me what I need to know."

His silence is all I need. I allow the tears that had been threatening to fall and look into the cerulean orbs that have never given me anything but love until today.

"Kole, can you grab my stuff?" I wait for him to walk back into the house. The connection I'm holding with Kane's gaze never wavers. When Kole is out of earshot, I continue speaking. "I deserve more than that, Kane. I'm not running. This isn't *me* running. This is me being strong enough to walk away even though I know it will hurt. This is me knowing that I'm worth everything and not just whatever you feel I'm allowed to know. And until you can give that to me, we have nothing left to say to each other."

"Willow," he begs, desperation making my name come out like a deep sob.

"No. You asked me to trust you, but you can't put that same trust in me. I get that your word means everything to you, but guess what, Kane? If you loved me, truly loved me, you would have found a way to be completely open and honest with me before the painful truth was allowed to scar me."

Kole walks back out of the house with two of my suitcases and my purse over his shoulder. He doesn't look at Kane, nor does he look at Kyle. He heads right over to me, and after asking me if I was sure, he takes me to his car and helps me fold into the passenger seat. He stuffs the suitcases in the trunk and makes his way to his side. The whole time, my eyes never leave Kane. I can see the pain in his whole demeanor. The connection that had always felt so strong between us pulls tightly against my own chest as the gravity of the situation hits me. My tears pick up speed as I let out a heaving cry.

It isn't until Kole has pulled his sleek sports car through Kane's gate that I allow my sobs to join the tears as I leave the only man who will ever hold my heart behind.

CHAPTER THIRTY-THREE

KANE

SO THIS IS WHAT IT feels like to have your heart ripped out of your chest and stomped on. A pain greater than I have ever experienced tears through my body with enough force that my chest feels like my heart has been pulled straight from it. Looking down at Kyle, I make myself pull him from the ground and drag his heavy as shit body inside the house.

I shouldn't care. I should be able to just leave him out in the elements and hope some wild animal tears him limb by limb. But despite his actions tonight, he's still my brother.

And part of the reason that I'm now standing here with a black fucking hole where my heart once was beating.

I stomp through the house, leaving Kyle passed out on the floor just inside the front door. I might not have left him outside, but I'll be goddamned if I'm going to go out of my way to make sure he's comfortable.

I should call his fucking wife and make her come get him, but I know from Kole that Jessica is in Europe for some photo shoot.

"Fuck!" My hand flies out with my outburst, and I slam it into the wall just inside my living room. The sheetrock gives way and my fist leaves a hole in my dark gray wall.

She said she wasn't running, but she left. What the fuck am I supposed to do with that? Not that I should expect any differently. She gave me the chance to explain and because of my pride, I didn't. All because of a promise I made to Mia three months before I even started this with Willow. A promise made with good intentions because of how much was at stake not just for Mia, but for my family as well.

I kept my mouth shut and let the best thing I've ever held in my hands walk away.

Fuck.

My footsteps thunder through the house as I retrace my steps since arriving home, and search for my cell. I had dropped it shortly after walking through the door, forgetting about the device instantly. Until right now. I note the time, just past eleven, before I press what I need and bring the phone to my ear.

"I hope you know what time it is," the tired voice says in greeting.

"I do. I also know that I just watched my fucking girlfriend leave with Kole while I stood there like a mute bastard and let my promise of silence, *to you*, rip our hearts to fucking shreds, Mia."

"Shit," she mumbles. I hear the sheets rustle. "I'll be right there."

Even though I'm so pissed at her right now, I can't allow her to put herself in danger. "No. I don't know what the media situation is like at my front gate and you don't need the stress of dealing with Kyle, who I should add I knocked unconscious when he was feeling the need to let it all hang out earlier. I just … fuck, Mia. I have to tell her. I know I gave you my word because not only was it no one's fucking business, but that's my blood growing inside of you and I had no problem keeping silent to protect the both of you. But now, I can't lose her forever because of this."

Mia sighs, and I know she's feeling bad about asking me for silence months ago. Making me promise while she sobbed in my arms, the positive pregnancy test clutched in my shocked hands. The same way I know it kills her that the media has been rabid for us to confirm the pregnancy to them, to solidify the rumors that they had spread about the life she is growing and my part in it.

"You know she deserves to know. I love you, Mees, but if I keep silent, not only will I lose her, but I'm going to lose myself as well. She's it for me, and I should have had this conversation with you weeks ago when I realized that Willow would never be going anywhere. I tried, but you've been avoiding the subject just as hard as I've been trying to talk about it. Any time I tried to bring it up, you pushed and refused. I should have tried harder, I know that, and I now have to live with the consequences. Look, I know it's because you're scared of what will happen when I tell her, but you know me and I wouldn't be asking you to put your faith in her if I didn't believe with everything that I am that she's strong enough to weather the storm."

Her heavy breathing comes through the line, and I wait for her to accept what I'm asking. "I know you trust her. The little I've gotten to know her tells me she can be trusted too, but Kane …"

"Listen to me, Mia. I know I'm asking a lot, but this secret is killing me. Can't you understand that?" I hear her muffled sobs, and I hate myself. "I'm asking you to allow me to break my word, Mia. Begging you. I'm not asking you to let me hold a fucking press conference and tell the world. I'm just asking you to let me have back the promise to stay silent long enough to tell the woman who I fucking hope to spend the rest of my goddamn life with the truth!"

I pace around the room, my chest tightening painfully with each second of Mia's silence. For the first time, I actually consider saying fuck it all and going back on my word regardless of what she says, but I know I never would. Even if that means I have to let the woman I love go. I felt the same fear for the last four weeks that I had been trying to get a hold of Mia when Willow wasn't around in order to have this conversation. I knew that the innocent life inside her needed to be protected from the pain that will undoubtedly come when the baby grows up and wonders why its mother allowed herself to fall pregnant by a man who would never love her like she deserved to be loved.

"Okay, Kane."

My shoulders slump as the relief of being let out of my vow hits.

"Do you need me to be there?"

"Mia," I start.

"No," she interrupts. "It wasn't and isn't fair for me to continue to demand so much from you when you've made it clear from the beginning how you felt about her. I should have given you the go-ahead to tell her weeks ago. Especially since I've talked to her myself, and I know she isn't going to do anything to hurt you … including letting this go past her. But I think it might be time to let it out, Kane. She might believe you, but the press is going to eat her alive without us confirming something."

Shit. She's right. Because of everything that had happened since we touched down in Santa Monica earlier, I hadn't even thought about the new rumors being added to the ones that had been simmering for a while.

Instead of them just speculating about Mia's and my relationship, whether the baby is or isn't mine, it's turned into a love triangle where Willow is the star villain.

"It's time, Kane. It's going to be okay. God, I'm so sorry," she sobs.

"Don't apologize. It's an impossible situation because we're in the spotlight, so no matter what, someone is going to lose. But it's not going to be you. It won't be Willow or me. And it won't be the baby. Let me call Kole and find out where she is. I'll talk to her and then we can figure out what to do."

"No, I'm coming over. She needs to hear it from you, but I also need to explain to her why I allowed this to happen. You aren't the only one at fault for it."

"Yeah." I laugh bitterly. "And neither are you."

When I hang up, I don't feel any lighter knowing that I can freely break my word to Mia and tell Willow what I had been holding back. If anything, I feel even more trepidation because I know if we can't figure out what to do about the media, the baby will be the least of my worries when it comes to repairing things with Willow.

CHAPTER THIRTY-FOUR

WILLOW

WALKING AWAY FROM KANE WHEN he was obviously hurting was almost impossible. I know that the old Willow would have just rolled over and let his excuses and secrets stay his own, but not now. I know without a doubt, just because of the fact I was able to walk away from him, that I'm no longer allowing my fears to rule me. I deserve more, from him and for me.

The part I'm struggling with, the one slowly chipping away at my resolve to stay strong, is the very real fear that when I left, it might be forever. I don't doubt that he will find me, try and bring me back, but right now, I have no idea how I would be able to move forward with him when doing so is going to put me in a position that I'm terrified to be in.

I wrap my arms around myself, turn from the window I had been blindly looking out of, and move to the bed. I've spent the last hour or so locked away with my thoughts. Kole had kept silent during our drive, but he let me know in no uncertain terms that he would not allow me to go to a hotel. He's given me my space since arriving at his house, but I'm not sure how long that will last. Kole, like his brother, has too great of a protective instinct.

I knew Kane had been keeping something from me. Heck, he admitted it. But I let it go because I understood he planned to tell me and I assumed that he would once we arrived. I might not understand why he couldn't have just called Mia and taken care of this before we came, but I figured it had a lot to do with him worrying that I wouldn't be able to handle their secret.

That I would run.

And I basically proved him right.

No. You can't think like that, Willow. You left because you had to. You left because he wouldn't tell you even when faced with losing you. You left because you're stronger.

But am I?

Did leaving mean that I was strong or does that make me weak because I didn't want to face what was being thrown right in front of me. Or an even better question, if I'm able to forgive Kane and move forward, will I be strong enough to deal with what I can only guess will get worse before it gets better when it comes to the public perception of me—us—everything.

I knew that when our relationship was officially thrust into the spotlight, there would be many eyes on me. The fear of what they would think, the things they would say, and worst of all—the scorn that would come just by being with him … it had been at the forefront of my mind daily.

But I believed that together we would be able to get through it. I had no illusions that it wouldn't be without struggles, but I still believed. But I'm not just facing public scorn for being with Kane, taking him off the market, and what many will feel is with someone not worthy of him. Now, I fear it will all be so much worse because I haven't just stolen Kane's heart—according to his brother, I also stole him from Mia and their child.

God, just the thought of Mia and her baby—Kane's baby—makes my stomach churn.

Was Kyle right? Kane didn't deny it, but his actions went a long way in confirming. Can I stay with him knowing that just months ago, he was with Mia? Sure, maybe he was telling the truth when he told me that they didn't have a relationship, but what if they did at one point?

I had thought, until today, the hardest part of overcoming my old self would have been eradicating the ghosts that had haunted me. Pushing past the fear that ruled me. Letting go of the pain I had felt over losing my mom, accepting that what 'family' I had left would never be a true family, forgiving the ones that had played the part in dragging me to rock bottom, and most importantly, learning to love every part of me. That last one being the hardest, but with Kane's help, not only did I see myself in a new light, but also the constant anxiety I had been carrying around worrying about the judgment of others *had* disappeared completely.

But now I know that the hardest part of overcoming is going to be in believing in the strength I had just found. Now, forced to test the boundaries of that strength and faith in myself, I'm afraid I'm not going to win this time.

Because, like it or not, the key to unhooking the final chains that held me captive for so long is right in front of my face. I felt that key turn when I was able to leave Kane, recognizing that I deserved better than secrets.

"No time like the present, Willow," I mumble to myself and grab my phone. I feel those imaginary chains dig in and tighten around my chest, the fear getting thicker as I type Kane's name into my search browser.

When the screen fills with links, my stomach pitches and almost shoots out my mouth.

"Oh, God."

Kane leaves Mia alone, pregnant, and scared.
What's next for Mia and Kane?
Mia in danger of losing Kane's child.
Who is this mystery woman?
Mystery woman revealed!

The first few headlines don't cause me nearly as much anxiety as the last. I can confidently move past those because I know there is no way that they will hold anything other than speculation meant to sell papers. Kane wouldn't have kept the paternity of Mia's baby a secret from me and just verified them to the media. There's no way. It gives me a little peace that regardless of what those say, it's all just lies until I hear it from him.

I feel a little lighter with that realization, but just looking at that last link—the least damning of all of them—makes me feel seconds away from a panic attack.

I've been afraid of this. What the public thinks about me. And whether I'm strong enough to handle it.

Because I know that regardless of how big Kane's secret is

and what it means for our relationship, if I'm not able to hack it emotionally when everyone is judging me freely—then there is no point in even continuing.

If I can't be strong enough to handle their words, then I might as well be the Willow who Kane met two months ago. I have to prove to myself that it isn't him I'm hiding behind to avoid being strong for myself. In a way, I should be thanking Kyle for slapping me in the face with the truth. It's forced me to realize I have to be strong alone, with no one holding me up.

Hovering my thumb over the link to the widely popular tabloid blog, I hold my breath as the page loads.

The world was abuzz today when news hit that confirmed bachelor, Kane Masters, 35, was officially off the market. Of course, no one had been able to confirm that rumor until today. It was to everyone's shock that the award-winning actor is stepping out with someone other than his on-again, off-again love, Mia Post, 34.

Masters has recently been dodging the rumors that he and Post are about to be parents. Neither one of their reps would offer comments on the matter, but the pictures of them both seen leaving the woman's clinic to the stars, and the fact that Mia herself is very pregnant, I would imagine that official word wouldn't be far away for the pair.

Good God, the picture that follows shows Mia during a recent talk show appearance. She looked stunning, but it wasn't her flawlessness that held my attention; it was the very round, pregnant belly that even the baggy dress couldn't hide. The date under the picture puts it as just two weeks prior.

She looks to be five or six months pregnant, and if that's the case, then Kane wouldn't have been lying if he told me that they weren't together when we met, but that doesn't mean that they weren't together months before Kane and I met.

I sigh and continue the article. My anxiety is through the roof, and instead of holding my breath, it comes out in a whoosh when I read the next part.

However, all of those rumors seemed to vanish in one second when a source close to the Masters camp came forward and confirmed that he is most definitely in a relationship, just not with Mia Post.

Masters has been on location in Georgia for his film, Impenetrable. *This will be his first time in the director's seat and already there has been rumors that the film, due out this coming summer, will be the frontrunner for many Oscar noms. It's said that during his time down South, he met and began a relationship with Willow Tate, 29, of New York City.*

It's unclear what this means for Mia and her baby, but the insider close to the couple said that Masters and Tate couldn't keep their hands off each other during their recent trip to visit her stepfather, owner of the Logan Agency, one of the top modeling agencies in New York. The couple was pictured leaving New York from a private airstrip close to the city, headed to California to finish filming.

Chills hit me when I realize that this insider had to have been Dominic or Ivy. To link me with them and use me as a tool for publicity when they had never had use for me before. They turned a spotlight on Logan at the same time trying to hurt me by going to the media about my relationship with Kane. I handed them the ammunition from which they so clearly used for personal gain.

I should have seen that coming. Knowing they wouldn't just let me have the last word and that they wanted to strike back where it would hurt—by throwing me to the wolves and sharks that would do their dirty work for them.

I let the hand holding my phone fall on my lap and let the fact sink in that the family who has never wanted me used me in order to put their name out there. Kane had told me that Dominic would most likely lose Logan soon. I knew for myself that he had been struggling. The competitive market is too great for him to control, and his own riches starting to dwindle to nothing.

Picking up the phone, I reread the last section and smile when I realize they gravely miscalculated. I know they're trying to hurt me, but because the article doesn't even mention them past just a fleeting comment, I know their use was over. They were only named to give a little credibility to the source, but if they had planned better, they could have used me to breathe some life back into their dying sails.

It shouldn't feel as good as it does to know that they will fail in their aim to hurt me. And honestly, now that I'm faced with the reality they tried, I don't care.

I really don't care because I meant it when I said that by telling them I forgave them, I would be able to move on and they couldn't touch me anymore. I feel lighter as I continue to read.

They continue to speculate on the seriousness of Kane's 'new relationship,' but it's obvious they don't know much because, besides the grainy pictures of us, there are no real facts.

I return to my search page and thumb through a few more

articles. None of the other links giving any more information than the fact Kane has another woman in his life who isn't Mia Post.

And then I find the fan-driven page full of comments about Kane's new woman. Not all of them negative, but a great number comparing me to Mia. I skim through the comments and feel sick at the number of them that voice the same fears I had at the beginning of our relationship.

That I'm not worthy of him.

That he can do better.

And more comments than I can count comparing me, my body, and my looks to Mia.

Surprisingly, when I finish, there is no residual pain from seeing them rip into me. The fear that I wouldn't be strong enough to handle what the public had to say about me, the judgment that I had forever tried to avoid from others, means nothing. For once, I don't care what others think about me because if I've learned anything in the last two months, it's that the only opinion that matters is my own.

Those chains that had been keeping me from finally letting go of my past and growing into someone stronger snap the instant my phone is lowered to the bed. I know now that no matter what happens next, I'm strong enough to handle it. I might be scarred, and I might come away with burns that will never heal, but if I walk away without fighting for Kane and our love, then I might not ever be able to move on with my life.

I became the change that I had wanted for myself. Two months, four years, a decade ago—I never would have believed this was possible. I would have ran and hidden behind my fears. And even though I long for Kane and the added strength his love gives me, I deserve so much more than what I had been prepared to live with.

I deserve all of him just as I've given him all of me.

I lie down, pulling the covers tight against me as a few tears fall from my eyes. Even with the knowledge I'm no longer weak and afraid, I'm still so full of fear that I will lose Kane in the end. Part of me wants to run back to him and tell him that it doesn't matter, I don't need the truth as long as I have him, but I know now that I would never be able to live with myself if I didn't prove to myself that I know I deserve more.

He might not have been completely honest with me because of a promise that he had made to Mia, but if he didn't tell me because of the child, I'm not sure what that means for us. How can I compete with that? How can I expect him to choose me when this child would need its father?

It's time to face the fact that no matter how great our love might be it just might not be able to hold up when faced with the very real possibility that Mia might be carrying his child.

"God, what now?"

CHAPTER
THIRTY-FIVE

KANE

GODDAMN VULTURES.

Mia called an hour after we hung up to let me know that reporters had swamped my gate. The paparazzi are in full bloodlust over the rumors of my 'love triangle.' I had spent enough time looking at the shit on the web to know they were painting Willow as the other woman while Mia was suffering through my infidelity.

What a bunch of bullshit.

Lies I'm at the mercy of because I can't say shit. A bed I made for myself because I didn't do anything to ensure that Willow would be prepared for them when the news hit. But even if I had and she was by my side, I would never throw Mia to the wolves by giving life to their scandalous rumors.

My publicist had told me to keep my mouth shut, deny it all and let my little fling just go home. His advice was to use this to keep the fire blazing while he uses the attention to get *Impenetrable* into as many hands as possible when they started asking questions. Turning my personal hell into his gain.

Needless to say, he was fucking shocked when I fired him right then and there. No one, and I mean no one, will use Willow in a negative way just to pad his pockets. I could give a shit about *Impenetrable* right now, not when my future is hanging on by a thread while this shit storm boils over and starts to take out everything around me.

"Let's go, Cam," I shout through the house and wait for him to come into view.

"Didn't Kole tell you it might not be a good idea?"

I look over at Cam sharply. "Does it look like I give a shit?"

Cam's all-knowing glare is the only response that I get.

"I can't just sit here and not go to her, Cam." I lean back against the wall that takes us to the garage and drop my head back. "What am I supposed to do? Just bring Mia here and let the press go ape-shit that on the heels of Willow's exit Mia came running to me?"

"That's not what I'm saying."

I open my eyes and take a deep pull of air. What I wouldn't give to get this helpless aggression out. "What should I do then?"

His usually impassive face breaks into an eerie grin; the look in his eyes cool and calculated. "You give her the grand gesture."

Cocking my head, my brow pulls tight. What the fuck is he on?

"You know, if you spent more time reading those romance books, you would have figured this out before now. You're a man who is known to avoid those assholes. You never comment when asked to confirm whatever it is that they want. Willow knows that, you've told her that, but what you haven't showed her is that the chance you had her take on you would be worth it because you believe in it enough to finally allow the world to have you without hiding. I get it, Kane. Your whole life is out there for their sick pleasure to feed themselves on every move you make. You deserve to have your own shit, but there is nothing wrong with telling them they're right about Willow. You can give them that and still keep your privacy. More importantly, you can give *her* that."

"Grand gesture?"

"That's what I said."

Stepping away from the wall, I walk over to where Cam's standing, trying to figure out where in the hell my silent friend went. "And what am I supposed to do about Mia?"

He sighs. "I'm not telling you to go out there and give them all of you. Just do what you need to in order to leave no doubt about what is between you and Willow. The rest of them can fuck right off."

It sounds so easy. Open my mouth and confirm my relationship.

"Let me call Mia," I say and walk back toward the front of the house while I wait for her to pick up. I step over Kyle and just barely resist kicking him in his stubborn head.

"Hey. Are you almost to Kole's?" she asks, a loud yawn ending her question.

"Mia, just go home. You need your rest."

"No. I need to fix the mess that I've created. Plus, I can always crash in one of Kole's many guest rooms."

I look through the door and see nothing but darkness outside my house. The front gate sits too far from my house to give me a view of what's waiting for me. "How bad is it out there?" I ask knowing that she will understand.

"Not too bad if you consider the police were showing up when I passed your street. I didn't even turn down there knowing they knew my car, but you could see them even a half mile out."

"Shit," I bark.

"Are you having trouble leaving? I'm sure Cam could just call the local PD and have them take care of it."

"It's not that. Cam had an idea, and I think it might work. Especially knowing how many of those motherfuckers are out there."

Her sigh comes through the line, and I know she's just gearing herself up. I wait, needing the time myself to deal with the fact that I'm actually considering this.

"What's the idea, Kane?"

"I'm going to walk out there and give them what they want?"

She gasps. "The baby?"

I'm shaking my head before I remember she can't see me. "Fuck, no. I wouldn't do that to you, Mia. I'm going to go out there and tell them with no uncertainty that yes, I'm with Willow Tate, and they can fuck off."

"Maybe you should leave that last part off." She laughs.

"Yeah, you're probably right."

"What did Trace say about this?" Her question spikes my temper when I remember how he wanted to play my life like a fucking puppet master.

"Trace got fired about an hour ago. For once, I'm not thinking about what is best for my career, Mia. It could fuck off because all that matters is making sure the woman I love knows just how much."

"Well, then, Kane, let me settle in and wait while you go do the big badass romantic scene to win the girl."

I let out a rough laugh. "Very funny. I know, I used to make fun of these scenes when I got stuck playing some lovesick pussy, but I'm willing to admit that it was easy to make a joke of a character's actions when you had no fucking clue what it was really like to feel the emptiness that led to their declaration. I would do a lot more if it meant she was back in my arms, Mia."

"I'll take your word for it. Text me when you're headed this way. Kole let me in and I'm going to lay down until you get here."

I hang up, pocket my phone and call out to Cam.

He comes stomping into the room, his booted foot just missing Kyle's head. "Well?"

"Get the car ready, and I'll meet you down at the gate. Keep it running and when I'm done, we head to Kole's."

Cam gives me a nod and turns to go to the garage, but not before I see that creepy-ass grin back on his face.

CHAPTER THIRTY-SIX

WILLOW

MY MIND SLUGGISHLY STARTS TO wake. I jolt when I feel another poke against my back. Swatting behind me at the annoying sensation, I burrow deeper into the pillow. I start to relax when the sharp poke hits me again.

"Willow!"

My name, accompanied with another jab, makes me jump, and I almost fall off the side of the bed in my haste. Turning my head, I squint through the darkness at the intruder.

"Kole?"

His white teeth shine brightly in the dim lighting, and his head bobs in affirmation.

"Is everything okay?"

He bends and clicks on the lamp next to the bed, soft lighting bathing the room in a muted glow. He's rumpled from sleep, and my eyes almost bug out of my head when I realize he's only wearing some low-riding sweat pants. I quickly avert my eyes and look away, hearing his deep chuckle as my face heats.

"I need you to come with me," he tells me before bizarrely standing and walking over to the door. "I figured you would want something more comfortable to wear instead of that … well, that," he says and points at me.

I look down and gasp when I see the state of my appearance. I had thrown off my jacket when I came in here earlier and because my bra is the most painful thing ever, it followed. I left my pants and top on, but given that I had been sound asleep, the top had shifted and now one of my nipples was dangerously close to giving Kole a show.

"Oh, God. I'm sorry," I rush out in embarrassment and grab the sweatshirt he had been pointing at. "Holy crap."

"Don't worry about it. Nothing I haven't seen before, but do me a favor and let's not mention that to my brother."

At the mention of Kane, my humiliation fades, and the pain I felt earlier returns. God, it hurts. My whole body feels bereft without his presence.

After pulling the sweater over my head, I move toward where Kole is waiting and follow him through the hallway and into what I assume to be his office. He points at the chair behind the enormous monitor and waits for me to sit. I look over my shoulder at him curiously and wait for him to clue me in to why he woke me up. His hand moves over the mouse and the computer wakes, making my eyes hurt when the brightness hits me.

"Sorry," he mumbles and pulls the wireless keyboard over to him.

I keep watching his movements on the screen as he brings up

the browser and then I move to his fingers as he quickly starts typing.

When I see the address for a very well-known tabloid site, I gasp and look up at Kole.

"Trust me," he says with a wink.

He has no way of knowing, but hearing that in a voice so similar to Kane's and followed by his wink, cracks my heart a little deeper.

God, I miss him.

"Here we go," he drones, and I look up to see him nodding to the monitor.

When I see the scene unfolding in front of me, I scoot closer and take it all in. I'm shocked at what I'm seeing, but my heart responds to the image of Kane instantly by picking up speed and all but bursting out of my chest.

What the heck is he doing? Walking out of his front gate and into the madness screaming and yelling questions so rapidly you can't decipher what any of them is actually asking.

My gaze drinks him in and I try to understand the expression on his face. He looks nothing short of determined with his body held tall and sure with each step he takes past his now open gates and closer to the cameras. A strobe light of flashes dances in the darkness as he willingly walks, alone, into the crowd. It isn't until he stops and holds up one hand to silence the group in front of him that I get a good look at his face.

To the world, he looks like Kane the movie star, confident in every move he makes including this one, but to me, all I see is the man who is falling apart.

"Holy crap." I gasp when those eyes I love so much seem to

look through the screen and right into my soul.

Kole grunts out a low laugh, but neither of us speaks, waiting and watching the live feed on the screen.

"I'm sure you have better things to do than to sit at my gate," he starts, looking around him at the reporters in his path. "As you know, there have been a few reports about my private life today that have created some unpleasantness for me and those I love." The crowd starts to buzz at the mention of those rumors, but he continues before anyone can question him. "While I hope you understand I won't confirm everything that is out there, I want you all to just shut up and listen to what I have to say."

Kole laughs loudly at his brother's hard tone and passive-aggressive dig at the invasiveness that their very existence brings him.

"Today, the woman I love found out the hard way just what your tactless reporting can do when you take just the smallest grain of truth and twist it into whatever you want. She was hurt because of my life, and I won't allow anyone the chance to question her value to my life. Not by you, my fans, and not even from herself. My private life is none of your business. My happiness and hers are the only things that concern me. So while I have your attention, allow me to set the rumors to rest. Yes, it's true that I am without a doubt spoken for. The beautiful woman who fell into my life earlier this year owns every part of me, my heart, and my future. You might think that's newsworthy, and you can try to find drama to fill your stories with, but I'm here to let you know you won't find any. The woman I love gave me the greatest gift when she opened herself up and took a chance on me. Go home and wait for the next story to break because you will not find it with Willow and me."

He keeps his eyes on the cameras in front of him for a few

beats and then turns, walks to the car I hadn't noticed idling just inside the gate, and climbs in the passenger seat. I can see Cam's face, a huge smile in place, as the cameras start to flash rapidly as he inches forward and the feed cuts off.

"Did that just happen?"

Kole closes the browser and turns his head. "Fuck yeah, it did."

I shake my head at his overwhelming happiness. I play back what I just watched, wanting to pinch myself because it feels like there is no way that was real. Kane just not only created a scene most romance movies would kill to generate with the passion and conviction in which he just professed his love—for me—to the world, but he also did something that I know he hated. He opened up his privacy in order to show me that he feels just as strongly about our love and me as he had said.

I know there is still uncertainty between us, but there is no doubt in my mind anymore that he's gearing up for a battle to prove to me that he understands I meant what I said. I deserve everything, and he's giving me just that.

"How did you know this was happening?" I question Kole. He walks around the desk and drops down into the plush couch against the wall. He yawns and I look at the clock on the monitor. "How were there even that many people there at almost one in the morning?"

"The vultures don't sleep when there's a juicy story to be found. And to answer your question, Kane called. Woke my ass up and demanded I get you in front of the computer in five minutes. I did my job, and now, we wait."

"Wait?" I sputter.

He nods, winks, and folds his hands behind his head. "Yeah,

shouldn't be much longer."

I nod when I have no clue what I'm actually nodding for and stand from the chair.

"Oh, no. You can't leave."

"I'm not leaving. I'm just not sure what I should do. Duck for cover or look for armor."

He barks out a laugh but doesn't say more.

His silence is almost worse than my imagination right now. I know Kane's coming. I could feel it even if I didn't have Kole hinting it. My body is a mix of nerves and excitement after watching that. Is he coming to tell me the same thing or is he coming to give me more?

"What am I supposed to do now?" I all but shriek at Kole.

"Uh ... maybe calm down?"

My eyes narrow. "I can't just calm down. How many people saw that?" I ask and point at the computer behind me.

He shrugs. "I don't know. In this country, maybe a couple billion or so. More overseas with the time difference and all."

"A couple billion," I stammer. "A couple BILLION!"

Holy crap.

"I don't know, maybe more. Baby brother goes big when he sets his mind to it."

"Kole, look ... I don't know you, but I'm kind of freaking out right now, and I need you to be serious. Why did he do that?"

He leans forward and braces his elbows against his spread knees. "My guess is he was letting his woman know just how much he loves her. But, I mean, I guess we could have been watching something different just then."

"You aren't as funny as you think you are."

His smile just widens.

"I never doubted his love, Kole."

His expression grows serious before he speaks. "Didn't you?"

"Me leaving wasn't about that." I sigh. "I know he loves me. He just didn't love me enough to give me all of him."

He stands and walks over to me. I look up into his somber face. "I'm pretty sure, Willow, that he just did."

I bite back a groan of frustration. "That's not what I meant. He's keeping something from me."

He nods, a dark flash of understanding in his eyes. "Yeah, but maybe ask yourself if he's keeping it from you to protect you just as much as he is trying to protect the others involved. He wasn't just telling the world that he loves them. It was you. Let that be enough to hear him out."

If only it were that easy.

CHAPTER THIRTY-SEVEN

WILLOW

TEN MINUTES OF PACING INSIDE of Kole's office wasn't enough to prepare me for Kane when he burst through the door, slamming the heavy wood against the wall with his force.

I almost jump out of my skin and can barely hear Kole laughing through the loud roar of blood rushing through my body. Kane steps into the room and his wild eyes hold me still until he reaches out to pull me to his body. His arms wrap around me as he bends his body to curl around me. His large frame dwarfs mine as his trembling body holds tight.

My hands come around him, and I fist his shirt, breathing him in and trying to calm my racing heart.

I'm not sure how long we stand there, but when he pulls back, I can see the distress deep in his eyes. "I'm so sorry." His voice quivers and his eyes beg me to forgive him.

"I know, Kane. I know."

"I fucking hate this, Willow. Hate knowing that I'm causing you pain and that I could have done everything a lot differently, but you have to know I'm not keeping things from you to be cruel. I've been beating myself up about this, but I couldn't say anything. It is just so much bigger than our lives."

I nod. "You couldn't or you can't?" The sadness I had felt earlier ebbing slightly at his words. My earlier courage to face this head-on gives me the drive to push through, even though I'm terrified of what will come to light.

Will I lose the man I love? Why is this baby such a secret that he couldn't tell me before now? I just can't figure out what piece of the puzzle I couldn't find to fit the whole picture together.

"Couldn't."

I give him a small nod but wait for him to say more. He doesn't ease his hold on my body, almost as if he's afraid I'm going to bolt if he does.

"I tried, baby. God, I tried to tell you, but you have to understand that I had given my word to Mia that she could trust me with something this big long before we ever started our relationship."

"How could you have tried, Kane? You avoided talking about your relationship any time that I asked. I gave you the trust you asked for. I even spoke to her myself. I can't see how hard it was to just tell me."

"Maybe I can answer that." I jump in his arms when the female voice intrudes into our moment.

My eyes round and his own beg me silently to hear her out. To listen to what they both have to say. My stomach heaves violently when Mia walks into the room.

I feel seconds away from hyperventilating when she walks the rest of the way from the doorway to where Kane is still holding me. My skin flushing hot and cold so rapidly that it's making me ill.

Her dark blond hair is pulled back into a sloppy mess of a bun, and her tired face is still gorgeous in its natural beauty. Her green eyes imploring as she stops just a few feet from us. I allow myself to look down and that sick seed of dread bursts inside me until I feel like it's going to explode from my mouth.

Her clothes are baggy and more for comfort than anything else. Black leggings, boots, and a simple tee shirt. But it's the shirt, wrinkled and loose everywhere except where it stretches tight against her swollen belly, which holds my attention.

"I wish we could have finally met under more pleasant circumstances, but it's still lovely to finally meet the woman who makes Kane so happy."

I mutely gape at her, not trusting my own body and its turmoil. I'm more worried that I'm about to throw up over all of us in some grossly accurate depiction of *The Exorcist*.

"Do you want to sit?" Kane asks, his raspy voice rumbling from his chest, and I finally look away from Mia and into his vulnerable eyes.

"No." I gulp.

"Where do I start?" Mia asks, and I know she isn't talking to me. How the heck would I know where to start; I'm having a hard enough time just trying to remember how to breathe.

"Just start from the beginning, Mees. You know you can trust her with all of it."

I don't take my eyes from his, the wretchedness making my already violent nerves spiral widely. He doesn't just look torn. He looks like just the thought of hearing what she has to say is going to tear him up a lot more than it will me. How is that even possible?

"Okay," she says softly, and I see her move to sit on the couch.

Movement on the other end of the couch tells me that Kole hasn't left either. I don't look away from Kane because I know that whatever is said now, what is between us and trying to salvage it is more important than who is witnessing it. Plus, it's probably not as if Kole is unaware. Right?

"Kane and I had just wrapped on a film that we had been working on together. I'm sure you know the movie, even though it isn't important, but it was a big deal because we hadn't worked together for almost five years. *Like the First Time* was a fun movie for us, but it was more like a reunion because it was the first time that Kole had also been cast with us. This time, Kole beat Kane for the lead, which was pretty hilarious."

Kole lets out a low burst of hilarity at the memory, but Kane just keeps searching my eyes. His troubled gaze darkening with each word that Mia speaks.

"The wrap party was pretty wild. Not indecent or anything, but the liquor was flowing and I'm pretty sure there wasn't a single sober person in the house. The whole Masters family was there, even though Christian and Becca left before things got crazy. I don't remember where Kole went, but by the time I realized I had too much to drink, I was past the point of rational thought."

Oh, God. I'm really going to be sick. My eyes widen, and Kane's fill with helpless sympathy as trepidation overcomes me.

"It's funny what you remember when faced with something traumatic. To me, each moment is burned into my brain, but even with the violent end to my night, I don't regret it."

Her words register, and I pull back in confusion. I finally look from Kane and meet her sad eyes, her hand rubbing absentmindedly against her abdomen.

"He acted like he didn't even remember," she continues, almost to herself. I see Kole's body tighten, and he looks over at her in shock. "I didn't know what to do, but I knew that Kane would protect me and help me through it. Regardless of how much it killed him."

"What?" I gasp. Does she mean? No. There is no way the Kane I know is capable of something like that.

She wipes her eyes and looks from the spot she had been blindly staring into and locks eyes with me. A sad, vulnerable smile lifts her lips, almost like an apology before she speaks the words.

"A month after that night, I sat on the floor and cried as Kane held me. The trust of that night held in his hand as he looked at the positive pregnancy test. It was then that I begged him and selfishly took his promise of silence, using it to help me find a way to come to terms with my new future."

"What the fuck," Kole harshly whispers.

I look from Mia and back to Kane. The pain is still present, but a fire of rage starts to build behind it.

"He kept my secret not only because I was asking him to help and shield me, but also because I knew that if anyone felt the same protectiveness I do toward my son, it would be Kane. He would have done that even if my child didn't share his blood."

"Oh my God," I sob, the sound coming out like a low whine.

"You son of a bitch," Kole seethes.

"Fuck," Kane bellows and turns his face from mine to narrow his eyes at Mia.

There's a moment of silence and each thud of my heart feels

like it's slowly breaking.

"Oh, oh! No. Shit. I didn't mean it like that," she rushes, and my tear-filled eyes move from Kane's chest and I look over at her. "The baby isn't Kane's."

"What?" I meekly question, the pain in my chest and stomach almost making me want to pass out.

"The fuck, Mia!" Kole yells over me.

"It's Kyle's. The baby is Kyle's." She looks from Kole with a wince before glancing toward me, her eyes brimming with tears. "I'm so sorry, Willow. I never should have asked him to keep it from you, but I selfishly let the knowledge that he was the only one who knew my son was conceived by a man who drunkenly took advantage of my inebriated state make me feel better. A married man who blamed me for the life he helped to create and wanted me to 'take care of it.' There are so many lives that will never be the same now, but it was safer for us to let the world assume it was Kane's than rip open everyone's lives and have my son, their nephew, be born with a black mark against him. I can never tell you how sorry I am for ever letting it get this far when I should have been strong enough to fight this without involving Kane."

My fists loosen against his shirt, and for the first time since he walked in the room, I start to pull from his embrace. I know he's taking my retreat the wrong way because he curses under his breath and his arms let go of my body to cup my face, bringing my attention back to his.

"God, Willow. I'm so sorry. Please, baby, don't pull away." He presses his lips to mine and I return the kiss, but I pull back and step back. "I should have told you, and you will never know how much I regret not making sure that this talk happened weeks ago, but I wasn't keeping it from you to hurt you."

"No," I start, and he snaps his mouth shut. Panic blazes brightly as his eyes plead with me not to pull away. "Stop, Kane." I move from his reach completely and walk over to Mia. A woman who I had always thought was living the perfect life. One I envied from afar and prayed to have just a sliver of her fearless confidence now sits before me looking like the weak, fearful, depressed woman that I had been when I was making those prayers. I know what she feels. Maybe not in the same capacity, but I know what it's like to live a life full of anxiety just thinking about the future. Not being able to see a single ounce of safety to help ease those feelings.

Until I learned what it was like to truly believe in myself.

But I also know I would have done the same thing in her shoes and reached out to hold on to anything that helped me function.

I recently learned I was the person who could have helped myself all along.

I sit down and reach out to pull her into my arms and we both sit there silently offering the other person something different. I'm sure for her this is her way of building the bridge of forgiveness that I needed to walk across in order to get to the future Kane was promising. I'm thankful for her ability to tell me her story even though I know that wasn't easy. For her to fearlessly trust I won't use it against her.

But for me, this embrace is a lot more than just forgiving her, Kane, and the impossible situation that almost ruined us. This is about me trying to show her that no matter how lonely she feels at her bottom, she will never be alone. There is always someone there to help you climb back up to your feet. It's a lesson that sometimes people never learn. I was lucky enough to have my own savior help me find the strength I needed to see my own worth, so I can only hope I'm able to give a little of that to Mia.

CHAPTER THIRTY-EIGHT

WILLOW

THE HEAVINESS AROUND US CONTINUED when I let my arms fall from Mia. She looked so lost and frightened that I wanted nothing more than to make everything better for her.

I glance around the room, examining Kole's pained face for a beat before I look over at the man who has held the weight of the world on his shoulders while keeping this secret. And he held the burden of Mia's pain knowing he could have very well lost his own happiness in the process. It amazes me just how selfless this man is. He was willing—is willing—to put up with the lies and rumors in order to protect his family. And that's just what this is, his family. Mia might not be a Masters by blood, but I see now that she has always been like a sister to him. Even if this baby wasn't Kyle's, I feel confident that Kane would have done the exact thing.

My strong and altruistic man. I had feared the worst, but the reality was so much more heartbreaking than I could have imagined. Not for me, but for Mia. I don't blame Kane for feeling the need to hold on to his promise, regardless of the fact that his word means so much to him because this was so much bigger than just a pregnant friend.

This secret can ruin so many lives.

And the weight of it has broken the woman held captive in the center of the storm. She may have been a confident woman at one point, but the one breaking down in front of me is at the bottom of her barrel. A place I know all too well is the worst kind of living hell to be trapped in.

"I promise, I'll find a way to fix this," Mia sobs, interrupting my thoughts. "I won't let this tear you guys apart."

Her words spark an idea that had been pushing its way to the forefront of my mind since this horrible story began to unfold. One that now, as I close my eyes and try to keep it together for Mia's sake, I feel the steady resolve of my decision take root.

This is an unfathomable situation facing us all. The repercussions of our choices from this moment on will shape the path of all of our lives, but the most important one of all being the innocent child who deserves more than having its existence turning into a public mockery of shame that will always haunt him his whole life. Mia didn't ask for this, and while I have no doubt that she loves her unborn son, she has no idea how to shield him from the monsters of the world. Monsters that I know firsthand will do nothing but make sure you never feel an ounce of happiness. Until recently, I had been terrified of them, but now I feel a power I never knew possible when I think about being able to keep that pain from touching someone else.

"No, Mia." I reach out and hold her hand in mine. The second her cold and clammy skin touches mine, my decision to fight for someone else becomes an all-consuming kind of determination. "You have nothing to fix."

Her sobs grow, and I take my hand from hers to pull her to me, her head falling to my chest as she cries. Huge, body-jolting sobs, which have pinpricks of emotion pushing up my throat, burning my nose, and stinging my eyes. I take a deep swallow, pushing through that emotion, and attempt to calm myself in order to take on the hardship that is slowly killing this woman.

Kole and Kane share a heated stare, both looking powerless and unsure of how to proceed. This is so much more than not knowing how to soothe a woman. These men aren't just watching someone they care about vulnerably break. If I had to guess, they're in just as much pain right now. Kole, having just found out about the truth behind Mia's pregnancy and his older brother's role in it, might not have the magnitude of emotions that I'm sure Kane has. Yet. But I have no doubt they will hit. I know that Kane is hurting for Mia, having just relived this through her words, but he's been searching my eyes since he arrived. His expression is one of confused anxiety and pleading desperation as he tries to gauge my thoughts in order to figure out what this new truth means for us.

I look away from the Masters men and bend my head so that Mia can hear me over her cries. "I can't imagine what you've been going through, Mia. I know that it wasn't easy to tell me, but thank you for trusting me with this. You have my promise that your secret is safe with me."

I see Kane's head bows and his shoulders slump. I wish I could go to him, but he needs to understand that I'm able to handle this without him. Regardless of how badly I want his arms and protection to shield me, I know now that I'm stronger than I had ever imagined. I need him to see that in order to believe what I'm about to say. To have no doubt that I'm now the one who's ready to take someone else's metaphorical hand and help guide her to a beautiful future.

Just as he did for me.

"We're not telling anyone," I tell the room with conviction.

Mia gasps and both Kane and Kole look over at me with disbelief.

"Willow, you don't know what you're saying," Kole responds, breaking from his own shock first.

"He's right, baby. This isn't going to go away. Just because I publicly and undoubtedly confirmed our relationship, the fact that they still believe Mia's baby is mine is only going to get worse unless we figure out a way to address it without hurting Mia or the baby."

I shake my head and give him a small smile meant to soothe his worries.

"No. We won't let this go past this room until Mia wants it to. This is so much bigger than having some rumors and stories printed about us, Kane. So much bigger."

He moves from the middle of the room and crouches in front of me, his hands splaying against each of my thighs as his eyes implore me to understand him.

"I know you're worried about how I'll handle the public backlash that will come with our silence, but that concern is misplaced, Kane. I promise you that I'm not making this decision lightly. I know the reality that we will be inviting by doing this and allowing them to paint me in a light that will not be pretty. But we know the truth. The only people who matter are in this room. And at the end of the day, their lies and speculations will never touch what we have."

His head drops into my lap, and I reach out with the hand that isn't holding Mia to me and run my fingers soothingly through his hair.

"If you would have asked me a year ago to allow others to freely judge me, I wouldn't have believed it possible to be strong enough to handle that. Just the fear of their judgment alone would have had me running, but Kane, if you have taught me anything, it's that no one else's opinion matters if I'm happy with myself and my life. This isn't me taking on someone else's burden, this is me helping shoulder someone's pain when it's so unbearable that the thought of going forward without giving help is more daunting than anything some stupid magazines will say about me. I'm not offering what I don't want to give."

"Baby," he hoarsely mumbles, his hands tightening and his head rocking against my lap. "This will never go away unless we admit I'm not the father. This might follow our lives for years to come."

"Look at me," I command, and he lifts his head slowly. "This *will* go away. It will eventually fizzle until they become bored or someone else does something to get their attention. But even if it doesn't, the only thing that should matter here is that your nephew is able to live a life that isn't started with a scandal. I'm strong enough, you're strong enough—*we* are so strong together that we're unbreakable. That is all that we need in order to move forward and power through. So what if it follows us, Kane? It won't follow *him*." I reach out and place my finger on Mia's stomach, letting what I'm saying to them sink in.

"God, Willow." His voice is thick with emotion.

"I don't care what they say, Kane. I know the truth and the only people who matter are this family. We say nothing. You all have given the world so much of yourselves. Your lives have been open for them to rip apart for far too long. Not this time."

"Willow, you … you have no idea what you're offering," Mia brokenly whispers. She pulls her body up, and my hand drops. "You have no clue."

I soften my expression and turn to address her, letting her see for herself that I mean what I'm saying. "I understand exactly what I'm offering you. I know because I was in your same position of helpless fear not too long ago. I endured, but only because I wasn't alone. I found my strength again because I had others who helped remove the pain I was living in until I could become tough enough to hold myself up alone. You aren't alone, and you never will be."

Her eyes fill with tears again.

"You're sure," Kane questions, his tone more steady than before.

"Positive, Kane. This doesn't define our relationship. No one but us has that power. This only comes between us if *we* allow it. You showed me what it was like to live a life free of the anxiety. Anxiety that had held me captive in fear that I had been desperate to break free from. I couldn't see past what was hurting me at that moment in order to see there was something better out there. I had your help to become free of all the pain I had felt in my life, and I'm now able to be the help someone else needs now. The help Mia needs."

He searches my face, looking for the tiniest hint that I might not understand what will follow if we allow the media to continue assuming that Mia's child is his and that I'm the other woman. "So what now, Willow?" he finally asks.

"Now, we make sure that Mia has what she needs and all of us move forward in our lives, but we don't do it alone. They will speculate and they will want us to give them anything if it means their lies can grow. We don't hide. Mia doesn't hide. None of us do. We go on and freely enjoy our lives. As far as I'm concerned, they could turn us into the next sister wives, but no matter what, this baby will never have to deal with the kind of stuff they would say if they knew just how he was created."

"And Kyle?" Kole asks.

"He needs help," Kane interjects before I can speak. "And honestly, as far as I'm concerned, he is no brother of mine. I haven't been able to stand to be in the same room as him since Mia told me what happened. I know you deny that he raped you, Mia, but the bottom line is that he forced himself on you when you weren't in the right frame of mind to voice your objections. Just because you didn't say no doesn't change the fact it wasn't consensual sex. He didn't believe Mia when she told him anyway, so as far as I'm concerned, he doesn't matter."

"What if he changes his mind and all of this means nothing?" Mia weakly inquires. "What if he wants us ... the baby?"

"Do you really think he would do that?"

Kane's question isn't meant to hurt her, but she flinches anyway.

"No. He won't. He hates dealing with the media even more than you do, but puts up with it because of Jessica. And we know that he wouldn't want Jessica to find out that he had been unfaithful. Not when there isn't a prenup and she would clean him out. Fuck, he's drunk constantly anyway, so it's not like anyone takes him seriously." Kole's pissed voice confirms what I thought about Kyle.

"And Mom and Dad?" Kane asks his brother.

Kole looks at him, and I know they both hate the thought of keeping this, their grandson, from their parents.

"I think they should know. They deserve to know," Mia speaks, and we all look at her. "If you're serious about not letting this be public knowledge, the next biggest scandal to rock Hollywood, then the only other people who should know are them. But that is my load to carry. I refuse to let you guys do that. By keeping this from your parents, it would only hurt them. By not knowing, they would miss out on knowing their grandson and he would miss out on their love. Regardless of how he came to be, it would be heartless to keep him from them."

I give her a reassuring hug, feeling so proud that she was able to come to a decision on her own.

"Then it's settled. No more secrets between us, but the world will never know. This is no one else's business but the Masters family," I tell the room and instantly feel like some of the heavy currents that had been filling the room dissolve around us.

This won't be stress-free to withstand. I'm sure the coming days and months will even be painful at times, but I know without a shadow of doubt that for me, this will be the easiest hardship I could endure. I'm strong enough to handle whatever is gossiped and lied about me and my relationship with Kane. I would be able to stand tall alone, but with Kane at my side, I know there is nothing that could ever be said to tear us apart.

I know the truth.

We know the truth.

And the love that wraps that truth up in a protective bond is stronger than anything that could ever attempt to knock it down.

CHAPTER THIRTY-NINE

KANE

WE LEFT KOLE'S HOUSE NOT long after we had all agreed to Willow's plan. I know I'm not the only one who hates this, but seeing the determination she has to not only bear this load, but also to come together in order to hold Mia up when she isn't able to do it herself has me falling in love with her all over again.

I wasn't kidding when I told her this wouldn't go away. That it will get so much worse before there is even a possibility they forget about us. This is entertainment news gold.

I've lived this life for so long that nothing the media says fazes me anymore, but it wasn't always like that. When I was young and impressionable, the lies they would come up with about my personal life made my desire for privacy take a backseat. I fed into every rumor, lie, and truth, giving them all of me until I had nothing left. Then I realized that they would say what they wanted regardless of my denial or verification.

They want blood, and it didn't matter who is sliced and damaged in the process. From that moment on, I never opened my mouth to give them gasoline to build a fire. Until earlier.

But my sweet Willow has never had to deal with this.

Until recently, she couldn't even see past the hurt a few people in her life had inflicted upon her in order to see her own beauty and worth. Their judgments, on such a small scale, had changed the way she was able to see herself. Those lies became a false reality. All because she let those judgments break her.

I'm not stupid. I know how far she's come. She went from hiding herself from me to openly giving. She's gone from the safety of shadows and stepped into the spotlight. All of this she did by herself, but still, I would be lying if I said I wasn't worried about what will happen when the judgment and scorn are on a much larger scale.

She's throwing herself to the wolves in order to protect my family and giving up her reputation in the process. She will, without my confirming that the baby isn't mine, be labeled as the woman who broke up Kane and Mia, even though there was never a Kane and Mia to break. They will search her past for dirt. Rip apart everything about her. From how she is dressed, to her hair and makeup, and what she eats. Worst of all, knowing this was one of her biggest mental weaknesses, I know they will take the body I love and throw some bullshit label on her. They will turn her healthy, curvy, fucking perfect body and deem her unworthy because she doesn't fit the mold that society has put on a woman.

I fucking hate this. I hate every second of what she's suggesting. However, I also know that she's right. It kills me to admit that even knowing what will happen. But, in order to protect my nephew, his life has to start off without the backlash that will follow if the real story of his conception was out there. This isn't just some sordid story about me meeting another woman when my supposed girl-friend is pregnant with my child. That would be forgotten about. Hell, it happens all the fucking time. No, this is much worse. This wouldn't be forgotten. They could milk stories out of this for years.

The supermodel who was cheated on.

The brother of Kole and Kane Masters, two widely famous names in Hollywood, being a dangerous drunk who all but raped a woman.

The 'bastard' child created in a drunken rage.

What my nephew would have to deal with would follow him his whole life. So like it or lump it, I know what Willow is demand-ing is the only way to keep him safe and allow him to live a some-what normal life.

So yeah, this doesn't just fucking kill me because of what could potentially hurt the woman I love. It's a big part, but it's not the only working piece determined to tear me in two.

My brother's drinking problem has become something that is a danger to those around him. He has not only shamed his mar-riage during this, but in my eyes, no matter what Mia says, he raped her and foolishly created a life. He had been spiraling out of control long before this—to the point that I don't even recognize him anymore. He is a monster, and in order to follow through with Willow's plan, we would be protecting him as well as the son that he demanded Mia abort when she told him the baby was his.

"It's going to be okay," Willow whispers into the darkness, eas-ing my mind as if she had been able to see inside my head while I fell apart beside her.

I give Cam a glance as he drives through the empty roads toward home before dipping my head closer to where hers has been resting against my shoulder. Making sure her ears are the only ones that can hear me.

"I know, baby," I tell her even though I hate it. The words burn as they fall from my mouth, leaving behind a taste of pure acid.

"We'll talk when we get home, and I'll make sure you actually believe those words."

I can't help it. Even though I feel like I might physically vomit right now, leave it to Willow to strip it down and call me out.

By the time we pulled up to the gates, it was going on four in the morning. The once-crowded entrance to my house now only held a few stray reporters, which was typical in the early morning hours.

On a normal day, it is never like this. A circus that holds you locked in your own home as they swarm around. Sure, you see them around, but they don't hunt you down like they did tonight. I know it has everything to do with the news hitting about my relationship with Willow. Because of my show earlier, it probably won't be dying down completely for a few days.

They had never seen me act like that. Even when I didn't hold on to my privacy with everything I had, I still didn't confirm a relationship as I did tonight. Fuck, even with Jenn, the only other woman they had been able to confirm, I was never the one who verbalized it. I let my reps do the job for me just like with anything else big in my life; it had never really meant enough for me to put myself out there.

Until Willow.

And I would do it again and again if that were what she needed.

But now that I've made some hugely publicized romantic move, they're going to think that means I'm now an open book. They'll stick around, for a few days or maybe a week, and hope that my newfound sharing will also include Mia's pregnancy.

It's this next wave of invasiveness that I'm the most worried about.

"Okay, Kane. Out with it. Tell me what's had you silently brooding since we left Kole's." Willow pulls off the sweater she had been wearing, and I almost swallow my tongue. Her thin strapped shirt thing the only thing under that sweater. Had I known that the breasts I love so much had been free this whole time, it might have been able to calm my nerves.

No, I think when she moves to sit on the bed to remove her heels. There's no fucking way this sight would have been able to calm me down. Her chest sways with each movement she makes, and I'm pretty sure I don't even remember my name anymore when she bends forward to do something with her shoe. Those full, huge tits strain against the tiny little straps and become best friends with gravity, almost slipping free.

"Shit," I groan and feel my cock harden. The last thing I need right now is a hard-on when this conversation is so important, but she should know better than to give me a view like that. I close my eyes, drop my head back on my shoulders, and start to imagine every nasty and disgusting image that I can.

"Are you doing that on purpose?" I accuse incredulously.

She giggles softly under her breath, and I know she is very aware of what she's doing to my body.

"Fuck."

Her chest jiggles with the laughter she's trying to keep in only spiking my desire for her to immeasurable heights.

"As much as it pains me to say this, please cover up, baby. You know how much I love your tits, and right now, the temptation is almost too much. Right now, as much as I want nothing more than to sink inside you and reassure myself that we're going to be okay, I need to be able to talk to you without distraction."

She sits up, those tits continuing to sway in that red shirt like she's a matador taunting the hungry bull inside me. Her own arousal for what I want is written all over her face. Her eyes the darkest of brown chocolate, her pale skin pink and glowing, and her lip held between her teeth.

"On second thought," I say and pull my own shirt off while toeing out of my shoes. I keep my eyes locked on hers as I work the button on my jeans and swiftly kick them off before standing before her completely bare. Her eyes widen, the lip falls from her teeth, and her gasps shoot around the room in a breathy echo. "Get up," I command.

She stands instantly and together we work at removing the few things left in my way. Our chests heave and the air that is rapidly falling from our lips dances between us. Her eyes never leave mine. We stand just a touch away from each other, but I feel her surround me.

This isn't about me wanting her body, which fuck I do. This is all need. My need to feel her warm and real against my body when just hours ago, I was terrified I would never have this again.

My hands grab her hips, dig into the soft skin around them, and I lift her up my body. Her own hands come to my shoulder as she lifts her legs around my hips, opening herself to me completely. Her pussy settles against my waist and my hard cock settles in heaven. My eyes close and a low moan thunders in my chest when the sensation of having her warm wetness cradling me shoots a fire-like dance up my spine.

When I feel her ankles lock behind me, one hand slowly glides up her spine until I cup her neck and pull her head into my shoulder, dropping my lips to her neck when the movement exposes the silky skin to me. I wrap my other arm tight around her waist and move to sit on the mattress.

After settling us so that my back is resting against the headboard, not letting her move an inch from my hold, I let out a deep breath.

This right here is everything.

The woman I love, the one who loves me back, wrapped around me. Our hearts pound against each other's chests while we take comfort in the adoration between us. It feels so much more profound than that. When I have her, skin against skin, heart against heart, I feel like everything in my body and mind becomes complete.

Our connection pulls tight on the invisible cords that link our souls until there is nothing left to do but become one.

This right here is all I need to know that all is right in the world.

"It's going to be okay," she mumbles against my neck, the words muffled.

At this moment, I believe her. I still need to explain to her just what could happen and get her reassurances while she's right here in my arms. Nothing between us while we strip more than our clothes off, open ourselves completely, and have a conversation so raw we're going to need this physical grounding to one another.

"Willow." I sigh and tighten my arms around her, pressing her tighter into my body. "They're going to do everything they can to keep this story front and center in everyone's eyes and mind. Trust me, I know this needs to happen, but I need you to really understand what will be coming while you selflessly throw yourself on the media's sword."

She tries to lift her head from the hold my hand has on her neck, and I grudgingly allow her to lean up but shift the arm that had been holding her neck to her shoulders and only give her enough space to lift her head and turn to meet my eyes.

"I understand, honey." She comforts me with a small smile. "I have no illusions about what will happen when I'm not just Kane Masters' girlfriend, but the woman who allegedly broke up what they believe was Hollywood's two top players and their love child."

"Baby." I sigh and drop my forehead to hers, keeping our eyes locked. "They're going to do whatever they can to hurt you because you will be the villain in this scenario. Regardless that I've confirmed our love, they will see Mia as the 'woman scorned' and they won't forget. Look at Brad and Angelina. She will always be the other woman, even if in their case it was true, regardless that they're very happy now, married, and have children. It's been years. She was ripped apart and knowing that will without a doubt happen to you, it fucking unmans me, Willow. I can't protect you in this situation. They win."

Her arms loosen from the hold she had around my neck and she shifts with the small leverage I allow until her hands cup my face and her lips are moving against mine as she speaks.

"You're wrong. We win. Our love wins. They can say what they want. Hate me, make me the villain, and do their worst to try to rip me apart. They only win if we let them, and that will never happen. I know you're thinking of the worst here and trust me, I thought the same things, but nothing they can say about me or us would devalue our love. When I look in the mirror, I won't see the things they will most likely say about me. I'll see me, Willow Tate, the woman who isn't perfect, but she is perfect in her imperfections. They are not allowed to have that from me. I'm not weak. I no longer fear words meant to tear me down because I'm better than that. I love me for me. I love me for you. And I love you because you were the one who gave me this beautiful love, taught me how to see myself, and there is no one who could ever come between that."

My hold on her tightens until I know it couldn't be comfortable for her, but she continues to hold my jaw, her lips just barely on mine, and our eyes refusing to break their connection until I show her that I believe her words. She gives me a wobbly smile and presses her lips against mine before tucking back against my chest.

I can't hold back the overwhelming flood of emotion that hits when I realize just how beautiful she is right now in the naked confidence that she's showing me. Bared in every way that she could be to leave no doubts between us that we will weather whatever storm follows because what we have can't be broken. Not when I'm holding the strongest woman I know in my arms.

With her held tight in my arms, I lean my head back. I only let go long enough to lift my hips and pull the duvet out from under us, wrapping it around our bodies and settling in. I keep her against me as the sun starts to climb high in the sky and not even then do we part. We both sleep, peacefully, with the knowledge that nothing will come between us.

Not now.

Not ever.

CHAPTER FORTY

WILLOW

GOOD GOD, WHAT IS THAT noise?

I move my head from the warm pillow of Kane's chest and lift my body, my muscles complaining when I move from the same position I had been in when I fell asleep.

Kane's erection makes me jolt upright when the hardness hits me roughly against my clit. He lets out a long moan with the friction created by my movement.

The noise that had woken me from the best sleep I've ever had powers through the silence around us and I jump again. Kane just rolls his head as an even deeper moan falls from his lips.

All thoughts of the ringing phone are forgotten when his lids lift and his normally bright blues are simmering a light navy with the hunger his lust is building.

"Is that yours or mine?" he asks, his voice thick with sleep and arousal.

"Mine." I gasp when his hips move, gliding his erection through my wetness.

He leans his head forward and gives me a wicked grin. "Then up you go. If that's who I think it is, they won't stop until they talk to you, and I want you interruption-free."

I gulp and then regrettably climb from his lap with his hands guiding me by their firm hold on my hips. His eyes continue to burn into mine, and I doubt I'm the only one feeling empty without the physical connection we had held through our early morning rest. Just as our relationship has proved when we're together, even in sleep, just the thought of being apart isn't bearable. Our bodies crave one another just as fiercely as our hearts do.

"The phone, baby," he reminds me with that thick, deep voice full of unspoken promises.

"Right." I nod but don't move. My eyes roam over every exposed inch of him, making it impossible to look anywhere else.

My phone stops its annoying ringing. I watch the ridges of Kane's abdominal muscles flex as he silently laughs. His arms move from their relaxed position next to his body and fold behind his head. I follow the movement slowly before letting my stare move to his face. He cocks a brow, in either question or some sort of silent dare. My pulse spikes, and I let my perusal of his body continue, sweeping my eyes from his to the stubble along his jaw. His dimple comes out, knowing that I'm getting drunk off him.

His tan skin, lightly peppered with dark hairs, makes my palms itch to roam over his chest. I continue down, back over the hard angles and planes of his form, until I see the evidence of his arousal standing long and thick against his body. His long legs, thick thighs, and those big feet end my journey of his flawless masculinity.

I step forward, ready to climb back on him, but my phone picks that moment to remind me of why I had ever left the bed—his arms—to begin with.

"Crap." I sigh, as longing drips from my exaggerated exhale.

I turn, reluctantly walking from the man my body craves greedily.

I search in my purse for the offending device and grab it as another burst of noise sounds.

I give him a silent apology when I see he was right about the caller and press accept, then speaker, before returning to the bed. I give in to my need for his touch, crawling in and tucking my body to his side. My head against his chest, arm on his abs, I sigh when I see his erection still in my line of sight around the phone.

"Damn." I groan, vocalizing my frustration at being kept from the part of him that I want.

"Willow Elizabeth! Did you just say a wordy-dirty?!" Eddie gasps loudly through the line.

"She did, I heard her," Kirby's voice chimes in, and I frown at the phone.

"Three-way, baby," Kane whispers loudly, his chest moving before the he lets out a low chuckle.

"I knew that," I defend, lifting my head and looking over to roll my eyes at him, which only making his laughter grow.

"Oh, that's a hot sound. Did you just wake up, Mr. Masters?" Eddie asks wistfully.

"Don't perv on Willow's man, Edward. That's just wrong."

"No, it isn't. You heard it. That sounded like a sex voice. Say something. Come on."

Kane bursts out a loud bark of hilarity, and I narrow my eyes at the phone.

"Shut up, Edward," Kirby orders.

"You never let me have any fun," he whines.

Clearing my throat, I wade in before they start going back and forth. When those two get going, there's no telling how long it will last. They're worse than siblings are.

"Is there a point to this chat or did you two just call so that Eddie could flirt with my boyfriend?"

"She said boyfriend, Kirby. Did you hear that?"

I roll my eyes, again, at Eddie.

"I did! Isn't it adorable?"

"Hey! Come on!" I growl some sort of annoyed noise deep in my throat, the chest that I'm lying on quivering again. "You are all hilarious. Very hilarious. Let's all poke fun at Willow this morning."

"Oh, come on, Wills. We're just happy for you, that's all."

"Happy and flirting with Kane?" I snap back at Eddie.

"Well, you open those pretty little eyes and look at him. You would do the same."

He's right.

"Is there a reason you two are calling me nonstop?"

"Yeah, Wills," Kirby responds, the lightness in her voice gone.

I lift up and look at Kane in question, but he just shrugs. "And are you going to tell me what that might be?"

Eddie clears his throat. Kirby lets out a deep sigh.

"Well?" I continue.

"We saw the news this morning. You can't miss it, honey. Every entertainment station is either playing some sort of highlight reel or using those little black tickers on the bottom of the screen to spread the word. You two are the top story on three morning shows and that doesn't even count the Google alerts I have on Kane that have been going *insane* since late last night."

I let that sink in before I respond to Eddie. "You have Google alerts set to Kane?"

"Uh, duh."

"Right. Okay. That's not creepy or anything."

"We're getting off track," Kirby complains. "Kane, I know you're there and listening and even though you're my boss, I'm about to step all over that line of professionalism here."

"I wouldn't expect anything less," he calmly answers.

"I know," she smugly says. "Let me just cut to the chase. While I commend you for that big spectacle you made last night—or early this morning, whatever—I'm a little concerned about Willow, and I wanted, no, we wanted, to make sure she's okay."

I settle back down, letting the tension out of my body. "I'm perfect," I tell them, meaning every word.

"Wills, honey, there are some pretty intense things being said."

"Being?" I request.

"Willow," Kane exhales in warning.

Leaning back up, again, I look him in the eye. "I'm okay," I mouth. He doesn't look happy, but nods and holds himself tense.

"Well, Wills," Eddie starts, clearly unsure if he should repeat the rumors.

"Shit. Okay," Kirby interrupts. "They're saying that even though Kane confirmed he is very much in a relationship with his new lady friend, there is already trouble in paradise because of the strain this affair has had on you two in the wake of his cheating being the reason he split with Mia. It's not pretty, Wills, and I hate to ask you this, but are they true?"

I should be mad she's asking. She has spent time with Kane, with the two of us together, and with each of us separately. She shouldn't be so easily fooled.

"Kirby," I warn.

"I know, I know! I'm sorry. But, Willow, there are some really nasty things being said. I just have to know that you're okay. Kane, I'm sorry again, but it has to be said. They're saying that an insider has confirmed Mia's baby is his! I'm just worried about you."

Kane's whole body is rigid. I know he hates this, but I also know he's still a little anxious about what will happen now that his worries are coming true.

"We love you, Willow," Eddie says through the line. "I just want you to be happy. I know this is a lot to take, and we're both worried. Is … is the baby his?"

I sigh. Not because I'm upset they're invading our privacy, but because I know they're only worried about me because they love me. They've seen me at my worst, and if anyone would know how bad I would have reacted in the past, it would be them.

Lifting completely from Kane's side, I move my leg over his hip and straddle his waist. I let the silence linger, ignoring the worried mumbling of my two best friends and focus on the man who holds my heart.

I rest the phone on his chest, my hands roaming over the corded muscles in his pecs before I move over his tense shoulders and lean forward, curling my fingers around his neck. Holding my weight off my hands and centering my body. My hips rock involuntarily against his. Some of the sharpness in his features fades when my warm center slides over his erection.

I keep my expression open so that he can see, with no doubt, that this isn't upsetting to me. I knew what was happening and he needs to see I meant every word. It doesn't matter what they say, *we* know the truth, and that is all that I need. He is all I need.

"Willow!" Eddie snaps, my silence too long for him.

"I love you both," I start, keeping my eyes on Kane. "I love that you're worried about me, and I know that you both have the best intentions. You've seen what it's done in the past when I was the center of others' judgments, but I need you two to also respect me when I tell you that this is none of your business. I'm not that person anymore. I know you're only acting out of concern, but trust me when I tell you that it isn't needed. I'm happy. So happy. It doesn't matter what's being said because the only person's happiness that is more important than mine is Kane's."

The tension drains from his face, and his hard expression makes way for a look of pure love and pride.

"Willow, the baby," Eddie cries in exasperation.

"Is none of your business," I interject. "The only thing that you need to know is that Kane and I are perfect. I need you to respect the fact that I will not now, or ever, talk about anything else in our relationship. You guys and your friendship means the world to me …" My eyes roam Kane's face as I continue to talk. The reverence that is now mixing with his love is filling me with my own sense of pride. "I can tell you, both of you, that there is no doubt in my mind that Kane came to me freely, entered our relationship freely, and his love comes with no conditions. The rest of the rumors, I'm sorry, will never be anyone's business but our own."

They both sigh. I can hear weeping, and I know by the girlish cries that it isn't Kirby.

"I feel like the world is at my fingertips, and I have a contentment in my soul that has never been there before. You don't need to worry about whatever is being said because I'm happy. We're happy. And nothing or anyone will change that."

"Oh, God." Eddie weeps, and I smile when his sobs grow distant while he gets himself together.

"Okay." Kirby breathes. "Okay."

"Okay," I echo.

"A contentment in your soul?" she whispers.

"Freedom from my darkest days," I confirm, and this time it isn't Eddie muffling his emotions; Kirby's soft hiccup-like sob now joins him.

"If you two don't mind," Kane strongly calls in the phone. "I'm going to hang up now and wake my girl up properly now."

He goes to grab the phone off his chest, but I swat his hand away, laughing.

"Eddie, check your schedule and let us know when you can come out to California. Kirby, I'll see you Friday."

I don't give them a chance to respond before disconnecting the call with a jab of my finger. They got what they needed, and right now, I'm about to get what I need.

I don't move after ending the call. The phone sits on his rapidly moving chest as I hold myself over his body and look deep into his eyes. The deep blue storm brewing deep within them.

There are no words spoken, and none needed.

Gliding my hands over the hardness of his chest and abdomen, I let my nails rake over the hard ridges of his abs, teasing the deep V right above where my body settled on his. He jerks his hips, pulls in deep gasps of air, and lets me worship his body.

I move my hands up, and on the way, I grab the phone and toss it over the side of the bed. The clatter of the wood floors the only other sound mingling with our rough breathing.

When my hips rock against him, only then do his hands fly to my body. He holds me against him as I continue to give him my love. I can feel his erection harden even further and moan when my movements have the sharp bursts of ecstasy shooting from my center and firing throughout my whole body.

My head falls back as my movements pick up speed. Not fast, but a harder rock; still gentle but just what I need to continue to feel the pleasure spiking.

When my neck rolls and I bring my eyes back to his, I gasp at the greedy rapture in which he is watching my move.

His hooded eyes lock to where our bodies are creating the most delicious friction before slowly moving up my torso and stopping on my breasts. His mouth opens, hanging there, as a rumble sounds deep in his throat. I can feel my breasts moving, swinging softly with each roll of my hips and quivering with each gasp I pull sharply into my lungs. I look down to see what is causing such a fierce reaction from him.

His fingers are curled into my hips, my soft skin giving to the pressure and his thumbs making deep impressions against my flesh. The sight of all my suppleness doesn't shame me. Not while he's looking at me with such voracity. The parts of me I had once hated have now become my favorite features because I know with just baring myself to him that he craves me fiercely.

He doesn't hold back how much he loves my body. I glance back at him and watch his face as I bring my hands up and cup my heavy, sensitive breasts. Pinching my nipples between my fingers, squeezing the skin and letting out a shameless cry. And because I'm watching him, I'm instantly rewarded.

His eyes drink my actions in, the deepness in his harsh breathing reverberating through the room, as the color in his skin heats. His nostrils flare, and I know he might not be able to hold back much longer.

I look down my body, past my hands still torturing him with my fondling and to where the tip of his hard erection peeks out with each backward rock of my hips. The flesh red, swollen, and angry looking. Wet with my own desire as well as what I'm sure is a good mix of his.

Seeing our bodies, connected without being completely fused, makes my whole body tremble with need.

I drop my hands and lift my hips, his erection instantly springing free. The hardness hits my entrance. The jolt is so strong from the contact that it's almost as if his body is begging me to drop and impale myself on him.

I look away from the sight between my legs and up to his face. The strain in his neck prominent and it looks like every vein in his body is visible as he is filled with the same overwhelming need that I am.

"Nothing between us," I demand, and the harshness of his breathing picks up even more. We already talked about it, and since I'm covered, there is no need to continue allowing anything else from feeling each other completely.

"Never." His gravelly voice moans low and deep in his throat in agreement.

My hips lift, just a little more, and as his fingers dig into mine with a pleasure-filled pain, I slam my body down on his length and that moan turns into dual groans of pure euphoria.

Our eyes never leave each other. I ride his body free of fear of what I might look like because the love blazing from his gaze leaves no uncertainty that I'm the most beautiful woman in the world to him.

My movements falter when he hits a spot so deep inside of me that I can hear my wetness with each slam of my hips. The pleasure is so intense I can no longer move on my own accord. Seeing my struggle, he knifes from his back and the next thing I know, my back is hitting the end of the bed and his hands are curling around my neck, holding my face still as he looks deep into me.

Searching as his hips power between my legs. Our cries bleeding together as we share the air between our lips.

No words are needed. Not when you can feel the love we have for one another with so much influence that it's almost tangible. There isn't anything between us at this moment. Our bodies move as one, our hearts beating in sync, and our souls finally coming home.

When the pleasure becomes too much, my mouth opens and I shatter. My whole body tightening, firing, and bursting in an explosion so bright that the heat only drives me higher and higher until I'm no longer sure I'm even breathing.

His own groans mix with my hoarse cries, and with one last powerful thrust, I feel the warmth of his climax spilling inside me.

It's at this moment, right here, as we pant in the rawness of our lovemaking, that I know nothing will ever be able to take this from us. What we have is a once in a lifetime love that can never be broken. The world outside our happiness will never penetrate what we have built. There is no force strong enough out there that could ever sever what we share.

I feel supremacy in that knowledge. A solidification in what I have become. Everything I had gone through has brought me to this moment in his arms. Every spiral I fell and pain I endured made me worthy of not only my own love, but his as well.

I know that our world will be full of imperfection, but I've found my little slice of flawless love and happiness here in Kane's arms. His love makes every second yet to come of our perfectly imperfect life something I know will never get old.

Our connection will never fade.

The magnificence that we both see in each other will only intensify the beauty we see in ourselves.

He was right when he said that it took two imperfect souls to form perfection together.

And with a deep sigh, I look up into his sapphire eyes and tell him, "I love you, Kane Masters."

"And I love you, Willow Tate." His contentment-filled smile is the last thing I see before he turns our bodies, wraps me tight in his arms, and I feel his words on my lips before he slants his head and takes my mouth in a deep, perfect kiss.

EPILOGUE

WILLOW

To say the last year and a half had been drama free would be like saying an ice cube took down the Titanic. It wasn't easy. Sometimes, it was unbelievably hard. But even on the darkest of those days, it was still the unbelievably beautiful. The serenity, even through the rumor mill wringers, couldn't be beat.

The decision to keep the father of Mia's son a secret from the world didn't come without its struggles. Christian and Becca had been devastated. But even though it broke their hearts to know what their eldest son had done, they were over the moon with their first grandchild on the way. I think it helped to soften the blow … and, honestly, it made the following months worth it.

Kyle spiraled.

No, he didn't just spiral, he hit rock bottom and decided to pick up a shovel and find a way to dig his own grave.

Literally.

Six months after Mia told me about the baby, and two months

after Milo Robert Post was born, Kyle decided to get behind the wheel after drinking himself stupid for hours. He lost control of his vehicle on a lonely stretch of coastal twist and turns just two miles from Kane's home.

At the time of Kyle's death, his brothers hadn't spoken to him once since they paid him a visit to let him know that Mia and the baby were none of his concern. Kole shocked us all when he threatened Kyle to ensure his silence. When Kane told me that Kole had said he would publicly claim Milo, making up something so juicy that the media would eat right out of his palms, I had been shocked. Sure, Kyle could have called his bluff, but I think he knew that with Kole's popularity, everyone would have believed him.

I asked Kole what he would have done or said. Kole just gave me a lopsided smile and shrugged. But later, Kane told me what Kole was planning *if* it came to where he had to go public.

Kole had never made it a secret that he would never marry or have children. He enjoyed his life and knew that it would be hard to find a woman who could put up with everything that came with his celebrity status. Not to mention, bringing a child into his world would be dangerous since he currently had one crazy stalker. So he just didn't want it and had always made it known. But, if it came to it, he was prepared to not only claim Milo, but he would fabricate a story so insanely graphic and juicy about his love triangle with his own brother, it would be like a Lifetime movie being played out for the world to see. He was right. The story of Kyle, the brother who was notorious for avoiding the press, cheating on his wife and fathering a love child would never have held a candle to Kole's rendition.

It was a risk, but just like the day we decided to keep the identity of Milo's father a secret, we knew the only thing that mattered was making sure he lived as normal of a life as possible and that it began with as little of a scandal as possible.

For months after Kane's and my relationship went public, it seemed like we were in the news daily. Pictures surfaced of us on dates, on the set of *Impenetrable*, even some creepy stalker-type pictures from someone who had followed us when we took a little vacation to the mountains. It was insane. But it was actually exhilarating.

When it became clear that not only was Kane very much in love, but that we also both had a great friendship with Mia, they abandoned their attempts at painting our relationship as some sordid triangle. It didn't come overnight, but it happened, and for the last two months, we've had nothing but support for our relationship.

Of course, the biggest reason for that was probably because of me.

Yup. Me.

When Kyle died, regardless of the fact that Kane had made peace with the fact he would never have a relationship with his brother again, it still cut him deep. He sunk into a depression, and I didn't know how to help. Weeks of chopped conversations, nightmares, and eventually silence. I had no idea how to help him get past that. Until Mia. She decided I needed to help him see the good things in life, or more specifically, give him something that would shock him enough to move on and remember the happier times.

Kane didn't even notice that I had left him alone for the first time in weeks, but he sure did take notice when I slapped one of the most popular entertainment magazines down in front of him a week later. Mia had reached out to the editor, a friend of hers, and explained that I was interested in doing an interview. Not just an interview, but also a bare all expose of myself—in lingerie of all things. I had just stood there, sputtering my shock, seconds away from passing out in panic … until she explained to the editor that this would be an inspirational piece that would show the struggles with body image, self-hate, and finally overcoming it. Hearing her put it that way—even though I was still absolutely terrified about being photographed in skimpy underwear—the thought of helping just one person who felt the way I used to pushed me to go through with it.

She had been right, God love her. Not only did Kane snap out of it when faced with his very bare girlfriend on the front page of the most popular tabloid magazine around, but also he had been so turned on by my confidence that he didn't leave the bedroom for two more days. Locking himself away for a whole different reason. And I enjoyed every rough, sweaty, arousing moment of it.

Since that interview, I had gone from the woman who *may* have broken up the rumored Kane and Mia relationship to a woman who became the face of learning to love your own skin. It was weird, and uncomfortable, at times, but every single letter I got from someone who told me that my story helped them to heal made it worth every second.

It was then that Ivy and Dominic made their final strike. We knew it would probably happen, especially after his attempt to keep the Logan Agency afloat on Kane's coattails had failed. Ivy had tried to sell a story to some low-rate tabloid that I had never had my so-called body issues. She claimed the true story was that I had been a bully to her making her so insecure that she paid thousands in plastic surgery to 'correct' the things I had told her were ugly.

That backfired terribly when numerous of the employees of the now bankrupt and closed down Logan Agency had come forward to not only deny, but also turn it back on Ivy, Dominic, and even my ex-husband, Brad.

I shouldn't have been happy that they not only failed but also lost everything. I shouldn't have spent a whole night drinking with Kane, Kirby, Eddie, and Kole. I probably shouldn't have cared at all.

But I did. I'm not proud of it, but I celebrated karma's brilliance in a drunken rage of laughter, facemasks, and nail polish.

So even though the last year and a half has held a lot of ups and downs, I'm so happy that it's ridiculous.

I was going to pass out.

It's quite possible I might actually puke, which would be absolutely horrifying given our current surroundings.

I look to my right and take in the calm man sitting next to me. He looks almost bored, which makes no sense because I know he's been a ball of nervous excitement all day.

This was so much easier the other times we found ourselves seated in a darkened theater, surrounded by the who's who of the entertainment world. Not once did I feel the need to purge my nerves in a very disgustingly graphic way. Of course, last year we were sitting here for another film for which Kane's acting had been nominated. It's so much different now that we're here for *Impene-*

trable. Not only because it's a film we're both insanely proud of, but because for Kane, this is the first time he's been nominated for his screenplay and directing.

'Award season' was like nothing I had expected. The red carpet was a full-speed chaos-filled madness of shouts, flashes, and small interviews. I played my part and stuck by Kane's side. I smiled when I was told to pose, and I stepped back to the side when Kane's new PR rep told him to turn on his charm and talk about *Impenetrable*, a film that climbed the charts in a frenzy of popularity. I don't think anyone was shocked when the nominations started rolling in.

So now here I sit, waiting as the names are being announced for the director award category. I can't even enjoy the moment long enough to freak out about the two stars chatting away on stage.

Nope.

I'm about to freak out.

Alessandra had already won the first award of the night, given for Lead Actress in a Motion Picture, just as I knew she would. I swear Kane had tears in his eyes when he gave the younger actress a hug. I know I did. We didn't win the nomination that the film had in the Lead Actor category. I could tell that Logan was bummed, but the reality is that even though he's now one of the most lusted over young actors, Alessandra stole the film and everyone knows it. The emotions she was able to bring to the surface, the power in which she broke before she healed were exceptional in their brilliance.

And we were still over the moon excited when that award went to Kole. So even though I know Kane would have loved to take another win for *Impenetrable*, when Kole stepped around me and hugged his brother before taking the stage, I could tell all thoughts of his own film not winning were gone.

When Best Screenplay was up, I wasn't as nervous as I am now. I clapped like a mad woman and silently wiped the tears when Kane took the stage to give his acceptance speech. He left the stage with a wink toward where I was seated in the darkened audience just as a seat filler had sat down. I was—thankfully—used to this from last year, but it's still weird to have some stranger sit next to you just so there are no empty seats. I don't think I'll ever understand Hollywood.

I know that winning for Best Screenplay was an incredible honor, but I felt like all of my eggs were sitting in the basket of unease for his next nomination. This film is his baby. Something that eerily matched my own life, a fact Kane had not missed. So while all the other awards are something to be so proud of, the one for Best Director is not only proof that the film had been a phenomenal success, but also gives Kane the validation that he's not *just* an actor.

He's created this film word for word.

He crafted its beauty.

And he deserves this moment.

Which is why by the time he had finished his behind the scenes obligations, I had hit a whole new high in my anxiety. Why does this have to be one of the last awards of the night? I've sat here for hours about to come out of my skin in sick anticipation.

His hand squeezes mine when they say his name, giving away his unease. I know the exact moment the camera must be showing us to all the viewers watching on television because I feel a rush confidence from his body. I look over, making sure I have a smile on my nerve-stricken face, and watch my man work the camera angled his way from the aisle. You would never guess how much he wants this by the easy, handsome smirk on his face.

"And the Golden Globe for Best Director, motion picture, goes to," the female voice says, her voice echoing around us.

Oh, God.

"Kane Masters for *Impenetrable*!"

"Oh, God!" I exclaim, jumping up at the same time that he slowly stands.

When he turns to me, I smile at him through the tears running down my face. His lazy smile grows, dimple comes out, and he wraps his arms around me before giving me a hard press with his lips against mine.

"I'm so proud of you," I whisper, just for him, before I shove him playfully into the aisle.

I can see his broad shoulders moving as he chortles, walking toward the stage with so much power in his controlled steps. Each one that he takes so sure and steady, as if he isn't facing one of the biggest recognitions in his career right now. I don't know how he isn't skipping down there while sobbing like a baby. Okay, so Kane isn't a skipper *or* a sobber, but still. I have apparently decided to take over the sobbing in happiness end of the emotional gauntlet while he deals with the thankful happiness.

I watch him hug both of the presenters before turning toward the audience, his deep laugh of disbelief as he holds the award up in reverence. I swipe at my face, removing the tears from my vision so I can memorize this moment. He brings his free hand up to run it through his hair, losing that messy-like perfection that his stylist had created. I'm sure if the camera were to show my wet, makeup ruined face, Kirby would be throwing things at the television, which I hope isn't the case since I'm a fan of the ninety-inch screen in Kane's media room. I can only imagine the elation flowing through that room now with Kirby, Eddie, Kane's parents, Mia, and little Milo making it party central.

Kane's shoulders pull back, and I know he's trying to control his emotions, but when he looks up from the award and into the crowd, I know he's losing.

"When we started filming *Impenetrable*, I had no doubts in this film. I knew that we were creating magic, and hopefully, through Allison's journey, we were creating freedom. Freedom for every person who is fighting the battles she did. We had filmed for a solid two months when the magnitude of that hit me. I believed in my film, the actors, and the message, but it wasn't until I witnessed the reality of becoming impenetrable that I was able to truly see its brilliance. At that moment, I knew this wasn't and would never be just a film to me. Not when I still have the very definition of it living in my guest house fifty yards away."

My body heaves when his meaning becomes clear and with a loud sob, my hand comes to my mouth and those darn tears leak again. I think back to the moment he's talking about when I first sat down next to him on the set in Georgia.

He continued with his speech, thanking his cast, production team, and everyone within Kane Entertainment for all of their hard work on the film. His little jokes making my hand fall and my smile grow. I'm finally able to breathe again when it looks as if he's about to stop talking. The pride for him at this moment is insurmountable.

"And lastly, to my beautiful Willow," he starts, looking toward my direction again, searching. "Without you by my side, I don't think that I would have been able to make *Impenetrable* as powerful as I know it is. I'm the luckiest man in the world right now. Well, almost."

He bizarrely stops talking as a secretive grin fills his face. He continues to look in my direction, and when he steps away from the mic, turning toward the stage stairs instead of following the presenters and that fancy dressed award show version of a traffic director, he stomps back down the aisle. He's headed back to where I'm seated as a dull roar of whispers starts filling the shocked theater.

"What in the world is he doing?" I gasp and look to my left at a very smug looking Kole.

"My guess is this would be another one of those embarrassingly romantic grand gesture things he seems to be so fond of."

"What?" I gasp again, turning back toward the advancing Kane. Kole continues to let out deep grunts of laughter as Kane takes the last few steps, stopping in the aisle directly in front of me and causing the seat filler to hurry out of the way.

He hands his brother the shining gold award, my eyes tracking its movements before looking back up to his face, only to find him no longer standing.

What the heck?

The room goes electric as the whispers turn into a mix of shocked gasps and excited cheers. I feel Kane grab my hand, and I look around the room before my shocked eyes move down to where Kane is now kneeling in front of me.

On one knee.

With his hand holding one of mine and the other hand in the

air.

Holding a ring twinkling from the lights dancing off it between his fingers.

An engagement ring.

Oh. My. God.

"Kane," I breathe in shock.

His smile brightens. "Well? How about you help me out here and make one of the greatest nights in my life even better. It's time to move out of that damn guest house and marry me."

"Is that a question?" I blurt.

He throws his head back and lets out a booming laugh. "Willow Elizabeth Tate, I love you. Will you marry me?"

I start nodding before he's even finished, and his smile grows even larger. I feel him slip the cold metal on my finger and then I'm in his arms. His hands cradling my face as he takes my lips in a deep kiss.

When he lifts his head, his lips dance across mine. "You're finally moving out of my guest house?"

"Oh, yeah." I giggle.

"Tonight, we celebrate in *our* bed."

I know the crowd can't hear his words, but he's once again giving the world confirmation of our relationship with one heck of a show. God, I love this man. I throw my head back and laugh with so much carefree abandon. He steps away, takes his award back from Kole, and with a nod to his brother, he turns and walks back toward where the producers are about to go insane to move him backstage. They might have been annoyed by his show-stealing moment, but when the ratings hit, they'll be thanking him for running over the allotted time.

They cut to a break seconds after Kane disappeared from view, and when the seat warmer drops back down in the seat she scampered out of when Kane came stomping toward us, I jump. The stranger is clearly frazzled by the turn of events. I give her a wobbly smile before looking down at my hand and the ring that now adorns it.

"I would say that's about as grand as it gets, *sister*," Kole whispers.

I turn to him and the feelings of overwhelming happiness that roll through my body make me feel like I'm the winner of every single award given out tonight.

The smile that fills my happy, tear-filled face doesn't falter once for the remainder of our evening. When Kane takes the stage once again with his cast and they collectively accept the award for Best Motion Picture, it still doesn't fade. I clap and beam up at the man who truly has proven to the world that when you believe in the possibility of becoming impenetrable, you can overcome anything and win.

I, Willow Tate, soon-to-be Masters, have truly won.

I have the love of the greatest man and his family. But most of all, I have the love of my own self and each and every perfectly imperfect moment I've lived, loved, and won.

THE END.

Thank yous…

To my family. Always to my family. You love me even when I'm overcome with voices and locked away in the office. When I come out a few days later confused about the sun shining or what day it is, you still love me. To the late night dance parties in my office while I work and even raiding my candy stash – you guys make every moment a little brighter. I wouldn't be able to do any of this without you.

To Felicia Lynn. I kind of like you, Cinderella. I mean, even though you are STILL pressuring me to cuddle you (even after I put it in print that it would never happen) I'll keep you around. Let's face it, if I didn't, who would I feed to the zombie bears in my woods when I took a break in the middle of the night? ☺ Seriously though, you make late night writing marathons so much more fun. Put up with my freeze out temps, AND love me even though I'm crazy. Win win.

To Sommer Stein. I never have the right words to tell you how much you mean to me. When I came to you with PI and basically just said 'no people on this cover, have fun' I knew you would knock it out of the park. You have created NINE stunning covers for me, but this one…this one is ALL your brain child and I can't thank you enough for creating something so stunningly PERFECT.

To Stacey Blake. I'm so blessed to have you on my side. I always know, no matter what, when I send you my final manuscript to format that the end result will be a piece of art in itself. You, my love, are amazing.

To Jenny Sims. Thank YOU for taking Perfectly Imperfect and dealing with the insane deadlines that I seem to always find myself in. And for all the little things that you do during the editing process that make it so much easier when I get the edits back. You rock, girlfriend.

To Lara Feldstein and Hollie Stubblefield. You guys read my 'baby' every step of the way. Put up with me every single time that I told you I changed this or that. I couldn't imagine this process without each of you to bounce plot things with. (Even though I'm pretty sure Lara might kill me one day because of how much I tease her.)

To Kim Ginsberg and her eagle eye. Hey – at least I learned my lesson about TOWARDS! Thank you for giving PI a whirl, you rock!

To Sofie Hartley. Where do I even start with you? Thank you. Not just for loving PI – but for once again making teasers that look so beautiful I just want to look at them all day. And let's not forget One Direction GIFs. I mean, that right there...

To Emma Hart and Rachel Brooks. Thank you for reading PI before it was released. For believing in a story that means the world to me and being willing to pause your insanely busy lives to meet Willow and Kane. My love for you two is huge.

To each and every reader that took a chance on a standalone and a cast that was completely unknown. It's because of the love that I've always gotten from my amazingly loving readers that gave me the strength to tell this story. One that is so personal to my own struggles that I never thought that it would see the light of day. You guys…you make me push myself to heights that I never thought possible. So, my biggest thank you of all goes to you. Each one of you.

And…to Willow.
You've lived inside of me for so long that I think it became easier to live with you than to face you. But, Willow, you have taught me so much during each and every one of these 110K words. I hope and pray that by setting you free, you can teach and help others that might have a little of you hiding inside of them as well.

xoxo

Made in the USA
San Bernardino, CA
16 March 2016